ORCS
Bad Blood III

Inferno

STAN NICHOLLS

First published in Great Britain in 2011 by
Gollancz
An imprint of the Orion Publishing Group
Orion House, 5 Upper St Martin's Lane,
London WC2H 9EA
An Hachette UK Company

This edition published in 2012
by Gollancz

1 3 5 7 9 10 8 6 4 2

A CIP catalogue record for this book
is available from the British Library.

ISBN 978 0 575 08865 8

Typeset at The Spartan Press Ltd,
Lymington, Hants

Printed and bound by CPI Group (UK) Ltd,
Croydon, CR0 4YY

www.stannicholls.com
www.orionbooks.co.uk

Praise for Orcs:

'Wall to wall action . . . gritty and fast-paced'   David Gemmell

'Fast, dirty, very funny, often surreal'   *Guardian*

'Buy now or beg for mercy later'   Tad Willams

'Excellent fantasy with a twist'   *SFX*

Also by Stan Nicholls from Gollancz:

Orcs: The Omnibus Edition
Orcs Bad Blood I: Weapons of Magical Destruction
Orcs Bad Blood II: Army of Shadows
Orcs Bad Blood III: Inferno

For Jacob Harry Fifer,
who will hopefully read this one day,
and probably wonder what the old boy
was up to.

Into the Fire

Discontented with life in pastoral Ceragan, orcs warband the Wolverines were intrigued to receive a message from Tentarr Arngrim, the wizard known as Serapheim, who had previously aided them. Arngrim described a world where orcs were brutally dominated by human invaders. Worse, their oppressors included Serapheim's depraved daughter, the sorceress Jennesta, once the warband's ruler, whom they believed dead. Although suspicious of Arngrim's motives, Stryke, the Wolverines' captain, persuaded his band to embark on a mission to help their fellow orcs, and possibly exact revenge on Jennesta.

The Wolverines held five peculiar artefacts called instrumentalities, created by Serapheim, which they referred to as stars. The means by which the band was deposited on Ceragan, the stars could carry their possessors between worlds, though Stryke was untutored in operating them. But he also had an amulet, taken from the body of Arngrim's murdered messenger, and its markings provided a key.

At full strength the warband consisted of five officers and thirty privates. Stryke commanded. Beneath him were two sergeants. Haskeer was one; the other, Jup, the band's solitary dwarf, had stayed behind in Maras-Dantia, the Wolverines' anarchic birthplace. There should have been a pair of corporals too. Coilla, the only female member and its Mistress of Strategy, was present. But her counterpart, Alfray, had fallen in battle. Death had also taken six of the privates.

To get the numbers back up, Stryke recruited a clutch of Ceragan novices, and replaced Alfray with an ageing orc called Dallog. This was less than popular with some of the Wolverines. They were even more disgruntled when local clan chief Quoll forced his popinjay of a son, Wheam, onto the band.

Bidding farewell to his mate Thirzarr, and their hatchlings Corb and Janch, Stryke first took the band to Maras-Dantia to search for Jup, in hope of him resuming his role of sergeant. They succeeded, and Jup, along with his partner Spurral, rejoined. But one of the new recruits, and Liffin, a veteran member, were killed by marauders. Haskeer in particular blamed Wheam and the other tyros for this, and openly expressed contempt for them.

Before they left Maras-Dantia the band encountered two humans, Micalor Standeven and Jode Pepperdyne, who posed as merchants. In reality, Pepperdyne was Standeven's slave, and they were running from tyrannical ruler Kantor Hammrik, to whom Standeven was indebted. Standeven's plan was to steal the orcs' instrumentalities to pay off Hammrik. Stryke would have abandoned the duo, or worse, had they not warned him of an impending raid; and in the fight that followed, Pepperdyne saved Coilla's life. So when the Wolverines had to quickly exit a life-threatening situation, using the stars, Pepperdyne and Standeven went with them. Their destination was the world of the warband's mission.

The Wolverines were unaware that an indefinite number of instrumentalities existed, scattered across endless worlds. Nor did they know that a clandestine group, the Gateway Corps, was dedicated to tracking them down. The activation of Stryke's stars was detected by the Corps, and its human leader, Karrell Revers, ordered his deputy, female elf Pelli Madayar, to recover them at any cost. Accompanied by a multi-species snatch team, and armed with potent magical weaponry, Pelli set off in pursuit of the Wolverines.

Arriving in Acurial, a world as luxuriant as Maras-Dantia was corrupted, the Wolverines were horrified to discover the orc populace had had their martial spirit bred out of them. Playing on this docility, and the ploy that Acurial possessed non-existent weapons of magical destruction, Peczan, a human empire, had invaded.

Tangling with the occupiers, who had a command of magic – rare among humans – the Wolverines found that not all orcs in Acurial were placid when they were rescued by a resistance group whose members' fighting instincts had reawakened. It was headed by Brelan and his twin sister Chillder. Its leader in hiding was their mother, Sylandya, Acurial's deposed ruler. The Wolverines joined the insurgency. They trained the rebels, and Coilla formed an all-female warband dubbed the Vixens.

Opposing the resistance were General Kapple Hacher, Governor of what Peczan regarded as a province; and Brother Grentor, High Cleric of the Order of the Helix, wardens of the magic. As heads of two of the empire's main pillars in the prefecture, the military and the spiritual, Hacher and Grentor were often at odds. But the arrival of Jennesta, Peczan's pitiless emissary and both men's superior, overshadowed their differences.

Pelli Madayar's Gateway Corps unit also arrived, covertly observed events and plotted to seize the Wolverines' stars.

The resistance discovered that a comet named Grilan-Zeat, which had appeared at crucial points in Acurial's history, was soon to return. Their hope was that it would be seen as an omen, and along with a call to arms from Sylandya would inspire the submissive populace to revolt. A prophecy was attached to Grilan-Zeat. It said that a party of liberators would accompany the comet. Some in the resistance believed the Wolverines might be these longed-for champions, and portrayed them that way to further encourage the citizenry.

With comet and prophecy as carrots, the rebels applied a stick. They increased harassment of the occupiers with the intention of bringing down their wrath, which in turn would spur the masses to react. The Wolverines were involved in a succession of attacks on the invaders. Until one particularly ambitious raid went badly wrong; an attempt to assassinate Jennesta was foiled, ending with her snatching four of the five stars. Stryke wondered if there could be a spy in the resistance, or even among the Wolverines themselves. Then the fifth instrumentality, in Coilla's care, was stolen from a rebel hideout. There was little doubt that this was also Jennesta's doing. As the comet became visible it looked as though the Wolverines would never see Ceragan again. They had no choice but to fight on alongside the resistance. And in the weeks that followed, the bellicose nature of the orcs of Acurial began to resurface, to their human oppressors' cost.

The Wolverines didn't know that Jennesta had used esoteric sorcery to duplicate their instrumentalities. But the Gateway Corps was aware through their own magical means that another set of instrumentalities had been brought into play, making their mission of containment all the more urgent.

Despite the animosity between their races, Coilla and Pepperdyne grew close as the insurrection built, and the normally reticent human related some of his history. He was a Trougathian, a member of an island race on Maras-Dantia whose misfortune was to occupy a strategic location between rival nations. Trougath was afflicted by war for generations, until finally betrayed by a supposed ally, and broken. Its population scattered, and some were enslaved, with the upshot that Pepperdyne became little more than Standeven's chattel. The largely nomadic Trougathians were maligned and reviled, not unlike orcs.

Events in Acurial took a dramatic turn when, in a resistance safe house, Standeven was found with the dead body of an orc intruder, though he denied any wrongdoing. The mystery deepened when the dead orc turned out to have Coilla's stolen instrumentality. Wolverines and resistance alike were suspicious of what Standeven might have been up to, but nothing could be proved.

Their spirits lifted by regaining the star, the band set out to get the others back from Jennesta. Staging an ambush, they achieved this; although some in the band thought it went a bit too easily.

Sick of Hacher's running of the province, Jennesta transformed him into one of her zombie bodyguards. She had Brother Grentor murdered. And when Sylandya came out of hiding to rally the populace, Jennesta assassinated her. That proved a miscalculation. Far from stifling revolution, it stoked the flames.

With the resistance close to victory, Jennesta and a group of loyal human followers fled for the coast, the Wolverines in pursuit. But as the band prepared to attack her, the Gateway Corps appeared and Pelli Madayar demanded the Wolverines' instrumentalities. Stryke's refusal unleashed an onslaught of powerful magic from the Corps. Sandwiched between them and Jennesta's advancing force, Stryke activated the instrumentalities, though he had no time to set their coordinates.

The band travelled through a succession of hostile realities, staying in each only long enough to randomly reset the stars and escape. Finally arriving in a barren but unthreatening world, Stryke calibrated the instrumentalities properly. His plan was to return Pepperdyne and Standeven to Maras-Dantia, then take the band back to Ceragan.

But the stars inexplicably deposited them in a world of islands, on an isle inhabited by dwarfs. The orcs' seemingly miraculous arrival saved them from massacre by the dwarfs, who took them for gods.

Shortly after, the island was raided by human slavers, the Gatherers, who carried off a number of dwarfs, including Spurral. Securing two boats and a crude map, the Wolverines set out to rescue her. The Gateway Corps, who had followed the warband to this world, were on their trail.

Spurral found herself at the mercy of the Gatherers' ruthless leader, Captain Salloss Vant. She immediately began fermenting mutiny among her fellow captives, one of whom, a lame female called Dweega, was thrown overboard by the slavers. Picked up by the Wolverines, Dweega was able to tell them the Gatherers' course. But the band had to fend off a seaborne attack by the Gateway Corps before continuing their hunt. And Standeven was growing morbidly obsessed with the warband's stars.

On board the Gatherers' ship the dwarfs rebelled, and Spurral faced up to Vant and killed him. Taking control of the vessel, the dwarfs began sailing it back to their home. En route they were attacked by a fearsome creature called the Krake – one of 'the Lords of the Deep' – and the ship was sunk.

One of their boats having been damaged by the Corps, the Wolverines landed on a nearby island for repairs. It turned out to be occupied by a group of goblins who held captive a number of kelpies who, despite being sentient, were traded as meat. The orcs made common cause with them and killed the goblins. Learning that the Gatherers sailed a predetermined route, and the kelpies' island was their next port of call, to gather slaves, the Wolverines took a goblin ship and headed there. They didn't know that Spurral and a handful of other dwarf captives, having survived the shipwreck, had washed up on the kelpies' island, and been nurtured by them.

Jup and Spurral were finally reunited. Feeling honour-bound, Stryke agreed to return the liberated dwarfs to their island home. On the way, Coilla and Pepperdyne's friendship, frowned on by many in the band, escalated and they secretly became lovers.

Shortly after the orcs reached the dwarfs' island, the Gateway Corps appeared, and Pelli Madayar again demanded Stryke's instrumentalities. His refusal sparked a battle, with the Wolverines facing the Corps' sorcery. The band narrowly avoided being overwhelmed when Jennesta arrived with her force, and magical combat broke out between her and the Corps.

At the height of the chaos, Jennesta confronted Stryke. And to his astonishment she was with his mate, Thirzarr, who was in an hypnotic trance, one step from the full zombie state, and under Jennesta's control. With horror, Stryke realised that Jennesta must have travelled to Ceragan to capture Thirzarr, and could have inflicted untold destruction on his adoptive world.

Jennesta offered Stryke a deal: surrender the Wolverines to her, for conversion to undead servitude, and Thirzarr would be freed from her bondage. Refuse and Thirzarr would become a zombie, never to recover. Stryke struggled with the proposition, and turned it down. At which point Jennesta declared that the outcome would depend on one-to-one combat between Stryke and Thirzarr. At Jennesta's command, Thirzarr launched a murderous attack on Stryke. He desperately fought to suppress the killing instinct that could have had him slaying his mate. Only chance, and the intervention of Coilla and Wheam, prevented it.

Rescued from Jennesta's malign presence, Stryke yielded to despair. The Wolverines, retreating in disarray, saw no prospect but failure.

Five years earlier

Events were finally coming to a head in Maras-Dantia.

Jennesta had led an army to the snowbound north, into the shadow of the advancing glacier. Once there, they laid siege to Ilex's great ice palace.

She didn't care about the fate of her Manifold Path army. An alliance of humans, orcs and mercenary dwarfs united in common cause against the God-fearing forces of Unity, the Manis were no more than a convenience to her. The only thing that interested Jennesta was inside the palace.

The situation had been compounded by treachery. Mani dragon mistress Glozellan had sided with Jennesta's enemies and brought her charges into play. A squad of leathery behemoths, saw-like wings beating furiously, spewed gouts of flame over the army. And Jennesta's father, Serapheim, used his sorcery to paint the grim sky with images that grossly lied, to sway her militia and break its spirit. Though she expected no better from that quarter.

As more snow began to fall, stinging the troops' flesh and blinding their vision, she grew impatient. Accompanied by her orc commander, General Mersadion, and half a dozen of her ablest Royal Guardsmen, she gained entry to the palace.

Its murky corridors held the stench of age-old corruption, and aberrant, inhuman sounds echoed through the crumbling pile.

Jennesta and her group were not the first to get in. Several advance parties of Manis had entered before them. Their corpses littered the place. Without exception they were terribly mutilated, and in many cases it looked as though they had been partially consumed. Despite his orcish spirit the general's disquiet was palpable, and the guardsmen, holding aloft oil-fed lanterns, were plainly anxious. Jennesta paid no attention.

They had hardly penetrated the labyrinth of twisting passageways and cavernous chambers when misshapen figures began moving from the shadows.

The Sluagh, a loathsome shape-changing race reckoned by many to be demons, infested the palace. Alien in form and in deed, they were entirely merciless. As they swiftly proved when the two hindmost guards in Jennesta's party were brought down and torn apart. Ignoring their screams she hurried on, the general and the other troopers, ashen-faced, close behind.

They hadn't gone far before the creatures struck again. Lurching from the gloom, fibrous hides glistening moistly in the dim light, one of them snared a guardsman with sinewy tentacles. At the ready this time, the soldier's comrades and the general turned to hack at the Sluagh.

'Leave him!' *Jennesta snapped.*

Their fear of her outweighed any feelings of solidarity. They abandoned the shrieking trooper. Glancing back, Mersadion caught a glimpse of the man's fate, and shuddered.

There was a respite as Jennesta strode on, looking for a way to reach the palace's lower levels. But it was short-lived. Turning into a narrow passage they found a pack of Sluagh ahead. Slavering and giving off a confounding babble, the beasts advanced. With her own safety at stake, Jennesta acted, fashioning a spell with an intricate movement of her hands, though with an air of blasé impatience rather than any kind of dread. A searing flash lit the darkness. The Sluagh burst open like ripe melons sliced with an invisible axe, liberating their steaming viscera as they fell.

Jennesta continued walking, lifting the hem of her gown above the mess. The others followed, gingerly stepping over the carcasses, hands pressed to their faces to keep out the stench.

They came to an arched doorway opening on to a flight of steps that went down into pitch blackness. A faint rhythmic throbbing could be heard from below. Jennesta ordered two of the three remaining troopers to stay at the entrance and stand guard. From the expressions the pair wore it was obvious they didn't know whether to be relieved or alarmed. There was no such ambiguity on the third soldier's face when she pointed to the stairs and told him to take the lead.

After descending for only a short time there was a commotion from the guards left above. It began with yells and ended in screams, quickly stifled. Unmoved, Jennesta told her two surviving underlings to keep going. The light from the lamp carried by the leading trooper wavered in his unsteady hand, casting grotesque shadows on the moist walls.

The periodic throbbing grew louder the deeper they went. But now it was mixed with other, discordant sounds; the grind of stone on stone and the creaking of timbers. There was a trembling underfoot. Tiny fragments of ice started to fall, shaken loose by the vibration. The sensation was like a minor earthquake.

The stairs came to an end, depositing them in a wide corridor that ran into darkness in both directions. Except not quite. To their right, there was a weak glimmer of light. Jennesta ordered the guardsman to extinguish his lamp. In the ensuing blackness the pulsating light could be seen clearly, outlining the shape of a sizeable door. They went towards it.

Small chunks of debris were falling now, and seeps of dust. The rumbling grew, pounding the soles of their feet. And there was something strange about the air. It felt charged, oppressive, and far too warm given the chill atmosphere.

There was a movement to their rear. Looking back, they could make out one of the Sluagh at the foot of the stairs, and several more behind. The guardsman lost his nerve. He dropped the snuffed lantern and ran, past the door bleeding light and along the passageway. His dash lasted less than twenty paces. A Sluagh's feelers whipped down from the ceiling, snared him and hoisted him up. Howling, legs kicking, he disappeared into shadow.

Taking advantage of the distraction, Jennesta hurried to the door, General Mersadion in tow. It was unlocked, but heavy and hard to move. She let him take the brunt of shifting it. On the other side was another, much shorter corridor, leading to an archway. The space beyond was bathed in beating light.

She got him to secure the door, then said, 'Looks like it's just you and me, General.'

Pointing at the source of the light he asked, 'What is it, my lady?'

'Think of it as a . . . gateway. It's very old, and it was what inspired my father to create the artefacts that rightly belong to me.'

He nodded, as though he understood.

'Activating the portal has released the energy that's destroying this palace,' she added offhandedly.

Mersadion looked no more comfortable for the explanation.

They approached the arch. It led to a set of wide steps that swept down to a capacious chamber that housed five massive, rudely worked standing stones, arranged in a semicircle. At its centre was a low granite dais, studded with what appeared to be gems. Issuing from the dais' surface was something wondrous.

It was as though a waterfall had been upended. But it wasn't a liquid cascade. It was light. Countless millions of tiny multicoloured pinpoints, spiralling, twisting, surging upwards in a never ending, constantly replenished flow. The dazzling vortex was the source of the throbbing beat, and a sulphurous odour hung in the air.

There were a number of beings present. Standing just beyond the arch, Jennesta scanned them. Her father, Tentarr Arngrim, known to the covert world of sorcery as Serapheim, was at the forefront. Jennesta's sister, Sanara, the most human in appearance of Arngrim's brood, was by his side. The rest were Wolverines, the wretched orc warband who had subjected Jennesta to the bitterest of betrayals. All were transfixed by the glittering spectacle.

Jennesta saw the female orc, Coilla, standing close to the dais and staring at the torrent. Coilla mouthed, 'It's beautiful.'

Standing next to her the dwarf, Jup, nodded and said, 'Awesome.'

'And mine!' *Jennesta declared loudly as she lost patience and strode down the stairs, Mersadion in her wake.*

All heads turned to them. For a split second Jennesta's steely poise faltered. But she was confident in the superiority of her magic over anything here, spell or weapon.

'You're too late,' Serapheim told her. His tone was cooler than Jennesta cared for.

'Nice to see you too, Father dear,' she returned acerbically. 'I've a contingent of Royal Guards at my heels,' she lied. 'Surrender or die, it's all the same to me.'

'I can't see you passing on the opportunity to slay those you think have wronged you,' Sanara said.

'You know me so well, sister.' She thought how prissy Sanara was. 'And how pleasant to see you in the flesh again. I look forward to despoiling it.'

The Wolverines' leader spoke. 'If you think we're giving up without a fight, you're wrong.' He indicated his troop with the sweep of a sturdy hand. 'We've nothing to lose.'

'Ah, Captain Stryke.' She cast a derisive eye over his warband. 'And the Wolverines. I've relished the thought of meeting you again in particular.' Her voice hardened with the tenor of authority. 'Now throw down your weapons.'

There was a flurry of movement. Someone came out of the host, sword drawn. Jennesta recognised him as the band's healer, an aged fool of an orc called Alfray.

Instantly, Mersadion was there, blocking the attacker's path. The general's blade flashed. Alfray took a blow. He swayed, his eyes rolled to white, and he fell.

There was a moment of stasis, an immobility of all present as they took a collective intake of breath.

Then Stryke, Coilla, Jup and the bulking brute Haskeer fell upon the general and hacked him to pieces. The rest of the band would have joined them if it hadn't been over so quickly.

Jennesta saw no reason to spend any of her magic intervening. But she quickly acted when the vengeful orcs turned to her. An apple-sized ball of fire manifested on the palm of her outstretched hand. Its intensity immediately grew, the brilliance hurtful to the eyes of everyone looking on.

Serapheim cried, 'No!' *at the backs of the advancing Wolverines.*

Jennesta hurled the fireball at them. They scattered and it missed, passing close enough to several that they felt its scorching heat. The fiery globe struck the far wall and exploded, the sound of its report filling the chamber. Chunks of masonry came down with a further resounding crash. She had already begun forming another fireball when Serapheim and Sanara stepped in.

Jennesta wrapped herself in a cloak of enchantment, a conjured field of protective vigour, near transparent save for the slightest tinge of shimmering green. Her father and sibling did the same, and a duel of sorcery commenced.

Blistering spheres and searing bolts were exchanged, needles of energy and sheets of power were flung. Some volleys the bubble-like defensive shields absorbed; others were deflected, causing the hellish munitions to ricochet. Multicoloured streaks sliced the air. There were intense detonations throughout the chamber, cleaving wood and stone.

All the orcs could do was take shelter. Except for a small group, oblivious to the mayhem, who clustered around their fallen comrade.

Under the onslaught, and the building power of the vortex, the palace was beginning to destruct. The rumblings grew louder. Fissures rippled across the flagstone floor, cracks appeared in the walls.

The combined might of Serapheim and Sanara was proving too strong for Jennesta. Her forehead was sheened with perspiration, her breath was laboured. She fought to maintain concentration. Her stamina, and her confidence, were waning.

Sensing that she was weakening, her father and her sister increased the ferocity of their assault. Her protective shield started to waver. When its emerald tint slowly changed to a pinkish crimson Serapheim and Sanara knew the sign. They upped their barrage.

Jennesta lost her hold. The shield silently burst into a golden nimbus that dissolved to nothing. She staggered slightly, then steadied herself with an effort of will. She let out an exhausted breath.

Serapheim darted forward and grabbed her wrist. She was in too much of a daze to stop him. He began dragging her across the chamber.

The Wolverines wanted to kill her. They came forward with blades in their hands.

'No!' Serapheim bellowed. 'She's my daughter! I've a responsibility for all she's done! I'll deal with this myself!'

Reluctantly, they obeyed.

Serapheim was pulling Jennesta towards the dais and the sparkling portal. When they were almost there she came to herself, and realised what he intended doing. She showed no fear.

'You wouldn't dare,' she sneered.

'Once, perhaps,' he told her, 'before the full horror of your wickedness was brought home to me. Not now.' Holding her in an iron grip, he thrust her hand towards the portal's cascading brilliance, the tips of her fingers almost in the flow. 'I brought you into this world. Now I'm taking you out of it. You should appreciate the symmetry of the act.'

'You're a fool,' she hissed, 'you always were. And a coward. I've an army here. If anything happens to me you'll die a death beyond your wildest imagination.' She flicked her gaze to her sister. 'You both will.'

'I don't care,' he told her.

Sanara backed him.

It seemed to Jennesta that they might have had tears in their eyes. She thought them weaklings for it.

Serapheim said something about evil and some prices being worth paying. He pushed her hand nearer to the sparkling flux.

She looked into his eyes and knew he meant it. She tried to conjure a defence, but nothing came. Her cocksure expression faded and she began to struggle.

'At least face your end with dignity,' he said. 'Or is that too much to ask?'

She spat her defiance.

He thrust her hand into the vortex, then retreated a pace.

She squirmed and fought to pull her hand free but the gushing fountain of energy held it as tightly as a vice. A change came over the trapped flesh. It began to liquefy, releasing itself as thousands of particles that flew into the swarm of stars and spiralled with them. The process increased apace, the vortex gobbling up her wrist. Rapidly she was drawn in to the depth of her arm, which likewise disintegrated and scattered.

The band was rooted, their expressions a mixture of horror and macabre fascination.

Her leg had been sucked in now, and it was melting before their eyes. Strands of her hair followed, as though inhaled by an invisible giant. Jennesta's disintegration speeded up, her matter eaten by the surging vortex at a faster and faster rate.

When it began to consume her face she finally screamed.

The sound was instantly cut off as the energy took the rest of her in several gulps.

She was plunging down an endless tunnel. A tunnel that sinuously twisted and turned. A tunnel without walls, like a vast, transparent tube; transparent but faintly iridescent. Outside, if the word had any meaning, there was both nothing and everything. Nothing in the sense of being utterly devoid of recognisable points of reference. Everything in that the dark blue velvet beyond the walls was peppered with countless stars.

She fell, helplessly. And caught a glimpse of a pinpoint of light, far, far below. It grew at a remarkable rate, rapidly swelling to the size of a coin, a fist, a shield, a wagon wheel. Then it was all-embracing and rushing at her, obliterating everything else.

She dropped, not into light, but complete darkness.

To her amazement, she woke up.

She was on her back, lying on what felt like soft grass. The air was balmy, and she could smell the sweet perfume of flowers in full bloom. Other than distant birdsong, all was quiet. Blinking at the sky, she saw that it was a perfect blue, adorned with a smattering of pure white clouds. The sun was high.

Two revelations occurred as her mind began to clear. First, she was alive. Second, this obviously wasn't Maras-Dantia. It also dawned on her that she was naked.

Her limbs were leaden, and she felt battered, though it seemed she had no major injuries. She tried to raise her head, but she was weak and nauseous, and found it too much of an effort. Her sorcery was also apparently depleted. She struggled to conjure the simplest of rejuvenation spells, and got nothing.

But she had enough of her senses intact to feel the power coursing through the ground beneath her. The raw magical energy in this place was of a strength and purity that far outdid the almost spent vitality of Maras-Dantia.

So she had no option but to lie where she was, in hope of regaining her vigour naturally.

She couldn't tell how long she was there; she was feverish, and such rational thoughts as she had were on matters other than the mere passing of time. They mostly concerned the retribution she would exact on her father, her sister and the hated Wolverines. If she ever got to see them again.

The day slid into evening. It began to get dark, and cooler. Overhead, stars were appearing.

She heard a sound. It took a moment for her to identify it as an approaching horse. The animal was plodding slowly, and coupled with the squeak of wheels and the jangling of chains it became obvious it was pulling a wagon. It came to a halt close by. Someone dismounted. There was the crunch of boots on gravel, then an absence of sound as whoever it was walked onto the grass.

Somebody gazed down at her. She could only make out that it was a human male, and he was robustly built. He stared for what seemed an age. Not just at her nakedness, but her general appearance. By any yardstick she was beautiful, but her beauty had aspects most observers found disquieting. Her singular eyes were part of it, as was the perplexing configuration of her features: a face a mite too wide, particularly at the temples; a chin that came almost to a point; a vaguely convex nose; a shapely but overly broad mouth, and a mass of coal black, waist-length hair. But it was her skin that was most arresting. It had a slight silver-green lustre, and a dappled character that gave the impression she was covered in minute fish scales.

She was fully aware of the depraved nature of the man's race, more than once having admired their inexhaustible cruelty. If his intentions had been dishonourable in any way there wouldn't have been much she could have done about it.

But instead of subjecting her to lust or brutality he performed an act of compassion he would later, albeit briefly, regret. Stirring himself, he spoke. His tone was kindly, concerned. When there was no reply he bent and wrapped her in his rough cloak. Then he gathered her up with the ease of a mother lifting her child, and as gently. He carried her towards his wagon.

Jennesta finally got a better idea of where she was. Even in the dying light she glimpsed a verdant landscape. She saw meadows, cultivated fields and the rim of a forest. Not far away stood a range of rolling green hills.

They came to a road, and the wagon. The man put her aboard tenderly, slipping a couple of folded sacks under her head as a pillow. When they set off he drove carefully.

Lulled by the swaying of the cart, she lay, fatigued, looking up at the rising stars. Despite her fever and her weakness she turned the same thought over and over in her mind.

She had had the luck to come across a good man.

The following week was a blur.

She had been taken to a farmhouse. It was modest, and needed thatching. There were chickens and pigs in the yard. In the house was the farmer's wife and her brood; four youngsters, all boys.

The farmer and his wife tended Jennesta. They fed her, bathed her and spoke soothingly to her until she got back her senses.

She feigned memory loss, and let them assume she had been attacked and robbed of everything. They just about accepted that the odd greenish patina of her skin was the result of a childhood malady, and soon seemed to ignore it. And it wasn't so outlandish, they told her, in a world that had orcs in it.

The reference to that particular race revitalised Jennesta. She interrogated the couple, demanding all sorts of information. Where were these orcs? Were they the only non-human race in this world? What was the humans' political set-up and where did its power lie? They found her questions baffling, and couldn't understand why she didn't know the simplest of facts. Jennesta blamed her contrived amnesia, pretending to recall a blow to the head.

What she learned was that she was in Peczan, the cradle of a great empire. It was incomparably mighty, though it had its enemies. Most of these were barbarian kingdoms, often at each other's throats, and of little account. Peczan's only possible rival was the orcs, who occupied a far-off land called Acurial. But even they posed little threat, Jennesta was told, given their aversion to warlike ways. Naturally she couldn't accept her hosts' talk of the orcs of Acurial being docile, and felt sure they spoke from ignorance. But she held her tongue on the subject.

What she learned set her planning. Now there was a goal, and she turned her will to achieving it.

She had almost entirely recovered physically. Her magical abilities were another matter. They had started to return, but feebly, though she still felt the land's amazing fecundity. Her plan could hardly be realised from a decrepit farmhouse in the middle of nowhere. She needed to move on. That meant fully regaining her powers, and the use of people to serve her purpose.

Jennesta applied another kind of power to the oafish farmer. His conquest took just days. Once seduced, he was clay in her hands, and she remade him in her own image. Where there had been humanity, now there was only a dim-witted devotion to her whims. Where there had been tenderness towards his family, now there was callous indifference.

Such was her hold on the man that he willingly conspired in replenishing her powers. In the event, his wife's contribution was poor fare, mean and stringy. But the hearts of the four boys proved extremely nourishing. Her abilities restored, Jennesta had no further need of the farmer. She dispensed with him by simply removing the cloud from his mind and allowing him to see what had been done. His suicide provided her with a fleeting distraction.

The farmer was her first acolyte. There would be many more.

She had heard of a nearby town, and lost no time getting there, taking the farm's wagon and what little money she could find. The so-called town turned out to be not much more than a village. But it did have a tailor. Finally rid of the farmer's wife's drab hand-me-downs, she made sure her new clothes included a hood and a veil, should her appearance be an issue.

She also learned something she found intriguing, and which the farmer hadn't bothered mentioning. Unlike the vast majority of humans in Maras-Dantia, in this world they had a command of magic. At least, some did. These adepts belonged to the Order of the Helix, a sect with as much sway in the empire as its political masters.

The Order's nearest lodge was in the region's administrative centre, a provincial city a day's ride away. Compared to the sleepy hamlets and villages she passed on the road, its bustling streets gave her a measure of anonymity. More importantly, it connected her with a strand of the empire's web.

Jennesta had no trouble finding the Helix lodge; prominently located, it passed for a major temple. She was less lucky trying to penetrate it as anything other than a supplicant. The Order was male dominated. There were females in its ranks but they were few, and hardly any had real power. Rebuffed, she looked for a weak spot.

The Order's local overseer was an elderly, addle-headed bachelor who had never met anything like Jennesta before. She captivated him with ease. In half a year she had become his indispensable aide, and was grudgingly admitted to the Helix ranks under his patronage. By year's end she occupied his position, thanks to the judicious administering of poison.

She had a power base.

The ruthless efficiency with which Jennesta ran the lodge, and reports of her outstanding magical abilities, attracted the attention of the Order's upper echelons, as she intended. The upshot was a summons to the capital, and Helix's headquarters.

Competition for preferment was much stiffer once she entered the Grand Lodge, and advancement was frustratingly slow. Applying pressure on obstructive officials, swearing oaths she would later break, forming fragile alliances, corrupting the susceptible, bullying the weak and eliminating rivals needed all her guile. It also took time.

Another two years went by before the Order of the Helix was hers.

She immediately turned her attention to infiltrating government. As magic and politics intermingled in Peczan, she had already earned a certain notoriety that opened previously slammed doors. By virtue of her position at the pinnacle of Helix, she was automatically granted access to the citadels of the ruling class and the parlours of the influential, despite their thinly-veiled resentment of a female. Once again, she set about climbing.

A further year of machination and murder passed. She completed it as an upper-ranking official; a position of considerable power, though short of the highest. Any hopes she might have had about reaching the apex of empire were allowed to slip away. It wasn't that she didn't have an insatiable appetite for power. It was simply that she had all she needed, and saw no point in wasting more time laying siege to the summit, where she would be too noticeable in any event.

Jennesta never stopped thinking about orcs. She thought of the Wolverines in terms of revenge. And she thought of the orcs of Acurial as an opportunity.

It had long been her ambition to command an unparalleled army, and given their inexhaustible passion for warfare, no race was better suited to fill its ranks than the orcs. In this, Jennesta was perpetuating the dream of her mother, the sorceress Vermegram, who long ago mustered the orcs of Maras-Dantia. With such a force, and armed with the instrumentalities, Jennesta saw no limit to conquest. But like Vermegram, the magical means to totally control the race had eluded her. The orcs who served her in Maras-Dantia were kept in line with iron discipline and brutal punishments; the doctrine of fear Jennesta applied to all her underlings. That had proved insufficient, as the actions of the cursed Wolverines attested. The irony was that she had all but perfected a method of control when her father consigned her to this world. A world whose only orcs inhabited a distant land.

So she was intrigued, during her fourth year, when she started to hear rumours about military action against Acurial. This wasn't because Acurial posed any kind of threat to the empire or its interests. It was motivated by a desire for expansion, a hunger for natural resources and to bolster Peczan's influence in the region. But even a dictatorship must occasionally placate the opinion of its subjects, particularly when planning to send their young into combat. The orcs reputed passivity went some way to assure people that an invasion would be a walk-over, but a pretext was needed.

It was Jennesta's idea to put out that the orcs had magic at their disposal, destructive enough to menace the empire. Ignorance about far-off Acurial was so prevalent that this story was widely believed. Jennesta earned kudos for the ploy, but her request to accompany the invasion force was ignored. She set about fresh intrigues to get what she wanted.

The invasion was launched, and succeeded, with minimal Peczan casualties. Which seemed to confirm that Acurial's orcs were too passive to resist; something Jennesta still found hard to believe. The empire's bureaucracy ground into action and started to administer what was now a province. Draconian laws were enforced. Helix lodges were established. While all this was going on, Jennesta fought to curb her impatience, never an easy task, and continued her campaign to get to Acurial.

Half a year into the occupation she gained a concession. On the principle of knowing your enemy, she had argued for being allowed to study the orcs. Her hope was that this would take her to Acurial. It didn't. But Peczan shipped back a sizeable number of orc captives. They were paraded through the streets of the capital as living tokens of the empire's triumph, then handed over to Jennesta for what was officially referred to as 'appraisal'.

She was confounded by what she saw. These orcs did indeed seem passive, even submissive. Her instinct was to test their apparent meekness to its breaking point. On her orders they were humiliated, demeaned, beaten, tortured and subjected to arbitrary executions. The majority offered no more resistance than cattle sent for slaughter. But a few, a very few, snapped out of their apathy and tried to fight back with a ferocity she knew of old. This convinced her that the race's martial tendencies were not so much absent as dormant, and could be reawakened.

She told her superiors about it. She demonstrated it to them by having selected subjects goaded to fury. The fact that at least some orcs were capable of defiance was no surprise to them. The situation in Acurial was becoming troublesome. There had been organised attacks on the occupying forces, and they were escalating. Jennesta persuaded them of the need to send an emissary to shake things up in the province. Her Helix reputation, and not least her ruthlessness, landed her the role.

But shortly before she was due to leave, she saw her father.

From time to time, Jennesta would walk the streets incognito, usually at night. She did it partly to gain a sense of the city's mood, but mostly to hunt for victims when she felt in need of sustenance. She went out alone, certain that her powers could better anything the city might threaten, though there were those who would have assassinated her given the chance.

She found herself in one of the more sordid quarters, as she often did. Such places tended to have an abundance of people who wouldn't be missed. There had been the usual minor inconvenience of men trying to approach or harass her. Most turned away when they saw her look. The persistent were given a taste of the Craft, leaving them stung or injured or worse. Jennesta remained unperturbed.

Weaving through a street that seemed to house nothing but taverns and bordellos, something caught her eye. A man was walking some distance ahead. Like her, he was hooded, and he had his back to her. But she thought she recognised his frame and gait, although there was sign of a slight limp. Certain she must be mistaken about who it might be, nevertheless her curiosity was stirred, and on impulse she followed him. He was doing his best to keep to the shadows. She did likewise.

After trailing him for some time through bustling streets they came to a quieter but no less run-down district. At one point the man slowed and looked back. Luckily for her, Jennesta was able to take refuge in the gloom of a cloister. Hidden by a crumbling column, she got a fleeting glimpse of his face. It was thinner than when she last saw him, and he looked drawn. But there was no mistake.

Very little shocked Jennesta. This was a rare and notable exception. But surprise was soon replaced by cold fury.

It seemed her father hadn't seen her, and continued his journey. She followed, doubly careful not to be spotted. He led her deeper into the low neighbourhood. Others lurked in the shadows here, but father and daughter both radiated something the night dwellers found unsettling, and they went unmolested. The streets became lanes and the lanes narrowed to twisting alleys. At last they arrived at a blacksmith's shop with adjoining stables, so ramshackle they were presumably abandoned. Her father paused at a side door and again looked back. Jennesta was well hidden. Satisfied, he pushed the door just far enough to slip in, then quietly closed it behind himself.

She lingered where she was for a moment. There was no question that she would act. Her dilemma was how. Remembering the last encounter with her father, she considered summoning Helix and military reinforcements. But there was a good chance he wouldn't still be here when they turned up. More importantly, he looked far less robust than he used to, and perhaps not so much of a challenge. Although she didn't know who else might be in there with him, of course. In the end her rage at his presence, and a hunger for vengeance, overrode any other considerations. She made for the door.

It wasn't locked, and opened at her touch. Inside was a short wooden passageway leading to another door that stood slightly ajar. She approached it stealthily. Peering through the crack, she saw a barn-sized interior lined on two sides with stalls for the horses, all derelict now. Ahead of her were stacks of powder-dry bales of hay. She crept to them and hid there.

There was a murmur of voices. The interior was ill-lit, but she could make out two figures. One was her father. The other was a much younger man, no more than a youth, with a striking mop of red hair and a freckled face. Like Serapheim, he carried no obvious weapon. The pair were conversing earnestly. Serapheim dug into a pocket, took out an amulet on a chain and handed it to the youth. The young man stared at it for a moment, then put the chain around his neck and tucked the amulet into his shirt. They carried on talking, and Jennesta, keeping low, moved forward in an effort to hear.

Serapheim held up a hand to halt whatever the youth was saying, then turned in her direction. 'You can come out,' he said, his voice clear and steady.

Jennesta cursed herself for thinking he wouldn't detect her presence. She stepped out of hiding. The youth looked shaken. Her father displayed no such reaction. He seemed calm as she walked towards them, though she judged his appearance as weaker than when they last met.

'You look a mess,' she told him.

'You haven't changed,' her father replied.

'Thank you,' she gave back wryly.

'It wasn't a compliment.'

'I thought you were dead.'

'Don't you mean hoped?' He didn't wait for a response. 'Luck and the Craft got me out of the palace. Just.'

'And not without cost, by the looks of you.' He said nothing and she added, 'So how do you come to be here? Or need I ask?'

'I thought the . . . task was done in Ilex. It was only later that I realised you hadn't perished, or had at least arrived somewhere you could do no harm. And when I saw what you were up to in this world . . .'

She wanted to say You can do that? *but bit it back. 'You can't be that far-looking if you weren't aware of me tracking you tonight.'*

'I let myself be preoccupied. Humans do that. We're not perfect.'

'That wins a prize for understatement. I assume your arrival at this particular time has some significance?'

'I've been here a while. I've watched you. I know you're intending to go to Acurial.'

'Ah. Your beloved orcs. So that's why you came here.'

'We owe them, Jennesta. For what we've done to them. What Vermegram tried to do.'

'My mother was a visionary!' she snapped. 'I'll never understand why she got entangled with a weakling like you.'

'Perhaps I was weak in turning a blind eye to her . . . misguided notions. But I believe she came to see the error of her ways.'

'There was no error in her ambition', Jennesta replied icily. 'It was right, and she almost achieved it.'

'I can't allow you to carry on what she started.'

'And how do you think you'll stop me? By repeating what you did to me in Maras-Dantia? You failed.' She rapped her chest with a fist. 'I'm here, in front of you. You'll fail again.'

'I'll have allies.'

'Not in this world. None in the empire and certainly none in—' She checked herself as a thought struck.

His thin smile seemed to confirm her suspicion. 'Not all orcs are like those in Acurial. As you well know.'

No, *she thought,* not in this world. *She turned her attention to the youth, as much to give herself thinking time as anything. He looked awed. 'And is this one of your . . .* allies?' *she asked, contemptuously.*

'Parnol's an apprentice; a very promising one.' He laid a hand on the boy's arm and fixed Jennesta with an even gaze. 'And he's under my protection.'

She didn't think her father would have made that point if this Parnol was capable of defending himself magically at any high level. So he had to have another function. She was beginning to guess what that was. 'Careful, Father,' she said. 'You don't have Sanara here to help you.' She flicked a glance at the youth. 'And he doesn't look comparable.' Parnol shifted uncomfortably.

'I'm warning you, Jennesta,' Serapheim bristled.

'Do it now.'

'What?'

'If you're so confident you can defeat me, why bother with plots and schemes? We can settle this now. Right here.'

'It doesn't have to be this way,' he reasoned. 'Reflect on the course you're taking.'

'Oh, save your breath, old man,' she retorted disgustedly.

'If you can see the light,' he persisted, 'as your mother did—'

'To hell with this.' She swiftly brought up her hand and lobbed a fistful of flame at him.

For all his age and brittleness, Serapheim was faster. A swathe of energy instantly appeared, embracing him and his apprentice. When Jennesta's searing volley struck, it dissipated harmlessly. She summoned a defensive shield of her own and continued her fiery assault. At first, her father didn't respond, until, under the increasing salvo, he retaliated. Blast and counter blast illuminated the cavernous barn.

It was all too reminiscent of their duel in Ilex, but Jennesta was determined on a different outcome. She invested all her concentration and considerable skills in overcoming her father's defences. Yet despite her resolve, and Serapheim's apparently diminished state, she couldn't break through.

Then she noticed her father produce an object from the folds of his cloak. Or rather, a cluster of objects, interlocked. In a heartbeat she realised it was a set of instrumentalities. Her eyes widened at the sight. She burned with frustration at having what she most desired so near yet beyond her reach.

Her aggravation heightened when she saw that her father was manipulating the artefacts. He had them directed at Parnol, who was doing little beyond looking terrified. Jennesta guessed what was about to happen, and nothing in her magical armoury seemed able to pierce Serapheim's barrier and prevent it.

In a rush she realised the flaw in her father's strategy. The barricade of energy he conjured was focused solely on repelling magic, which left another possibility. But Serapheim was slotting the last instrumentality into place, and she had just seconds to do something about it. More in desperation than in hope, she acted.

The sunburst spell she unleashed was simple. It was merely the generation of an eruption of light, but blindingly intense. When she opened her eyes she saw that it had left Serapheim and Parnol in disarray, and both had instinctively turned their backs on her. But her father was still fumbling with the instrumentalities. Gathering up her gown, Jennesta plucked out the dagger she kept strapped to her thigh. She drew back her arm and flung the blade with all the strength she could muster.

In that speck of time, two things happened simultaneously. Serapheim activated the instrumentalities, and his apprentice, still dazzled, lurched into the dagger's path. Unimpeded by the shield, it struck the youth square between his shoulder-blades. Serapheim cried out. Parnol staggered from the blow, then whipped away by the power of the instrumentalities, he vanished.

Shocked by what had happened, his concentration broken, Serapheim lost his hold on the protective shield. As it dissolved, Jennesta began to conjure a further, lethal strike. Her father hastily adjusted the instrumentalities, and with a last look mixing sorrow and anger, he disappeared too.

She stood alone. There was disappointment at not having eliminated her father, and particularly at letting the instrumentalities elude her. But she judged it at least a partial victory.

The sulphurous tang of magic hung in the air. It mingled with the smell of burning timber, stray bolts from their battle having started several fires in the building.

She left it to burn.

Jennesta set out for Acurial not long after, and many were glad to see her go.

She had no way of foreseeing what would unfold there. No hint that she would triumph in her quest for the instrumentalities, yet see her other plans ruined, thanks to the intervention of the detestable Wolverines.

Nor could she imagine that she would eventually find herself on a corpse-littered beach on a world of islands, poised between the prospect of victory and having everything turn to ashes.

1

There was chaos.

All across the island, battles were raging between Jennesta's loyalists and the Gateway Corps. Most of the dwarfs who inhabited the isle, and who had survived the initial clash, had fled to their boltholes or the upper slopes of the sacred volcanoes. Seashore and jungle resonated with the flare of magic and the ringing of blades.

The Wolverines were gathered in the strip of pebbly land between beach and tree-line, sheltering behind an outcrop of rock. They were still reeling at what Stryke and Coilla had told them.

Two of the band's best scouts, Hystykk and Zoda, had been dispatched to discover Jennesta's whereabouts. They returned crest-fallen.

'She's not where you last saw her, Captain,' Zoda confirmed. 'There were too many of her troopers about for us to look much further afield.'

'So where the fuck is she?' Haskeer said.

Coilla shrugged. 'Could be anywhere by now.'

'This island's not so big,' Stryke told them. 'We can find her.' As the effect Jennesta's spell had on him wore off, it was being replaced by pure anger.

'Where's she likely to have gone?' Pepperdyne asked.

Haskeer gave the human a venomous look. 'If we knew that, pink face, we wouldn't be flapping our gums here.'

'I mean, figure it out. It wasn't as though she was actually winning the battle, was it? It was a draw at best. And it looks to me like that elf's group holds the beach. So she'd maybe think twice before going for her fleet.'

'Makes sense,' Coilla said.

'Trust you to back him,' Haskeer muttered.

Coilla shot him a dagger look but kept quiet.

'So what does she do?' Pepperdyne went on.

'Goes inland,' Jup supplied.

'Not a lot of choice,' his mate Spurral added, lightly ribbing him.

Pepperdyne nodded. 'Right. But is she going to tramp about in the jungle? I don't think so. She'd make for something more practical.'

'The dwarfs' village!' Wheam exclaimed.

The others had worked that out already, and he didn't get the hurrah he expected.

'What do you think, Stryke?' Coilla asked.

'I think we're wasting time,' he snapped, 'when Thirzarr needs me.'

'Yeah. So, the village?'

He sighed. 'As good a place as any, I s'pose.' To the rest he announced, 'We're moving out! We run into anybody, we cut 'em down!'

'Don't we always?' Haskeer wondered.

'She won't be alone,' Dallog warned, drawing another contemptuous look from Haskeer.

'I know,' Stryke said. 'We can deal with it.'

'What about Jennesta herself?' Jup asked. 'What happens if—' He saw Stryke's expression. '—*when* we find her? How do we handle *that*?'

'I'll think of something,' his captain returned gruffly, and without further word turned and set off at a pace.

The band fell in behind him.

Coilla slipped an arm around Pepperdyne's waist as they walked. It drew looks.

'How bad was it back there?' he wanted to know.

'Pretty bad. I've never seen Stryke so . . . out of control.'

'He seems all right now.'

'Don't kid yourself. Take my advice: steer clear of him. He's just about bottling the fury.'

'Can't blame him after what happened to his mate. I know how I'd feel if something like that happened to . . . somebody I care for.' He smiled at her.

Coilla returned it, then sobered. 'It's not just Thirzarr. He's got Corb and Janch to think about too. His hatchlings,' she added by way of explanation. 'And who knows what mayhem Jennesta might have wreaked in Ceragan. This is one pissed-off band, Jode.'

'How can I tell?'

'What'd you mean?'

'You're orcs. Pissed-off seems to be the natural state.'

She grinned again, despite herself. 'Not all the time.'

'Thankfully, no.'

'Mind you, it was good that Wheam got pissed-off back there just when we needed it.'

'Sounds like he did well.'

'Yeah. Not that Haskeer believes it.'

They glanced at Wheam. He was jogging along next to Dallog. But Dallog seemed more interested in Pirrak, one of the other tyros from Ceragan, with whom he was engrossed in conversation.

'Looks like Dallog's neglecting him,' Pepperdyne observed.

'He has to mentor all the newbies.'

'I've noticed he's spent a lot of time with that one recently.'

'Maybe Pirrak needs some kind of guidance. The fresh intake are new to this, remember.'

'Been quite a baptism of fire for them, hasn't it?'

'Yes. It's a wonder we haven't lost more of 'em, thank the Tetrad.'

'The what?'

'You've not heard any of us say that before? It's our congress of gods. There are four of them. I'll explain some time, if you're interested.'

'I'd like to hear about it. And you . . . believe in these gods? You appeal to them?'

'Usually when somebody's trying to part me from my head.'

Pepperdyne smiled. 'I know that feeling. It was the same with my people.' He cast an eye over the trudging band. 'I guess there's a certain amount of appealing going on right now.'

'You bet.'

'So how do your— *Damn.* Heads up.' He nodded.

Coilla followed his gaze and saw Standeven elbowing their way. She rolled her eyes.

Pepperdyne's one-time master arrived sweating. 'I need to talk to you,' he insisted to Coilla in an undertone.

'About what?'

He looked around, anxious not to be overheard. 'The instrumentalities,' he mouthed.

Pepperdyne groaned. 'Not this again.'

Standeven glared at him and turned indignant. 'I only want to ask the Corporal here if they're still safe.'

'What's it to you?' Coilla said.

'A lot. As it should be to everybody here. Our only chance of getting home depends on—'

'I know. They're safe. You'd have to kill Stryke to get 'em. Unlikely in your case.'

He ignored the jibe. 'And has he mastered them yet? Has he worked out what's wrong with them?'

She jabbed a thumb in Stryke's direction. 'Why don't you ask him?'

Standeven looked to Stryke, forging ahead at the column's prow. He saw the broadness of his back, the rippling muscles and, when he turned his head to scold those following, the murderous expression he wore. 'I'll . . . wait until he's free.'

'He does have a couple of other things on his mind,' Pepperdyne informed him dryly.

'But they're secure, right? The stars, they're—'

'*Enough*. You're getting obsessed with the things. Give it a rest.'

Standeven flushed redder. 'There was a time,' he grated angrily, 'when you wouldn't have dared speak to me like that.'

'So you keep telling me. And I keep saying that time's past. Live with it.'

Shaking with impotent fury, his old master fell back in the column, where he was given a wide berth.

'I think he's going crazy,' Pepperdyne said, at least half seriously.

Coilla shook her head. 'Don't know about that. I do know the effect the stars can have.'

'Effect?'

'Spending too long with 'em can make things a bit weird. We've seen it in the band.'

'Weird?'

'You turned into an echo, or what?'

'Just explain, Coilla.'

'Later. It's a long story. But the stars have the power to get a hold on some, make 'em act . . . well, a bit like Standeven.'

'What about Stryke? He's with the things all the time.'

'Yeah, and that's a worry. But like I said, it affects some, not all. He seems to handle it. Most of the time.'

'Oh, great.'

'What I'm saying is, keep an eye on Standeven.'

'I usually do.'

They marched in silence after that, turning things over in their minds.

Stryke was leading the band along the upper lip of the beach, keeping the jungle to their right. Soon they would reach a line of sand dunes marking the point where they needed to turn inland, onto the path that headed toward the dwarfs' settlement.

As dwarfs themselves, Jup and Spurral felt a natural sympathy with the natives, but their empathy was with Stryke. Marching four or five ranks to his rear, they found themselves eyeing him constantly.

'He looks in a state,' Spurral commented, 'near frenzied. Is he going to hold it together?'

'Course he will. He's tough. What beggars belief is how history's repeating itself.'

'Me and the Gatherers.'

Jup nodded. 'So I know how he feels.'

'He helped you get through that.'

'Yeah. I owe him.'

'Now you can repay. He needs your support. And maybe more down the road, depending on how this plays out.'

'There's no going near him at the moment, the mood he's in.'

'Well, you'll just have to—'

'*Wait!* Look.' He pointed at the sand dune they were approaching.

A number of humans were swarming over it, their Peczan uniforms marking them as Jennesta's followers. Several of her undead slaves were with them. Their movements were lumbering and jerky, and their deathly pallor was evident even at a distance. The looks of surprise on the troopers' faces testified to this being an unexpected encounter rather than an ambush.

'*Damn*,' Spurral said. 'Just what we needed.'

'Yes, it is,' Jup told her.

'More *trouble*'s what we need?' She drew her short-bladed sword.

'Better to be at the enemy's throats than each other's. It'll bleed off the tension. 'Specially Stryke's.'

As Jup spoke, Stryke rushed at the troopers, bellowing a war cry. The rest of the band took it up and thundered after him. All but Standeven, who hung back, looking fretful.

The two lines met in a bellowing roar and the clatter of steel.

Stryke tore into the human ranks like a hot cleaver through pig fat. A pair of troopers went down in a brace of heartbeats, and instantly he was engaging a third. He fought like a berserker, oblivious to whistling blades and lunging spears. His only aim was rending the flesh of anything in his way.

Coilla and Pepperdyne worked in unison, carving a path deep into the enemy's ranks, until they ran into one of the undead. The process by which Jennesta magically created her zombie adherents endowed them with a strength and stamina most lacked in life. This one was an exceptional example, and must have been hulking even before he met his fate. Armed with what looked like a tree trunk, he took a hefty swipe that caught Pepperdyne off guard. The blow was glancing, but enough to bring him to his knees. A follow-up would have brained him, had Coilla not rushed in, sword swinging. She struck the zombie at its waist, cutting deep. Back on his feet, Pepperdyne rejoined the fray, adding his weight to the fight. Together they hacked their foe to pieces.

Jup and Spurral also fought in harmony. Given their height, this was as much necessity as choice. Employing a well-practised technique, Jup used his staff to crack kneecaps, toppling opponents and bringing them in range of Spurral's blade.

Haskeer had no truck with anything like finesse. Having felled a trooper with a thrust to the man's chest, he had his sword dashed from his hand by a stray blow. Menaced by a trio of advancing soldiers he swiftly hoisted the corpse and hurled it at them. They went down like a row of skittles. Snatching up his sword, Haskeer followed through.

The new recruits instinctively fought as a group, with Dallog marshalling them, and gave a good account of themselves. Even Wheam, his confidence growing, managed to inflict some damage.

The whole band, steeped in frustration, vented their anger with orcish fury. They stabbed, slashed and pounded at the enemy mercilessly, intent on nothing short of a massacre.

At length, Stryke wrenched his blade from the innards of the last human and stood panting as he surveyed the slaughter.

'Feeling better?' Coilla said.

He wiped blood from his face with the back of a hand. 'Some.'

Jup arrived. 'Casualties light,' he reported. 'Dallog's patching up those who need it.'

Stryke nodded. 'Then let's keep moving.' He set off.

They took the jungle path leading to the dwarfs' village, alert to any further danger. The journey was uneventful until they were almost at the settlement, when they spotted columns of black smoke beginning to rise above the trees. Shortly after, they entered the clearing.

All but two or three of the huts were burning, and a dozen or so dead dwarfs were scattered about. Some of the band caught the briefest glimpse of movement in the jungle. It was judged to be natives fleeing to their hiding places. Coilla called out to them, but got no reply. The remaining huts were searched, along with the surrounding terrain, and proved deserted. Lookouts were posted, and the private with the best head for heights, Nep, was ordered to climb one of the taller trees to spy out the land. Stryke set half a dozen grunts on the more or less endless task of finding suitable wood to replenish their store of arrows. The rest of the band gathered around him.

'No Jennesta,' Haskeer said tightly, glaring at Pepperdyne. 'So much for your brilliant plan.'

'It was a reasonable assumption,' the human protested.

'And nobody had a better idea,' Coilla added.

Haskeer switched his baleful stare to her. 'That's right, take his side. As usual.'

'It was the best idea,' she repeated deliberately.

'Yeah, right.'

'If you've got some kind of beef, Haskeer, let's hear it.'

'I'm not keen on humans having a hand in how this band's run.'

'I haven't,' Pepperdyne told him. 'I was just trying to help.'

'And a fat lot of good that turned out. We don't need your *help*. So why don't you—'

'*Shut it*,' Stryke warned, his tone ominous. 'We're all in this together, and I'll have no bickering.'

'Now *you're* taking his part,' Haskeer grumbled.

'I said *shut . . . it*. There'll be no indiscipline in this band. And if anybody thinks otherwise they can step up now.'

Haskeer looked as though he just might, except they were interrupted by a shout from Nep at the tree top.

'What?' Stryke bellowed back.

'The ships! They've gone!'

'Which?'

'All but ours!'

Stryke signalled for him to come down.

'So Jennesta *has* left the island,' Jup said.

'And that other bunch too, by the sound of it,' Spurral put in.

'Shit,' Haskeer grated through clenched teeth.

'*Now* what do we do?' Coilla said.

2

The Gateway Corps ship had sailed beyond sight of the dwarfs' island. But the Corps elf commander, Pelli Madayar, who had taken the wheel herself, was uncertain which course to set. For that, she looked to her goblin second-in command, Weevan-Jirst. He was gazing at a plump, gleaming gem nestling in his palm.

'Anything?' Pelli asked.

'Nothing.'

'Take the wheel. I'll try.'

They swapped places. She warmed the gem in her hand, then stared hard at it. Its swirling surface was cloudy.

'Is something wrong with it?' Weevan-Jirst asked in the rasping timbre peculiar to his race.

'There shouldn't be, given the quality of its magic. I'll check.'

'How?'

Pelli was aware that although high in the Corps' magical hierarchy, her deputy still had a lot to learn. 'By comparing it with a set of instrumentalities we already know about,' she explained.

'Those held by the orc warband?'

She nodded. 'You're aware that each set of artefacts has its own unique signature; what some call its song. We know the tempo of the ones the Wolverines have. I'll see if I can attune to them. One moment.' Face creased in concentration, she softly recited the necessary spell. At length she said, 'There,' and showed him the gem.

Images had appeared on its façade. They were arcane, and continuously shifting, but to adepts their meaning was plain.

'The orcs' instrumentalities,' Weevan-Jirst interpreted, 'on the isle of dwarfs.'

'Yes. Which confirms that the fault doesn't lie in our method of detection.'

'I see that. So why can't we trace the artefacts Jennesta has?'

'Because I'm now certain that she's done something unprecedented, or at least extremely rare. The instrumentalities she's using are copies, presumably taken from the originals the orcs have. Their emanations are unlike those given off by the genuine articles, which is why we're finding it difficult to track them.'

'Copies? That would be a remarkable achievement.'

'Oh, yes. There's no doubting her extraordinary magical talent. Moreover, I believe she's also tampered with the originals in some way, giving her a measure of control over them.'

'Which would explain the erratic way the Wolverines were world-hopping before arriving in this one.'

'Indeed it would. She's toying with them.'

'But I'm puzzled.'

'How so?'

'Our mission is to retrieve the orcs' instrumentalities, and we know where they are. So why have we left them behind on the island?'

'We now have not one, but two sets of instrumentalities in irresponsible hands. And Jennesta's ability to duplicate them is potentially catastrophic. Imagine dozens, scores, *hundreds* of instrumentalities in circulation. The Corps could never control a situation like that.'

'It doesn't bear thinking about,' Weevan-Jirst agreed gravely.

'We've two options. We can go back to the island to tackle the orcs again, and run the risk of losing Jennesta for ever. Or we concentrate on her, knowing we can find the orcs as long as they have the artefacts, which they're unlikely to part with.'

'We don't know where she is.'

'I think we can find out by recalibrating our detection methods on the basis that her instrumentalities are copies.'

'Is that possible?'

'In theory. Only it might take a little while. But there's something else that could work to our advantage. Jennesta has Stryke's mate, and we can almost certainly count on him pursuing her too. With luck, we'll be able to bag both sets at the same time.'

'How will *they* know where she's gone?'

'Don't underestimate how tenacious a race the orcs are. I'd put a large wager on them working it out.'

The goblin looked doubtful. 'Isn't this deviating from our orders?'

'I have autonomy in the field, to a degree.'

'Yes,' he hissed, '*to a degree*. Are you going to consult higher authority?'

'Karrell Revers? No. At least, not yet.'

'Can I ask why not?'

'I have total respect for his judgement, but he's not here.'

'You mean he'd likely order you to stick to our original mission.'

'Probably. And we'd lose precious time while the situation's debated on homeworld.' She gave him a concerned look. 'Of course, I appreciate that you might be unhappy with my plan. But I'll take full responsibility for—'

'I'll be glad to abide by any decision you make, Pelli. For the time being.'

She decided not to pursue that comment. 'Thank you. Meantime, we have something else to attend to.' She looked along the deck. The bodies of three of their comrades were laid out, wrapped in bloody sheets. 'Then we have a score to settle with Jennesta.'

There were dead on Jennesta's ship too. Some walked and breathed, after a fashion. Others would never do either again.

Several of the latter were being pitched overboard by a party of the former.

The corpses being disposed of were dwarfs, broken and bloodied following Jennesta's creative interrogation methods. Apart from mundane necessity, the fate of the discarded cadavers had the additional effect of chastening her followers. But although Jennesta embraced, indeed revelled in the appellation tyrant, she was coming to understand the value of tempering stick with carrot when it came to her subordinates' loyalty. This took several forms. The promise of power and riches under her dominion was one way. Another was the dispensing of pleasure, her sorcery being capable of conferring sensations of wellbeing, even ecstasy, as readily as terror.

But there was a kind of follower for whom neither punishment nor bliss was the spur. These rare individuals shared her taste for cruelty. And Jennesta had found one. His name was Freiston. He was a young low-ranking officer in the Peczan military, one of those who had thrown in their lot with her in the hope of extravagant rewards. He was a human, so naturally she distrusted him. Not that she didn't distrust all races, but she was especially suspicious of humans. After all, her father was one.

Freiston had caught her attention because of his skill as a torturer, and his passion for it, which had proved useful. On the strength of that she promoted him to her notional second-in-command.

Following the debacle on the island, they were in Jennesta's cabin. She was seated, regally; he was required to stand. Also present was Stryke's mate, Thirzarr, who lay insensible on a cot. She looked as though she was sleeping, but it was a state only Jennesta's sorcery could rouse her from.

'Did you get what you want, ma'am?' Freiston asked.

She smiled. 'My wants exceed anything you could imagine. But if you mean the information I needed to set our course, then yes.'

'If I may say so, my lady, it's ironic.'

'What is?'

'That those dwarfs should have given their lives for something as mundane as a location.'

She gave him a withering look. 'It's hardly mundane to me. But it was a case of making them understand, rather than them trying to withhold what I wanted. Not that you're complaining, surely? You obviously enjoyed it.'

'I'm ready to serve you in any way necessary, ma'am.'

'Perhaps you should have been a diplomat rather than a soldier.' He started to respond. She waved him silent. 'We'll be in a combat situation at landfall. I need my force in good order and well briefed on what they'll be up against. You'll see to it.'

'Ma'am. We're going to be a *little* under strength in a couple of key areas due to a few of our people being left behind on the dwarfs' island.'

'Do I look like someone who cares about that? If they were too slovenly to obey my evacuation order I don't need them.'

'Yes, m'lady. Can I ask when we'll reach our destination?'

'In about two days. What I seek turned out to be nearer than I suspected. So you're going to be a busy little man, Freiston.' She rose.

'Let's set the wheels turning.' Glancing at Thirzarr's recumbent form, she led him out of the cabin.

From the deck, the other four vessels in her flotilla could be seen, ploughing in her flagship's wake. On the deck itself, one of Jennesta's undead stood motionless over a dwarf's body. She swept that way, Freiston in tow.

Approaching, she saw that the zombie was General Kapple Hacher. Or had been. He was staring at the cadaver. Freiston showed no emotion at seeing his one-time commanding officer so hideously reduced.

Jennesta was furious. 'What are you doing, you *dolt*?' she raged. 'You had your orders. Take that—' She jabbed a finger at the corpse. '—and cast it overboard.'

The drooling hulk that had been a great army's general and governor of a Peczan province carried on staring.

'Do it!' Jennesta insisted, further incensed. 'Obey me!'

Hacher lifted his gaze to her, but otherwise stayed motionless. Her patience exhausted, she continued haranguing, and took to cuffing him with a rings-encrusted fist, raising puffs of dust from the tatters of his decaying uniform. After a moment his eyes, hitherto glassy, flickered and showed something like sentience, and perhaps a hint of defiance.

Freiston's hand went to his sword hilt.

'Do . . . as . . . you're . . . told,' Jennesta commanded, fixing Hacher with a look of smouldering intensity.

The light died in his eyes and they returned to insensible. With a kind of rasping sigh he bent to the corpse. He lifted it with no sign of effort and, straightening, tossed it over the rail. There was a distant splash.

'Now get back to your duties,' Jennesta told him.

Hacher slowly turned and trudged away, heading for the prow and a group of fellow zombies hefting supplies.

Jennesta saw Freiston's expression and answered his unspoken question. 'Sometimes, when their original force of will was strong, subjects can be less compliant.' She indicated the party Hacher was joining. 'They're imperfect beings; far from the ideal I have in mind.'

'Can they be improved, ma'am?'

'Oh, yes. In the same way that a peasant using poor clay makes poor pots, this first batch has flaws that carried over from the material I was forced to use. But with the right subjects, and refinements I've made to the process, the *next* batch is going to be far superior. As you'll soon see. But you have something on your mind, Freiston. What is it?'

'We have the orc's female,' he replied hesitantly.

'Stryke's mate, yes. What of it?'

'If he's as pig-headed as you say, my lady, won't his band be after us?'

'I'm counting on it.'

'Ah.' He knew better than to query her reasoning, but ventured another thought. 'And the group that attacked us? Who *were* they?'

'They can only have been the Gateway Corps. I thought they were a myth, but it appears not.'

'Aren't they another threat?'

'They're meddlers. Self-appointed so-called guardians of the portals. There'll be a reckoning for what they did today.'

Freiston had doubts about that, given that Jennesta had just had to retreat from them. But naturally he kept his opinion to himself.

'Neither orcs nor a ragbag of interfering elder races are going to stand in my way,' she went on. 'There's going to be a very different outcome the next time our paths cross.'

3

Stryke's fury had subsided. Cold purpose took its place.

He set about getting things organised. As it was nearly dusk, the dwarfs' remaining undamaged longhouses were commandeered and the surrounding area secured. A group was sent to the goblin ship the band had arrived in, to replenish its rations and to guard it. Scouting parties were dispatched to comb the island.

Having done as much as he could for the time being, Stryke sat down on the steps of one of the longhouses and fell to brooding. Everybody in the band knew better than to approach him. With one exception.

Jup came to him with a steaming bowl and a canteen. 'Here.' He offered the food. Stryke barely looked at it, and said nothing. 'You've got to eat,' the dwarf told him. 'For Thirzarr. You'll be no good famished.'

Stryke took the bowl. He stared at its contents. 'What is it?'

Jup seated himself. 'Lizard. The jungle's full of 'em. That other stuff's leaves and roots,' he added helpfully. 'There's fruit too, but I figured you need meat.'

Stryke began eating, without enthusiasm.

After a moment, Jup ventured, 'About Thirzarr . . .' He ignored Stryke's baleful expression and pushed on. 'I'll tell you what you told me when Spurral got taken. Your mate has a value to Jennesta. And you don't damage something of value.'

'What value? Why should Jennesta give a damn about Thirzarr's life?'

'Don't know. It could be as simple as antagonising you. What's important is that Jennesta kept Thirzarr alive; she didn't leave her lying on the beach back there.'

'But the state she was in. Like one of the bitch's damned undead.'

'Not quite. Jennesta *threatened* to make Thirzarr that way. But she didn't do it. That's more reason for hope, Stryke.'

'We don't know she hasn't. And it's not just Thirzarr. There's Corb and Janch. What value are *they* to her?'

'There's no reason to think—'

'And Ceragan itself; what might she have done there?'

'Stryke.'

'Come to that, what if—'

'*Stryke.* Could she have made Ceragan more of a shit hole than Maras-Dantia?'

Jup was gratified when that drew a thin smile. 'Where do we go from here?' Stryke said.

'Not sure. We just have to believe that a way's going to open for us. But you know we're with you, Stryke. The whole band. Whatever it takes.'

Stryke nodded and went on eating mechanically.

They sat in silence.

Not far away, just inside the jungle's lip, Coilla and Pepperdyne were foraging.

He stooped and ripped up a handful of purplish leaves. 'Do you think these are all right?'

Coilla looked, then sniffed the bouquet. She made a face. 'I wouldn't risk it unless you want to poison everybody.'

He tossed the clump away. 'This is harder than I thought. Things seem more or less the same in this world as ours, but when you take a closer look . . .'

'Yes, there are differences in the small stuff. But think about how big some of the differences were in those other worlds we went to. We were lucky with this one.'

'Talking of which, you started to tell me how what we call our home world isn't really *your* home world, despite you being born there. What the hell was that all about?'

'It's not the real home of any of the elder races. As we were told it, it rightly belongs to your race.'

'And?'

'You want to hear it now?'

'What else is there to do? Unless you'd prefer to—' He reached for her.

She wriggled free, laughing. 'Whoa! Steady. All right. It's complicated, and I don't even know if it's true, but—'

'It's just a fairy story then.'

'The stories *they* tell would freeze your blood. No, we reckon what we heard's probably true, but . . . who knows?'

'So spill it.' He sat, then patted the sward next to him and she sat too.

'All right.' She gathered her thoughts. 'The story goes that the world we both come from was the humans' world. All we knew was our land; what we called Maras-Dantia and your race called Centrasia. We thought Maras-Dantia belonged to all the elder races living there, and that humans came from outside much later and fucked everything up.' She saw the look he gave her. 'No offence.'

He smiled. 'None taken. So what was the truth?'

'There were humans in Maras-Dantia before the great influx, or at least a few. One of them was Tentarr Arngrim, who calls himself Serapheim.'

'*Before* the influx? You said he set you off on this mission. How *old* is this man?'

'Very, I guess. But he's a sorcerer, so . . .' She shrugged. 'Anyway, Serapheim's mate was a sorceress called Vermegram. Whereas he's human, she was . . . I don't know. Something else. They had three offspring, all female. One was Jennesta. Then there was Adpar, who was part nyadd.'

'What's that?'

'A kind of water sprite. Jennesta killed her.'

'Charming.'

'The third sister's Sanara, who must take after her father 'cos she looks human. She helped us out of a fix in Maras-Dantia.'

'What's all this got to do with—'

'I'm getting to it. What we know about those early days—'

'What you *think* you know.'

'Yeah, right. Now shut up. Serapheim or Vermegram, or maybe both of 'em, found a way to move between worlds. It's what led to the stars Serapheim made. Or discovered.' She waved a dismissive hand. 'It's all a bit vague. But their messing around opened . . . sort of cracks between worlds. Holes, if you like. And elder races fell through from their worlds to Maras-Dantia.'

'Including orcs.'

'Yeah. Which set us on the road to servitude, and wound up making us the backbone of Jennesta's army. But that's another story. The one I'm telling you ended with Serapheim and Vermegram falling out . . . somehow. Some say they turned from lovers to enemies, and there was a conflict. I don't know anything about that. Vermegram's reckoned to be dead, though nobody's sure how or when.'

'Hang on. You said she wasn't human.'

Coilla nodded. 'You only had to look at Jennesta and Adpar to see that.'

'How could she be anything *but* human if she was in Maras-Dantia before the elder races arrived?'

'Fucked if I know, Jode. I'm not an oracle.'

'What you said about your people going into servitude; how did—'

'Enough questions. Some other time, all right?'

He was taken aback by the sharpness of her reply, but shrugged and said, 'Sure.'

She changed the subject and softened her tone. 'It's getting cooler.'

He slipped an arm round her. She moved closer and laid her head against his shoulder.

There were shouts from the clearing.

'Damn!' Pepperdyne complained. '*Every* time we get a quiet moment together . . .'

'Come on,' Coilla said, scrambling to her feet.

They headed back to the village.

One of the scouting parties had returned. They had four human prisoners with them, their hands tied behind their backs. Looking terrified, their uniforms dusty and tattered, they were forced to their knees. The band gathered around them, Stryke to the fore.

Orbon, who led the scouts, reported. 'Found these stragglers further along the beach, Captain. There was no fight left in 'em.'

Grim-faced, Stryke approached and walked slowly along the line of crouching captives. All of them avoided his gaze and kept their heads down.

'I've just one question,' he told them. 'Where has your mistress gone?'

A couple of the prisoners glanced nervously at each other, but none of them spoke.

'I'll make myself plain,' he said, walking back and forth in front of them, his unsheathed sword in his hand. 'I get an answer or you get dead.' He went to the first in line. 'You! Where's Jennesta?'

The man looked up. He was trembling. 'We . . . That isn't . . . the sort of thing she'd . . . tell the likes of us.'

'Wrong answer,' Stryke told him. He drove his sword into the prisoner's chest. The man toppled, and lay twitching before he was still.

Stryke moved on to the next human. 'Where's Jennesta?' he repeated, his gory blade pressed to the captive's throat.

This one was more resolute, or perhaps it was bravado. 'You can go and fuck yourself, *freak*,' he grated, and made to spit in Stryke's face.

He didn't have the chance. Stryke brought back his sword and swung it hard. The blow was savage enough to part the man from his head, which bounced a couple of times before rolling to a halt at Standeven's feet. His face drained of all colour and he hastily stepped back, looking queasy. The decapitated torso sat for a moment, gushing, before it fell.

The next man in line was older than the others and wore an officer's uniform. He was splattered with his dead comrade's blood.

Stryke turned to him. 'Has that loosened your tongue? Or do I do the same to you?'

The man said nothing, though it was as likely from fear as courage. Stryke drew back his blade again.

'Wait!' Pepperdyne yelled, pushing his way forward. 'What the *hell* are you doing, Stryke?'

'This is band business. Stay out of it.'

'Since when was it your business to slaughter unarmed prisoners?'

'You've a lot to learn about orcs, human.'

'I thought I'd already learned that you were honourable.'

That seemed to give Stryke pause for thought, but he didn't lower his sword. 'I need to know where the bitch's taken Thirzarr.'

'You'll not get anything out of dead men.'

'Force is all their kind understands.'

'My kind, you mean. And isn't that what humans say about orcs?'

'We *do* understand it,' Haskeer protested.

Pepperdyne jabbed a thumb at the dead prisoners. 'Not working too well here, is it?' He turned back to Stryke. 'Let me try. Come on. I'm one of *their kind*; maybe they'll open up to me.'

'Why don't you keep your snout out of this?' Haskeer said. 'You're not in this band.'

'He's proved himself,' Coilla told him. 'I say we give it a chance.'

'Here we go again.'

'And what's that mean?'

'You're backing him. Again. Seems to me you should be siding with your own, not outsiders.'

'*We're* outsiders, you idiot! Everybody shits on us, curses us, hates us. You might think of that when you're busy judging. Jode's suffered as much as we have, in his way.'

'You're talking about a human. They're more shitters than shat upon, I reckon.'

Jup burst out laughing. 'Sorry.' He tried to sober himself. 'But . . . *shitters*? *Shat upon?* You outdo yourself, Haskeer.' He started laughing again. Several of the privates joined in. He made a better fist of composing himself. 'Coilla's right. Maybe Jode could make 'em talk.'

Haskeer was seething now. 'You too, eh?'

'What have we got to lose? If it doesn't work we can move on to cutting off a few of their fingers or toes or . . .' He glanced at the pair of alarmed prisoners. 'Failing that, Stryke can finish 'em.'

'What is it you want, Stryke?' Pepperdyne asked. 'Information or revenge?'

'There's a lot to be said for revenge.'

'My people have a saying: "If you go out for revenge, build two pyres." '

'I'll build a hundred,' Stryke replied coldly, 'a thousand . . .'

'Make the biggest for Jennesta. But you won't learn where to find her from dead men.'

Stryke slowly lowered his sword. 'Try. But be quick.'

'Thanks. Might be better if you all left us. I think you're making the prisoners nervous.'

Stryke snapped an order and everyone retreated to the other end of the clearing, Haskeer mumbling unhappily as they went. Pepperdyne crouched by the two remaining humans and began some earnest talking.

The band settled down to wait.

Stretched out on the compacted earth of the clearing, Haskeer said to no one in particular, 'How do we know he ain't plotting with 'em?'

'What?' Coilla said. 'When did you swap your brains for horse shit? Jode's trying to *help*.'

'Yeah, we know how helpful humans can be.' He looked sharply at Standeven, sitting nearby, making him fidget uneasily.

'You're full of it, Haskeer. You should wise up about who our friends are.'

'Friends, Coilla? Are you trying to tell me that—'

'You're bruising my ears!' Stryke declared. 'Give it a rest, you two.'

Haskeer and Coilla fell into aggrieved silence.

The band quietened down too. Pepperdyne carried on talking with the prisoners.

The orcs were just starting to get restless again when one of the perimeter sentries, Gant, called out to them. The second scouting party had returned.

It was led by Dallog, who had the tyro Pirrak at his side. Wheam walked alone, further back. But what caught everyone's attention was who the scouts had with them; a party of dwarfs, three of them youngsters.

Spurral stood. 'Isn't that Kalgeck? And those kids who got us the map?' She ran towards them, Jup and some of the others close behind.

Kalgeck, with whom she had suffered captivity by the Gatherers, rushed forward to meet her and they embraced. The children, Heeg, Retlarg and Grunnsa, gathered round too.

'Am I glad to see you,' she told them, speaking in Mutual, the universal tongue. 'Are you all right?'

Kalgeck nodded. 'We managed to get to one of our hideaways. It was close though. We ran into some human soldiers, like those over there.' He pointed at the captives with Pepperdyne. 'They would have killed us, except some of that other bunch with all the different races came along. Who were they?'

'We don't know,' Spurral admitted. 'Not exactly.'

'Anyway,' Kalgeck went on, 'they protected us. They sort of sprayed fire at the soldiers and scared them off. Then they told us to run and hide.'

Coilla looked thoughtful. 'Interesting.'

'Heads up,' Jup said. 'Here comes Jode.'

Pepperdyne arrived, clutching a small piece of parchment.

'Luck?' Stryke asked.

'Some. It didn't take much for them to see the light. They know roughly where Jennesta's gone, but not why. One of them drew this.' He handed Stryke the paper.

It was a roughly drawn map, showing a cluster of islands, with one island, set apart from the rest, bearing a cross. The only other thing was a rudimentary set of arrows indicating the compass points.

'So it's east of here,' Stryke said. 'But how far?'

'They weren't sure, but thought it was a couple of days' voyage. So not too far.'

'Why not compare it with the map we've already got?' Spurral suggested. 'The one these kids found for us.'

'Just about to,' Stryke told her. He fished it out of a pocket.

They unfolded it, laid it on the ground and compared the two.

'There,' Pepperdyne said, pointing to one corner.

'Yeah,' Stryke agreed. 'They match, more or less.'

'We know about that island,' Retlarg announced.

'Do you?' Coilla asked. 'How come?' All three children started to clamour. She held up a hand to still them. 'Kalgeck? You know anything about this?'

'Yes. A couple of the elders were with us for a time when we were hiding. We heard them talking about it.'

'What did they say?'

'The humans, those soldiers, they were trying to find out where the island was. They took away some of our tribe to make them tell.'

'What's so special about it?'

'It's where your kind live.'

'What do you mean?'

'He means orcs,' Spurral said.

The youngsters all nodded vigorously and chorused agreement.

Pepperdyne, who had picked up enough Mutual to have a sense of what was being said, looked taken aback. 'There are orcs in this world?'

'Why not?' Coilla reckoned. 'There seem to be plenty of races here, just like in Maras-Dantia.'

'This is all about Jennesta's scheme to create a slave orc army, isn't it?' Jup put in.

'Orcs wouldn't let her,' Coilla declared.

'Unless they're a bunch of pussies like that lot in Acurial,' Haskeer contributed.

'How likely is that? They'd wipe the floor with her.'

'Yeah? With her magic—'

'We're wasting time,' Stryke said. 'We've got a destination. Let's get to it.'

Pepperdyne indicated the prisoners. 'What about them?'

'We'll leave 'em to fend for themselves.'

'How'd you feel about that, Kalgeck?' Spurral wanted to know.

'There are parts of the island that are deserted. They can go there. We won't interfere with them if they leave us alone.'

'Fair enough,' Stryke said. 'Now let's get to the ship.'

4

Rather than wait for dawn, Stryke insisted they set sail that evening. There was a crimson sunset as they upped anchor and moved away from the island, promising a torrid following day.

So it proved. Even at dawn it was hot, though a constant, moderate wind gave some relief and kept the sails full. The cabins and cargo holds were stifling, and most of the band preferred the relative comfort of the deck. In scattered pairs and groups, the main topic of whispered conversations was Stryke's treatment of the prisoners. Some backed him, others had doubts. Stryke himself spent most of his time alone at the prow, as though willing the ship onward.

Pepperdyne was amidships, at the wheel. As an islander born and bred, it would normally have been a pleasure, had not Standeven been plaguing him.

'You saw what he did to those soldiers. Didn't that alarm you?'

'Stryke did what he felt he had to do,' Pepperdyne replied, his response measured. 'I can't say I liked it, but—'

'It was the act of a savage.'

'I'd take what you're saying more seriously if you didn't have a cloud over you about that dead orc back in Acurial.'

'How many times do I have to tell you—'

'Yeah, sure.'

'Those two Stryke killed were *human beings*,' Standeven persisted. 'Our kind.'

'And not just a lowly orc, eh?'

'Forget that! My point is that Stryke's the one with the instrumentalities.'

'Here we go again.'

'They're our only way home.'

'And there's no way you're getting them.'

'That's not it. I'm saying is he the best one to be in charge of them?'

Pepperdyne laughed. 'It should be you, is that it?'

'No! But he's unstable. He showed that yesterday.'

'Maybe he is, maybe he isn't. But he's what we've got, whether you like it or not. No way is he going to give them up.'

'Of course he isn't. But I'm thinking that if we spoke to him, reasoned with him, maybe we could get him to take us back home before we get dragged deeper into this madness.'

'You say *he's* unstable then you come up with an idea like that. It's not going to happen, Standeven. Do you really expect him to break off searching for his mate to ferry us home? Not to mention how erratic the stars have been. How could he be sure of *getting* us home? Or of getting himself back here?'

'So you're admitting he can't control them.'

'I'm not sure anybody could. Anyway, I'm not inclined to run out on the band. Not now, when they're trying to find Thirzarr.'

Standeven was puzzled. 'Why?'

'It's called loyalty. A notion you're not familiar with.'

'What about loyalty to Humanity? To *me*.'

'It has to be earned. The band's done that. You haven't.'

'Your trust in these orcs is misplaced. This . . . relationship or whatever it is you're having with Coilla; they're laughing behind your back about it, you know. Those who don't hate you for it, that is. Why don't you stick with your own?'

'I think you just answered that question yourself. For all of what you call their savagery these beings aren't devious like you and most of our race. Whatever you might think, they don't hide their true opinions behind mealy-mouthed words. They speak plain and act out what they feel. I quite like that.'

'And that's your excuse for your disgusting union with one of them, is it?'

'I don't have to explain myself to you or anybody else. And I don't have to listen to this shit. Now clear off.'

'Since when did you get to give orders?'

'I'm the skipper as far as this vessel's concerned, and that makes my word law.' Pepperdyne gave his erstwhile master a flinty look. 'And if that isn't enough for you, I can back it with this.' He took a hand off the wheel and made a fist of it.

Standeven blanched, then, mumbling curses, turned and stamped off. Coilla was coming up the stairs to the wheel as he went down, and he pushed past her wordlessly.

'What was *that* about, Jode?' she asked.

'The usual.'

'Still keen on the stars, eh?'

'He says he isn't.'

'Yeah, right.'

'He said something else.'

'So stop creasing your brow and spit it out.'

'What do you reckon the rest of the band think about . . . us?'

'Do they know?'

'Standeven said they did, and that they're not happy about it.'

'Nobody's said anything to me. Well, apart from Haskeer. But he's always moaning about something, and humans aren't his favourite race.'

'Maybe we should be a little more discreet.'

'Why? What the fuck's it got to do with them?'

'Well, it's not as though our situation's that normal, is it?' He saw her expression and started rowing back. 'Not that there's anything *abnormal* about it, of course. I mean—'

'All right, you can stop digging now. It's rare, yes, but that's no reason for anybody to get sniffy about it. Anyway, Standeven's probably just trying to vex you. Don't let him get under your skin.'

'Expect you're right. But I'd be happier if—'

'Hold it. Here comes Wheam.'

'Damn it. It's busier than a town square on market day up here.'

She favoured him with a smile. 'Give the kid a break. He looks low.'

Wheam trudged up the steps dejectedly.

'Why so glum?' Coilla asked.

'Oh, this and that,' the youth replied.

'Anything in particular?'

'Dallog just chewed me out.'

'Why?'

'He says we haven't got enough drinking water on board, 'cos we left in a rush and didn't load enough, and everybody's drinking more in this heat.'

'How's that your fault?' Pepperdyne said.

'He's not blaming me for it. But he sent me to tell Stryke.' He glanced at their brooding captain at the bow.

'And you're not keen on the job?'

Wheam shook his head.

'Why can't Dallog tell Stryke himself?' Coilla wondered.

'Dunno. He seems to be more involved with the other tyros right now. Well, one; Pirrak.'

'That's his job, isn't it? Looking after you neophytes.'

'S'pose.'

'How low *is* the water?'

'Not enough to get us where we're going, he says.'

'All right. I'll talk to Stryke about it.'

'You will?'

'Sure.'

Wheam broke out in a grin. 'Thanks, Coilla. I was hoping you'd say that.'

'I figured. Now lose yourself while I sort it.'

He went off with a lighter step.

She looked to Pepperdyne. 'Where's the map?'

He hauled it out of a pocket and handed it to her. 'Think you can get Stryke to wear a stopover?'

'Sounds like we've no choice.'

'Rather you than me.'

'He'll see the sense of it.'

'In his present mood?'

'Leave it to me.' She unfolded the map. 'Where are we?'

He leaned over for a look, then pointed. 'Around there.'

'So the nearest place to stop would be . . . here?' She jabbed at a string of islands, two quite large.

Pepperdyne nodded. 'They seem as good as any. Assuming they have water, of course.'

'How far are they?'

'Half a day. Less with a favourable wind.'

'Right.' She waved the map under his nose as she left. 'I'll bring this back.'

'Good luck,' he muttered.

Coilla was aware of the band's eyes on her as she made her way to the prow.

Stryke must have heard her approaching, but he didn't turn or speak.

'Stryke?' she said, then more firmly, '*Stryke.*'

'Come to tongue-lash me about those prisoners?'

'No. That's done.'

'What, then?'

'Something you need to know, and act on.'

He turned to face her, and she saw that he looked haggard. 'What is it?'

Coilla drew a breath. 'There's been a screw-up on the rations.'

'*What?*'

'We left in such a rush—'

'We can do without food for a couple of days.'

'Sure. But it's the water.'

'*Shit.*' His features darkened further. 'Whoever's responsible should get a whipping for this.'

'Give it to yourself.'

'That's close to insolence, Corporal.'

'Maybe. But it's closer to truth. If we made a mess over the provisions it's because you were driving the band too hard.'

'I'd drive it to its bloodied knees when I'm trying to find Thirzarr.'

'When *we're* finding Thirzarr. You seem to have lost sight of what we are. We're the Wolverines. We look out for our own. But we won't get a chance to do that if we die of thirst.'

Stryke mulled over her words. At length he said, 'Where do we get water?'

She showed him the map. 'We're here. The nearest islands are these.'

'When would we get there?'

'Jode reckons not long after noon.'

'Suppose we rationed the water.'

'Dallog wouldn't have raised the alarm on this if he thought that'd work. I know you're frantic about Thirzarr, Stryke, and any delay's a pisser, but we've no option.'

Again he weighed things up. 'Do it. But I don't want to spend any more time there than we have to.'

'Got you.' She jogged back towards the wheelhouse.

They altered course immediately. The winds stayed friendly, even increasing by a few knots, and they made good time. Not long after the sun passed its zenith they spotted one of the necklace of islands. It was tiny, little more than a rock jutting out of the ocean, and they passed it by. The next two or three were about the same. When they reached the first of the bigger islands it proved almost as barren, and in any event there was nowhere to land, unless they wanted to climb sheer cliffs. A couple more minor islands came into view, and true to form they were tediously small and desolate. Everyone on board started to worry. Stryke paced ominously.

The second large island was a different proposition. Even from a distance they could tell it was verdant, so Pepperdyne steered the ship towards it. Stryke ordered the ship to circle the island, and they found that it, too, was protected by tall cliffs. But not on every side. There was a long stretch of beach, its fine, almost white sand stroked by gentle, foam-topped breakers. The beach stretched to a dense, sun-dappled jungle. Stryke had Pepperdyne take them in.

They dropped anchor as near to the shore as they could. The three boats their stolen goblin ship carried were unlashed and lowered. Stryke decided on leaving just a skeleton watch and taking most of the band as the landing party. He wanted a quick excursion, and the more hands the better. Standeven was one of those left on board, to his and everyone else's relief, and the rest of the watch were told to keep an eye on him.

Before setting out, Stryke told Haskeer to hail the island.

'Why warn 'em?'

'Because we've come peaceably. If anything lives here I want them to know that.'

'Our ship's done a pretty good job of announcing us anyway,' Jup said.

'I still want to make ourselves known,' Stryke insisted. 'Do it, Haskeer.'

'Why me?'

'You've got the biggest mouth,' Jup told him.

Haskeer glared at him, then cupped his hands and bellowed.

Stryke got him to repeat several times. There was no response.

'We saw no signs of habitation, and there are no ships. It's got to be deserted,' Jup argued.

'Probably,' Stryke agreed. 'But we won't take any chances. There'll be three search parties. Haskeer, you lead one; and you, Jup. I'll take the third. We'll decide the groups once we hit the beach. Now move.'

They swarmed over the side and filled the boats.

The trip was brief, and soon they were splashing ashore through the shallow, crystal-clear water, colourful fish darting from their path. On the beach, Stryke addressed them.

'Our only job is to fill those.' He pointed at the heap of canteens and cow-gut sacs they'd brought. 'You know what to do; look for natural springs or anywhere that might catch rainwater. And hurry. I don't want us lingering here or—'

Jup was signalling him with one hand and pressing a finger to his lips with the other. He pointed at the jungle. The whole band quietened and looked that way.

They stood in silence for some time, scanning the greenery. It got to the point where they began to think it was a false alarm. Then there was movement in the foliage. Restricted to just one or two places, making it unlikely to be the wind, it was accompanied by a rustling and the snap of dry twigs.

In the undergrowth there was the briefest flash of what appeared to be a pair of vividly red eyes.

'Looks like we're not alone after all,' Coilla said, reaching for her blade.

5

'Spread out!' Stryke bawled. 'And have your weapons ready!'

The band fanned out, swords, axes and spears in hand.

'Do we go in?' Haskeer asked, nodding at the area of jungle where they'd seen movement.

'No,' Stryke decided. 'If they're friendly they'll come to us. If they're not, it's a trap.'

'We can't stay here for ever,' Coilla said.

'I know that,' Stryke came back irritably.

Minutes passed. Nothing happened.

Pepperdyne broke the silence. 'Whatever's in there, how likely are they to come out when we're standing here fully armed?'

Spurral nodded. 'Good point.'

'Yeah,' Jup agreed, 'perhaps if we looked a little less confrontational . . .'

'Stryke?' Coilla said.

He sighed. 'All right, stand down. But *stay alert*.'

The band relaxed, or at least made a show of it. Some sat, or leaned on their axes, though their eyes stayed fixed on the jungle.

More time passed.

Stryke grew increasingly restless, and finally declared, 'I can't be doing with this.'

'And?' Coilla said.

'I'm thinking we should go in and deal with whatever we find, friendly or otherwise.'

'Just say the word, chief,' Jup replied.

Stryke took up his sword again. 'Right. Forget groups; we're going in mob-handed. Anything tries to stop us, we down 'em.'

The band brightened. They were keen to relieve their frustrations with a fight.

''bout time,' Haskeer mouthed, speaking for them all.

Stryke at their head, the band moved towards the tree-line.

'*Hold it!*' Dallog yelled. 'Look!'

A figure was emerging from the jungle. It walked upright and was taller than most of the orcs. As it came nearer its features were revealed. From the waist upwards it resembled a human, albeit with a thin covering of dark fur. Below the waist it had legs resembling a goat's, with a thicker, gingery pelt, that ended in hooves. It had a long tail, similar to some kind of monkey. The creature's beard, like the hair on its head, was black, curly and luxuriant. A small pair of horns, again like a goat's, protruded from just above the hairline. Its face was close to a human's, excepting small, upswept ears and eyes with intensely red orbs.

'What the hell is *that*?' Pepperdyne whispered.

'A faun,' Coilla explained. 'Back in Maras-Dantia they're forest-dwellers.'

'Are they friendly?'

'We've not had a lot to do with them. Though we've killed a few in our time.'

'I suppose that's not having a lot to do with them.'

The faun approached boldly, seeming undaunted by the sight of a heavily armed orc warband accompanied by dwarfs and a human. His step was certain, and he wore an expression that could have been called imperious. He bore no obvious weapons.

Stryke went forward, raised an open hand and addressed the faun in Mutual. 'We're here in peace. We mean you no harm.'

'You come well armed for beings with peaceful intent,' the faun replied. There was a commanding edge to his voice, a tone that suggested he was used to being obeyed.

'It's a violent world. But you're right.' He made a gesture and the band put away their weapons. Though more than a few did it with reluctance.

'Who are you?' the faun asked.

'I'm Stryke, and this is my . . . these are my companions, the Wolverines.'

'I am Levanda. If you really are here in peace, welcome.' He looked them over, his gaze lingering on Jup, Spurral and Pepperdyne. 'If I may say so, you seem rather broad-minded in your choice of . . . companions.'

'We like to get on with everybody,' Stryke replied, straight-faced.

'Why are you here?

'We need water. Nothing more.'

'Of course.'

'We'll trade for it if—'

Levanda waved the offer aside. 'Your presence is payment enough.'

From behind her hand, Spurral said to Jup, 'Bit of an old smoothie, isn't he?'

'You will honour me by accepting our hospitality,' Levanda told Stryke, 'for which the fauns are renowned.'

'Thanks, but we've pressing business elsewhere. So just the water. No offence.'

'My clan will be disappointed. We put great value on visitors. Come.' He turned and made for the jungle.

Exchanging glances, the warband followed.

It was much cooler, and a lot darker, when they entered the greenery. At first, trailing the faun, they had little sense of where they were heading, beyond it being deeper into the tangle. But at length they met a well-trod path and the going became a mite easier. The path meandered, veering round large clumps of bushes, dipping through gullies and over vegetation-smothered hillocks. Eventually it calmed and widened, and led them to an open space. This housed dozens of sturdy, mature trees, and the trees cradled dwellings. They looked a little like huts that had somehow been hurled and caught in the trees' embrace. A mixture of timber, wattle and wicker, many of their frontages had loggias. There were fauns clustered on these, looking down.

More were in the clearing below. They were going about their daily occasions; preparing food, tending several fires in pits, or just lounging and passing time. One sat on a stump playing softly on a bone flute. Every so often fauns scampered up and down stout ropes dangling from the trees. Despite their ungainly physiques, they did it with remarkable ease.

As the band arrived, the fauns stopped whatever they were doing and stared.

Looking around, Pepperdyne said, 'I can't see any women. Or do they all have beards too?'

Coilla stifled a giggle. 'There aren't any females.'

'What, they hide them?'

'No, there are no female fauns. That's how it was in Maras-Dantia anyway.'

'No females? How do they—'

'It's said they breed with nymphs. But they only come together when they need to. So I guess there's an island in these parts where nymphs live.'

'You saw those other islands. Nothing lived on them.'

'Well, further away then.'

'Yet these fauns don't seem to have ships, or even boats. We didn't see any.'

'Maybe the nymphs come to *them*. Does it matter?'

'I suppose not.'

The piping of the flute tailed off as the band halted. There were many fauns present, but they kept their distance, standing all around. They were silent.

'Where's the renowned hospitality?' Jup mumbled.

'Where's the *water*?' Spurral said.

Stryke echoed that. 'If you'll just show us to your spring, Levanda, we'll be on our way.'

'Are you sure I can't press you to food and drink?' the faun replied.

'Like I said, we're in a hurry.'

'Pity. It could be your last chance for a while.'

There was a smattering of laughter from the fauns surrounding them.

'What do you mean?'

'We like to fatten up the merchandise.'

More laughter, and louder.

'We've no time for jests.' Stryke's anger was rising.

'Oh, this is no joke. Not for you, anyway.'

'So what the hell is it?'

'Trade. With his kind.' He nodded at Pepperdyne. 'Gatherers.'

Given recent events that was particularly inflaming to Stryke, and to Jup and Spurral.

'*What?*' Stryke grated.

'The Gatherers bring us nymphs in exchange for whatever beings fetch up on our shores. Your race is a valuable commodity; we'll get a good price. All you have to do is surrender.'

Again, Haskeer spoke for them all. 'You can kiss our arses, goat breath.'

'We know you to be a belligerent race, but you can see that you're outnumbered.' He pointed at Haskeer. 'Throw down your weapons, or we'll disarm you.'

'We do the disarming,' Stryke told him. In one smooth, rapid movement his sword was out and swinging.

The blade sliced through Levanda's outstretched arm. He screamed, staggered back and sank to his knees, blood gushing from the wound. His severed limb lay twitching wetly on the ground.

There was a split second of shocked immobility on the part of the fauns. Enough time for the Wolverines to draw their weapons.

Then all hell broke out.

Producing hidden blades, the fauns rushed in on all sides, and the band spun to meet them.

It wasn't the orc way to stand and wait for the tide to hit, and Stryke was the first to move. He charged at the oncoming wave, sword and long-bladed dagger in his hands, a roar in his throat. And there was no fancy swordplay or mannerly rules when he met the foe. His only aim was carnage and he dealt in it wholesale.

Under his onslaught a faun collapsed with a split skull, and the next took steel to his gut. Advancing in unison, a trio tried to bring Stryke down. He dispatched the first with ease, slashing his neck with a vicious blow. The second he came at low, hamstringing him; and the third succumbed to a thrust to his chest. Vaulting over their bodies, Stryke set about another opponent.

The rest of the band weren't idle. Coilla employed the store of snub-nosed blades she kept in her arm sheaths. Confirming her status as the best knife-thrower in the band, her first couple of lobs were true, striking a faun square between its eyes and another in the windpipe. Her third effort merely wounded, though grievously. Then the enemy were too close for throwing knives and she switched to her sword.

Pepperdyne fought beside her, their blades expertly carving flesh as the fauns kept coming. Wrenching his sword free from a foe's innards and spinning to face the next, he caught a glimpse of Haskeer. He had a hatchet in one hand and Levanda's amputated arm in the other, which he was using to bludgeon a particularly muscular adversary. Sprawled in a crimson pool, Levanda himself looked on, his expression a mixture of agony and open-mouthed amazement.

As was their practice, Jup and Spurral worked as a team. Favouring his staff, Jup cracked heads adroitly, or used it to tumble opponents, bringing them within range of Spurral's wickedly keen pair of knives. In unison, the dwarfs penetrated deep into the fauns' ranks, leaving a trail of dead and injured in their wake.

The new recruits had also got into the habit of fighting together, like a small band within the band, less able but improving with every engagement. Wheam, Keick, Pirrak, Harlgo and Chuss, steered by Dallog, gave a good account of themselves, valour making up for their lack of experience.

No sooner had the Wolverines bettered something like half of their attackers than a further group emerged from the jungle. Armed with spears and battleaxes they swept towards the fray. The veteran band members needed no order to react. Those who could, peeled off from the battle and headed for the fresh incomers; Seafe, Gleadeg, Prooq, Gant, Reafdaw, Nep and Breggin among them.

Leaving Pepperdyne to deliver a death thrust to a wounded faun, Coilla caught up with Stryke. He stood over his latest kill, eyeing a bunch of circling foes.

'Need a hand?' she asked.

He gave her a sidelong glance and she saw that he was in a killing state, an almost dream-like reverie that came on when the bloodlust took hold. It was something she knew and respected.

No words were necessary. Together, they advanced. One of the fauns who had been holding back warily lost his nerve and fled. It was enough to trigger the others. They turned and ran, and it had a knock-on effect. Those fauns still standing began to withdraw.

'I think they've broken,' Coilla said.

Stryke was coming to himself. The crazed look was leaving his eyes. 'Maybe. But we have to—'

There was a high-pitched whistling sound. Something hit the ground close by.

'Archers!' Coilla yelled.

Several more arrows winged from the tree houses, peppering the sward.

'Everybody down!' Stryke bellowed.

Those of the band who weren't still actively engaged with the enemy dived for whatever cover they could find. Several, including Stryke and Coilla, used faun corpses for shelter, meagre protection as that was.

Band members armed with bows, principally Reafdaw, Eldo, Zoda and Finje, immediately began returning fire.

The advantage wasn't entirely with the faun archers. They had to avoid hitting their own kind remaining below. The orcs had no such restraint.

A faun was struck and fell, drawing a ragged cheer from the orcs. Seconds later another plunged to earth.

'We'll never get 'em all at this rate,' Coilla complained. 'They could keep us pinned here till doomsday.'

Arrows continued to rain down.

There were shouts behind them. Stryke and Coilla looked to their rear. An orc had taken an arrow.

'Can you make out who it is?' Stryke said.

'One of the tyros,' Coilla told him. 'I think it's Chuss. But it looks like it's just his arm.'

'And who the hell's *that?*'

A Wolverine was dashing towards Chuss. He was running a zigzag path, trying to avoid the arrows zinging all around him, and it was hard to make out who he was.

'It's another newbie,' Coilla realised. 'Harlgo.'

'Take cover!' Stryke shouted at him. *'Get down, Harglo!'*

Too late. An arrow pierced Harglo between his shoulder-blades. The impact threw him off his stride but he kept going. Slowing, his stride uncertain like a drunk's, he managed a few more steps before a second arrow struck the back of his neck. He went down, a dead weight. It was the fauns turn to cheer.

'Shit!' Coilla hissed.

'Burn 'em!' Stryke hollered. *'Burn 'em out!'*

The Wolverine archers were prepared. Their kit included bolts wrapped with tarred cloth. Quickly striking sparks, they began igniting them. In seconds, flaming arrows zipped towards the tree houses.

It must have been some time since rain, because the dwellings were tinder dry, as was the foliage they nestled amongst. The burning arrows hit the houses' walls, and passed through open doors and windows. Fires instantly broke out.

Even as the houses blazed the fauns carried on showering arrows on their tormentors. The orcs likewise continued sending up their fire-tipped bolts. Soon almost all the lofty huts were alight and the fauns were forced to bail out. Some climbed down, braving orc shafts. Others fell, in many cases burning and shrieking.

It was the final blow for the surviving fauns in the clearing. Those who were capable fled into the jungle, chased off by vengeful band members.

But the Wolverines' triumph was tempered.

Stryke and Coilla stood and jogged to Harglo. He was surrounded by a group of kneeling comrades. Dallog was there, wearing a grim expression, and as they arrived he looked up and shook his head. As they suspected, Chuss' wound was nasty but in no way life-threatening. It made the loss of Harlgo bitterly ironic.

Stryke came away from the huddle and headed for Levanda, who still lay where he fell. A number of the band tagged along, Jup and Spurral among them.

They gathered around the faun chief. He was conscious, but had lost a lot of blood, and his eyes were growing dull.

Spurral pushed her way to the front and gazed down at him. 'You know the joke?' she said. 'There are no Gatherers anymore.' Then she took her blade and plunged it into his heart.

No one begrudged her. But Haskeer looked disappointed at being cheated out of the act himself. He made do with spitting on the corpse.

'Yeah,' he said, wiping the back of a hand across his mouth. 'Don't mess with orcs, shithead.'

6

'I say it's *your* fault,' Haskeer contended, aggressively jabbing Dallog's chest.

'And how do you work *that* out?'

'You're supposed to be looking after these rookies, ain't you?'

'That's the job Stryke gave me, yes, but—'

'Not doing it too well, are you?' He pointed to Harglo's body.

'Not fair,' Dallog countered, trying to contain his own fury. 'We were in a battle, and that means casualties.'

'*Battle?* That was no battle, it was a skirmish. Not that you'd know the difference. You're wet behind the ears for all your great age.'

Half of the band looked on, waiting for a fight.

'We Ceragan orcs might be new,' Dallog said, 'but we've paid our dues on this mission. Harglo isn't the first we've lost, remember. There was Yunst and Ignar too.'

'Proves they weren't up to it!' Haskeer came back triumphantly. 'And talking of remembering, *we* lost Liffin. All 'cos of you, and him.' He nodded Wheam's way. The youth looked at his feet, shamefaced. 'But I blame you more. You should have known better.'

'You're staining Harglo's name. He was brave.'

'Stupid, more like.'

'I resent that.'

'Resent it all you want.'

'Take it back!'

Haskeer balled his fists and leaned in menacingly. 'Make me.'

Dallog raised his own hands. 'Any time.'

At that point Stryke arrived and roughly separated them. 'What the fuck's the matter with you two?' he demanded. 'I turn my back and in no time—'

'Just a few home truths,' Haskeer told him.

'If there's any truth telling to be done, I do it, Sergeant!'

'I'm just saying—'

'You say too much. I don't care what your beef is, either of you. All I'm interested in is getting out of here and finding Thirzarr. If that's too much for you both, I'll leave you here to fend for yourselves.'

They knew he meant it, and that seemed to sober them.

Noskaa and Vobe trotted up.

'We found the spring, Captain,' Vobe reported, 'a couple, in fact. We got all the water we needed, and the fauns kept well away.'

Noskaa grinned. 'Yeah, they're shy of us now, and they've enough to do fighting the fires.'

'Good work,' Stryke said. He turned to Dallog. 'How's Chuss?'

'He'll be fine,' the corporal answered sullenly.

'Any other casualties?'

'Only minor.'

'Right, we're leaving.'

'What about Harglo?'

'We haven't got time for a proper send-off for him. Sorry.'

'We're not going to leave him here?'

'Sometimes, when an orc dies in the field, we've no choice.'

'It wouldn't take long to build a pyre. If we all—'

'No.'

'I've got to face his kin when we get back, Stryke, *if* we get back, and I don't relish having to tell them we couldn't dispatch him decently with a few words said.'

'I feel as bad about it as you do, but we've got to move,' Stryke insisted.

'Do you?' There was an edge to Dallog's voice.

'Can I suggest something?' Pepperdyne said. All heads turned his way, more than a few looking resentful at a human apparently interfering in something so orcish. 'Why don't we take Harglo with us and bury him at sea? That'd give you time to do it properly and have whatever sort of service you want. It's what my people used to do.'

'We're not your people,' Dallog muttered.

Stryke nodded. 'All right, we'll do it.'

'We can't,' Dallog protested. 'An orc should go out of the world in flame, or at least be buried deep. Not flung into the sea like some—'

'It's that or we leave him.'

For a moment it looked as though Dallog would keep arguing. Instead he replied, 'Whatever you say, Captain.'

They loaded the water and caught the tide. The winds were fair and they made good progress. Even from afar, tall columns of black smoke could be seen rising from the fauns' island.

When they were well under way they turned their attention to Harglo. Dallog insisted on taking care of everything. As keeper of the band's standard he carried spare pennants. A couple were stitched together and used as a shroud, tightly bound.

The band gathered on deck. As the mate of a Wolverine, there was no objection to Spurral being present. But Stryke worried that having humans there could antagonise the band. So Pepperdyne stayed up on the bridge, along with Standeven, although they could hear what was said.

Dallog carried on the tradition started by his dead predecessor, Alfray, and conducted the ceremony. Given the respect for Alfray, and the hostility some felt towards the new intake, that didn't please everybody; particularly Haskeer, who stayed sour faced throughout.

After saying something about Harglo's character, qualities and clan background, Dallog evoked the Tetrad, the orcs' quartet of principal deities, commonly known as the Square. The young recruit's spirit was commended to Wystendel, god of comradeship, Neaphetar, god of war, Aik, god of wine, and Zeenoth, goddess of fornication. Then the corpse, sliding from a tilted plank, was consigned to the depths.

Normally this would have been followed by the taking of excessive amounts of wine and pellucid, accompanied by overblown stories about the deceased's exploits and the singing of heroic songs. But given the circumstances this was deferred to a later date. Wheam announced that he was composing an epic ballad honouring Harglo, the performance of which was also deferred, to a date to be decided.

When it was over, and the band had scattered to their duties, Stryke took Dallog aside.

'That was done well,' he said.

'Not well enough for some in the band, I think,' Dallog replied frostily.

'It's true you're not Alfray, and a few begrudge that. But you're your own orc and you did as good a job as he would have, in your way.'

'The belief seems to be that I don't care for my charges as well as he did.'

'Don't listen to Haskeer. Harglo's death wasn't your fault. None of them were.'

'No. Yet I feel liable. It seems . . . unjust that they should pass so young when I've reached the years I have.'

'Call it fate, or the whim of the gods. We all live in the Reaper's shadow.'

'But think how good it would be if we didn't.' There was a spark of real passion in the corporal's eyes. 'If we could turn back the years and cheat death . . .'

'It comes to us all, Dallog, sooner or later.'

'It's unfair, this rapid piling on of time. One instant you're young and strong, the next near dotage. Least, that's the way it feels.'

'Most of us orcs don't have the luxury of ageing, living as we do. Born as fighters, despised, all hands against us. A short life's the likely outcome. You've survived. Count yourself lucky in that regard.'

'But if only—' He had been in a kind of reverie as he spoke, now he came out of it. 'Forgive an old one's rambling, Stryke. You've got enough on your platter worrying about Thirzarr without my musings.'

'Anybody would think you had one foot in the pyre. There's life in you yet.'

Dallog gave a thin smile and nodded, and without further word they parted.

At the other end of the ship another meeting was taking place. Coilla had made it her business to seek out the tyros, to offer them condolence on the loss of their comrade. Only Pirrak had eluded her, and now she found him. He was at the rail, staring out to sea.

'Pirrak?'

He started and spun to face her, and he seemed alarmed. 'Corporal?'

'Steady. You look as jumpy as a frog on a hot griddle. You all right?'

'I'm . . . yes, I'm fine. I was just . . . You startled me.'

'You're pale.'

'Am I?' He touched a hand to his cheek, self-consciously.

'Thinking about Harglo?'

'Harglo. Yes. Yes, he was on my mind.'

'Did you know him long, back in Ceragan?'

'Since we were hatchlings.'

'That makes it harder.'

Pirrak nodded.

'You're young,' Coilla went on, 'and you've not seen as much action as the rest of us. You'll . . . well, you won't get used to losing a comrade but you'll learn to accept it. It's one of the costs of what we do. Of who we are.'

'That's what Dallog says.'

'He's right. And you can take some comfort from the way Harglo died. He was trying to help Chuss. That showed good fellowship. He was brave.'

'Yes. Brave.'

'Look, if you ever need anybody to talk to—'

'Yes, thanks. I'm all right. Really.'

'Well, take it easy.'

Coilla turned and left him, but couldn't help noticing that he went straight to Dallog, further along the deck.

She climbed the stairs to the wheel, and Pepperdyne. Standeven had gone off to fill a corner somewhere.

'You look thoughtful,' Pepperdyne said.

'I was just talking to Pirrak. He was really tense.'

'Can you blame him? He's a rookie, and going through a lot.'

'Yeah, s'pose. But sometimes I wonder about the tyros. Like, whether they're going to hold it together.'

'They have so far. And they've got Dallog. He seems grounded.'

'Hmm. I guess things are a bit fraught.'

'Yeah, we're all on edge.'

'You too?'

'Not as long as you're here to protect me.'

She smiled. 'Fool.'

Mid-morning of the next day they passed a group of mountainous islands. They were on the chart Stryke had and came as no surprise. What was unexpected were the three ships with black sails that came round the headland of the last island and followed them.

Orbon was at the wheel of the orcs' ship. He was one of the privates who had proved to have some talent for steering, and Pepperdyne was training him as a relief. Pepperdyne himself was down on the deck with the rest of the band.

'They look just like this ship,' he reckoned, shading his eyes with a hand.

'Goblins?' Jup said.

'A lot of them got killed when the band freed those kelpies,' Spurral reminded them. 'Could be more, out for revenge.'

'Maybe they're not goblins,' Jup suggested.

'They're goblin ships, ain't they?' Haskeer retorted.

'*We're* on a goblin ship. That doesn't make us goblins, does it?'

'Could it be that Pelli Madayar's bunch again? Coilla wondered.

'Well, I say we stop and face the bastards,' Haskeer declared. 'Whoever they are.'

'No way,' Stryke told him.

'You reckon this could be innocent, Stryke?' Coilla asked.

'Plenty of ships in this world.'

'Yeah, but *goblins* . . .'

'We keep going.'

'So what we going to do; lead them to our destination?'

'We'll deal with it.'

'But—'

'Fuck the goblins. Or whoever it is. All I care about is getting where we're going.' He looked to Pepperdyne. 'Can we have more speed?'

'We're going just about as fast as we can now.'

'Try.'

'I'll get up to Orbon and see what we can do.' He made for the stairs.

'I can't believe we're running from a fight,' Haskeer mumbled disgustedly.

Pepperdyne applied his skills and they did manage to put on a few more knots. Steadily, they increased their lead over the trio of ships. By the middle of the afternoon they had fallen back and out of sight.

Some time later the Wolverines came across a pair of islands. Again, they were marked on their map, and they were the largest islands they'd seen so far in this world. One was lush, with golden beaches.

The other was its complete opposite; rocky and stark, its shoreline nothing but shale. The islands were close together, separated by a narrow channel.

'You sure we have to go between them?' Stryke asked.

'According to the map this area's strewn with reefs,' Pepperdyne explained, 'except for this strait. Otherwise we'd have to make a big detour.'

They had to slow down to navigate the channel safely. No sooner had they entered when a grunt on lookout in the rigging began to shout. He pointed to the verdant island, on their starboard side. A large number of canoes were coming out to them.

That drew most of the band to the rail, straining to see. Given recent events, they assumed hostility.

'Can anybody make out who they are?' Stryke said.

'Think so,' Jup replied, squinting. 'They look like . . . elves.'

'Yeah,' Spurral confirmed, 'you're right.'

'They haven't given us trouble before,' Coilla said.

'Really?' Stryke replied. 'What about Pelli Madayar?'

'Back in Maras-Dantia, I meant.'

'Who knows how they are here? This place is full of surprises.'

'They don't *look* hostile.'

'I don't care. We're not taking any chances.'

'The speed we're travelling we can't stop them reaching us,' Pepperdyne told him.

'And we really can't go faster?'

'Too risky in a strait this tight.'

'Prepare to repel boarders, then.'

The band took up their weapons and watched as the armada of canoes approached.

When they arrived, the boats kept up with the slow-moving ship without too much trouble. They were numerous and carried many elves, along with heaps of trinkets, craftworks and general bric-a-brac.

'Do they want to trade?' Coilla wondered.

Jup shrugged. 'Dunno. But they've fallen unusually quiet for traders.'

He was right. The hubbub to be expected from hawkers who infested ports was absent. The elves had become muted as soon as they saw that the ship was crewed by orcs. Now most of them simply sat and stared. They seemed bewildered.

One of the boats was much bigger and more ornate than the others, resembling river barges the Wolverines had seen on their travels. Rowers were seated at the bow end. The stern held an elevated platform covered by a gold and blue fabric canopy. On the platform was a seat, and in it sat an elf of mature years, dressed a little more finely than the rest. Behind him stood a much younger elf controlling the rudder. With some difficulty this boat was manoeuvred until it lay alongside the orcs' ship.

'Stay sharp,' Stryke warned the band. 'This could be a ruse.'

'They don't look like ambushers,' Jup said, 'what with all that junk they're carrying, and no sign of weapons.'

'Anything's possible in this place.' He had ordered the archers to nock their bows; now he signalled them to stand ready. Then he hailed the boat. *'Who are you?'*

The regal-looking elf called back, *'I was about to ask the same question!'*

'Identify yourself!' Stryke repeated.

'Mallas Sahro! I'm the Elder of this clan!' He indicated the bobbing flotilla with a sweep of his slender hand. *'And you?'*

'Captain Stryke of the Wolverines!'

'You're orcs!'

'Obviously!'

'Then I confess to being confused!'

Stryke was puzzled by the exchange. *'Explain!'*

'We thought you were goblins!'

'You were expecting *goblins?'*

'Yes!' He pointed to the boats' cargoes. *'This is tribute for them!'*

'Do you think he means those three ships we saw?' Coilla asked.

'I don't know,' Stryke confessed. He yelled again. *'There are no goblins on this ship!'*

'I see that! It seems we are again mistaken!'

'Again?'

'You're not the first of your kind we've seen lately!'

'What do you mean? When?'

'Yesterday! Ships passed with humans on board, and an orc!'

Stryke's heart took a leap. He had to force himself to ask the question. *'Was it . . . a female?'*

'Yes! We glimpsed her standing on deck!'

'Could it be?' Coilla whispered.

'We need to talk!' Stryke called. *'Will you come aboard?'*

'I will not set foot on a goblin ship!'

'I said there are no goblins here!'

'It's taboo!'

'Shit,' Stryke hissed. *'This bellowing at each other is no good! How can we parley?'*

Mallas Sahro considered that. *'Come ashore! We'll meet on the beach!'*

'Careful,' Haskeer warned. 'Might be a trap.'

Stryke ignored him. *'All right, we'll trust you!'*

'As we will you! I return, you follow!' He signalled his rowers and the boat pulled away. All the canoes did likewise and headed back to the island.

'They seem harmless enough,' Coilla said as they watched them leave.

'So did the fauns,' Jup reminded her.

'We'll take no chances,' Stryke assured them. 'Bring us to a halt, Pepperdyne.'

'Are you sure? I thought we were in a hurry.'

'We are. But if these elves can tell us anything to speed our journey I want to hear it. Now do as you're told.'

The anchor was dropped and the sails taken up.

Stryke decided to leave Dallog and the tyros on board to guard the ship. The elderly corporal looked as though he thought this might be some kind of slight, but said nothing. Not knowing how the elves would react to humans, bearing in mind the Gatherers' reputation, Pepperdyne and Standeven were left behind too. Figuring dwarfs would probably be acceptable, Stryke included Jup and Spurral in the landing party. By the time all that was sorted out the elves had got back to their island. The band piled into their three boats and followed.

Mallas Sahro was waiting for them on the beach, seated in his throne-like chair. He had only a couple of functionaries or servants with him. The rest of his clan had pulled well back, to the tree-line, where they sat watching. None of them seemed to have weapons. Stryke took that as a promising sign of good faith.

The Elder greeted them with, 'You come well armed for talking.'

'Where have we heard that before?' Coilla whispered.

'We're always armed,' Stryke said, and tried to reassure him by adding, 'To us it's like the fine jewellery your clan wears.'

Mallas Sahro was indeed bedecked with rings, bracelets and necklaces, all fashioned from silver, though tastefully simple in design. From his expression he was less than convinced by the comparison, but replied, 'Very well.'

'I should tell you that we've dealt with the elven folk before, and they've had no cause to regret it.'

'And we know the orcs, for all your fearsome nature, to be honourable and fair.'

'Yeah, we'll kill anybody,' Haskeer muttered.

The elf raised his thin eyebrows.

'Don't mind him,' Stryke said, giving Haskeer a murderous sidelong glance, 'he's got an odd sense of humour. *How* do you come to know about our race?'

Mallas Sahro seemed puzzled by the question. 'The same way you know ours, I suspect. This is a world of many races, and many meetings.'

'Of course.' He saw no point in explaining that the Wolverines were not of this world. The Elder would probably think him insane. 'What concerns us is the orc you saw yesterday.'

'The female.'

'Yes. What did she look like?'

'We only had the briefest glimpse. She was tall, and straight, and her hair was like flame. I can't tell you more.'

'It could be Thirzarr, couldn't it, Stryke?' Coilla said.

'Perhaps. And you say she was with humans, Elder?'

'Yes.'

'Did you see another female with them? One of . . . unusual appearance?'

'No. But we did not linger too long near those ships. You see, we made the same error as we did with you today.' A troubled look came to his face. 'We thought it was *him*.'

'Who?'

'Gleaton-Rouk. A goblin with command of dark magic, and a nature utterly ruthless. More than once we've suffered his wrath.'

'That's who the tribute was for?'

'Yes. We're traders, not fighters. We make things, like this jewellery you admired. There are silver seams here and we mine them. The goblins have no such skills, or the patience to learn them. They only *take*. Their talents lie in cruelty and destruction, and we pay tribute to keep them from our door.'

'Yeah, we've encountered goblins before,' Coilla said.

'With respect,' the elf told her, 'I think even the formidable orcs would find Gleaton-Rouk a daunting foe.'

'So when you saw our ship you thought it was him,' Stryke reasoned.

'Yes. That and the fact that he's due.'

There was a commotion from the crowd of elves at the rear of the beach. They were pointing out to sea.

Three black sails had appeared on the horizon.

7

There was something close to panic on the elves' island. But the populace wasn't disappearing into the jungle; they were running down the beach towards their boats.

'What's happening?' Stryke said as they streamed past.

'We must meet them with the tribute!' Mallas Sahro replied.

'Or what?'

The Elder seemed not to understand. 'I thought I made that clear.'

'This Gleaton-Rouk's going to cut up rough.'

'To say the least!' The elf was agitated. 'He'll ruin our crops, burn our homes, put us to the sword!'

'Why?'

'Why?'

'Because he's threatened to, right?'

'Yes. And he's punished us in the past. Several of my clan have been killed by him.'

'That's tough, but it's a just few. He hasn't killed you all or burnt you out.'

'No, because we pay the tribute!'

'And if you didn't, or offered less, what would he do?'

Mallas Sahro was at a loss for an answer. 'As I said, he would kill us and . . .'

'Wrong,' Stryke said. 'If you were wiped out he'd have no tribute, no silver. Why should he do that? Can't you see what's going on here? He kills a few to keep you in line. The rest's bluster.'

The Elder threw up his hands. 'But what else can we do?'

'Ever thought of defying him?'

'We're not warriors!'

'We are.'

'This ain't our affair, Stryke,' Haskeer said.

'I reckon it could be. Remember what Spurral here said earlier, about them maybe being out for revenge on account of what we did to those goblin slavers. More I think about it, the more sense it makes.'

'I thought you wanted to waste no more time.'

'My hunch is we won't have the choice. And you were right, Coilla, about leading them to where we're going. We don't want that.'

Haskeer snorted, 'Oh *come on*, Stryke.'

'You're not up for a fight, Haskeer? *You?*'

'Well . . .'

'Please,' Mallas Sahro implored, 'I must go!'

Stryke grabbed his arm. 'You could put a stop to this now.'

'It's easy for you to say. We have to live here.'

'Living in fear isn't living.'

'And we're not keen on tyrants,' Coilla added, warming to the prospect.

'You're asking me to put my folk at risk,' the elf protested.

'I'm asking you to free them. With our help.'

'Those ships are moving at a hell of a lick,' Spurral observed.

They were much nearer than they should have been since the band last looked. Their black sails billowed fit to split.

'It's magic,' the Elder said. 'I told you he commanded powerful sorcery. Even the wind obeys him.'

'Don't you elves have magic too?' Coilla asked.

'Yes, but on a different scale. Ours is healing, benign, protective.'

'So use it to defend your clan and leave the fighting to us.'

'I don't know . . .' His eyes were darting to the shoreline. Most of the elves were with their boats now, obviously anxious, waiting for his order to set off.

'Does Gleaton-Rouk normally come in three ships?' Stryke wondered.

'What?' The Elder dragged his gaze back to him. 'Oh. Er, no. Usually just one. We thought yesterday was an exception, when we saw the female of your kind. Then today, when you—'

'Right. I've a hunch they've come in force because of us.'

'You?'

'They feel they owe us a debt. Of blood. Well, you going to make a stand?'

'You can't fight him. He has exceptional skills.'

Stryke slapped his sheathed sword. 'So do we.'

'I'm sorry. I appreciate what you're saying, but I can't take the risk. I have to think of my clan.' Head low, as though in shame, he hurried off accompanied by his keepers.

'You gave it your best shot,' Haskeer said. 'Let's get out of here'.

'I meant it when I said we've no choice. You think they're just going to let us sail away?'

'Not to mention that we can't leave these elves at the goblins' mercy,' Coilla added.

'What's more important to you, Stryke,' Haskeer rumbled, 'these elves or Thirzarr?'

'I'd knock you down for that if I didn't know you said it because you're an idiot. I figure it *was* Thirzarr the elves saw yesterday. If Jennesta's kept her alive this long there's a chance she'll survive longer. But before we can find out we have to get through this.'

Haskeer had nothing else to say.

They watched as the Elder's boat went out, surrounded by his clan's many canoes. The trio of goblin ships was near enough that figures could be seen on their decks.

'So what do we do?' Jup said.

'If I'm wrong,' Stryke told him, 'the tribute gets handed over and the goblins leave. If I'm right, then we do what we're best at.'

They looked on as the goblin ships drew nearer and the elves' boats headed for them. Then things took an unexpected turn. Manoeuvring nimbly, despite the narrowness of the channel, one of the ships changed course.

'Should they be doing that?' Spurral said.

'What the hell—' Jup exclaimed.

Without slowing, the two ships carried on towards the elves' motley fleet.

'This doesn't look good,' Coilla said.

The ships ploughed through the swarm of elves' boats. Many were swamped, overturned or shattered. Elves jumped from boats to avoid the oncoming prows. Soon the water was peppered with bobbing heads, wreckage and the debris of tribute. There were shouts and screams from the swimming elves.

Emerging from the chaos, the ships began coming round, to close in on the shore.

'Looks like they're not in the mood for trinkets today,' Jup said.

'It's us they want,' Stryke told him. *'Weapons!'*

The band filled their hands.

'Hey!' Coilla yelled, pointing. 'There!'

They hadn't been paying attention to the third goblin vessel. It was making straight for the orcs' anchored ship.

Those on board had been watching. They saw the pair of goblin ships sail into the elves' boats, sinking or upsetting scores of them, and leaving a trail of wreckage. Now the third ship was coming their way.

Pepperdyne glanced at his companions. Dallog, Wheam, Pirrak, Keick and Chuss; none of them veterans and one nursing a wound. And Standeven, who could be relied on to be useless or worse. So six defenders. He looked to the approaching ship. There were perhaps four times that number of goblins visible on its deck.

As Pepperdyne wasn't a member of the band, and the band operated on military principles, he had no authority. Dallog's rank put him in charge. Pepperdyne had his doubts about the wisdom of that, but rather than waste time arguing he opted for conciliatory.

'How do we handle this, Corporal?' he asked.

'The fewer who get aboard the better.'

'That's what I figured. How many archers we got?'

'Good ones? That'd be Keick and Chuss. But Chuss—'

'Yeah, right.' He glanced at the tyro. Chuss' wound meant his arm was bound and in a sling.

'I'm not too bad with a bow,' Dallog added. 'You?'

'I'm a blade man. But I can use a spear.'

'So me and Keick as archers, Wheam, Pirrak and you with spears. Chuss'll have to do what he can. Luckily it's not his sword arm.'

The goblin ship was coming alongside; no mean feat in so narrow a channel.

'Unless you're going to fight,' Pepperdyne told Standeven sarcastically, 'you'd better hide yourself.'

Standeven nodded, and avoiding the others' eyes, scampered for the hold.

'Here they come!' Dallog shouted.

The goblin ship glided in, its rail no more than a hand's span from the orcs'. A splash sounded as its anchor went down. Goblins were rushing forward with grappling hooks to secure their charge on the Wolverines' ship.

Dallog and Keick loosed arrows. One caught a goblin in the chest, the second found another's windpipe. They kept firing as Pepperdyne, Pirrak and Wheam used their spears to impede the boarding, while Chuss slashed at groping hands and jutting heads.

The first, modest wave of would-be boarders lying dead or wounded, a second dashed to the rail. Mindful of the first wave's fate, most of them carried shields. Now hits were rarer as orc arrows clattered against the shields and spears were deflected. The battle at the rail turned into a slog, and Pepperdyne discarded the spear in favour of his sword and knife. No goblin had set foot on the orcs' ship, but the battle to keep them off was steadily being lost.

The orc archers carried on firing and managed to drop a couple more of the enemy despite their shields. Then an arrow came at them. Not from the mob trying to get aboard but from above. The bolt penetrated the deck close enough to Dallog that its flights brushed his leg. They looked up. A goblin was high in the rigging of the attacking ship, armed with a bow and aiming again. They scattered as his second arrow pierced the deck.

Keick nocked a shaft and sent it up at the sniper. It missed. The arrow carried on and curved in a great arc to disappear over the other side of the goblins' craft. The goblin in the rigging returned fire, and would have struck Keick if Dallog hadn't barged him aside, narrowly avoiding being hit himself. Dallog swiftly took his turn at the goblin archer. His effort was a much wider miss than Keick's, who by then had his own bow drawn. Holding down the urge to let loose immediately, he took time getting his eye in. When he fired, his arrow sped true. It impacted in the goblin's midriff. He hung on grimly but briefly before plunging to his ship's deck with a shrill cry, landing on two of his comrades.

The distraction had taken Dallog and Keick's eyes away from the rail. Now they saw that it was a scrum, with several goblins aboard and more about to follow. They dropped the bows, drew their blades and ran to join the fight.

Because there were so few defenders to repel boarders they were well spaced out along the rail. Which meant Wheam was a good twenty paces from Pirrak, the next in line, and could expect no aid. He thought he needed it. Still clutching his spear, he was pointing it at an advancing goblin. The goblin was armed with an ornate double-headed iron axe and a boiling fury.

The tyro had the benefit of reach, but the goblin had the skill and confidence of a seasoned fighter. As he had been taught, Wheam used his spear to make it as hard as possible for his opponent to properly deploy his weapon. The goblin, his anger stoked by Wheam's determination to keep him at bay, tried to dislodge the spear with wild swings. When they connected, Wheam could feel the transmitted impact in his sweating hands, and struggled to hold on.

The goblin was dealing blows with the axe's flat, the better to knock the spear aside. Now he deftly flipped the axe, lurched to one side and swiped downwards. The spear was sliced in two, leaving Wheam clutching about a third of the broken shaft. Certain of a kill, the goblin advanced, still swinging. Wheam backed-off fast, lost his footing, stumbled and fell. Then the goblin was standing over him, a grimace of triumph on his face, the axe raised for a death blow.

Wheam still had the broken shaft in his hand. In desperation, bellowing with the effort, he thrust it upwards with all his strength. The shaft, unevenly severed so its head was like a stake, plunged deep into the goblin's belly. Crying out in shock and pain, he staggered rearward, the axe slipping from his horny fingers. Then he fell and lay writhing, his hands on the protruding shaft. Wheam scrambled to his feet, fumbled his sword from its sheath and buried it in the creature's chest.

He turned away. He was panting for breath and shaking. But he had never felt so good. More goblins were climbing over the rail. Wheam brought up his sword and prepared to meet them.

For Pirrak, the situation Wheam had faced was reversed. Many of the goblins now getting aboard carried their traditional weapon: a spear-length metal trident, its forks sharpened to a wicked keenness. Armed now with a sword, Pirrak was at a disadvantage, and he didn't dare try to retrieve his spear. So he took to dodging, stooping and sending in low blows. One such pass had him hacking into a goblin's sinewy leg, liberating a gush of dark, almost black blood. Wailing, his victim fell away, to be replaced by another trident-bearing goblin.

They circled, Pirrak turning away the trident's thrusts with his blade. The goblin lunged, driving the trident forward, and only Pirrak's nimble footwork saved him. He managed to hit the trident's metal shank a couple of times, but his blade merely raised a melodious din. Pirrak knew that at any instant he could be set upon by further opponents, but he couldn't overcome the goblin's defence or experience. He opted for a charge, dashing parallel to his foe, slashing as he went. The best he could do was catch the other's shoulder, opening a gratifying but superficial wound. That only outraged the goblin, who renewed his efforts to impale Pirrak.

The duel continued for what felt like an age to Pirrak. He was beginning to believe that he would be the first to weaken, or make a wrong move from inexperience. Feigning, thrusting, stabbing and swiping at each other, they moved through a bizarre lethal dance.

Suddenly it was over. In a brief hiatus at his front, Dallog looked for Pirrak. What he saw had him reaching for a hatchet. The goblin was closing in on Pirrak again when the hatchet struck the creature between the shoulder-blades. He spun and fell. Tyro and corporal exchanged a look, then both returned to fighting.

Dallog and Keick had entered the fray together and stayed that way. Their work was a grind of hacking and chopping, ducking and twisting. Keick slashed his blade across a goblin's face, forcing him back. Knocking a shield clear, Dallog plunged his sword into an opponent's trunk, crunching through its hard, almost insect-like carapace.

A sword and knife combination was Pepperdyne's choice. He could use them with a surgeon's skill or apply brute force as necessary. Facing a charging goblin, he employed both. Leaping aside at the last moment, he spun and brought his blade down on the goblin's outstretched arm. The amputated limb dropped still holding its trident. Howling, the wounded goblin fell away. Pepperdyne flicked his pair of blades into the deck and scooped up the trident. He hurled it at a goblin just climbing over the rail. The trident caught him square, propelling him backwards and out of sight. Pepperdyne plucked his quivering sword and knife from the deck, and looked for the next target.

For his part, Chuss made himself useful by finishing off the wounded left by the others. He had a hairy moment when one of the injured goblins seized his ankle in an iron grip. But the creature was dying, and a blow from Chuss' sword completed the job.

Shortly, the flow of boarders thinned and stopped. On the goblins' ship the remaining uninjured attackers withdrew and scrambled over the far rail. Presumably to wade ashore and join the fight there.

The defenders stood in silence, breathing hard, bloodstained, muscles aching.

'Is that it?' Wheam panted.

'Think so,' Pepperdyne replied.

'Could be more hiding over there,' Dallog said, pointing at the other ship with a gory blade.

'We'll check. But I think we got the better of them. I reckon they underestimated us and didn't want to spare many from the main assault on the beach.'

Dallog nodded. 'Likely.'

Pepperdyne looked at the tyros. 'I have to say your charges gave a good account of themselves.' He touched the hilt of his upright sword to his chest, saluting them.

They looked bashful. Youngsters again.

'They're orcs,' Dallog replied. 'They come alive in blood.'

'I should make sure Standeven's all right,' Pepperdyne said. 'Though why I bother . . .'

He went to one of his former master's favourite hideaways; a storage locker under the bridge. Wrenching the door open, he found him curled up inside.

'Have they gone?' Standeven asked tremulously.

'Yes, you're safe.'

'It's not me I'm worried about,' he came back with faux indignation.

'No? Then who?'

'Not who, *what*. Do you think Stryke's keeping the instrumentalities safe? I mean, with all this fighting going on—'

Pepperdyne slammed the door on him and rejoined the others.

'I wonder how things are going on the island,' Dallog said.

'Should we join them?' Keick wondered.

'I don't think Stryke would be very pleased if we abandoned our post,' Pepperdyne replied.

'He's right,' Dallog added. 'We should stay put. They're on their own.'

8

On the beach, Stryke and the rest of the band were watching.

They saw their ship attacked by the goblins, during which Coilla at least had concerns for those on board. Now the goblin ship, which almost completely blocked the view of the orcs' own, was being evacuated.

Jup pointed at the goblins jumping or lowering themselves over the side on ropes, then splashing towards the shore. 'Looks like Dallog and the others did well.'

Coilla nodded. 'Good for them.'

'Yeah,' Stryke said. 'But we've got our own problems.'

The other two goblin ships were anchored, and their crews were also wading to the beach, their tridents held above their heads. Elves were arriving too, staggering out of the waves, some supporting kin.

'It's too open here,' Coilla decided. 'We're better off facing them inland.'

'*Run away?*' Haskeer growled.

'A strategic retreat to a position that benefits us.' She nodded at the unfolding scene. 'Look at their numbers.'

'Coilla's right,' Stryke said. 'We're not at full strength. Makes sense for us to pick the terrain. We'll get ourselves into the jungle back there and waylay the bastards.'

Spurral was looking at the surviving islanders struggling ashore. 'Let's hope the elves stay clear.'

'No worries there,' Haskeer sneered. 'They've no guts for a fight.'

As the band jogged towards the greenery, the first of the goblins were emerging from the water.

Once into the coolness of the jungle, Stryke had the band gather round. 'This is how we're doing it. Four groups. There . . .' He pointed to a large downed tree. '. . . there . . .' A big, moss-covered rock. '. . . there . . .' A thick stand of trees just inside the lip of the jungle. '. . . and there.' The remains of an abandoned elf cabin, rotting in the tropical climate. 'They likely saw us come in so they'll be following. And they'll be expecting a trap, so we need to be well hidden and *quiet*.' He glanced at Haskeer. 'Archers fire at my order, not before. We don't want to give 'em a chance to retreat. Sergeants, get the groups sorted.'

Jup and Haskeer quickly divided the reduced band into four units and headed one each. Haskeer's group took the rock as its hideaway, Jup's the fallen tree. Coilla led the third unit, and made for the ruined hut. Stryke's group hid themselves in the stand of trees. He had chosen the hides because they formed the four sides of a corral or box. The task for Stryke's group was to secure the fourth side, the corral's gate, once the enemy were in.

They took their positions and waited.

What seemed like an age passed, and Stryke wasn't alone in thinking the goblins would simply wait them out. Then there was movement in the boundary between beach and jungle. Leaves rustled and dry bark cracked. Dark shapes could be made out.

The goblins came into the jungle. They used a measure of stealth, but seemed more reliant on their greater numbers. The orcs bided their time, well hidden and silent, waiting for the enemy to enter the snare. Soon, as many goblins as were likely to had moved into the area, and they were starting to fan out. The trap had to be sprung while they were still bunched.

'*Fire!*' Stryke bellowed.

The archers had been spread across the hiding places. Now they let loose from all sides. Arrows slammed into the outermost of the pack of goblins. A good half dozen fell, dead or wounded. No sooner had they gone down than a second wave of arrows came in. At which point practically all of the goblins went down, whether hit or not, to avoid the shower of bolts. Some had bows. Kneeling, they began to return fire. But the orcs were playing shoot and hide. Bobbing up or round their cover, they fired then instantly ducked back out of sight.

This went on for a while, and not to the goblins' advantage. Their only hope was to break the impasse. At an order gutturally barked, presumably by one of their commanders, they rose and charged. Like the blooms of some exotic black flower bursting open, goblins hurtled towards all four hides.

The orcs got off a few more shots, but things were about to get too intimate for bows. Blades and hatchets took their place.

The greatest number of goblins headed back to where they entered the jungle, hoping to regain the beach. They were confronted by Stryke's unit, the gatekeepers, slipping from the trees to block the exit. This group was slightly larger than the other three, given it would bear the brunt, but it was still desperately small compared to the pack of charging goblins. And it wasn't only the goblins' numbers that gave them an edge; many had tridents.

The orcs met them head-on, a resolute line of barbed steel, determined to deny a way out. It was a savage clash, and Stryke was to the fore. His first encounter was short and brutal. A goblin charged, trident levelled. Stryke nimbly side-stepped, batted away the trident and followed through with a second swipe, to the creature's throat. No sooner had the goblin been floored than it was instantly replaced. Stryke and his unit stood their ground, dodging and downing the press of opponents.

The slab of rock sheltering Haskeer's group was swarming with goblins, while others were trying to round it. Attrition was the name of the game. The goblins were bent on overrunning the orcs, and the orcs were as keen to stop them. With fighting up close and vicious, tridents proved too cumbersome, and most were discarded. The goblins switched to their serrated, snub-bladed swords and crimped daggers. But trying to scale the barrier was a challenge. The rock ran with blood, making traction difficult.

A cleaver in each hand, Haskeer swung at the encroaching goblins, cracking skulls and shattering bones. When one of the hatchets caught in the hilt-guard of a goblin's sword it was wrenched from Haskeer's grip. Enraged, he struck out with the remaining hatchet, scything the creature's belly and releasing its stinking contents. Swiftly bringing up the weapon he swiped at another goblin, striking him on the side of the head with the flat of its blade. As he fell, others took his place. Haskeer's detachment fought on.

Jup and Spurral were in the vanguard of the group stationed at the fallen tree. Compared to Haskeer's unit their cover was minimal. But they were just as resolute. They stood behind a barrier bristling with blades and spear-tips, and clad with shields, which the frantic goblins all but threw themselves against. Dispensing with staffs, the dwarfs employed their short swords and knives, thrusting and slashing at goblin flesh.

The pummelling on the Wolverines' shields was as relentless as a rainstorm on a field of wheat. And when one of the rangy goblins struck Spurral's shield particularly hard it was dashed from her hands. The creature followed through with a lunge to her breast. Fortunately, Jup's reactions were quicker. He blocked the blade; and Spurral, swooping low, buried her sword in the goblin's guts.

The shuffling of the combatants' feet caused her shield to be kicked away, beyond reach. A goblin tried exploiting that vulnerability, slashing his blade as he moved in on her. She could expect no further help from Jup, who had his own problems with an axe-wielding opponent. Not that she needed it. Her stocky, robust physique belied the speed and agility she was capable of, as her foe discovered. Ducking, weaving, she eluded the blade, then gave the goblin's shin a couple of hefty kicks. It was enough of an irritant to jolt the creature, and let Spurral deliver a lethal thrust. The vengeful goblins kept coming.

At the decaying lodge, Coilla perched on a heap of collapsed timber, looking down at the raging conflict. She was picking off goblins with her cache of throwing knives, plucked from her arm holsters. Choosing her mark, she lobbed a blade and struck a creature's head, downing him. On reflex born of experience she instantly yanked out another knife. There was no shortage of targets, and her next shot winged to a goblin's exposed neck.

She got a bead again, and threw. But the goblin it was aimed at managed to raise his shield. The knife bounced off it and landed a few paces away. Stooping, the goblin retrieved it, and swiftly hurled it at Coilla. It was an able throw, though not quite good enough. The blade embedded itself in the lodge wall, a hand's breadth from Coilla's head. That enraged her. As the goblin charged her way she tugged the quivering knife free, and with a grunt of effort pitched it at him. The blade caught him in the eye. Coilla reached for her sheath. There was one knife left. She flung it at the nearest attacker. It struck the creature's midriff, not killing but inflicting a grievous injury. Her arsenal spent, she drew her sword and jumped into the fray.

Fighting raged on, close quarters and bloody. The orcs took wounds, but could have suffered worse had they not had the protection of their hides. Even so, the unfavourable odds were starting to grind them down.

A cry went up from the goblins engaging Stryke's group at the trap's entrance; a rasping, keening outburst quite unlike the gruff roar a similar-sized mob of orcs would have made. It was a yell of triumph. Stryke and his unit had given a good account of themselves, but finally, perhaps inevitably, they buckled. The goblins had broken through. With no choice but to withdraw as they flooded out, Stryke's crew readied themselves to continue the battle as a brawl. But the corralled goblins stampeded past them and spilled onto the beach, leaving the killing floor littered with their dead and mortally wounded.

Stryke bellowed an order, calling the other three teams to him. They jogged his way, trampling over the corpses and cutting down the injured still game for a fight.

'Let's finish it!' Stryke yelled, pointing seaward with his sword.

They gave chase, emerging from the jungle's rim and dashing for the beach. What they saw there stopped them.

The fleeing goblins had joined the rest of their incoming contingent, a group of almost equal size, and they were forming up to face the orcs.

'*Shit*,' Coilla mouthed.

A hush fell as the two groups eyed each other.

Then a goblin pushed through the ranks and swaggered out into the separating gap. He was more finely dressed than the others, and had a long bow slung over one shoulder. It was black, elaborately embossed with tiny hieroglyphs in gold, and made from a material it was hard to identify, appearing to be neither wood nor metal. At his waist was a leather quiver holding arrows that were likewise black and marked with golden symbols.

'Who leads you?' he demanded, his voice coloured by the distinctive sibilance peculiar to his kind.

'I do,' Stryke said, stepping forward.

The goblin looked him over, a contemptuous expression on his face. 'I am Gleaton-Rouk.'

'I guessed that.'

'You owe me,' the goblin grated.

'How?'

'You killed some of my brood siblings.'

'The ones using kelpies for meat, you mean.'

'Whatever they were doing wasn't your concern.'

'We made it our concern.'

'And for that you owe a debt of blood.'

'You think you're going to collect it?'

'Have no doubts on that score, orc. Now throw down your arms.'

The Wolverines broke into derisive laughter.

Stryke's smile melted. 'That's something we don't do,' he informed the goblin evenly.

'Give yourselves up or die.'

'Like fuck we will,' Haskeer said.

The goblin glared at him. He indicated his force with a sweep of his bony arm and hissed, 'Consider the odds.'

Stryke coolly appraised them. 'Yeah, it does seem a bit unfair on your lot.'

Gleaton-Rouk began to seethe. 'So you refuse?'

'What do you think?'

'Then suffer the consequences.'

'Fine by us,' Stryke told him.

The goblin turned his back on them and headed for his line. His parting shot was 'So be it! Ready yourselves for hell!'

'See you there!' Coilla piped up cheerily.

The goblin ranks parted for him and he disappeared.

'Not taking the lead himself, I see,' Jup observed.

Haskeer nodded. 'All mouth and breeches.' He spat on the ground contemptuously.

The Wolverines watched as the goblins prepared for an attack. They could have fallen back to the jungle and faced them there, or stayed put and met them with a defensive formation. But their blood was up.

Stryke didn't need to give an order. By a kind of osmosis, intent spread through the band like a contagion.

As one, they charged.

Bellowing and whooping war cries, the Wolverines thundered towards the startled goblins.

They struck their lines at speed, wrong-footing the enemy and throwing them into confusion. The orcs laid into them with savage fury, severing limbs, piercing lungs and hacking off heads. Unprepared for wrath on such a scale, dozens of goblins fell like corn before the scythe.

Coilla worked a pair of swords as she ploughed through the chaos. She stove in a ribcage to her right, crushed a skull to her left. One blade slashed a goblin throat as the other slid deep into his comrade's belly. Weapons ranged against her were dashed aside, their wielders' impertinence paid for with cold steel. Like the rest of the band she was driven by bloodlust, the matchless trait of her race.

The ferocity was shared by Jup and Spurral, who battled with a berserk fierceness that near equalled the orcs'. They had become separated when they penetrated the enemy line, but proved as formidable fighting singly as they had as a team. For Spurral, the goblins were so much flesh to nourish her ravening blade. Jup, brandishing a pair of daggers, followed in his mate's wake, bringing down her leftovers. Blocked by a particularly obstinate foe, he came at the goblin low and with force, toppling the creature onto Haskeer's waiting sword.

Typically, Haskeer had attacked with as much, if not more frenzy, than any in the band. Heaving his blade from the goblin Jup tossed his way, he swiftly reemployed it, severing another's leg. The mass of targets kept it busy.

Stryke had made it his business to seek out Gleaton-Rouk and settle with him. But there was no sign of the goblin chieftain. And now Stryke's attention was on his band. The shock of their charge was wearing off and the goblins were rallying. A counter-attack was beginning, pushing the Wolverines back by sheer weight of numbers, and the band was taking wounds.

To Stryke's right, no more than a good spit away, one of the veterans, Bhose, was tussling with a trident-wielding goblin. Bhose lost. The goblin breached his defence and struck him with the trident, its razor-sharp tines passing clean through the orc's shoulder. Bhose went down under the impact, causing his assailant to lose his grip on the lodged trident. The goblin leapt forward, stamped his bony foot on Bhose's chest and attempted to pull the trident out. Hands clasping its shaft, face wreathed with pain, Bhose struggled to stop him.

Stryke quickly disposed of the opponent he was facing, then waded Bhose's way. By the time he got there the goblin had wrestled his trident free and was raising it for a killing blow, while Bhose stretched a hand for his sword, lying just beyond his reach. Stryke buried his blade in the goblin's back. Retching blood, the creature collapsed.

Bhose wasn't the only orc to sustain a wound. For all their bravado and martial skills, the Wolverines were being too severely challenged by the recovering goblins and were close to becoming overwhelmed. Stryke judged it prudent to disengage and regroup. On his signal a couple of nearby privates took hold of the recumbent Bhose and began dragging him clear. Then Stryke yelled an order. As one, the band pulled back. All got clear, as much by luck as dexterity. Wary of some kind of ruse, the goblins didn't pursue them.

The Wolverines arrived back at the spot they started from. They were paying the toll of combat. Some had injuries, and all of them ached from the exertion of battle. They were blood-splattered and out of breath, and Jup and Spurral ran with sweat.

Stryke quickly assessed the wounded. Supported by a pair of comrades, Bhose looked the worse. Coilla was checking his shoulder.

'How is he?' Stryke asked.

'It's a nasty wound,' she told him, 'and it's bleeding a lot.'

'I'm fine,' Bhose protested.

'Pity Dallog's not here to dress it,' Jup reckoned.

'Balls,' Haskeer said. 'Who needs him? Anybody could staunch a wound like that.'

'Anybody but you, maybe.'

'How'd you like me to cut a piece out of you and try?'

'Shut it!' Stryke barked, jabbing a thumb at the goblins. 'Save your bile for them.' He turned to the grunts holding up Bhose. 'Get him to the rear.'

'I'm fine,' Bhose repeated weakly.

'Do as you're told.'

They hauled him away.

The goblins were forming up for an attack.

'Brace yourselves!' Stryke warned.

The orc archers had a few arrows left, and nocked them. Everyone tensed.

There would be no charge from the Wolverines this time. That tactic was spent. It was the goblins' turn.

Somebody on their side shouted an order. They began to advance, slowly at first, then with gathering speed.

'*Steady!*' Stryke yelled.

The goblins broke into a trot, then started to run.

When they covered about half the distance to the Wolverines, something strange happened.

An abnormality occurred in the space between orcs and goblins. The air itself seemed to turn heavy, and took on a ruddy, dusty glow. A film appeared, shimmering like the surface of a giant soap bubble, rippling with pulsing scarlet. It stood as a semi-transparent veil across the charging goblins' path.

Most slowed or stopped. Some, the brave, foolhardy or crazed, kept running. Deceived by the veil's translucence, these few dashed headlong, thinking to break through. Three or four of them struck the barrier simultaneously. It repelled them. They flew back as though flung by a giant invisible hand. And from the instant they touched the glistening wall, they ignited. Wreathed head to foot in flame, they landed heavily, to writhe and scream as they burned.

The Wolverines felt a wave of heat, and involuntarily stepped back.

Haskeer gaped. 'What the—'

Coilla pointed. '*There!*'

Farther down the beach a large group of elves had gathered. Mallas Sahro, their elder, was to the fore.

'They're using their magic,' Stryke said.

'So they do have some backbone,' Haskeer muttered.

The burning goblins' comrades were vainly trying to beat out the flames when another, stronger heat wave throbbed from the veil.

The band drew back again. They saw that the veil had emitted a sheet of fire that swept towards the milling goblins. When it reached the first of them, those tending the fallen, they too burst into flames. It didn't stop. Continuously regenerating itself, the burning curtain kept moving at a walking pace. Ignoring the agonised screams of those on fire, the remaining goblins backed away, then quickly retreated as it herded them in the direction of the shoreline.

The band noticed that one goblin risked himself to retrieve a dropped trident. He went for that particular weapon rather than any number of others, even though it put him in danger of contact with the advancing wall of flame. Once he had it, he ran full pelt for the sea, holding the trident high above his head as he splashed in. The others entered the water close behind. To their rear, the fiery veil halted at the shore's edge.

Stryke and the band watched as the mantle of fire slowly faded, along with its heat. Beyond it, the goblins were waist-deep, making for their ships.

Jup was shielding his eyes with a hand. 'Is that their chief?' he wondered.

A figure was standing on the prow of the biggest ship.

'Yeah,' Coilla confirmed.

'Fucking coward,' Haskeer murmured.

'What's he doing?' Jup said.

Coilla squinted again. 'Looks like he's drawing his bow.'

Haskeer gave a derisive snort. 'Bloody fool. What's he hope to hit from that distance?'

'What's up with them?' Spurral asked, nodding at the crowd of elves along the beach. They were shouting and gesturing, but they were too far away for their words to be made out.

'Probably celebrating,' Stryke suggested.

From his ship, Gleaton-Rouk loosed an arrow.

'It's way off target,' Haskeer sneered. 'Even if it got this far it'd miss us by a mile.'

Most of the Wolverines agreed, showing disdain with mocking jeers. Their scorn appeared justified as the arrow soared well to their right and far too high to do any damage except to treetops.

But then there was a change. Defying nature, the arrow altered course. It turned sharply and began to descend, heading straight for the band.

'Down!' Stryke bellowed.

Everyone dropped and hugged the ground. Bhose was already sitting, nursing his wound. One of the attending grunts gave him a shove and with a moan of pain he slumped onto his back.

The arrow soared towards them, and for a moment it looked as though it would pass overhead. Instead its trajectory became more acute. Impossibly gathering speed, it descended so fast they couldn't see it.

The arrow struck Bhose in his chest.

'Back!' Stryke yelled. *'Pull back!'*

The band hastily retreated, making for the trees, keeping low and dragging Bhose with them.

As soon as they reached shelter, Jup examined their comrade.

He looked up at the circle of Wolverines. 'He took it square to the heart. He's dead.'

Coilla gazed out at the departing goblin ships and said, 'How the *hell* did they do that?'

9

Surrounded by his brothers-in-arms, an orc lies dead on the edge of a beach, his blood seeping into the sand.

The sand consists of an untold number of grains. The number of grains of sand on all the beaches of all the islands is trivial compared to the number of worlds that exist.

The void between them is unimaginably great, and terrible. But tenuous, spider-web bridges connect the worlds, woven by the power of the instrumentalities.

An endless expanse. A blue-black canvas speckled with infinite points of light.

One speck, no brighter and no dimmer than most, was verdant. Ceragan, a blue-green world, was home to orcs. It was largely unspoilt, but a small part of it had been defiled.

At the encampment, they were still clearing up the damage. Their own dead had gone to their pyres; the attackers' corpses, far greater in number, had been disposed of less ceremoniously. Now the orcs were repairing their dwellings.

Nearly half of the lodges had been wholly or partly destroyed by fire. The corrals were broken and the livestock had scattered. Wagons were upended, and a barn stood in ruins. The carcasses of horses and cows were being hauled away.

The settlement echoed to the sounds of hammering and sawing. Timber was unloaded from overburdened wagons. Smiths pounded anvils next to braziers of glowing coals. Lengths of rope were woven and roofs re-thatched. New fortifications were being erected.

Wandering through all the activity were two young male hatchlings. They were siblings, the eldest over four summers old, his brother three. Each clutched a skilfully crafted hatchet. They were much smaller versions of the weapons carried by the adults, but just as sharp, and woe to anyone who tried parting the pair from them. Not that it would occur to orcs to do so.

The hatchlings roamed with no particular purpose, driven by boredom, curiosity and a certain amount of anxiety. Their parents had been snatched from them, and although they were being cared for, they were adrift and fretful. They were more careless than they would have been if adults they respected were watching over them. It showed in their mud-caked boots and mucky britches.

The younger of the two moved with less certainty than his brother. In common with the very young of many races, he walked like a small drunk, stumbling occasionally. Only when he toppled and couldn't right himself did his brother stretch out a hand to him.

They watched as roofs were fixed, fences rebuilt and debris heaved from the well. Some greeted them with a nod or a few distracted words. Most ignored them. Their offers to help were dismissed with gruff laughter or sharp words. They were resigned to staring.

'There you are!'

They turned at the sound of the familiar and not altogether welcome voice, and saw the clan's chief, Quoll, sweeping their way. He was still big and powerfully built, despite his advancing years, and seemed incredibly ancient to them. Festooned with the armlets, bangles and leopard-tooth necklaces signifying his position, he was accompanied by his usual entourage of kin and dogsbodies.

He stood over the hatchlings, his followers looking on. 'Where have you been?' he demanded.

'Right here,' Corb told him.

'You're the oldest. It's your duty to look after your brother.'

'He does!' Janch protested.

Quoll fixed him with an icy gaze, which to the youngster's credit he held and tried, less successfully, to return. 'Judging by the state you're both in I'm not sure about that. What have you been doing?'

'Just playing,' Corb replied casually.

'Hmmm. Getting under everybody's feet more like.'

'No we haven't,' Janch muttered, his eyes now on his own feet.

'The time is coming to put aside childish things,' the chieftain declared portentously. 'What with your parents lost and—'

'They're not!' Corb protested.

'Not this again. Listen to me, both of you. Part of growing up is learning to accept what the gods have in store for us. You have to resign yourself to them being gone.'

'Don't say that!'

'It's the truth, Corb. You must come to terms with it.'

'*No.* They're not dead. I *know* they're not. Don't care what you say.'

'*How* do you know?'

'They're great warriors. Nobody could kill them. I just . . . feel it.'

Janch nodded vigorously in agreement.

Quoll sighed, and his forceful tone softened a little. 'Yes, Stryke showed his valour many times; and Thirzarr matched him in bravery and skill. Look at the price paid by the force that took her. But look too at the commander of that force, the witch.'

Corb and Janch shuddered inwardly, remembering the stories their mother told about the witch, and the raid that confirmed them.

Quoll himself recalled the ferocity of her attack, but stayed master of his emotions. And he resolved not to criticise Stryke in front of the hatchlings, though he half blamed their father for bringing near ruin on them all. 'Going against a power like hers is pissing into a gale,' he continued, 'even for an orc. I admire your loyalty to your parents, and your faith in them. But it's best not to rely too much on hope.'

'What about Wheam?' Janch piped up.

The chieftain held his steadfast expression, no matter what was going on inside. 'I have to suppose that my son is lost too. He was a disappointment to me. My wish is that he met his end with some dignity, and courage, as an orc should.' He had spoken in a kind of mild reverie, avoiding their eyes. Now his clarity returned and he looked to them. 'Face it. Stryke and Thirzarr are probably dead, thanks to the witch.'

She was no witch. She was a sorceress, and resented being thought of otherwise. And Jennesta's resentment was not to be stirred up lightly.

She stood on a beach on a world unimaginably distant from Ceragan. Night was falling and the moons were beginning to appear. Not that she was in any way softened by the sight.

A figure approached. She recognised it as her latest aide, a major whose name she had already forgotten. He was another field promotion, his predecessor having been killed earlier in the day. This replacement was a younger man, and moderately bright for a human, but she saw little in the way of a future for him. He came to her with eyes averted and an uncertain step.

She didn't wait for him to begin his no doubt stumbling report. 'How are they?'

'They seem to have settled, my lady.'

'Not too much, I hope. I need their ferocity as well as their obedience.'

'Yes, ma'am.'

'You look uncertain, Major.'

'Well, my lady, they . . . they're a little . . . troublesome.'

'I'd expect them to be. Though more to my enemies than us. Come.' She turned and strode towards the island's heart, her aide following at a safe distance.

They came to a makeshift camp. Like youngsters caught in mischief her troops quickly turned solemn when they saw her, and presented themselves stiffly. She ignored them and swept past. Her goal was at the centre of the camp, adjacent to her own tent.

Several large wooden cages stood there. They were well built, and by necessity robust. Guards were posted all around them. Two or three of Jennesta's zombie servants were present. Trusted with simple tasks, they were pushing hunks of meat and water jugs through the slats. The captives stared at the offerings but showed scant interest in eating or drinking. Most of them were standing motionless. A few crouched in the dirt with vacant gazes, and one or two shuffled aimlessly. They came more to life, of a sort, when they noticed Jennesta approaching.

A kind of roar went up from them, part frustration, part fury, but strangely distorted, as though it should have been less muted. They became agitated, after a fashion, and moved to rattle the bars of their cages, still howling.

Jennesta raised her arms. '*Silence!*'

They instantly quietened. But they obeyed without exactly being cowed, and close scrutiny might have shown a tiny hint of something like defiance in their eyes.

'Good,' she said, studying them. 'They look promising.'

'Promising, ma'am?' the major ventured, shooting a nervous glance at the cage's occupants.

'I need their fire,' she explained. 'But there also has to be submission to my will. It's a balance.'

'May I ask what use these creatures will be put to, my lady?'

'Initially, revenge,' she replied, ignoring his impertinence in querying her. 'I've been exiled from the Peczan empire because of those terrorists in Acurial, and the Wolverines played their part in that. But it was an ill wind that's brought me nearer to attaining my goal. There'll be a reckoning the next time I encounter that wretched warband.'

'Begging your pardon, ma'am, but if we're to engage with them again we might have to consider the level of our forces. Not a few have fallen in your service. Today alone we lost—'

'I'm aware of that,' she informed him icily, and embedded in her tone was the inference that she didn't particularly care. 'But here, in front of you, is a beginning; the reinforcements to swell our ranks, more pliable and much more ferocious than those sorry efforts.' She indicated the trio of once human zombies milling near the cages.

One of them was Kapple Hacher, formerly a man of power and influence who had made the mistake of inviting Jennesta's anger. Her contempt seemed to faintly register with him. There was the merest flicker of recognition, an echo of the dissent in the captives' eyes. It went unnoticed.

'We're leaving here. Now,' she announced abruptly. 'Issue the orders.'

'Ma'am. And the Wolverines?' the major asked.

She glanced towards her grand tent. Its flaps were open. Inside, sitting in plain view, was Stryke's mate, Thirzarr. Her bearing was rigid and her expression was vacant.

'The Wolverines will come to me,' Jennesta said. 'And they won't be alone.'

Pelli Madayar was in a dilemma, and plagued with uncertainty. The dilemma was how best to act in what was an increasingly complex situation. The uncertainty came from questioning her own abilities.

She was at the rail of her ship, the many races of the Gateway Corps unit busy around her. Her second-in-command, Weevan-Jirst, stood by her side.

'You're making too much of it,' he hissed.

'Am I?'

'Your orders are simple enough: recover the instrumentalities.'

'You make it *sound* simple. The reality turns out to be a lot messier.' She gave him a sidelong glance. 'Or is that just my elven way of looking at things?'

'Perhaps. Then again, maybe we goblins have a tendency to see events as a little too black and white.'

Pelli smiled. 'That's quite an admission.'

'One thing about being in the Corps and mixing with other races is that it exposes you to different views. But I stand by what I said. Our mission has a plain objective.'

'It *did*. But now there are *two* sets of instrumentalities, and at least one other player in this drama. Those factors increase the variables. I'm in a quandary about how to tackle the problem.'

'We have the weaponry. Resolve to use it against the orcs and that sorceress alike. And not just a mild dose, like before.'

'Again, easily said. But it doesn't take into account the innocent casualties that could cause and—'

'It's not for me to remind you, but what the Corps believes in and what it expects is getting back instrumentalities, whatever the cost. If that can be done without harming the blameless, well and good. But it's not the primary consideration.'

'That's where my doubts set in. It's been generations since the Corps had to do anything like this, and those rules were formulated long ago.'

'That doesn't make them wrong.'

'I think they are. Which is why I'm wondering if I'm best suited to lead this unit.' She sighed. 'The way things are going, my first assignment looks like being my last.'

'Karrell Revers gave you this job because he knew you could do it. And you can, if you get over your scruples and see our work as being for the greater good.'

'So a few deaths of bystanders along the way is an acceptable price, yes, I know. I can't accept that.'

Weevan-Jirst studied her face, his own remaining typically expressionless. 'Who exactly are these bystanders?' He jabbed a lean hand at the ocean. 'How many true innocents are we likely to meet on the islands out there?'

'Enough.'

'Or is it that you have sympathy for one group in particular?' It was hardly a question.

'The orcs? You know I have . . . not sympathy, but some regard for the fix they're in.'

'You can't see *them* as innocent.'

'I see them as unwitting.'

'Don't forget they attacked us.'

'I don't think that was deliberate.'

'Not deliberate? You're talking about a savage, destructive race. One of a very few never granted membership or knowledge of the Corps.'

'Many races are maligned. There are those who would tar all goblins with the same brush because of the actions of a few.'

He nodded soberly. 'I'll grant you that.'

'So how can we be sure that what's said about orcs is true? And even if it is, it's the nature they were born with. Who are we to judge?'

'The Corps judges all the time. It decides who can't have instrumentalities, and the means necessary to enforce that. Having the instrumentalities fall into the hands of a race beyond the pale like the orcs, and that sorceress, is what the Corps was set up to prevent.'

Staring at the distant horizon, again she sighed, more in resignation this time. 'I suppose you're right. There is a bigger picture. I'll be mindful of it.'

'You will forgive me for what I am about to say. And I would not like you to think . . .'

She had never known him to be hesitant before. 'Yes?'

'I would not like you to think that my words are inspired by anything other than making our mission a success.'

'All right. Go on.'

'Gratified as I am to hear that you intend acting more decisively, I understand this might prove . . . difficult for you. In that event, I would be prepared to assume leadership of this unit.'

Pelli needed a moment to take that in. 'You're challenging my command?'

'No. I'm merely stating that if you're unable to fulfil your function I will step in.'

'That would be your duty in any event, if I were killed or badly wounded or—'

'Those aren't the eventualities I have in mind.'

'What is?'

'Your possible reluctance to employ the force necessary when it comes to the crunch.'

'I see.'

'I have the right to take over,' Weevan-Jirst reminded her. 'It's laid out in the Corps' tenets. You would be bound to give me access to your means of contacting Revers, and I would report your incapacity to him.'

'Did he put you up to this? I mean, were you briefed that you might need to take such action?'

'Only . . . in so many words.'

'So Revers doesn't trust me?'

'He mistrusts your inexperience. As a responsible leader, he had to plan for any . . . shortcomings.'

'At what point am I considered incompetent? Am I to make every decision with your reaction in mind? I can't see that making my position easier.'

'Naturally I would apply common sense. But if the success of this mission were to be threatened by inaction on your part, I would move to relieve you of your command. Not that I would lightly adopt such a course.'

If there was a way of telling when a goblin looked embarrassed, she didn't know it. But it was obvious he was serious.

'You won't have to,' she told him.

10

The Wolverines built a funeral pyre on the beach of the elves' island.

Stryke would have preferred to skip the ritual and push on. But the discontent about Harglo's burial at sea felt by many in the band was something he didn't want to rekindle.

Assuming the function that was once performed by his predecessor, the late Alfray, Dallog again conducted a ritual in which he entrusted their fallen comrade to the care of the gods. Not everyone in the band was happy with the corporal fulfilling this role; Haskeer in particular wore an expression showing more than simple grief. But he and the few other dissenters held their peace.

Bhose's corpse was laid on the pyre. His weapons, helm and shield were distributed amongst the band, as was the custom, but his sword was placed in his hand. Then Stryke said a few words, paying tribute to Bhose's courage and loyalty, and they consigned his body to the flames.

All the elves had gathered, watching from a distance in respectful silence. Mindful of not stoking tensions in the band, Pepperdyne saw to it that he and Standeven also stood apart. Coilla would have preferred Pepperdyne at her side, but throughout the ceremony contented herself with sidelong glances that caught his eye.

It took some hours for the pyre to do its work. The Wolverines stayed to the end, in a mood close to reverential, while the elves slowly drifted back to their settlement. At length, Stryke broke the spell with an order for the band to stand down.

As he passed, Haskeer said, 'Another good comrade gone.'

Stryke nodded. 'Yeah.'

'This mission's costing us dear in lives.'

'It's the price we have to pay sometimes.'

'Did Bhose have to pay it today?'

'What do you mean?'

'I don't know that the way we fought made much sense. Trying to box those goblins in, then taking it out to the beach.'

'What would *you* have done?'

'It ain't just that; it's this whole mission. It started simple. Now we're floating round these lousy islands with a bunch of hangers-on and the band bleeding members.'

'You're painting it too black. We fight and some of us die, you know that. It's the orcs' lot.'

'Yeah, but—'

'And we've no choice. At least, I haven't as long as Thirzarr's out there somewhere. Even if we were ready to leave we can't rely on the stars anymore. So like it or not, we're stuck with what we've got.'

'And if we don't make it home?'

'Then we'll settle for getting our own back on Jennesta.'

'Some chance.'

'Taking chances is something else we do, even slim ones. But you don't have to. If you don't like the way things are going you can stay here with the elves.'

'No, no. I only—'

'Or if you think you can do better at leading the band, be my guest and try.'

'Look, Stryke, I just—'

'*Otherwise*, stop bellyaching. Got it?'

Haskeer sighed and mumbled, 'Got it.'

'Right. Now let's see if we can find out what happened to Bhose.' He turned and walked away. Haskeer followed, and the rest of the band fell in behind them.

Stryke led them to the elves' village. It had become a sombre place. The elves had dead of their own, many of them, and the bodies were laid out in front of Mallas Sahro's lodge. He sat on an imposing, throne-like chair overlooking the scene, a couple of attendants at his side. When he saw the Wolverines approaching he rose to meet them.

'On behalf of my clan,' he said, 'allow me to express regret at the loss of your comrade.'

Stryke nodded. He glanced at the rows of elven dead. 'Your folk have suffered too. Our sympathies.'

'Thank you. We have an old saying: "There will be tears enough to rival the ocean". That never seemed more apt.'

'Why did you decide to use your magic after all?'

'The answer lies before you. In the past the goblins have taken a life here, a life there. Never before have they slaughtered us on such a scale. That, and because of what you said about us using our powers to throw off their yoke.'

'You aided us, and we're grateful. But it was our fault. They were here because of us. We brought you trouble, and for that we owe you an apology.'

'No, you don't. We already had that particular trouble. The goblins have plagued us for a long time, but it took today's events to force us to act. It was a lesson. A hard one, to be sure, but necessary.'

'I'm pleased you see it that way. Though you must be aware that they might return for vengeance.'

'In which case we have our defensive magic. Hopefully it will be enough to ward them off. In any event, given the beating you inflicted on them, I suspect it will be a while before they brave our shores again.'

'I trust you're right about that. But you probably aren't the only islanders in these parts to be tormented by them. You might think of making common cause with your neighbours. There's strength in numbers.'

'A wise thought. I'll set about it once our period of mourning ends.'

'Don't leave it too long,' Stryke cautioned.

'What we don't understand,' Coilla said, 'is what happened to Bhose.'

'Yeah, how the hell did the goblin manage a shot like that?' Jup wanted to know.

'Shadow-wing,' Mallas Sahro replied.

'What?' Stryke asked.

'The bow Gleaton-Rouk used. Its name is Shadow-wing. At least, that's one of its names. It has many.'

'And it's enchanted.'

'Of course. No ordinary bow could perform that way.'

'How does it work? I mean, why did it single out Bhose in particular?'

'Shadow-wing is subject to a very specific type of magic. The shafts it looses have to be daubed with blood from the intended victim. Once so anointed the arrow will always find its target. *Always.* It has nothing to do with the skill of the archer.'

'That explains something we saw when the goblins were retreating,' Coilla recalled. 'One of them risked himself to pick up a weapon.'

'It must have been the weapon that wounded your comrade during the battle. The blood on it would have guided Shadow-wing's arrow. In all probability the goblin retrieved the weapon knowing only that it had wounded an orc. It happened to be your comrade Bhose. It could have been any member of your band who sustained an injury that bled.'

'Why didn't you warn us about this bow?' Jup said.

He shrugged his shoulders. 'We simply didn't have the chance.'

'What do you know about the bow?' Stryke said. 'Where did it come from?'

'It was long thought to be a myth. Like all such fables, there are many stories attached to it, most contradictory. But the prevailing legend is that it was made by the goblins' gods, long, long ago. They have strange gods, as you know, and not a few of them dark.'

'How did these gods come to be parted from it?'

'Again, there are different stories. Some say it was stolen from them by a celebrated goblin hero, who himself has many names. Others hold that the gods gifted it to a goblin in gratitude for a task he performed. Or that it was used by one god to kill another, a rival, and the bow was flung from the clouds in disgust, and landed on earth to vex the world of mortals. The tales are legion. As are those surrounding Shadow-wing's passage through history. What the stories have in common is that corruption, treachery and death always attend the bow. Gleaton-Rouk is a master of those black arts, so I suppose it comes as no surprise that he has gained it. As I say, we thought the bow was just a story. I wish it could have stayed that way.'

'Well, we're heading away from here. Chances are we'll not see Gleaton-Rouk again, much as we'd like to have a reckoning with him. Likely it's you that'll have to face that damn weapon again.'

'If so, we shall be extra cautious about any of our blood that's spilt.'

'I wouldn't count on having seen the last of Gleaton-Rouk, Stryke,' Coilla suggested. 'He has a grudge to settle with us.'

'We're not going looking for him. Thirzarr comes first.'

'I thought this band believed in avenging its own,' Haskeer rumbled.

'We'll go after him once we've settled our score with Jennesta.'

'If we're still alive.'

'If we're able, I vow we'll cross paths with Gleaton-Rouk again.'

'And be careful not to bleed anywhere near him,' Jup added.

Spurral gave him a sharp elbow to the ribs.

'When must you leave?' Mallas Sahro asked. 'Can you stay and take refreshments, or rest?'

'We're moving on soon as we can,' Stryke said. 'Besides . . .' He looked at the elf corpses. '. . . this is your time for grief, not feasting with strangers.'

'At least let us supply you with food and fresh water for your journey.'

'That would help. Thank you.'

'And this,' the chief said, slipping a hand into a pocket in his robe. He brought out a bracelet. Made of a silvery, semi-rigid material, it was about as wide as an orc's finger was long, and was studded with blue stones of various sizes. There was a hinged clasp, indicating that it opened. 'This is a charm to ward off magical attacks. It, too, is old, though not as ancient as the bow. It won't repel the strongest magic, but might buy you a brief respite. Take it.'

'You're sure?'

'I know orcs have no innate talent for magic, as elves do, and we have other charms. I think that you might need this more than us.'

'We'll take any help we can get.'

'Be aware that once the bracelet is on your wrist it will be impossible to remove until either its protection is no longer needed or its power is spent.'

'I suppose it'll stop me losing it,' Stryke reasoned. 'But how long does its power last? And how will it *know* it isn't needed anymore?'

'If unused, its magical energy could last centuries. In the event of it having to counter really potent sorcery, it might be less than a day. As to how it will know when to release itself . . . it will know.' He stared hard at Stryke. 'So, your arm?'

Stryke obliged and Mallas Sahro clamped the bracelet on his wrist.

Once the clasp clicked into place the bracelet visibly contracted and tightened. Stryke felt it gently fasten snugly against his flesh.

'By the end of the day you won't even be aware of it,' the chief assured him.

Stryke looked it over, turning his wrist. 'I'm obliged.' His gaze went to the sea. 'We've got to be moving now.'

'I'll have the supplies brought out right away.' He nodded at one of his aides, who hurried off. 'And I have a suggestion. When they left, the goblins abandoned one of their ships; the one they used to try to board yours. It's not quite as big as the one you arrived in, but it's faster. Why not take it?'

'Good idea, we'll do that.'

'Go in peace then, and be assured that you will always have a welcome here.'

Not long after, the Wolverines were back at sea and the elves' island was out of sight. The wind was strong. With Pepperdyne in his usual place at the wheel, and a sleeker vessel, they made good progress.

Stryke was at the stern, sitting on the deck with his back to the rail, studying the bracelet. The chart was spread out on his lap. He had grown more morose since they set sail, and Coilla approached with care.

'Suits you,' she said, nodding at the armlet.

He smiled thinly. 'I was wondering if it protected just me, or all of us. Stupid of me not to ask.'

'Let's hope we don't have to find out.' She glanced up at the ship's black, billowing sails. 'They were right about this ship being faster.'

'I could wish for the magical speed it had when we first saw it.'

'Jode reckons we'll be there soon. Maybe as soon as late tomorrow. Hang on.'

'I've no choice.'

She crouched next to him. 'Stryke . . . about Bhose. I—'

'You're not going to sound off about that too, are you? It's bad enough listening to Haskeer grousing.'

'I'm not about to blame you for anything. I'm more worried that you might be blaming yourself for Bhose's death.'

'No more than when anybody in the band gets themselves killed.'

'So quite a lot then.'

'We're born to kill, and to flirt with our own deaths. It's the orcs' creed. But when you're in command you can't help thinking that some choice you made, an order you issued, might have been wrong and put the band in peril.'

'And Thirzarr?'

'Thirzarr as well. I've put her and the hatchlings in danger. I don't even know if they're still alive.'

'We all signed up for this mission. All right, Thirzarr and the hatchlings didn't, but they're orcs too. My point is: they know the odds.'

'Corb and Janch don't, not yet. They're too young.'

'The clan in Ceragan do. They'll be looking after them, the way we all watch each other's backs in the band.'

'If Jennesta left anybody alive.'

'You've got to have hope, Stryke. Why else go on?'

He pondered that for a moment, then said, 'You seem to be living on hope yourself.'

She was puzzled. 'What d'you mean?'

'You and Pepperdyne.'

'What?'

'You hope it'll work out. But you could be storing trouble for yourself, Coilla. Orcs and humans come from different worlds, and you know how much bad feeling there's been between them. The chances are you'll—'

'Oh, you're good, Stryke. You've managed to turn it from you to me. As usual.'

'I mean it. I just don't want to see you get hurt.' His words were not said unkindly.

Because of that, and the strain he was under, she bit back her anger. 'You found contentment,' she replied coolly, 'don't deny it to me.'

'I might have lost it.'

'For your sake, I hope not. But whatever passes between Jode and me is our concern, nobody else's.'

'Just think about what you're doing.'

'Yeah, right,' she said, getting to her feet. 'I'll catch you later.' As she left, Stryke went back to studying the bracelet.

She was fuming as she headed towards the prow.

'Coilla.'

'Yes?' she snapped, spinning to face whoever had spoken. 'Oh, Wheam. Sorry.'

'That's all right. It's been a tough day, what with Bhose and everything.'

'You're not wrong. I've been meaning to say: you did well helping defend the ship. We're all proud of you.'

The youth looked both pleased and embarrassed. 'Thanks, Coilla.' Then the cheer went out of his face. 'I wish everybody felt that way.'

'Who doesn't?'

For answer, he nodded. She followed his gaze. Further along the deck, Dallog and Pirrak stood close together. They were deep in conversation.

'Like I told you before,' Coilla said, 'Dallog has charge of all you tyros. You can't expect him to play favourites.'

'He doesn't seem to have any time for me these days. Only Pirrak.'

'Who probably needs special attention. You should be pleased you don't.'

Wheam brightened a little. 'I hadn't thought of it like that.'

'There's usually more than one way to look at things. Don't pick the worst.'

Haskeer arrived, his expression flinty, and would have passed them without a word had Wheam not spoken.

'Sergeant!' Haskeer stopped and stared at him. 'We've all been saddened by the loss of our comrade Bhose,' Wheam said, reaching for the goblin lute he habitually had slung on his back, 'and I've been honouring him in verse. Can I offer you a lament?'

'Only if I can offer you a kick up the arse,' Haskeer growled. He stomped off, scowling.

'Happy ship,' Coilla remarked. 'Don't mind him, Wheam. Why don't you get some sleep? There might not be much chance after we make landfall.'

'Yes, I suppose I should. But . . .'

'What now?'

'Some of the band have been talking about the Krake, and how it can pull a ship under and—'

'They should know better. Don't worry about it; we've more pressing concerns. Now get yourself to your bunk. And if we get attacked by sea monsters I'll give you a call.'

*

They sailed on through the night and much of the next day. Late in the afternoon they spotted a landmass.

'That has to be it,' Pepperdyne said, perusing the map.

Stryke nodded. 'So let's land.'

'We need to take care. This chart's not the clearest I've ever seen, but it looks like there could be hidden rocks off those shores.' He pointed. 'Here, see? We'll need to take soundings.'

'Do what you have to.'

They approached the island with caution, and Pepperdyne got one of the privates to measure the water's depth with a length of rope and a lead weight. It proved unusually deep, but there was no problem finding a path through any submerged rocks. Eventually they dropped anchor just off the main beach. A skeleton crew was left to guard the ship, along with Standeven, while the rest of the band waded ashore. They saw no signs of life.

'As islands go,' Coilla said, 'this one's not very big.'

'Big enough for a settlement,' Stryke replied. 'We'll head inland.'

The island's interior was swathed in dense jungle and at first they had to hack their way through. They would have expected to disturb birds or the myriad small animals that lived in the undergrowth, but there was only silence. Soon they came to an area where trees had been felled and the scrub cleared to form an open space. They found the settlement.

It was in ruins. There were perhaps a score of lodges and huts, and not one was undamaged. Something like half were burnt out. They saw the mutilated bodies of a few dogs, but no corpses of any other kind, and certainly nothing living.

'We're too late,' Coilla whispered.

'So what do we do now, Stryke?' Spurral asked.

He gazed about, a look of utter despondency on his face.

'Stryke?' Coilla urged.

'I don't know,' he said.

11

The elves' dealings with the outside world didn't end with the orcs' departure. The day after the Wolverines left, the Gateway Corps ship arrived.

Wary given recent events, the elves flung up their magical barriers. The strange, multi-species group of visitors dismissed these obstacles with almost casual contempt. There was alarm when the goblin Weevan-Jirst appeared; and bemusement at the sight of the elf, Pelli Madayar. Her presence, and her oath that they came in peace, gained a measure of the elves' trust. For their part, they told the strangers what had happened with the goblins, while casting edgy glances Weevan-Jirst's way; and they were honest about the Wolverines having been there. But they stayed loyal to the warband and refused to say where they were headed.

Pelli didn't linger. She took ship immediately and ordered their former course resumed.

Weevan-Jirst was displeased, and showed his irritation when they stood together at the helm.

'We should have *made* them tell us.'

'What are we,' she retorted, 'marauders? Anyway, we don't need a steer from them; we have our sorcery to help us follow the orcs.'

'So why did we waste time stopping there?'

'To gather intelligence.'

'We gained precious little in that respect.'

'I disagree. We confirmed that we were on the right trail, and learned about the Wolverines' tangle with . . .' She shot him a glance. '. . . members of your race.'

If her aide found the reference objectionable in any way he didn't show it. 'You could have pushed them harder. We might have learnt more.'

'Did you see the graves back there? And the number of them? It wasn't the right time for an interrogation.'

'It was exactly the right time, while they were weakened by grief.'

'I thought otherwise.'

'Because they're elves? Your own kind?'

'No. I give no more weight to my own race than any other,' she replied steadfastly. 'Any more than I would hold you to account for the wrongdoings of some goblins.'

He made a kind of low clucking with his bony jaw, the goblin equivalent of tutting or an exasperated sigh. 'The fact remains,' he hissed, 'that we are conducting ourselves with less than single-minded purpose.'

'I think you mean ruthlessness. As I said, I don't see that as an honourable way for the Corps to behave, and I wouldn't want to be part of it if it did.'

'Then perhaps you should consider your position as commander of this mission.'

'The one best placed to determine that is our leader.'

'Unless I, as second-in-command, judge you incompetent.'

'You've already made that point. I prefer Karrell Revers' counsel.'

'As you please.'

'And I'm overdue reporting to him. So if you'll excuse me . . .' Without waiting for an answer she turned on her heel and walked away.

When Pelli got to her cabin she locked the door, something she didn't normally bother with. Then she took out the crystal she commonly used to contact Karrell Revers. In moments, following the appropriate incantations, it was glowing in the palm of her hand.

The image of a mature human's face appeared on the crystal's surface. He spoke without preamble. *'It's been too long since your last report. What's happening?'*

'Events move apace here. Reporting hasn't been my first priority.' She wasn't in the mood to apologise.

Revers looked as though he was going to rebuke her for that. He contented himself with, *'So tell me now.'*

'We're in hot pursuit of the Wolverines. And I'm sure the sorceress can't be far away.'

'Have you actually engaged with either yet?'

'Not since our confrontation on the dwarfs' isle.'

'Which you could have won if you'd used the full potential of your weaponry.'

'I didn't feel it was appropriate. There were innocents present.'

'And orcs.'

'Yes, but—'

'And perhaps your sympathies for them could have stayed your hand?'

'No. I mean, you know I'm in favour of giving them the benefit of the doubt. My belief is that they're being manipulated. But that doesn't in any way compromise my—'

'We seem to have this conversation endlessly. Your one and only aim should be to retrieve the instrumentalities, both the original and duplicate sets. Any other consideration is secondary. Compassion for orcs certainly is.'

The crystal's magic was such that his words were audible both in her mind and, less loudly, in the cabin. It was something she always found a little disconcerting. 'I can get the instrumentalities back,' she replied, 'and if things are handled properly, without too much blood being spilt. Surely that's a better outcome for the Corps?'

'The only outcome that counts is gaining the artefacts. I think you're close to failing in that.'

'So why did you give me this job in the first place?'

'Because I believed you were capable of it, or at least that you'd grow into it.'

'My chances would be greater if my leadership wasn't being undermined.'

'What do you mean?'

'Weevan-Jirst. Did you order him to scrutinise my actions? And to relieve me of my command if he saw fit?'

'Pelli, you must understand that—'

'Did you?'

'There has to be a contingency plan for every mission. You are unproven. I needed to know our objective would be achieved, whatever the cost.'

'So you instructed my second-in-command to spy on me.'

'To keep a watchful eye on you. Just that.'

'And to take over this mission if he didn't like what he saw.'

'The Corps and our calling are bigger than any individual, Pelli. I make no apology for trying to ensure the success of this venture.'

'I gave my loyalty to you, and to the Corps. Is this how you repay me?'

'There would be no threat to your command if you acted decisively.'

'By which you mean taking no heed of casualties among the blameless.'

'Civilian losses are regrettable, but they're trivial in light of the havoc the instrumentalities can cause in the wrong hands.'

'I can't regard the death of innocents as unimportant. That's not what I thought the Corps was about.'

'If you don't know our sole purpose by now perhaps there is *a basis for questioning your judgement.'*

'It seems you're determined to believe that.'

'No, I think I've given you more than enough chances to prove yourself. But we've got to the stage where there's nothing more to say. I want to talk with Weevan-Jirst.'

Seeing no point in arguing further, Pelli simply replied, 'All right.'

She left the cabin, slipping the crystal into her pocket. But she didn't seek out her second-in-command. Instead she made for a quiet part of the ship and went to the rail.

She took out the crystal, holding it in her clenched fist and not looking at it. It was true there were other ways of communicating with Karrell Revers, but they involved invocations only she knew, and there was no way she was going to divulge them. The crystal was the simplest, most direct channel.

There was a moment of hesitation then, a realisation of the gravity of what she was about to do.

She looked around to see if anyone was watching. Then she dropped the crystal overboard.

The band was worried about Stryke.

He was in a frame of mind that mixed despair with flashes of belligerence. They left him to brood in the ruins of the deserted village.

At Coilla's instigation several scouting parties were sent out to comb the island. No one thought anything would come of it, but it was better than doing nothing. As it was comparatively small, the island didn't take long to search, and the scouts were soon back. They had nothing significant to report.

Calthmon had led one of the parties to explore the opposite side of the island. He had an observation. 'There are other islands, just off this one. Three or four of 'em.'

Pepperdyne had the map, loaned to him without protest by Stryke. He consulted it. 'Yes, we knew that. They're here on the chart. A way off, according to this.'

Calthmon shook his head. 'Nah. You could hit the nearest with an arrow. Water between's shallow, too. I reckon we could walk it.'

'I was worried that this map might not be very accurate. What's over there? Could you see?'

'Nothing. They're just rocky. Barren.'

'Doesn't help us much, does it?' Jup said.

'So what do we do?' Haskeer asked. 'We can't just sit on our arses waiting for Stryke to pull himself together.'

'Damned if I know.'

'Couldn't we go back to the elves' island?' Spurral suggested.

'Can't see that they'd be much help,' Coilla told her. 'Any other ideas? Anybody?'

'I suppose we could sail these waters in the hope of picking up a clue about where Jennesta's gone,' Pepperdyne said. 'Though I'm pretty sure that'd be fruitless.'

'Great,' Coilla sighed. 'Anybody else? No? All right. I think all we can do is hone our blades, check our kit and wait for Stryke to snap out of it. He'll know what to do.'

'Will he?' Haskeer said.

She ignored that. 'Anybody comes up with a better plan, sing it out.'

'If we're waiting, I'm doing it on the beach,' Spurral decided. 'There's more cheer there than in this place.'

Coilla looked at the ruined settlement. 'I'm with you on that.'

'What about Stryke?' Jup said.

'He'll be fine.'

Spurral headed off, and the rest of the band drifted along behind her. If Stryke noticed, he gave no sign.

On the beach most of the band settled down together. They

proceeded to overhaul their weaponry, and to discuss the situation in low tones. There was a general air of despondency.

Coilla and Pepperdyne sat apart from the others. Coilla spent the time cleaning the throwing knives she had retrieved after battling the goblins.

'What do you reckon?' Pepperdyne said. 'Can you see a way out of this?'

'Offhand, no.'

'What about Stryke?'

'What about him?'

'*Is* he going to snap out of it?'

'Course he is. I've seen him like this before, though not as bad. He just needs some time. '

'And what you said about him knowing what to do. Will he?'

'No idea. But if anybody can come up with something, it's Stryke.'

'So we wait.'

Coilla shrugged. 'What else can we do?' She glanced at the rest of the band. Like her and Pepperdyne, two others had chosen to sit to one side. 'I want to talk to somebody, Jode. Hang on here.'

He nodded. She stood and moved off.

Almost as soon as she left, Standeven arrived.

'What is it?' Pepperdyne snapped tetchily.

Standeven affected a hurt look. 'Do I have to have a reason for talking to my long-serving helper?'

'There's a motive behind everything you do. And *helper* isn't exactly the word I'd choose to describe our connection.'

'Words, words, words.' Standeven waved a dismissive hand. 'We put too much weight on them.'

'Words like *slave*, you mean? That one's light as a feather. Except to anybody it's applied to.'

'*Connection*. That's the only word you've used that's of any importance.'

'What the hell are you talking about, Standeven?'

'Whatever you want to call it, we do have a bond. We've been through a lot together, and we've always overcome anything and anybody who stood in our way.'

'*I* have, you mean.'

'Now we're in another fix.'

'That's a statement of the damned obvious. What's your point?'

'The instrumentalities.'

'Oh, for the gods' sake! Not *that* again. Don't you ever—'

'Hear me out. You think I want to get my hands on them.'

'I wonder what gave me that idea.'

'But all I really want is to get back to our world.'

'You haven't exactly hidden that ambition.'

'Be serious,' he returned sternly. 'I've got a plan.'

'And you're going to tell me about it.' Pepperdyne's tone was one of resignation.

Standeven leaned into him, too close for Pepperdyne's liking, and monopolised his ear. 'Stryke won't be parted from the instrumentalities, quite rightly, so he has to be persuaded to use them to take me back. And you too, of course,' he added as an afterthought.

'Persuaded.'

'Yes.'

'By you.'

'Well, given the way he thinks about me, it'd be better coming from you.'

'Me. And what am I supposed to say to him?'

'It's simple. All he's got to do is take me . . . take *us* home, then return here. We're out of his hair, he's still got the instrumentalities.'

'He's going to do this in the middle of searching for his mate, while his band are going down like flies and a weird bunch of sorcerers are stalking us. Not to mention a revenge-crazed goblin with an awesome bow.'

'It's not asking *that* much, seeing all we've been through with this gang of freaks.'

'This is *insane*. As I told you before, there's no way Stryke would agree to a harebrained idea like that. Get that through your thick head. And even if he did agree, by some miracle, you're forgetting something: there's no guarantee you'd get home. The instrumentalities aren't working properly.'

'So he says.'

'What?'

'We've only got his word for it. How do we know he isn't lying?'

'Why the hell would Stryke do that?'

'Who knows how these creatures' minds work?'

'Yours is more of a mystery. Look, if you want to try getting Stryke to take you back, go ahead and ask him. I think I can guess his answer. But don't involve me in your ridiculous schemes.'

'What about you? Surely you want to get back to our own world.'

'No. At least, not now.'

Standeven adopted a knowing expression. 'Oh, right. The female.' He gave a grotesque, leering wink. 'Prefer to go native with her for a while first, do you? Wouldn't appeal to me, I must say, but each to his own, and—'

'Say another word,' Pepperdyne informed him coldly, 'and I'll break your nose.'

One look at his face convinced Standeven that lingering there wasn't a smart idea. Muttering under his breath, he shambled away.

Further along the beach, Coilla approached Dallog and Pirrak. They sat together a little way from the others, engrossed in conversation, but stopped when they saw her.

Dallog nodded in greeting. 'Coilla.'

'All well?'

'Far as it can be, given where we are.'

'How about you, Pirrak?'

'Me, Corporal? I'm . . . fine.'

'You did well in the battle with the goblins. All you new recruits did.'

'Er . . . thanks.'

She turned to Dallog. 'Can we talk?'

'Sure.' He looked to Pirrak, who got up and left.

'He seems a little jumpy,' Coilla said, watching the tyro walk away.

'Aren't we all?'

'Yeah, I guess so.'

'What did you want to talk to me about?'

'No need to look so serious. I only wanted to ask about Wheam.'

'What's he done?'

'Nothing. It's just that he feels you've been a bit . . . distant from him lately.'

'Did he ask you to bring this up with me?'

'No. He doesn't know I'm talking to you about it. And I think we should keep it that way.'

'Well, it's true. Though I wouldn't call it distant.'

'What would you call it?'

'I'm trying to help him grow, Coilla. You know his story.' He counted off on his calloused fingers. 'He's got a powerful sire who's always on his back. His belief in himself's low. He's got no inborn talent for fighting, despite his orc nature. He's wet behind the ears and—'

'He's getting better.'

'Granted. He's come on a lot since this mission started. But he won't rise much further as long as he's leaning on somebody. I reckoned the time was right to cut him loose.'

'So it's about getting him to stand on his own feet.'

'And he won't do that as long as the props are there.'

Coilla nodded reflectively. 'I can see that. One other thing. It seems to bother him that you're spending so much time with Pirrak.'

'He's bound to resent being replaced by one of the other tyros, as he looks at it.'

'Why are you so interested in Pirrak?'

'Unlike Wheam, he still needs his props.'

'Why?'

'In his way, he's as uncertain of himself as Wheam. Only he's better at hiding it. Mostly. You said yourself he was jumpy.'

'So you don't believe in the tough approach in every case.'

'They're different orcs. Wheam's had his nurturing. Pirrak's isn't over just yet.'

'Can we rely on him? In a fight, I mean.'

'As surely as any other in the band. He's already proving himself. Like Wheam.'

She weighed his words. 'All right. I'm obliged, Dallog.'

'You're welcome, Corporal.'

Coilla left thinking he was a wise judge of character. She was impressed.

Heading back towards Pepperdyne, she saw Standeven shuffling away from him. Halfway there, Spurral joined her.

'Know what I'm thinking?' she said.

'Nope,' Coilla replied. 'Mind-reading's not one of my talents.'

'I'm thinking how much Stryke's search for Thirzarr mirrors what happened to me and Jup.'

'When the Gatherers took you, you mean. S'pose it does. It was a hard time for you both.'

'Yes, but that ended happily.'

'You think this won't?'

'I don't know. I hope it will, of course. But the difference between my situation and Thirzarr's was that you had some idea of where I was being taken.'

'Yeah, it's tough knowing what to do next.'

'Coilla, do you ever wonder . . .'

'What?'

'Do you ever wonder what you'd do if the same thing happened to you and Jode? If you were parted and—'

'It hadn't occurred to me. Go a bit nuts, I expect.'

'You feel that strongly about him, then.'

'That's a sneaky way of getting me to open up about it, Spurral.'

'Sorry.'

Coilla grinned. 'I don't mind.'

'Does anybody else?'

'What do you mean?'

'You must know there are some in the band who frown on what you're doing.'

'You one of them?'

'Me? Come on, Coilla, you know me better than that, I hope.'

'Well, I don't give a damn what any of the others think.'

'Nor should you. And Jode feels the same way?'

'I guess so. Why do you ask?'

'To give you a little support, if you need it, and to say I know how Jode might feel as an outsider. Like me, a dwarf in an orc warband.'

'Do we make you feel like an outsider? Or Jup?'

'No, far from it; and I wouldn't expect it from orcs. If anybody knows what it's like to be outcasts it's your race. But when all's said and done you've got your ways and we've got ours. We can't help our differences. Though it has to be said that dwarfs are more acceptable to orcs than humans, given your history.'

'I can't argue with that.'

'Mind you, Jode doesn't seem typical of his kind.'

'No, that's Standeven.'

They shared a low, conspiratorial chuckle over that, and both of them glanced at Standeven, picking his way through surly groups of Wolverines lounging on the sand.

'I just wanted you to know somebody in the band backs you,' Spurral said, 'and I suspect Jup and me aren't the only ones.'

'Thanks, Spurral.'

'Hey, look, here comes Stryke.' She nodded in the direction of the jungle's fringe.

'Let's hope he's bearable.'

As he drew nearer, Coilla's impression was that Stryke seemed a jot restored. There was a hint of purpose in his gait that had been missing earlier.

He acknowledged them with a slight bob of the head. 'What's happening?'

'We were hoping you'd tell us,' Coilla replied. 'Got a plan?'

'An issue of brandy tots to buck up the band. They look as though they could use it.'

'That's not much of a plan, Stryke.'

'For where we go next, no, it isn't. That I don't know. What I do know is that this fighting unit works best, and figures things out best, when it's in good order. Let's get 'em up and busy.'

'Then what?'

'We'll see.'

Spurral felt a little superfluous. She wandered away, just a few paces, and stared at their ship, gently swaying at anchor offshore.

She noticed splashes of foam on the otherwise calm surface. As she watched, the splashing became more of a commotion. Others saw it, too. Orcs were standing, and some were calling out.

Stryke and Coilla joined her.

There was a great disturbance in the water now.

'What the hell's going on?' Stryke wanted to know.

A large area of the sea was churning. Through the misty spray they caught a flash of glistening, leathery skin.

Spurral whispered, 'My gods . . .'

'What is it?' Coilla said.

Something very big and bulky was rising out of the water.

Spurral tried to speak, but nothing came.

'*What is it*?' Coilla repeated.

Turning to her, Spurral managed, 'The . . . Krake.'

12

For what seemed an eternity the band was rooted, staring at the spectacle.

The mass of grey, rubbery flesh rose ever higher, streaming cascades of seawater. Thick as mature tree trunks, a dozen tendrils emerged and swayed menacingly.

Stryke was the first to come alive. *'It's moving this way!'* he yelled. *'To arms!'*

The band took up their weapons. Coilla and Pepperdyne found each other, as did Jup and Spurral. The tyros gathered around Dallog. Standeven backed away, stumbling in the direction of the jungle, hands shaking.

With amazing swiftness the creature came towards the beach. Its progress threw up a vaporous haze, but beyond it was the impression of multiple eyes as big as hay-cart wheels and rows of fangs the size of gravestones. The forest of tentacles wriggled horribly and gigantically like independent organisms. Water displaced by the leviathan's bulk rushed towards the island and lapped its shore.

At Stryke's order seven or eight members of the band fired their bows. They used bodkin arrows, the meanest they had. All struck, but at least half simply bounced off the toughened skin. Others lodged but didn't seem to have any effect. The archers kept firing.

'We have to do better than this,' Jup said.

'We can't fight the thing,' Spurral insisted.

'If it lives it can be killed.'

'I dunno about that.'

'Oh, come on, Spurral!'

'I've seen what it can do. We have to retreat!'

But retreating was the last thing on the band's mind. Several of the heaving, sucker-encrusted limbs were towering over the beach. Others began to probe it, sliding in like enormous, bloated snakes. A group of orcs ran to the nearest with axes drawn. It lashed out, swiping them with enough force to bowl most of them over. Scrambling to their feet, they set to hacking at the appendage and succeeded in severing it, releasing a dark green, foul-smelling fluid. The remainder of the writhing limb was quickly withdrawn, leaving a trail of the glutinous liquid to soak into the sand.

The whole band pitched in, attacking the advancing tentacles with swords, spears and hatchets. It was Reafdaw's misfortune to get too close to one particular limb. Quick as fury it whipped around him. Trapped in a crushing embrace, and bellowing, the grunt was dragged seaward. His sword was lost, but he held on to a dagger. He slashed at the tentacle, and what passed for the creature's blood flowed copiously. But it didn't weaken its grip.

A bunch of his comrades gave chase, Stryke in the lead. Catching up, they cut, stabbed and pummelled the limb. Its hold on Reafdaw stayed firm. Then it began to rise, hoisting the struggling grunt off the ground. Its destination was obvious: the creature's cavernous maw.

Stryke leapt, caught hold of the tentacle and scrambled astride it, as though riding a horse. Its upward motion stalled a fraction. The other orcs got the idea. They followed their captain's example, jumping to the raised limb and hanging there until their combined weight brought it down again. A frenzied onslaught saw the limb hacked off, freeing Reafdaw. There were vivid red sucker marks wherever his flesh was bare. He stumbled to snatch up his dropped sword and rejoined the fray.

Haskeer's approach was direct. Scaling a large rock embedded in the sand, he threw himself at one of the questing tentacles. The spear he was holding, tip down, penetrated the thick hide and passed clean through. Temporarily pinned, the squirming limb was chopped to pieces by a swarm of grunts.

Emboldened, Haskeer tried it again. Launching himself from another rock, clutching his spear, he fell towards a snaking tentacle. The spear struck, and snapped in two. He was propelled sideways by the awkward impact, landing heavily on the beach. For a moment he lay there, the wind knocked out of him, his head swimming. Until he felt something nasty brushing against his leg.

The tentacle darted at him. Thicker than he would have been able to hug, had he wanted to, it moved with shocking speed. Haskeer rolled clear, narrowly avoiding its embrace. He kept moving, backing off, hands pushing at the sand, feet kicking; scuttling like a crab, the need to move outweighing his inability to get up. The tentacle came after him. He took a chance and scrambled to his feet, a whisker shy of getting caught. Still retreating, engaged in a grotesque dance to avoid being seized, he tried staving off the thing with a hastily drawn dagger.

Wheam arrived, along with a couple of the other tyros, Keick and Chuss, the latter still game despite nursing his wounded arm. They laid into the tentacle.

'What kept you?' Haskeer barked.

They were too busy to reply. He added a hatchet to his knife and joined in.

Pepperdyne and Coilla battled a rearing tentacle. Their blades slashed it in a dozen places, yet still it came on. After much dodging and swerving they managed to get either side of it. Their determined, coordinated hacking separated a goodly length of flesh, releasing its foul odour. The rest of the tentacle pulled away. But there was a legion of replacements

'This is hard work,' Pepperdyne said. He was panting.

'It's gonna get harder,' she told him, pointing.

The Krake had got a lot nearer. It was not far off the shore now, a mountain of quivering grey flesh, uncurling more of its tentacle emissaries.

'Can it come on land, d'you think?'

She shook her head. 'I don't know.'

'We have to pull back!'

'Too right.' She looked around, spotted Stryke. 'Stryke! *Stryke!* Look!'

He saw, and began bellowing orders.

The Wolverines disengaged, leaving the beach to the fleshy invaders, and headed his way.

'Inland!' he cried, urging them on. *'To the trees!'*

Haskeer was the last to retreat. Passing a hunting tentacle on his way, he gave it a mighty kick, which proved ineffective but satisfying.

As the band ran for cover the shadow of the Krake fell across the beach. They crashed into the jungle, and kept going until Stryke judged they had penetrated far enough and called a halt. A movement in the undergrowth had them raising their weapons. Hoisting out the source, not too gently, few were surprised to find it was a cowering Standeven.

'What now, Stryke?' Jup wanted to know.

'I guess we wait it out.'

'That's it, is it?' Haskeer said. 'We hide in here and hope that thing goes away.'

'Got a better plan?'

'Fight it.'

'You go ahead.'

'It's what we *do*, Stryke. We don't run from a fight like frightened hatchlings.'

'And we don't waste lives going against something we *can't* fight. Maybe we'd stand a chance if we were an army and not just a warband. But we're not.'

'Well, I reckon—'

There was a sound from the direction of the beach. A rustling, splintering noise. Something was moving their way.

'Look!' Coilla exclaimed.

A tentacle ploughed through the jungle. It came to a particularly large tree, wrapped itself around it, uprooted it with ease and tossed it aside. Hardly slowed, it continued towards them. Some way to their left a second tentacle appeared, destroying all in its path.

'Back!' Stryke ordered. 'Everybody back!'

They needed no urging. As they retreated deeper into the jungle the sounds of destruction kept pace, from behind and on either side. The vegetation was much thicker here, and the air was fetid with the sickly sweet smell of rotting things and stagnant water. A reminder that living places were also dying places.

A little further on, the commotion of the pursuing tentacles still plainly heard, they passed a small clearing. At its centre stood a modest-sized altar, made of stone and simple in its design. Four icons were carved on its face. To most in the band there was a familiar look about it.

They pushed on, everyone alert. The band were using swords to hack through the foliage; Jup and Spurral preferred to beat obstructions aside with their staffs. As usual the tyros stuck together, with Dallog to the fore. Wheam plodded grimly, his precious lute strapped to his back. Standeven shadowed Coilla and Pepperdyne, as though the latter was still his beholden protector. In the event, any rescuing Pepperdyne did was confined to hauling up Standeven every time he tripped over a root.

The next attack came with little warning, save a rustling in the green canopy overhead. Suddenly, a tentacle jabbed down like an angry giant's finger, hit the ground and surged in their direction. The band lobbed spears, and peppered it with arrows. Coilla tugged out one of her throwing knives and tossed it with sufficient force to penetrate the tough flesh. The limb withdrew. Not completely, but enough for them to continue their flight.

'Looks like we slowed it down a bit,' Pepperdyne remarked to Coilla as they battled through the jungle.

'All I've done is lost a good knife,' she complained.

'Those tentacles are blind. Obviously, they've no eyes. So how do you think they home in on us the way they do?'

'Who knows? Instinct?'

'Maybe they can detect movement. You know, vibrations or—'

'Does it matter? Getting clear of the things is more important, isn't it?'

'Yeah, course.'

They kept going, and the sounds behind them grew more distant.

'Reckon it's given up, Stryke?' Jup asked.

'Don't know. Could be.'

'How far do you think those limbs can reach?' Coilla wondered.

'An incredibly long way,' Spurral told her.

'More good news,' Haskeer grumbled.

Stryke looked doubtful. 'Not this far, surely?'

'I wouldn't count on it,' Spurral said.

'This isn't that big an island,' Jup reminded them, 'and it's much longer than it's wide. So wherever we go we could be within its reach.'

'Perhaps not,' Pepperdyne replied.

'What do you mean?'

'A creature the size of the Krake would live in deep water. It might not even be able to come on land, the same way a fish can't. Which is why it uses its tentacles to snare prey.'

'How does this help us?' Stryke wanted to know.

'Those islands not far from the shore we're heading towards. The scouts said the water's shallow enough for us to wade across.'

'There's nothing but rock over there.'

'The important thing is the depth of the water around the islands. It wouldn't be deep enough for something as large as the Krake.'

'You're guessing that. Like you're guessing those tentacles couldn't stretch as far as the islands.'

'If they can,' Jup said, 'with no shelter over there we'd be ripe for the plucking.'

'You're right,' Pepperdyne said, 'I'm guessing. But has anybody got a better idea?'

The ensuing silence was broken by a fresh upheaval behind them. Two or three tentacles were coming their way.

'We'll do it,' Stryke decided. 'Let's move.'

They had to travel faster, whatever the obstructions; the limbs were noisily closing the gap. After what seemed an age the jungle began to thin. The trees were sparser and they had glimpses of a much brighter, open space beyond.

Shortly after, they burst out of the jungle. They were on a beach, meaner and more pebbly than the one they had started from. Not far offshore, perhaps a decent arrow shot away, was the nearest of the adjacent islands. It was much smaller than the one they were on, and completely stark.

Snatching a spear from one of the grunts, Haskeer hurled it high and arcing, so that it came down about a third of the distance to the island. It landed almost upright, less than half its length submerged.

'If it's the same all the way across,' Coilla said, 'we shouldn't be more than waist deep.'

Haskeer jabbed a thumb at the dwarfs. 'Except for these two short-arses. It'll be up to their necks.'

'We'll manage just fine,' Spurral told him coldly.

'Even if it is too deep to wade,' Standeven said, making a rare contribution, 'couldn't you swim?'

'With all our weapons, all our kit?' Pepperdyne retorted.

'All right, all right. I only asked. It's not as though I can swim anyway.'

That drew a chorus of groans.

Pepperdyne glared at him. 'Just . . . shut up.'

Ominous sounds were still coming from the jungle, faint but distinct.

'Are we going to get on and do this, Stryke?' Coilla asked, eyeing the barren island.

'Yeah.'

'Suppose those tentacles *can* reach this far,' Haskeer said. 'If we get caught out there we're done for. '

'Then don't linger,' Pepperdyne told him.

'If you're wrong, human . . .'

'Do we have a choice?'

'Let's go,' Stryke ordered.

They moved forward and entered the water, many of them holding their weapons above their heads.

About a third of the way across, one of the grunts cried out and pointed. Everybody looked back. A couple of tentacles were rummaging around the beach they'd just left. As the band watched, several more appeared, twisting high above the trees.

'They're not following,' Coilla said. 'Maybe they've come to their limit.'

'Maybe,' Stryke replied. 'Let's not hang around to find out.'

They carried on, casting anxious glances over their shoulders. The Krake's arms stayed where they were, exploring the terrain like snuffling hounds, and a couple more emerged from the jungle to join them.

At length the Wolverines reached the desolate island and dragged themselves onto its rocky shore. They climbed to its highest point, actually a very modest elevation, and kept watch.

'Suppose it doesn't go away?' Wheam said.

'If it's like any other animal,' Stryke replied, 'it'll tire or get hungry and look for easier prey.'

'How long's that likely to be?' Jup wondered.

'We'll see.'

They settled down, their damp clothes steaming in the heat of the sun.

Enough time passed for their clothing to dry, and tempers to start growing thin, before anything happened.

'Heads up!' Jup shouted.

As one, all the tentacles were rapidly withdrawing.

'It's gone,' Dallog said.

'Hold your horses,' Stryke cautioned, 'it's not over yet. Now we wait and see if the water really is shallow enough to keep that thing away from this side.'

'Yeah,' Haskeer said, casting a hostile glance Pepperdyne's way.

Again they waited. And Stryke made it a long wait, to be sure. The shadows were lengthening when he judged the time right for a move. Cautiously, the band waded back to the main island. They did it in silence, save for Haskeer's muttered grumbling about getting soaked again. Once there, Stryke sent Nep, Eldo and Seafe ahead as scouts.

Before the band got to the beach where their ship was anchored, the scouts were back.

'It's left,' Seafe reported.

'You sure?' Stryke said.

'We couldn't see it. And it's too big to miss.'

'Good.'

'We don't get off that light though, Captain. Our ship's been damaged.'

'Shit. Bad?'

'Well, it's still floating. But it's messed up. Reckon the Krake gave it a slap before it went.'

Stryke sent a party out, including Pepperdyne, to assess the damage.

'It looks grim, but I think most of it can be repaired,' the human explained a little later. 'It's taking on some water, and the main mast took a whack. They're the most important things to take care of.'

'How long?'

'Couple of days.'

'Too long.'

'Might get it down to one if we all sweat.'

'What do you need?'

'Timber, mainly. There's wood in the jungle here that'd do. Not ideal, but—'

'Let's get started.'

'It's not far off night. You want us to work in the dark?'

'Needs must.'

'Stryke, once the ship's righted, then what?'

'We'll get to that.'

'We don't know where to go. Not to mention we could be braving the Krake again once we leave here.'

'I said we'd get to it.' There was enough of an edge in his voice to put Pepperdyne off taking it further.

Stryke sent most of the grunts into the jungle to look for suitable wood, both for repairs and for fires to work by. The privates had been gone no time when Breggin came running back.

'What is it?' Stryke demanded.

'We're not alone!' The grunt was breathing hard.

'Who? How many?'

'Dunno. One. Maybe. Couldn't make out what. Just saw something moving in the undergrowth, that way.' He pointed. 'It gave me the slip.'

Drawing his sword, Stryke headed for the jungle at a dash. The rest followed; even Standeven, though he kept well to the rear. In the rapidly darkening interior a number of the scouting grunts joined them. Stryke had them spread out and comb the area. He pushed on, the other officers, the dwarfs and Pepperdyne flanking him.

They didn't have to go very far.

It was dark enough that, at first, Stryke wasn't sure what he was seeing. Then he realised there really was a figure standing in the shadows. He approached warily, and as he got nearer he saw that it had its back to him. It stood completely still, though by now whoever it was, unless deaf, must have heard him and the others approaching.

'No sudden moves!' Stryke barked at it. 'Turn round. And keep your hands in sight.'

The figure remained as immobile as a statue.

Stryke took a couple more steps. 'Show yourself!'

Slowly, the figure turned.

Nearer now, Stryke was sufficiently close to see its face. What he saw made him doubt his sanity.

He was looking at himself.

13

Stryke was too stunned to speak.

He stared at the being he faced. It was like gazing into a mirror. The features were his, identical in every detail. Only the slightly ill-fitting, nondescript clothes his double wore were different: a cloth jerkin over a cotton shirt, thick russet-coloured trews tucked into knee-high leather boots. No weapon of any kind; at least, none that could be seen.

Stryke's reverie was broken by Haskeer yelling, '*Sorcery! Kill it!*'

Blades drawn, he and the others began to advance. Stryke himself stayed rooted.

The stranger who looked exactly like him held up his hands and, in a calm, melodious voice quite unlike Stryke's, said, 'You can lower your weapons. I'm not a threat.'

'We're supposed to take your word for it, are we?' Jup replied, keeping his staff at the ready.

Stryke gestured for them to stay their hands, and he found his voice. 'Who . . . what are you?'

'Forgive me,' his likeness told him. 'It's a little artifice on my part. Now hold, and don't be fearful of what you see.'

Haskeer's wasn't the only chin that jutted in indignation at the remark.

'Watch out!' Coilla warned. 'It's doing something!'

The stranger began to change. Its features became oddly indistinct. The flesh seemed to melt, to run and refashion itself. There was the sound of what could have been cracking bones as the body twisted, contracted, expanded. In a moment the figure was transformed.

What stood before them now was more slender and taller than the imitation Stryke it had just been. Its face was much nearer human than orc, though not entirely so. But there was an androgynous look about the creature that made its gender indistinct. The eyes, green as emeralds, had a distinct slant; the nose was small and a little upturned. Auburn hair had emerged, abundant and collar length. It was a well proportioned face, with finely drawn features, and could be called either handsome or beautiful if its owner's sex was defined.

'What in hell are you?' Stryke said.

'A friend.' The creature's voice remained the same.

'So you say,' Jup muttered.

'My name is Dynahla.'

'You're a fetch, aren't you?' Coilla ventured. 'A shape-changer.'

'I have the ability to assume other appearances, yes.'

'Why make yourself look like me?' Stryke asked.

'Self-defence. In my experience most beings are reluctant to attack someone who looks like themselves.'

'You a he or a she?' Haskeer said. 'Or can you change that too?'

Dynahla smiled. 'I can see you'd be more comfortable dealing with a masculine being.' As it spoke, another change occurred, though it was minor compared to what they had just seen. The flesh ran more subtly, altering features in small ways. The chin, cheekbones and brow all hardened somewhat; the body grew modest muscles and the hips reduced. The result was more obviously male, while retaining a measure of ambiguity.

'I hope you're not going to keep on doing that,' Spurral remarked.

'What're you doing here?' Stryke demanded.

'I was sent,' Dynahla replied.

'By that bunch of sorcerers tailing us?' Haskeer wanted to know.

'The Gateway Corps? No, I'm not with them.'

Stryke was puzzled. 'The what?'

'You have a lot to learn, Stryke, and if you bear with me there'll be explanations.'

'How do you know my name?'

'I know all your names.' Dynahla pointed a trim finger at one after another of the band. 'Coilla, Haskeer, Jup. You must be Spurral. Dallog. That is Jode Pepperdyne, and—'

'How come you know so much about us?'

'It *is* sorcery,' Haskeer declared. 'There's magic at work here and I don't like it.' He half raised his blade.

'No,' Dynahla said. 'Or yes, rather. But not in the way you mean. Benign magic. And it isn't mine. I'm talking about the one who sent me here.'

'You haven't said who that was yet,' Stryke reminded him. He had decided that thinking of this being as male was less confusing.

'Someone you're familiar with, and who means you no harm. I was sent by Tentarr Arngrim, the one you know as Serapheim.'

'*He* sent you?'

'To aid you.'

'What are you to him?'

'Interesting question. An . . . acolyte.'

'A claim like yours is all the better for proof,' Jup said.

'I can prove it. To everyone, Stryke, or do you wish us to be alone?'

'No. We're all in this together.' He gave Pepperdyne a fleeting glance, and Standeven, skulking some way back. 'Whatever you've got to say is for everybody.'

'Then perhaps you would like to gather them.'

He nodded. 'But not here. Let's get back to what's left of the light.' At his order, Dallog gave two blasts on his horn to summon the scouts home. 'You're going under armed guard,' Stryke told Dynahla. 'I don't trust you. Whether I do depends on your so-called proof.'

'I understand.'

'If you start to change—'

'I won't.'

They headed back to the beach.

Sword at the ready, Coilla was one of those flanking Dynahla. Turning to him, she said, 'Fetches are very rare, aren't they? Least they were on Maras-Dantia.'

'So I'm told.'

'They say that seeing a fetch in your likeness, the way Stryke just did, foretells your death.'

'And they say that you orcs can't tolerate daylight.'

'Bullshit.'

'Precisely.'

No more was said until they reached the shore. As the last of the scouts started to return, Stryke asked some more questions.

'Are you of this world?'

'No.'

'How did you get here?'

'The same way you did.'

'You have stars?'

'Serapheim transported me, as he did my predecessor, Parnol.'

'Who?'

'Another acolyte. You knew him only in death. He was the messenger Serapheim sent to you in Ceragan.'

'The human with the knife in his back.'

'Yes. Jennesta was responsible for that.'

'No surprise there then,' Haskeer said.

Stryke's hand went to his throat. 'I've got his amulet.'

'Good,' Dynahla said. 'That was enterprising of you.'

'But it's no use. The stars don't work properly.'

'You still have them?'

'Yes.'

'Have they had any . . . effect on you? You can be truthful. I know that they have affected you in the past, and Haskeer.' He looked at the sergeant. He returned a scowl.

'No,' Stryke replied. 'I've felt nothing.'

'That's good too. Hopefully you've become attuned to them.'

'What does that mean?'

'Each set of instrumentalities has its own signature, what some call its song. A being spending any amount of time in their presence either suffers or harmonises with them, as perhaps you are doing. Do you understand?'

'I think so.'

'But it's not wise to be within their range of influence for too long, even if their effect seems to be benevolent.'

'Why not?'

'Because the instrumentalities embody an unimaginable power. A power that even the most adept of sorcerers do not fully comprehend.'

'I'm not surrendering them,' he insisted, sensing the way things were going.

'I'm not asking you to.'

'Anyway, as I said, they don't work. Not the way they should. Do you know why?'

'Yeah,' Jup added, 'and does Jennesta have anything to do with it?'

'What about this Gateway Corps?' Coilla pitched in. 'Who are they? What do they want?'

'And where's Thirzarr?' Stryke demanded.

Dynahla raised a hand to still the clamour. 'These matters are best addressed by the proof I have to offer. Is this all your band, Stryke?'

He looked around. The last couple of stragglers were jogging their way. 'Yes.'

'Then you're about to have some answers. But don't expect everything to be resolved immediately.'

'That doesn't sound too promising,' Coilla remarked darkly.

'Trust me,' Dynahla said.

As they watched intently, hands on weapons, the fetch took a small silken pouch from his pocket and poured the contents into the palm of his hand. As far as they could see it was sand, identical to that on the beach. He threw it into the air. It didn't fall, but hung there in a cloud. Then it rearranged itself, forming a kind of flat canvas, no thicker than an individual grain, suspended just above their heads.

Suddenly it was no longer sand, at least in appearance. It became a rectangle of gently pulsing white light, which in turn gave way to a succession of primary colours, flashing through the spectrum. When it calmed, an image came into focus, raising gasps and exclamations from some in the band.

The human Tentarr Arngrim, Serapheim to the fraternity of wizards and seers, gazed down at them.

Wheam looked terrified. Dallog, the other tyros, Spurral, and Pepperdyne and Standeven, none of whom had much if any knowledge of the sorcerer, were almost as awed.

'This image is recorded in the grains of sand,' Dynahla explained. 'You cannot converse with him.'

'Like back on Ceragan the last time,' Haskeer whispered.

Stryke shushed him.

Serapheim spoke, his voice loud, almost booming, and all could hear. *'Greetings, Stryke; and Wolverines, I salute you. You are to be congratulated on your efforts in Acurial. Your actions there played a not insignificant part in freeing your kind from the shackles of oppression.'*

'Didn't get us Jennesta though,' Jup muttered under his breath.

As though responding, Serapheim's likeness went on, *'It's regrettable that you had less success in your dealings with my daughter. But do not reproach yourselves for it, and take heart from knowing that aspect of your mission is far from over.'* The sorcerer paused briefly. When he resumed, his tone was less formal, and betrayed a degree of weariness. *'I've much to tell you, although I fear not all your curiosity's going to be satisfied. Not yet.'* He grew more matter-of-fact. *'First, let me commend Dynahla to you. You've a faithful, dependable ally in this adherent, who has my complete trust, and deserves yours. Dynahla's powers can be of great help to you. All I ask is that you don't allow my most steadfast servant to come to harm. I'd be devastated should Dynahla suffer an end as miserable as Parnol's, whose fate you have doubtless now learnt.'* There was something that could have been a sigh before he carried on. *'As with so much that is corrupt, Jennesta was behind Parnol's death. Just one more casual murder to her, but a grievous blow to me, and to our cause.'*

'We have a cause?' Coilla mumbled.

'I know that, for a time, Jennesta had possession of the instrumentalities you hold,' Serapheim continued, *'and since you regained them they've failed to work properly. Didn't you wonder at the ease with which you got them back? I mean no slur on your abilities, but had she been determined to keep them you would have had a much harder fight on your hands. The fact is that Jennesta wanted you to recover the instrumentalities. For two reasons. First, she has mastered an ancient magical process that allowed her to copy them. Second, she placed an enchantment on the original set she allowed you to take back. A spell which accounts for their erratic behaviour, and may even let her track your movements.'*

There were some knowing nods at that. It was more or less what smarter members of the band already suspected.

'As far as I can tell, the fake instrumentalities Jennesta possesses have as much power as the genuine ones. I don't have to tell you that this makes her even more dangerous. As far as the influence she exercises over your instrumentalities is concerned, Dynahla has the skill to counter it, though in a limited way. I expect to fare better, but only if you bring the instrumentalities to me.'

'Why didn't you come here yourself?' Haskeer said.

'He can't hear you,' Dynahla reminded him.

'Oh, yeah.'

Several of the others glared and waved him quiet.

'As you know by now,' Serapheim's image said, *'we are not the only ones with an interest in the artefacts. The group hunting you are members*

of a fraternity called the Gateway Corps. They are an incredibly ancient order, active for perhaps as long as there have been instrumentalities. Their sole purpose is to locate and seize the artefacts. This they do from the best of intentions, and given the power of the instrumentalities their concern is understandable, but they pursue their goal with utter dedication, akin to fanaticism. They, too, are dangerous. Their magic is very potent and they command advanced weaponry.'

'You're telling us,' Coilla remarked.

'Again, Dynahla may be able to provide some measure of protection as far as the Corps is concerned. Though your best strategy would be to give them as wide a berth as possible. Let me repeat that you can trust my acolyte, in this and all other matters. Allow yourselves to be guided by Dynahla, who will lead you to me. Be of good heart, and keep faith that your path will lead you to victory.'

Serapheim's image vanished. The shimmer went out of the grains of sand and they fell, a tiny gritty shower pattering down to the beach.

'What about Thirzarr?' Stryke demanded angrily. 'He didn't say anything about her. Where is she?'

'Serapheim warned you that not all your questions would be answered immediately,' Dynahla said.

'Lot of good that does me.'

'But it doesn't mean those answers can't be found. That's one of the reasons he sent me to you; to help you find the truth.'

'The only truth I want is the whereabouts of Thirzarr and our hatchlings.'

'If it's any comfort, we believe your hatchlings are safe.'

'How can you know that?'

'Serapheim has his ways of knowing.'

'But he can't tell me where Thirzarr is?'

'Your mate is within the influence of Jennesta's magic. It cloaks her, and makes her harder to trace. But Serapheim's working hard to penetrate that barrier.'

'What was that about us going to Serapheim?' Coilla asked. 'Why should we want to do that?'

'Because apart from me, he's the only ally you can rely on,' Dynahla replied, 'and the most powerful.'

'So why didn't he come here himself?'

'There are good reasons. You'll see.'

'Where is Serapheim?' Stryke said.

'Our way to him is on this world.'

'What does *that* mean?'

'It isn't far. But first we need to take to sea. And your ship must be repaired for that.'

'Tell me something I don't know. But where are we going?' Stryke repeated.

'West.'

Pepperdyne still had Stryke's map. He got it out and consulted it. 'Where exactly in the west?'

Dynahla looked, then pointed. 'There.'

'There's nothing in that region. It's just open sea.'

'Only according to your map.'

'I know this chart's a bit vague in places, but—'

'There is much it doesn't show. Trust me.'

Stryke wasn't alone in wondering if they could. 'What if we decide not to go with you?'

'You're wiser than that. You know you have no other option.'

He had to concede that. But he didn't say so.

'What about that Gateway Corps outfit?' Jup said.

'Yeah, what about 'em?' Haskeer put in. 'They gonna cause us any more trouble?'

'They'll never stop hounding you until they gain the instrumentalities,' Dynahla explained, 'or you kill every last one of them. Given how powerful they are, that's unlikely, even for a warband of orcs. Of course, that assumes you can avoid the clutches of the Krake. Then you can steel yourselves to face Jennesta.'

'Sounds like a piece of piss,' Coilla remarked sarcastically.

Dynahla smiled mirthlessly. 'Nobody said it would be easy.'

14

The Wolverines worked hard repairing their ship, labouring through the night and well into the next day, with Stryke driving them mercilessly. Shortly after noon they were close to having the vessel seaworthy.

As the only really experienced sailor present, Pepperdyne was given the task of overseeing the work. Anxious to be under way, Stryke had him come ashore to report on progress.

'How much longer?'

'We're all but done,' the human told him. 'Just a few minor chores left, and we need to get supplies of fresh water over there, along with any food we can scavenge from the jungle.'

'I've got the band working on that. You sure the ship's up to the voyage?'

'It's not a perfect job, but it should serve.'

'That's all we need.'

'Some of the repairs are only temporary, mind, and they're not likely to last too long. I'd like to carry them out properly first chance we get.'

'I don't know when that'd be. For now we make do.'

'And . . . the band.'

'What about 'em?'

'They've been working like dogs all night. They could do with rest.'

'No time.'

'They're dead on their feet. If they don't get—'

'You take care of the ship,' Stryke emphasised his words with a finger jab to Pepperdyne's chest, 'and I'll worry about my band. They're used to hard work. Anything else?'

'Nope.'

'Then get back to it.' He turned on his heel and left the human.

As he walked away, Stryke caught a glimpse of Dynahla, standing further along the beach and staring out to sea. Having no appetite or time for any more riddles he let the creature be.

Then he spotted Haskeer, returning at the head of one of the foraging parties. They were rolling barrels towards the shore, and some carried sacks. He went their way.

'Done yet?'

His sergeant nodded. 'Just about. There's plenty of water, but lean pickings far as food goes.'

'We'll get by.' He looked to the group Haskeer had just been leading. 'Thought I told you to take along some of the tyros.'

'Yeah, well, I didn't.'

'That was an *order*, Haskeer. I want the new recruits mixing in more with the band; they're not learning fast enough. Where do you get off ignoring me?'

'You can't rely on 'em. They're greenhorns.'

'What d'you expect if we don't teach them?'

'I'm a fighter, not a wet nurse. Let Dallog suckle his own brood.'

'What is it with you and him? Why're you so down on the tyros?'

'Well, he ain't no Alfray for a start.'

'Shit, not *that* again. It's time you got your head round Alfray being dead and gone.'

'More's the pity. And who we got instead? A puffed up, self-satisfied—'

'Dallog's not trying to replace Alfray. Nobody could.'

'You're telling me.'

'You're being too hard on him. On all of them. The tyros have paid in blood on this mission. Ignar, Harglo, Yunst. All dead.'

'And we lost Liffin, and now Bhose. Either of which were worth a dozen of those rookies. If you wanna talk about dying, Stryke, maybe you should look at the band.'

'Meaning?'

'As if it's not bad enough having a bunch of learners to shepherd, we've a pair of *humans* tagging along.' He all but spat the word. 'And one of 'em an orc killer back in Acurial.'

'We don't know that for sure.'

'Yeah, right,' Haskeer sneered. 'You gonna defend the other one, too, and what he's up to with Coilla?'

'Whatever Coilla and Pepperdyne do is no business of ours, long as it doesn't endanger the band.'

'You sure it won't? This is a human we're talking about.'

'He's done nothing to make me distrust him. The opposite, if anything.'

'What he's doing with Coilla's enough for me. It ain't natural, Stryke. It's . . . *sick*. Now, on top of all that, we've got this fetch, or whatever it is, telling us what to do. Seems to me that all adds up to a pig's ear far as this band goes.'

Stryke was about to reply, or possibly end his sergeant's rant by knocking his teeth out, when Haskeer stared past him and glowered. Turning his head, Stryke saw that Dynahla had silently arrived.

'Am I interrupting anything?' the shape-changer asked.

'Not for me,' Haskeer said. He shoved past them and strode away.

Watching him leave, Dynahla said, 'He has a lot of anger.'

'We all do. What did you want?'

'It looks as though the ship's nearly ready.'

'Almost.'

'And we'll leave shortly?'

'Soon as we can.'

'There could be a problem. I sense that the Krake is still nearby.'

'That's another of your talents, is it, sensing things?'

'I have some ability to do that, yes. Not unlike the farsight dwarfs possess, though somewhat different in nature. But how I know doesn't matter. What's important is what you're going to do about the Krake.'

'Any suggestions?'

'Only that you'd do well to think of a strategy before setting sail. The creature might not bother us, but if it does—'

'Yeah, I get it. That all you've got to offer?'

'I might be able to cloud what passes for the beast's mind, and slow it a little. But not much more.'

Stryke remembered something. 'I've got this.' He showed the bracelet Mallas Sahro had given him. 'Could it help?'

Dynahla studied the bracelet, then bent and sniffed. 'Elf magic.'

'You can tell by *smelling* it?'

The fetch nodded. 'Different classes of sorcery have distinct aromas, if you know how to detect them. As to the efficacy of this totem; it could ward off minor magical attacks. Though you shouldn't expect it to offer any protection against Jennesta.'

Stryke pulled down his sleeve. 'And against the Krake?'

'A creature like that operates on pure instinct. We need a more physical method of hampering it. Perhaps your band can come up with ideas.'

'More time wasted,' he grumbled.

'Better that than facing the monster unprepared.'

Stryke had to agree.

Ordering most of the band to keep at work provisioning the ship, he hastily got together a conclave of his officers. Naturally that included Dallog, despite Haskeer's silent though palpable disapproval. He wasn't keen on Pepperdyne and Dynahla being present either, but knowing Stryke wouldn't tolerate any more arguments, he curbed his tongue.

'We're ready to leave,' Stryke told them. 'Only we've got a problem. The Krake's still out there.'

'What makes you think that?' Jup asked.

'Dynahla here can *sense* it.'

'Really?' Coilla said. 'You can do that?'

'Yes,' Dynahla confirmed.

'So how do we get clear of the Krake?' Stryke wanted to know. 'Any ideas?'

'We don't,' Haskeer offered. 'We kill the fucking thing.'

'Any *useful* ideas?' Stryke restated, ignoring the sergeant's offended glare.

'Can't we outrun it?' Dallog suggested, further stoking Haskeer's annoyance.

Pepperdyne said, 'Unlikely. Not from a standing start, even with a strong wind. Which we don't have off these shores. Though with a good enough diversion I reckon we'd stand a chance of getting away.'

'Such as?' Stryke prompted.

'Remember what the resistance used against the Peczan forces? Acurialian fire they called it, didn't they? Perhaps we could use that.'

'How?'

'Same way the resistance did; as a barrage, and maybe we could tip spears with it, and arrows.'

'That ain't gonna kill the brute,' Haskeer objected.

'But it might slow it down.'

'Do we know how to make the stuff?' Stryke said.

Pepperdyne nodded. 'It's similar to a weapon we had back on Trougath. Mostly it's oil. The other part's something mixed in to make the burning oil stick to its target. We used various things: tree sap, soap shavings, honey, certain gummy berries. Though I guess we'd need quite a quantity for something the size of the Krake.'

'There are plenty of barrels of lantern oil on the ship,' Jup recalled, 'along with pots and other containers to hold it.'

'And lots more scattered around the settlement back there,' Coilla said, jabbing a thumb at the jungle.

'All right,' Stryke decided, 'we'll try it. Let's get that oil ashore.'

'Why bother hauling it over here? We could do the making on the ship.'

'And what happens if the Krake pops up before we're finished? No, Coilla, I want us fully armed and ready when we set sail. So one party to bring the oil. Another to search out the tacky stuff to go with it. You seem to know about that, Pepperdyne, so go with 'em. A third party scours the settlement for pots and the like. The rest get making more arrows and spears. We need lots. And cloth or something, to wrap them with. Now move yourselves.'

Jup and Haskeer gathered the rest of the band and got them into groups. Everybody had a task, including Standeven and Dynahla. The human scavenged for rags; the fetch helped mix the brew.

Barrels were used to blend the oil and a variety of viscous fluids, some more successfully than others. Once they got the mixture right it was ladled into as many suitable vessels as they could find; pots, bottles, flasks, pitchers and jugs. Anything that would shatter on impact. Oil-soaked cloths, jammed into the containers' mouths, served as fuses.

Arrows and spears were made in prodigious numbers. This should have been straightforward, but proved tricky because the wood yielded by the jungle was of variable quality. Once hewed, their sharpened tips were hardened over flame. Nor were the band's usual weapons ignored. Swords, hatchets and throwing axes were whetted, and bow strings tightened.

All that remained was to test the Acurialian fire. Selecting a charged pot at random, Stryke positioned himself about fifty paces from one of the large, half buried rocks that dotted the beach. Fuse lit, he lobbed the bombard. It struck the rock near its crown and instantly exploded. The sticky, blazing oil covered a good two-thirds of the rock's surface, its intense orange flame billowing black smoke. It carried on burning a lot longer than they expected.

'They'll do,' Stryke announced. He turned to Pepperdyne. 'Is the weather right?'

'Tide's up and there should be wind enough. But if we don't go right now it'll have to be tomorrow. I wouldn't relish steering through those straits in the dark.'

Stryke bellowed the order and embarkation got under way.

Once everybody was on board he had the containers lined-up ready on deck. Braziers were stoked, for igniting the fuses. Archers and spear-carriers lined the rails. Jad was dispatched to the crow's nest, and other grunts swarmed on the rigging. The sails dropped and the goblin ship's peculiarly embellished anchor was raised.

Pepperdyne had taken the wheel. Coilla was at his side, clutching a bow. Stryke roamed the decks, scolding, encouraging, swearing. Dynahla stood alone at the prow, crimson hair flowing in the clement breeze.

They set off.

The band fell into a tense silence as the craft gradually started to move. Any exhaustion they had from working all night fell away as they scanned the waters, alert for the slightest sign of anything amiss.

At length, and painfully slowly, the ship nosed its way into the open sea.

'So far, so good,' Pepperdyne half whispered.

Coilla dragged her gaze from the ocean. 'Maybe all that work was for nothing.'

The sails were swelling. They started to pick up a little speed.

'At least we've got an addition to our armoury,' he said. 'This Acurialian fire could be useful if—'

They saw Dynahla's head turn their way. The shape-changer was shouting something, but they couldn't get the sense. A heartbeat later

Jad was crying out from the crow's nest and pointing. It was the prelude to a general uproar from those on deck.

Ahead of them, and off to starboard, the water was troubled. A leathery dome broke the surface, larger than any they had ever seen on a temple or a tyrant's folly. It rose inexorably, growing bigger, shedding water and glistening repellently in the light. Several tentacles appeared, thicker than a main-mast and garlanded with seaweed.

Pepperdyne frantically spun the wheel. Sluggishly, the ship began turning to port.

Dynahla was heading their way. Thundering up the stairs to the helm, Stryke got there first.

'Can we lose it?'

Pepperdyne shook his head. 'Don't know. Maybe if we'd been under way a bit longer . . .'

The Krake was still rising, water cascading from its coarse hide. The ship rocked in the swell.

Dynahla arrived.

Before the fetch could speak, Stryke barked, 'What was it you said about clouding that thing's mind?'

'How do you think we got this far? I've bought us a little time. Use it!'

Pepperdyne applied all his skill to manoeuvring the craft. The Krake was still ahead and a lot nearer. It wasn't in their path, but close to it. As the ship swerved to its new course, away from the creature, the Krake surged forward, as though to cut them off. It was hard to tell whose speed was the greater.

They avoided a collision, but found themselves uncomfortably close to the beast. They were still veering. It continued to advance. The gap was closing fast, and the Krake's tentacles stretched their way.

'We've no choice now,' Coilla said, glancing at Stryke.

'So we take the bastard.'

Even though he was coming to know the orcs better than most other humans had, Pepperdyne was taken aback at the wild, almost crazed smiles Coilla and Stryke exchanged. The orcs' hunger for a fight, whatever the odds, was as deeply ingrained in them as cruelty was in his own race.

'Try to keep us clear of it!' Stryke bellowed.

Pepperdyne nodded and bore down on the wheel. Coilla nocked a cloth-headed arrow. Dynahla clutched the rail and stared intently at the looming monster.

Stryke made for the stairs and the deck below. The Krake was a writhing mountain now, blocking out the light. The air had a fishy stink to it.

'Steady!' Stryke yelled at the band. *'On my order!'*

Spears and arrows were poised over the braziers. Torches were held ready for the bombards to be lit.

A tentacle brushed the side of the ship. To the Krake, it was no more than a tap, like a hatchling's gentle nudging of a toy boat. It felt like a small earthquake to the Wolverines. The ship listed violently. Several band members lost their balance and fell. Unsecured objects slid across the deck, and the port side took a drenching.

'Now!' Stryke bellowed.

The archers were first. A swarm of burning arrows streaked towards the groping tentacles. All struck. The range was close enough that many penetrated, sizzling as they delivered their blazing cargo. Those that didn't pierce still left a stamp of fire on the creature's moist flesh. The nearest tentacle, peppered with glowing, fizzling bolts, dropped back underwater. Another immediately replaced it, and a second cloud of radiant arrows soared its way.

The main bulk of the Krake, its ravenous eyes and gaping maw, could be seen clearly now beyond a growing forest of waving limbs. Arrows like darting fireflies sprayed them. Once the tentacles were running with flame they fell back, but the Krake was only slowed, not deterred.

Stryke was fearful that if it got into range the creature would dispatch tentacles under the ship to upend or crush it. And it was almost near enough to do that. His dilemma was that the Krake was still too far away for the bombards or spears to reach it. The point at which it would be near enough, yet not threaten the ship, was a fine judgement. All Stryke could do was urge on the archers and bide his time.

On the bridge, Pepperdyne and Coilla watched as the fiery rainbow of arrows arced towards the encroaching beast.

'The arrows can't last much longer, surely?' Pepperdyne said, spinning the wheel.

Coilla had an arrow nocked herself. She applied flame, aimed and sent it winging to the Krake. 'No,' she replied, plucking another shaft from her quiver. 'I'm surprised they've lasted this long, the rate we're using them.'

He looked to the mass of living flesh bearing down on them, then back at her. 'I don't know that we can get away from this thing.'

'If anybody can do it, you can.'

'I'm flattered, but your faith might be misplaced. The Krake's moving nearly as fast as we are, despite what we're throwing at it.'

'We haven't thrown everything yet.'

He gave the wheel another hard tug. 'Maybe we'd better start.'

Coilla unleashed her arrow.

A wave of displaced water swept in, rocking the ship again, and more violently than before. The orcs in the rigging had their work cut out hanging on.

Stryke judged the time right to strengthen the assault; the Krake seemed near enough. He just hoped his estimate of the gap separating them was accurate.

At his command, the band began lighting bombards' fuses. A moment later they were flinging them hard, adding their power to the volley of arrows. The distance was a challenge, and took all the throwers' strength, but most of the missiles found their target. On contact with the Krake they exploded with much greater force than the arrows. Some burst reddish when they struck, others yellow-blue or orange, depending on the glutinous liquid mixed with the oil.

'Best you can do?' Haskeer taunted.

Jup glared at him. 'I might be throwing less than you, but at least I'm hitting the bastard.'

'Yeah? Beat this.' He lit a fuse, drew back his arm and took aim. With a grunt he lobbed the flame-tipped pot.

They watched it streak against the darkening sky. It briefly disappeared from sight in the confusion of explosions, flaming arrows, smoke and thrashing limbs. It showed itself again when a reddish-orange bloom erupted on the side of the creature's gigantic head. Tendrils of fire rippled out from the blast, marbling the Krake's leathery hide.

Haskeer shot the dwarf a superior smirk.

'Stand back,' Jup said, hefting a bomb.

He launched it like a discus, spinning round for momentum and letting go with a roar. The projectile soared high and fast. It, too, impacted on the monster's glistening dome; a blood-red blossom, sending out rivulets of lava.

'Right,' Haskeer grated. He rolled up his sleeves and reached for a bomb.

Another wave hit the ship, sending a fierce tremor through it. The roll that followed was the most acute yet. Much of the clutter that was unsecured had already shifted to the port side. This bigger blow shifted some of the heavier objects, including the brazier Jup and Haskeer were standing beside. It toppled, spilling its red hot coals. As the deck was wet that wouldn't have mattered. Except that the jolt caused Haskeer to drop the bomb he was about to light. The pot shattered and its content instantly burst into flames. Leaping back, they were lucky to avoid being splashed by liquid as tenacious as a limpet and as scathing as acid. But they were confronted by a spreading wall of fire. They set about beating at it, Haskeer using his jerkin, Jup a piece of sacking.

Several of the grunts had been given the additional task of firewatcher. For Standeven it was his only job, and one it was thought even he couldn't make a mess of. As the nearest firewatcher he had to respond, and arrived clutching two buckets, one slopping water, the other filled with sand.

He took one look at the fire and froze.

Jup and Haskeer were on the other side of it, feeling the heat and unable to get to him. They had to content themselves with shouting curses. Standeven was oblivious.

Then Dallog was there with Wheam and Pirrak, and Spurral bringing up the rear. The buckets were snatched from Standeven and he was pushed aside, roughly enough that he went down and sprawled on the deck. They attacked the flames, thrashing it with clothing and sacks. Water was no good; pails of sand had to be chained over, until at last they were able to trample what remained of the fire and kill it.

Standeven was still on the deck, propped on his elbow, staring dazedly at the scene.

Haskeer dashed to him, grabbed him by the scruff and drew back his fist. 'You bloody useless little—'

Stryke arrived, panting. *'Leave it.'*

'This stupid bastard would've let us burn,' Haskeer protested.

'We've more important things to worry about. Get to your station.'

'But—'

'Do it!'

Haskeer gave Standeven a murderous glare, then let him go. The cowering, ashen-faced human slumped. Haskeer returned to the fight.

Casting Standeven a disgusted look of his own, Stryke ordered everyone back to their duties. He also had the spears brought into play.

The bombardment of the Krake carried on. What was left of the band's hoard of arrows continued soaring its way. The bombs exploded incessantly, joined by a cloud of blazing spears.

The creature was on fire. Not in patches, as before, but totally. A fetid smell of charred flesh hung in the air. Punctured by numerous spears and arrows, the Krake slowed its advance, and stopped.

To cheers from the band it began to sink below the waves. When it was completely submerged the fire could still be seen, permeating the water with a ghostly glow.

Stryke raced up to the bridge. Dynahla was still there, surveying the scene.

'Is it finished?' Coilla asked.

'Don't know,' Stryke replied, glancing at the turbulent water where the Krake had gone down. 'But we're not sticking around to find out.' He turned to Pepperdyne. 'It's up to you now, human. Get us out of here.'

Pepperdyne nodded and spun the wheel.

They headed west.

15

Not every landmass in the world of islands was populated. But one such, nondescript like so many others, was hosting surreptitious visitors.

Jennesta didn't want for comforts, whatever her followers had to cope with. While they bivouacked as best they could, her tented quarters offered a haven, and even a measure of luxury. But it was the privacy that she valued most when undertaking certain magical practices, as now.

She stood by a small table. On it sat a representation of the Krake; a miniature, crudely fashioned model. It was on fire. Flames played across its entire surface, but they would never harm the Receptive Matter Jennesta had used to fashion the creature's likeness.

For a moment she was spellbound, literally. She willed the enchantment to unravel, until the link between her mock-up and the real beast was broken, and her control gone. She had been gazing at the flames. With a slight movement of her hand she extinguished them.

She didn't see the encounter between the Wolverines and the sea creature as a defeat. She had harassed the orcs, as she had with the fauns, which caused them trouble and delay. It was an agreeable pastime. A satisfaction.

The Receptive Matter cooled instantly. If it had ever been hot. She picked it up, squeezed it in her palm and returned it to its usual shapeless, colourless state. It was displeasing to her touch, but had a sweet odour that was almost heady. She returned it to her precious stockpile, in its plain silver casket, then put the casket out of sight.

The effort of maintaining the spell had tired her. There would have to be sustenance soon. Preferably fresh, warm and still beating. But that would have to wait.

She wasn't alone, although she could have been for all the awareness her captive had. Thirzarr was seated at the far end of the quarters. She was stiffly motionless, her gaze vacant.

Jennesta moved to the tent's entrance, stopped just short of it and clapped twice, sharply. Shortly after, there was a scrabbling at the canvas flaps. A pair of her undead menials came through awkwardly, and awaited her pleasure, their expressions as vacuous as Thirzarr's.

'Take her back to the others in their cage,' Jennesta ordered, pointing at the orc.

One of the zombies obeyed, and began to shuffle in Thirzarr's direction. The other was Hacher, who remained immobile. Sluggishly, he turned his head towards Jennesta and fixed her with a dull but even stare. She repeated the order, more firmly, but still Hacher hesitated.

'What's wrong with you?' Jennesta snapped. 'Do as you're told!'

He slowly moved. Not towards Thirzarr, but Jennesta. She flicked a jolt of energy at him, as a herdsman might chastise livestock with a whip. The impact half spun Hacher, and he would have fallen if some buried instinct hadn't surfaced and made him reach out to the table for support. His hand came down hard on its edge, causing one of his desiccated fingers to snap off. It dropped to the heavily carpeted floor.

Jennesta laughed scornfully. 'Not much of an iron hand now, are you, General?' Her expression returned to harsh and she added coldly, 'Obey my order.'

Hacher had been staring dumbly at his disfigurement. He looked up when she spoke, and after a moment's wavering began to shamble in Thirzarr's direction.

Jennesta told Thirzarr to rise. In her almost catatonic state she meekly complied, and flanked by Hacher and the other undead was escorted from the tent, the trio moving at a languid pace.

Almost immediately a human officer entered, bowed his head and begged Jennesta's pardon for intruding.

'What is it?'

'Your . . . guest has arrived, my lady. Along with something of a retinue.'

'Send him in. Alone.'

'Ma'am.'

'And take that with you.' She indicated Hacher's severed finger.

Doing his best to hide his distaste, the officer gingerly picked it up with his thumb and forefinger. He left holding it out in front of him, as though he were a nervous scullery maid ordered to dispose of a drowned rat found in a pot of soup.

Jennesta didn't have long to wait for her next visitor. He strode in, his black bow slung over one bony shoulder, a quiver of arrows at his hip.

'I am Gleaton-Rouk,' the goblin declared sibilantly.

'Welcome,' Jennesta replied, a syrupy, artificial sincerity in her tone. 'I'm obliged to you for accepting my invitation.'

'It wasn't your words that brought me.'

'You found the gems and coin I sent spoke more eloquently. I understand. But that was a trifling gift compared to what you could gain.'

Avarice flashed in his dark eyes, along with suspicion. 'What do you want of me?'

'Two things. First, I need an additional ship.'

'Why?'

Jennesta fought down the impulse to tell this creature to mind his business. 'I'm recruiting a certain number of . . . *helpers* on my travels. I need another ship to transport them, and I understand you're best placed to supply one.'

'It could be possible. If you make it worth my while.'

'I've no shortage of funds.'

'I will see what I can do. You said there were two things.'

'I take it that's your famous bow,' she said, eyeing it and seeming to ignore his question. 'It's a handsome weapon.'

'It's not for sale,' Gleaton-Rouk hissed.

She laughed. 'I didn't intend making an offer.'

'Nor can it be taken from me,' he added charily.

'Really? Don't worry; I've no need of it.'

'Then why speak of it?'

'Partly out of what you might call a professional interest, as a practitioner of the ancient art myself.'

He gave a derisive snort. 'Any power you might command would be no match for Shadow-wing's.'

'Be that as it may, I didn't ask you here to debate the efficacy of magic. The bow touches on the second reason I wanted to meet with you.'

'How so?'

'I know you used it recently to kill an orc.'

'What is that to you?'

'I commend you for it. I, too, have a blood feud with the Wolverines, and particularly with its leader. Working together, you and I could bring about a reckoning.'

'I've no taste for being recruited.'

'I said working together. What I'm proposing is an alliance.'

'You have a small army, and you claim magical powers. Why do you need me?'

'Because you have something greater than mere magic. You have a passion for vengeance. As do I.'

'Yet you seek an ally.'

'I need one I can trust. I'm surrounded by fools.'

'And what would we achieve?'

'We could pour pressure on the warband, and bring about the death of its damnable captain, Stryke.'

'What's in it for me?'

'I should hope that the sweetness of revenge would be reward enough.' She noted his expression and added, 'Though of course I would also show my appreciation in the form of further riches.'

Gleaton-Rouk thought about it, and at length hissed, 'I agree. Subject to the details being to my liking.'

'Of course,' Jennesta replied smoothly, reflecting on how best to betray this new partner. She had no doubt he was thinking the same. 'And as a token of my good faith I would like to present you with a further pecuniary offering. As a down-payment, let's call it.' Having looted the treasury before fleeing Acurial, her apparent generosity was of no consequence. Besides, she could always get more, one way or another.

The goblin gave her the tiniest nod by way of acceptance. 'And for my part I shall make arrangements concerning the ship you require.'

'How long will that take?'

'It will be settled before the day's end.'

'Then I suggest you return here to continue our discussion.'

Gleaton-Rouk nodded, and together they left the tent.

There was a lot of activity outside. Her troops were going about their chores, along with a few of the zombies. The latter were watched with suspicion and not a little bewilderment by Gleaton-Rouk's entourage. They numbered about a dozen, and stood together not far from Jennesta's tent, clutching their tridents.

As Gleaton-Rouk headed their way, Jennesta stopped him with, 'There's one more small matter to clear up.'

'What might that be?' he said, turning to her.

'When my delegation approached you to arrange this meeting, one of them was killed.'

'A regrettable occurrence. We had no idea who this group of humans were, or whether they were hostile. We thought to defend ourselves.'

'I see.'

'It was no more than you would have done yourself, I expect.'

'Your feud with the Wolverines is over them having killed some of your kin, is that right?'

He was puzzled by the turn the conversation had taken, but replied, 'You know it is.'

Jennesta looked at his retinue. 'These are your kin?'

'Some are, some aren't. All are my clan.'

She pointed at a goblin. 'Is he kin?'

'Yes.'

'What about him?' She indicated another.

'Him? No, we do not share blood.'

Without a further word, Jennesta raised her open hand, palm up, and placed its heel against her chin. Like a child dispersing dandelion heads, she gently blew. A jet of black vapour streamed from her hand. As it flowed it solidified into something resembling a cluster of catapult shot. Faster than the eye could follow, the cloud of shot flashed towards the goblin she had singled out. It struck with tremendous force, riddling his body with a myriad of tiny crimson explosions. Many passed clean through him. Instantly he was rendered little more than pulp, collapsing in a gory heap.

Such was the precision of Jennesta's spell that the dead goblin's companions, although standing with him, were completely untouched, except by their comrade's blood. For an instant they froze, then they began brandishing their weapons, their faces twisted with outrage. Jennesta's followers tensed and reached for their own blades.

'You took one of mine, I've taken one of yours,' she told Gleaton-Rouk, her voice strident enough to be heard by his retinue.

For the first time since he arrived the goblin leader wore an expression that betrayed his true feelings. It was disbelief and awe. But as the realisation of what he was dealing with dawned on him it gave way to the kind of grudging respect one bully feels for another. The whole thing was fleeting, and he quickly returned to seeming passivity, but Jennesta saw.

'I understand the need for . . . compensation,' he said, signing his bodyguards to stand down with a flick of his bony hand. They did so uneasily. 'Let us regard this as a debt paid.'

'And I'll levy no interest,' she replied, giving him a smile designed to be charming without quite achieving it.

'Until later then.' He bobbed his head. Glancing at the lightly steaming remains of his dead follower, he added in a softer tone, 'You must teach me that sometime.'

'I might just do that,' she said.

They left, and she returned to her quarters.

Killing the goblin had fatigued her further. Not seriously, just enough to be annoying. But there was one more thing to do before she could take nourishment.

She ordered complete privacy, and in the cool of her tent enacted a ritual. One that forged a mental link with another party. Someone not too far away, and approaching.

Dynahla leaned against the rail on a quiet part of the orcs' ship, head in hands, crimson locks flowing in the breeze.

'*Hey.*'

There was no response.

'*Hey*. Dynahla!'

The shape-changer stirred and slowly turned.

'You all right?' Stryke asked. He was accompanied by Jup.

'Yes. I'm . . . fine. I didn't know you were—'

'What were you doing?' Jup said.

'Communing.'

Stryke frowned. 'You better explain that.'

'I was in touch with someone. Mentally, that is.'

'Who?'

'Serapheim.'

He was nonplussed. 'You can do that?'

'Under certain circumstances. Though it's not easy.'

'How do you do it?'

'We have a psychic link, you might say. It's hard to explain.'

'You said Serapheim couldn't talk to us directly,' Jup recalled. 'That's why you brought his message.'

'He can't communicate directly with any of *you*. There has to be the link, and even with it, it's difficult. But none of that's important. What he told me is.'

'So spit it out,' Stryke demanded.

'He has an idea where Jennesta is, and it's not far. We have to change course.'

'An idea?'

'More than that. A . . . sense.'

He slowly shook his head. 'I don't know . . .'

'I thought you wanted to find your mate more than anything.'

'I do. But I don't know if I want a wild-goose chase based on a hunch.'

'Trust me, Stryke, this is more likely to be right than wrong. Besides, what other option do you have?'

'You said that about us going to Serapheim,' Jup reminded him. 'And you said we needed him to help fight Jennesta.'

'Ideally, he'd be there. But she's nearer than he is, and we need to seize this opportunity before she's on the move again. What do you say, Stryke?'

'I thought we needed Serapheim's magic to stand a chance against her.'

'We'll have to make do with mine, and your band's undoubted martial skills.'

He thought about it. 'All right. But this better not be a waste of time. I'll get Pepperdyne to alter course.'

'I was just on my way up to take a turn at the wheel,' Jup said. 'I'll tell him.'

'All right, go ahead.'

'*What* am I telling Pepperdyne? About the new course, I mean.'

Stryke looked to the shape-changer. 'Go with him, Dynahla. I'll brief the band.'

Jup and the shape-changer made their way to the bridge in silence. As usual, Coilla was there alongside Pepperdyne. They were told of the change of direction and why it came about.

'Where exactly are we going?' Pepperdyne asked as he took out the well-thumbed chart.

'We need a southward bearing,' Dynahla explained, tracing a line with his finger. 'In this direction.'

'There's nothing there. Just like the last time we looked at this map, before setting our present course. You have a thing about invisible islands?'

'I don't think anybody's ever fully mapped out this world. There's a lot more to it than this chart shows. Believe me, our objective lies there.'

Pepperdyne shrugged. 'If that's what Stryke wants.' He began spinning the wheel.

'I'm supposed to have a turn at steering, remember,' the dwarf said. He glanced at Coilla. 'And yes, I can reach it.'

'I wasn't going to say a thing!' she protested. 'You're confusing me with Haskeer.'

Jup smiled. 'Yeah, I guess he's the one who'd offer me a box to stand on, the irritating bastard.'

'I don't think this is a good time for your lesson,' Pepperdyne said, 'given the change of course. Sorry.'

'It's all right. The prospect of a fight appeals to me more than playing sailors, to be honest.'

'I need to leave you,' Dynahla stated, as though their permission was needed. Nobody blinked, so he added, 'See you soon.'

They nodded and the shape-changer left.

'What do you think, Jode?' Coilla asked in a low tone. 'Is he on the level?'

'Dynahla? I don't know.'

'This new course seems rum,' Jup said.

'And again we're heading for somewhere the map says doesn't exist. Though I can't see what he'd get out of lying. We'd find out soon enough if there really isn't anything there.'

'Might do to keep an eye on him though,' Coilla suggested.

'I'm already doing that,' Jup told her.

'Good idea,' Pepperdyne said. 'There's always a chance that—'

Coilla shushed him, finger to lips. She flicked her head to indicate the stairs. Someone with a heavy tread was coming up them.

Haskeer clambered into view. When he saw Jup his features lit up with something it took them a moment to recognise. It was a smile.

'Jup!' he boomed. 'I've been looking for you.'

'If it's a scrap you're after,' Jup said, instinctively balling his fists, 'forget it. I'm not in the mood.'

'*A scrap*? You wound me, old friend. Why would I want to hurt you?'

'*Old friend?*' Coilla mouthed.

'You couldn't hurt me if I was a nail and you had a hammer,' Jup assured him. 'What's the game, Haskeer?'

'Is it a game to want the best for a friend?'

'You appear in an unusually good mood,' Pepperdyne commented dryly.

'And why not?' Haskeer boomed. 'I'm surrounded by good companions, not least our human comrades.' He lifted a hand. Pepperdyne tensed. But instead of the expected blow he was rocked by a hearty slap to his shoulder that made him stagger.

'I thought you hated humans,' Coilla said.

'How'd you get *that* idea? Aren't we all brothers in arms under the skin, ready to lay down our lives for each other?'

'You been drinking sea water?' Jup asked.

'Ever the joker, aren't you, old pal? My Jup. My little Juppy Wuppy.'

'That does it,' the dwarf decided. 'He's gone insane.'

'If I'm insane,' Haskeer intoned gravely, 'it's with the passion of the fondness I feel for you.' He broke into a broad grin and lurched forward, arms outstretched. 'Come on, gimme a hug!'

'Keep him off me!'

Haskeer stopped and began to chuckle.

'Just a minute,' Coilla said. 'There's something fishy about all this.'

Haskeer nodded. 'Caught me.'

A change came over his features. They softened, shifted and reformed themselves. An instant later, Dynahla stood before them.

'Sorry,' he said. 'I couldn't resist that.'

As their astonishment wore off, the others laughed.

'That was . . . impressive,' Pepperdyne admitted.

'You're telling me,' Coilla agreed. 'I could have sworn it was him. Except for the bullshit, that is.'

'How do you do it, Dynahla?' Jup wanted to know.

'How do you do farsight?'

'I was born with it. Like all my race.'

'But it improves with practice?'

'Well, yes.'

'Most beings are born with at least the potential for magic. True, it's stronger in some races than others. It's much more latent in orcs, for example, but it's there. The trick is to develop it.'

'That takes willpower, right?'

'The dominance of the will is the least important factor.'

'I don't understand.'

'Imagination is much more important.'

'Is it?'

'What's your favourite food, Jup?'

'Huh?'

'Let's say . . . venison. You're fond of it?'

'Yeah. Who isn't?'

'Do you feel hungry?'

'Now that you mention it—'

'I reckon we all are,' Coilla said. 'We've had no chance to eat.'

Dynahla smiled. 'Good. So picture a haunch of venison, turning on a spit, running with juices. See it in your mind. Smell that delicious aroma.'

'You're making my mouth water,' Jup confessed.

'Sink your teeth into the succulent flesh. Think of how good it tastes.'

'Hmmm.'

'Now let's suppose that you can't allow yourself to eat the venison. It's very important that you don't. Let's say your life depends on not eating it. You must use your will to resist wanting to eat that meat.'

'Easier said than done when I'm this hungry.'

'Use the power of your will. Really concentrate. Refuse it. Close your eyes if it helps.'

He did, and they all watched in silence for a moment.

'How did you do?' Dynahla asked.

'Well . . .'

'Not too good?'

'You put a pretty tempting image into my head. It's hard not to want it.'

'All right. Picture that hunk of meat again.'

Once more, Jup closed his eyes.

'Look at how delicious it is,' Dynahla went on. 'It's golden brown. Succulent. Smell that delicious tang of cooking meat. But hang on! What's this? Look closely. The venison's lying in a latrine. It's covered in filth, and swarming with maggots and beetles.'

'Yuck!' Jup made a face. Coilla and Pepperdyne didn't look too cheerful either.

'How easy did you find it to resist that time?' Dynahla said.

'No problem.' He looked a little queasy. 'I don't feel quite so hungry now. But what does it prove?'

'That sorcery is only partially about exercising the will. Much more important is imagining the improbable with enough intensity that you make it real. The imagination is *stronger* than the will. When you understand that, you're some way towards understanding magic.'

Jup found that intriguing, and began questioning Dynahla about it. Engrossed, the dwarf and the fetch waved vaguely at Coilla and Pepperdyne as they left the bridge together.

'Quite a character,' Pepperdyne said.

'Impressive though,' Coilla replied. 'It was the dead spit of Haskeer.' She grinned. 'And you've got to admit it *was* funny.'

'Yes. But one thing worries me, just a bit.'

'What's that?'

'Dynahla can impersonate any of us, perfectly. How comfortable are you about having someone like that in the band?'

16

The veil between the worlds is thin as gauze, unbridgeable as an ocean. It separates an incalculable number of realities, an infinite array of glittering pinpoints hanging in the velvet firmament. Seen closer, if that were possible, they reveal themselves as globes. Some are barren rocks, or beset with volcanic activity, or icebound. A few are fertile.

Two species lived beneath the blue skies and pure white clouds of one such world. The race of humans had carved out a far-flung domain, the Peczan empire, now suffering its first setback despite its great military strength and possession of magic. The newly liberated race of orcs, cause of that humiliation, occupied a more remote, much smaller segment of the planet. Bolstered by their reawakened martial spirit, they were resolved never to fall under human dominance again.

The orcs' land was Acurial. Taress, its largest city by far and the capital, had borne the brunt of the recent occupation. Free at last, the populace determined to erase all trace of Peczan's regime. Buildings that had been commandeered were returned to their original purpose. Structures built by the empire were being torn down, with detention camps, torture facilities and execution blocks the objects of particular fury. Guard stations, billets, signposts and anything else pertaining to the overthrown were demolished and consigned to bonfires, along with portraits of Peczan bureaucrats and military chiefs. Marble busts were pounded to smithereens.

At the same time, Taress was rebuilding itself. Invasion and rebellion had devastated many parts of the city, and legions toiled on reconstruction.

The main square had been one of the first areas to be reclaimed. Work there took a commemorative form. Statues had been erected.

The tallest, although in many ways the simplest, honoured the late Principal Sylandya. Acurial's ruler before Peczan's occupation, and leader of the resistance, her martyrdom was the spark that gave fire to the revolution. She was shown seated, but didn't give the impression of being enthroned, as would be expected of a head of state. Her attire and demeanour were humble, her expression mild. The sculptor had made no effort to flatter her memory by disguising her advancing years, as might have been the case with a more vain subject. Her frame was slight, even frail. Yet she exuded an unmistakable authority.

Two orcs stood at the monument's base, looking up at the figure. They were twins, male and female, and less than thirty summers old.

'What would she have thought of this?' Chillder wondered.

'Not much, I reckon,' her brother replied. 'Our mother had little time for the conceits of power. It was one of her many virtues.'

'So was dealing with the mountain of parchmentwork that plagues us now.'

'Not as exciting as fighting as rebels, is it?'

'No, Brelan, it's not.'

'But it's what running a state's all about. It has to be done.'

'You're more like mother than I am in that way. I think you *like* shuffling paper.'

He smiled. 'Like I said; it has to be done. Taking care of the formalities is a price we pay for getting our freedom back.'

'I wish she was here to guide us through it,' Chillder said, nodding at the statue.

'Me too.'

'And if it hadn't been for that bitch Jennesta,' she added bitterly, 'she would be.'

'I know. But our mother's death wasn't in vain. If she hadn't perished as she did the revolution might never have happened. '

'I'm not sure about that. Either way, Jennesta went unpunished, and that sticks in my craw.'

He gave her a moment, then, 'Come on,' he urged gently, 'we ought to be moving.'

They headed across the square.

'Of course, she might have been,' Brelan said.

'Who might have been what?'

'Jennesta. Punished. For all we know, the warband reckoned with her.'

'Or they might have suffered the same fate as our mother. The frustrating thing is we'll probably never know.'

They arrived at the shadow of another monument, and slowed to a halt despite the pressing nature of their business. It was larger than Sylandya's, though squat rather than tall, and housed on a pedestal no more than waist height from the ground. Five life-sized figures were depicted; four orcs, one of them female, and a dwarf. They were in heroic poses, weapons drawn. To the rear of the group was a low stone wall that acted as a backdrop. This bore a carving along its entire length, showing a further twenty or more of the principals' comrades. Controversially for many in Taress, it also showed a human.

The front of the monument was strewn with necklaces of fangs, pots of wine, embellished weapons, sketches of the heroes, not all of them crudely executed, and other offerings. In a not very orc-like gesture, there were even some bunches of flowers. The monument's base carried a plain inscription reading '*The Wolverines*'.

'And what do you suppose *they* would think about *this*?' Brelan asked, echoing his sister's earlier question.

'Haskeer would have liked it. Not sure the others would care much.' She turned to him. 'Where could they have gone, Brelan? Do you think they're still alive?'

'Well, you can bet they didn't return to their so-called northern lands. I never did buy that. As to whether they're still alive . . .' He shrugged. 'Who knows? I'm just grateful they came here when they did.'

'Except for the human. The slimy one.'

'Standeven.'

She nodded. 'Orc killer.'

'Maybe.'

'How can you doubt it?'

'You're probably right. But I can't help thinking even he wouldn't have been stupid enough to murder one of us in our own land.'

'The pity is we let him get away with it.'

'There was no proof.'

'How much did you *need*?'

'That's all water under the bridge, Chillder, and something else we can't do anything about. Now can we get a move on? We've a problem to deal with, remember.'

They resumed their journey.

The streets leading off the square were bustling. Extensive rebuilding work was going on and laden carts jammed the thoroughfares. Passers-by stared as Brelan and Chillder passed, and some waved. They were public figures now.

As they walked, Chillder said, 'I sometimes wonder whether we should be doing all this work.'

'Why wouldn't we?'

'Peczan's pride took a battering. How do we know they won't invade again, if only to save face?'

'We've got as many hands putting up defences as rebuilding. More. If the humans come back we'll know it, and this time they'd face a population ready to fight.'

'Would they? Grilan-Zeat's gone now. What worries me is that our warlike spirit's going to fade along with the comet's memory.'

'I don't think so. Our folk have had a taste of the freedom that fighting brought them. They won't easily forget that.'

'I hope you're right.'

'Trust me. We've more important things to worry about, not least trying to replenish our plundered treasury, thanks to Jennesta.'

'And now this . . . strangeness. What the hell's happening, Brelan?'

'Damned if I know. Maybe we'll learn something from this new event.'

They pushed on, moving away from the centre and entering less crowded streets. The further they went the more they saw of the defensive measures Brelan referred to. In piazzas, or open spaces where buildings had burnt down during the uprising, citizens were being drilled. Mobile road blocks, consisting of hay wagons loaded with rocks, stood at the side of major avenues. Rooftops were utilised as lookout points, and in some places purpose-built watchtowers were under construction. The threat of re-invasion was being taken seriously.

At last the twins reached a district previously given over to cattle yards and storehouses. Now a contingent of Acurial's newly-created regular militia were stationed there. In addition to an armed populace, a standing army was thought desirable, and former resistance fighters made up its nucleus. It was early days for the force; their uniforms were makeshift and their weapons ill-assorted. Their quarters were at a rudimentary stage too, and in common with the rest of Taress the area was a building site.

Waved through the compound's gates by saluting guards, Chillder and Brelan made their way to a recently erected barracks block. They were met outside by an officer, a comrade from the resistance days, who unlocked the barracks' door and ushered them in.

'Not that there's much to see,' he said.

There were only minor signs of disorder in the deserted interior. A couple of the cots were askew, a chair was upended and a few items of kit were scattered across the floor.

'This has been left exactly as it was?' Brelan asked.

The officer nodded. 'Just as you see it.'

'How many?'

'Eleven.'

'When?'

'Some time during the night. We only knew when they didn't show up at reveille.'

'You've searched the camp?'

'Of course.'

'Were any of them . . . dissatisfied in any way?' Chillder said.

'These weren't troublemakers. They were as solid and as loyal as any we've got.'

'Their arms went too?' She pointed at an empty weapons rack.

'Yes.'

'You've told no one about this?' Brelan said.

'No,' the officer replied.

'Good. Keep it that way. You can leave us now. And thanks.'

When the officer had gone, Chillder turned to her brother. 'How many times does this make?'

'Seven, I think. Possibly eight. That's just from Taress, mind. There are a few unconfirmed reports from outside the city. With this new lot I reckon we're talking upwards of seventy militia having gone missing, that we're aware of.'

'So what are we dealing with? Desertion? Hostage taking?'

'As far as we know there's no reason for any of them to have deserted. And I can't see abducting armed bands of warriors being that easy a task, particularly from inside a compound like this.'

'Did all the others go in similar ways?'

'Some did. From their quarters, just like whatever happened here. One group went out on a patrol and never came back. There were a couple of cases of disappearances on guard duty, and one where four, I think it was, vanished from a weapons dump. There's no real pattern. Except nobody saw anything.'

'Could Peczan be behind this? Might they have got agents in and—'

'Humans trying to hide among a nation of orcs? I don't think so, Chillder.'

'Or could it be our own kind? Traitors doing the humans' bidding.'

'It'd take a lot of them, not to mention a pretty big conspiracy. I don't want to think there could be that many traitors. I don't believe there are. There might be one or two turncoats, for some twisted reason, but not on this scale.'

'There's another possibility. Have you noticed the smell in here?'

A faint sulphurous aroma hung in the air, mingled with the scent of the barracks' new wood.

'I'm not sure.'

'Oh, come on, Brelan; you know what it is.'

'Magic?'

'*Yes.* Couldn't that be it?'

'I can't see how. Humans have mastery of magic, not orcs, and like I said; where would humans hide in Acurial?'

'Jennesta's not human. This could be her doing.'

'The same thing applies. I mean, she'd stick out, wouldn't she? Anyway, I don't believe she's still hanging around. The mob would tear her to pieces, never mind her sorcery. That's not a risk she'd take.'

'*What* then? Who's doing this?'

'Whoever or whatever's responsible, we're going to have to brace ourselves for more of the same.'

'You reckon?'

'We've no reason to think it might stop. Whatever *it* is.'

'How do we protect ourselves?'

'Short of gathering the entire army together and watching each other's backs, I've no idea. And who can say if even that would work?'

'There must be *something* we can do, Brelan.'

'We don't know what we're trying to protect ourselves against. All we do know—'

'Is that our comrades have disappeared as surely as the Wolverines,' she finished for him.

He nodded, looking grim.

17

Long after the sun disappeared, and the crisp night sky was speckled with stars, the Wolverines' ship ploughed on.

They used hooded lamps for such light as they needed and conversed in hushed tones. Dynahla was the only real guide to their destination, and as they were uncertain about how close they were, or whether there might be other craft abroad, they ran dark and silent.

Stryke gathered his officers in what had been the master's cabin, or whatever the ship's former, goblin owners called it. Its windows were kept firmly shuttered.

'What do we do when we get there?' Haskeer demanded before they all finished seating themselves.

'That's what we're here to figure out,' Stryke told him. 'Now sit down and shut up.'

Sullenly, his sergeant did as he was told.

'We don't know what we'll be up against,' Stryke said. 'So we need a plan. You're our strategist, Coilla; talk to me.'

'We *do* know what we'll be up against: Jennesta. Question is how best to overcome her and pull off our mission. And not get killed doing it.'

'Isn't that always the way it is when we tangle with her?' Jup asked.

'Yeah,' Haskeer chimed in, 'since when did we worry about odds when it comes to a fight? I say we go in with blades out and give no quarter, Stryke, like we usually do.'

'This is different. I want Thirzarr out of there and safe. That's what Coilla meant by the mission. This isn't just about killing Jennesta.'

'You don't want to fight?' Haskeer looked incredulous.

'*Course* I do. But I want to fight smart.'

'Could be we'll run straight into opposition,' Coilla said, 'in which case it'll be an all-out scrap. But if we can get ashore unseen, maybe a snatch squad's the best option to bring out Thirzarr.'

'What about Jennesta?' Jup wanted to know.

'Once we get Thirzarr clear we can tackle her force head-on.'

'Only trouble with that,' Stryke judged, 'is that it spreads us thin.'

'Yeah,' Coilla agreed. 'Three groups. Snatch squad, main body holding back 'til they get the word to attack, and a group defending the ship.'

'That could be us,' Dallog suggested. 'Me and the rest of the Ceragans. We could guard the ship.'

Haskeer sneered. 'Quick getting in with that bid, ain't you? Frightened of a fight?'

'*No.* It's just that we work well together. We've proved that.'

'You did a good job holding it last time,' Stryke conceded. 'That's your detail then.'

'We're better off without 'em,' Haskeer muttered.

'But I can't spare all of you,' Stryke added. 'Take Chuss, Pirrak and Keick. Wheam can come with us.'

Haskeer loudly groaned. 'As if we didn't have enough trouble.'

Stryke showed him a clenched fist. 'I won't be telling you again. We need all the bodies we can get. He's included.'

'Not in the snatch squad?' Jup said, faintly alarmed.

'No. He'll be part of the main force.'

'Who *is* in the snatch squad?' Coilla wondered.

'Me, you, Jup and a couple of the grunts. I'm thinking Eldo and Reafdaw. Dynahla should be in it, too.'

'Why?'

'He says he's got magic. We might need that. And before you say it; yes, we don't really know anything about him. I'll take that risk.' He looked to Haskeer. 'You'll head the main force.'

'So I get the pleasure of Wheam's company. Lucky me. Pepperdyne, too?'

'Yes.'

'What about the other one?'

'Standeven stays on the ship. You'll keep an eye on him, Dallog.'

Somebody rapped on the door and barged in. It was Finje, breathing hard from a dash.

'We can see it,' he reported. 'The island. It's in sight.'

*

'It's big,' Stryke said, peering at the long black slab of the island, outlined on the horizon by the spreading dawn. 'Funny it's not on the map.' He shot Dynahla a searching look, coloured with a hint of suspicion.

'There are lots of maps. I doubt there's one that charts this world accurately. Anyway, what's the worry? There it is.'

'You're *sure* Jennesta's there, and Thirzarr?'

'Yes.'

'Because Serapheim told you so.'

'Not just that. Now we're close I can sense the presence myself.'

'*You* can? How?'

'As with so much to do with the craft, it's hard to explain to the uninitiated. Let's just say that living things give out a certain . . . cadence, and some of us can detect it.'

'I can't pretend to understand that.'

'You'll have to take my word for it then. But be certain that Jennesta, and your mate, are on that island.'

They were at the ship's prow, and Stryke carried on staring at the island for a moment before speaking again. 'The plan's to send in a snatch squad to get Thirzarr out before we launch a full attack. Will you be part of the squad?'

'I think I ought to be. Though you should be aware that Jennesta's sorcery is stronger than you know, and quite possibly greater than anything I can summon.'

'That's better than nothing. But here's something *you* should be aware of. All I know about you is what you've told us. On the strength of that I'm trusting you. Betray that trust, or do anything that might harm Thirzarr, and you won't be coming back from this mission, whatever happens to the rest of us. Got it?'

'I understand. You can rely on me, Stryke. Now unless there's anything else, I'd like to prepare.'

'What does that involve?'

'Nothing too drastic. I just need to find a quiet corner for contemplation, to centre myself.'

'I need to do some preparing myself. I'll send for you when it's time.'

*

From the bridge, Coilla and Pepperdyne watched Stryke and the shape-changer part.

'Think we can trust him?' Pepperdyne said.

'Stryke seems to. Not that he has much choice. Though it'll go badly for Dynahla if this is some kind of trick.'

'It'd go pretty badly for us as well.'

'The band's used to being in tight spots.'

'It's not the band I'm worried about. It's you.'

'You're worried about an orc going into a fight.' She had to smile. 'That's like worrying about a bird flying or whether a fish can swim.'

'Hunters bring down birds and fish lose out to hooks.'

'I'm not a fish or a bird, so I've nothing to worry about, have I?'

'You know what I mean.'

'Look, Jode; my race lives for combat. It's what we do. Or hadn't you noticed? I'd have thought you'd understand, being a fighter yourself.'

'Only out of necessity.'

'And you get no pleasure from winning a fight? No rush of joy when you down an opponent?'

'Well . . . maybe. A bit. But I don't relish putting my life on the line every day the way you do.'

'It's in our nature. We fight, and we fight to kill. If death takes us, that's the price we pay. Though we do our best to make damn sure it's who we're up against that does the paying. We trust to our skill, and to luck and to the Tetrad. If you want an orcs' creed, that's as near as I can get to it in words.'

'I'm not arguing about your nature, Coilla. That's part of what I love about you, and I'd never change it. I only want you to be careful.'

'Why didn't you just say that in the first place?'

Pepperdyne slapped his forehead with the heel of his palm in a gesture of mock exasperation, and they laughed.

'So what's the plan?' he said. 'How are we going about this raid?'

'Stryke'll be briefing us shortly, but the idea's to anchor well offshore and go over in boats. If we get there without being spotted we split into our two groups and the game's on.'

'And if we are spotted?'

'Then it gets messy.'

*

It happened as Coilla said. All lights extinguished, the ship was anchored as far from the island as practicable. Dallog's unit was left in charge. The rest of the band cautiously lowered the boats, and likewise in darkness, made for the shore using muffled oars.

The sea was obligingly calm. It did little to reduce the tension of the crossing. Eyes and ears sharp, silence imposed, they expected the alarm to be raised at any moment. But they reached the shore apparently unseen. There was no sign of Jennesta's ships; the band assumed they were anchored on another side of the island.

The point at which they met the shore was rocky and too steep for a landing. So they moved along the coastline, keeping close, until they found a sandy beach. Clambering ashore, they headed for the shelter of trees, dragging the boats behind them.

To face Jennesta, they had to find her. Stryke sent out as many scouts as he could spare. Zoda, Prooq, Nep, Breggin and Orbon got the job. Treading lightly, they fanned out into the jungle. The rest of the Wolverines kept low and quiet, and waited.

It wasn't a long vigil. The island was large, but Jennesta had seen no point in penetrating its interior to set up a temporary camp. Her force was located a short distance inland, and to the west. There were guards, of course; and Breggin and Zoda, who got nearest, thought Jennesta's army might have grown. Stryke gave no time to wondering how that could be.

He ordered the band into its two groups. The larger, main force, lead by Haskeer, would follow the snatch squad but at a slower pace. At a prearranged spot it would stop and wait for its signal to attack. If the signal didn't come, no one doubted they would go in anyway.

It was full night when Stryke headed off, with Jup, Coilla, Dynahla, Eldo and Reafdaw in tow, the latter pair carrying bows. Dynahla refused any kind of weapon beyond a small decorative dagger he always wore.

Coilla shot Pepperdyne a quick smile as they left. He returned a wink, braving Haskeer's scowl.

The snatch squad travelled with measured speed, careful not to give themselves away. Soon they were out of sight of the main force at their rear. Following the scouts' directions, they forged on through semi-jungle conditions, aggravating but far from impenetrable, until they came to clearer land. Moon and star shine were more plentiful here, and the band moved sure-footedly. At last they arrived at a grassy rise. Going up it on their bellies, they peeked over its crest at the vale below. They saw a cluster of tents, tethered horses, and figures outlined in the glow of cooking fires and armourers' braziers.

Anticipating a possible refusal, Stryke left Dynahla out of dealing with guards. There seemed to be four, but they weren't fixed. Their patrolling took them across the orcs' path to the camp. Stryke thought to let Eldo's and Reafdaw's bows take care of them. The guards patrolled in pairs, which made the task easier. The trick was to eliminate one pair without the other knowing. That meant waiting until they were out of each other's sight.

The four guards, having completed their rounds, were bunched together. Any attempt to drop them by Stryke's two archers ran the risk of their targets raising the alarm before they could reload and re-aim. But finally the guards parted, each pair moving away in opposite directions. Stryke sent Reafdaw and Eldo to the right, to shadow the duo walking that way. Hunters and prey soon disappeared from view. The other pair of guards, heading left, had also gone beyond seeing.

'How good are your archers?' Dynahla asked in a hushed tone.

'Good enough,' Stryke said. 'It's why I picked 'em.'

'What we have to be wary of,' Coilla explained, 'is the guards going the other way.' She nodded to the left. 'When they come back and don't see the others—'

'It could be yelling time,' Jup finished for her.

Dynahla nodded.

They kept watching.

The wait was long enough that they were beginning to suspect something had gone wrong. Then Eldo and Reafdaw reappeared, giving the thumbs-up. At exactly the same time the two remaining guards returned. With frantic gestures Stryke and the others indicated this, and urged the grunts on. Doubled over, resembling loping apes, Eldo and Reafdaw started to run towards them.

The pair of guards returning from the left were in plain sight now. They were talking to each other, animatedly, and slowing. The absence of their comrades had been noted.

Eldo and Reafdaw arrived, breathing hard and scrabbling for arrows.

'Move it!' Stryke hissed. *'They know something's wrong!'*

The grunts had to rise above the crest of the hill to discharge their bows. As they did, one of the guards glanced their way and saw them. His mouth formed an 'O'. It was too late. The arrows winged towards them, hitting true, and they went down without a sound.

'Come on!' Stryke ordered.

The squad scrambled over the rise and down into the vale.

They checked that the guards were dead, retrieved the arrows and hid the bodies in the undergrowth. That done, they pushed on to Jennesta's camp, moving stealthily.

Using the shelter of a small copse, they had their first close look. They weren't in a good place. There was well lit, exposed ground ahead of them, and at least a dozen troopers were working or lounging in it. Further back, in the shadows, Stryke thought he caught a glimpse of what might have been goblins, and perhaps other non-human creatures. The others saw them too.

'Looks like Jennesta *has* been beefing up her little army,' Coilla said.

Stryke nodded. He turned to Dynahla. 'Feel anything? I mean, is she here? And where is she?'

'She's here all right. Down that way.' He pointed to the westward end of the camp. 'In one of those tents.'

'Doesn't take a wizard to figure that out,' Jup said.

Dynahla ignored him and added, 'We might be facing stronger opposition than we bargained for.'

'Maybe a few goblins and whatnot,' Stryke replied dismissively. 'We can deal with it.'

'I didn't mean them. There's more than one kind of magic here.'

'You sure?'

'Quite. They're of different orders, mind you, and different disciplines. Two unrelated races, probably. What Jennesta radiates is like a great black, angry ocean. This other source . . . I can't identify. But by comparison it's a lake. Filled with blood.'

'Sounds fun,' Coilla offered, deadpan.

'Facing Jennesta's dangerous enough. Going against *two* wielders of magic . . . well, that's asking a lot.'

'You wanna leave?' Stryke said. ''Cos if you're not behind this you can get out right now.'

Dynahla's gaze darted back to the camp, then returned to Stryke.

'No. No, I'm in. And I'll do what I can. I just wanted to warn you about what might be in store.'

'You've done that. Now let's get going.'

He led them in the direction of the cluster of tents. Having to keep hidden, their progress was slower than he would have liked, but eventually they arrived opposite the tents. There was less obvious activity here, save the occasional trooper wandering through. The area was dimly lit, being some distance from the cooking fires, though there were one or two braziers.

'I guess that must be Jennesta's tent,' Jup said, indicating the biggest and most ornate one.

'Has to be,' Stryke agreed. 'Doesn't mean Thirzarr's there though. Any idea where she might be, Dynahla?'

The shape-changer shook his head. 'It's much harder locating a being who hasn't any magical powers. What I can tell you is that Jennesta's in this part of the camp, but she isn't in that tent.'

'Can you tell *where* she is?'

'Not precisely. Except that she's close.'

Stryke sighed. 'All right. Then I guess her tent's where we start.'

'All we have to do is get to it without being seen,' Coilla said dryly.

'I'd like to do that without having to tackle any of the soldiers and causing an uproar. So we stay put until it gets clearer over there.'

'What if it doesn't?'

'We'll think again.'

Once more they waited, keeping well out of sight and never taking their eyes off the camp. As the night wore on, comings and goings grew less, apart from occasional guards making their rounds. There were no lights in the large tent they assumed was Jennesta's. Nor did anybody leave it or go in.

'This is as good as it's likely to get,' Stryke decided, eyeing the now deserted area between them and their goal. 'We'll get into the tent by the back.'

'What if it's empty?'

'You're full of questions tonight, Coilla. If it's empty, we keep looking. Jup, got the horn handy?'

The dwarf patted the satchel at his waist. 'You bet.'

'Be ready to use it when I give the word.' He scanned the camp again. No one was about. 'We go in pairs. You and Coilla first. *Move.*'

They scurried for the tent, making the most of shadows, and reached it without incident. Then they circled to its rear and were lost to view.

'Reafdaw, Eldo; you're next,' Stryke said. 'I want you taking care of the entrance. Can do?'

'No problem,' Eldo grated.

'Go!'

The grunts also reached the tent without trouble. Their position, at the front, was more risky, but they did a good job of melting into the gloom on either side of the entry.

'Now us?' Dynahla asked.

'Wait!' Stryke hissed, grabbing the shape-changer's sleeve. He pointed.

A sentry had appeared from the far side of the camp, and he was walking towards Jennesta's tent.

They held their breath as he approached. His pace was infuriatingly slow, but it looked as though he might bypass the big tent. That proved deceptive. When he was parallel to it, he turned and headed for the entrance. Stryke knew that at any moment Eldo and Reafdaw would be spotted. He tensed, ready to break cover and tackle the man.

'What do we do?' Dynahla whispered.

'Stay put. I'll deal with it.'

The sentry was almost at Jennesta's tent. Stryke half rose, hand on his sword hilt.

Eldo stepped into view, hands held up in apparent surrender. Startled, the sentinel drew his sword. But he didn't raise the alarm. Eldo walked slowly towards him, and he was saying something Stryke and Dynahla couldn't hear. Talking, holding the guard's attention, the grunt kept moving, describing a sly circle that had the man turning until his back was to the tent. At which point Eldo stopped.

Reafdaw sneaked out of his hiding place, a knife glinting in his fist. Swiftly, silently, he crept up behind the guard. In one fluid movement he clamped a hand over the man's mouth as he sunk the blade into the small of his back. The guard slumped to the ground. Eldo and Reafdaw quickly dragged his body away, dumping it amongst dense vegetation at the camp's edge.

'Right,' Stryke said, satisfying himself that there were no more guards about. 'Let's get over there.'

He and the shape-changer rushed to the tent. Reafdaw and Eldo, returning to their positions beside its entrance, gave them a wave as they passed. Stryke and Dynahla went round to the back, and found Coilla and Jup waiting there.

'What kept you?' Coilla said, mildly irritated.

'We were writing poetry,' Stryke told her. 'Now let's do this.' He drew a knife. 'Ready?'

The others nodded, and braced themselves for whatever might be inside.

Stryke jabbed the blade into the fabric and cut a long slash. He prised the two sides apart, making an opening big enough for them to look through. The interior was gloomy; only a faint illumination from the camp fires penetrated the tent cloth. Detecting no sound or movement, he slipped inside. The others followed.

Various items of plush furniture were scattered about, causing some stumbling in the dark, but it looked as though no one was there. Then Stryke spotted something.

At one end of the tent, in almost complete darkness, there was a shape. He padded towards it, and realised it was someone seated. For a moment he couldn't make out who or what it was. Once his vision adjusted to the murk, he rushed forward.

'Thirzarr? Thirzarr!' He clutched her hand. It felt cold. '*Thirzarr!*' He got no response. 'It's so damned dark in here!' he cursed.

'This might help,' Dynahla said.

He cupped his hands, and for the first time Coilla noticed how elegant and almost feminine they were. When he opened them again there was a purple fireball nestling between his palms, about the size of a hen's egg. It bathed the scene in a soft, eerie glow. It showed them that Thirzarr was sitting rigidly, and her eyes were open, though they were glazed and unfocused.

'*Thirzarr!*' Stryke mouthed anxiously.

'Jennesta's got her in a . . . kind of trance,' the fetch explained.

'Like the last time we saw her,' Coilla recalled.

'Can you bring her out of it, Dynahla?' Stryke asked.

'Possibly. But not here. We need to get her somewhere safe first.'

'What do we do?' Jup said, 'Carry her?'

'We might not have to. Tell her to stand, Stryke.'

'Will she?'

'She's in a highly suggestible state. The spell binding her should be answerable only to Jennesta's voice. But a familiar voice, one she knows intimately, might be as effective. Try it.'

'Stand up, Thirzarr,' Stryke said.

Nothing happened.

'Maybe we *should* carry her,' Coilla muttered.

'Try again, Stryke,' Dynahla suggested. 'A little more firmly. Order her this time.'

Stryke looked doubtful, but did it. *'Stand up! On your feet, Thirzarr. Now!'*

She stood.

'As long as you don't ask her to do anything complicated,' Dynahla added, ' she should do as you say.'

Coilla snickered. 'That'll be a first.' She sobered when she saw Stryke's face.

He addressed his mate, firmly but not unkindly. 'Thirzarr, come with me.' He took a few steps, watching her over his shoulder. She moved too, albeit stiffly, and began to follow him. 'It'll be easier if we go out the front way,' he decided. 'Check that it's clear, Jup.'

The dwarf went to the entrance and gave a low whistle. Reafdaw poked his head in.

'All clear out there?' Jup said.

Reafdaw nodded and pulled aside the flap for them.

Stryke took Thirzarr's arm and guided her. The others followed. Dynahla came last, closing his fist on the radiant fireball, snuffing it out.

Everything seemed quiet outside. Even the noises from the other end of the camp had died down.

'Now we get Thirzarr away and hidden,' Stryke told them. 'Then we call the main force in. Come on.'

He headed for the perimeter as briskly as he could while still holding Thirzarr's arm.

They were hardly under way when there was movement in the darkness at the camp's edges. Figures emerged. A large number, toting weapons. They approached from three sides, and Stryke didn't doubt more were coming in from the rear. The figures brought light with them, thrown out by blazing torches scattered about their ranks. It grew bright enough to reveal Jennesta in the forefront.

She halted ten paces short of Stryke's party. Her followers took her cue and also held back.

'You're full of surprises, Stryke,' Jennesta said. 'I didn't think you had the wits to find me. You're certainly witless in believing you could walk in here without me knowing.'

'You would have known it.'

'Ah. This is a *raid*, is it? An attack with . . . six of you. Or are you counting on your mate bringing it up to the dizzy heights of seven?'

'What have you done to Thirzarr?'

'I find it so touching that beasts like you can display actual feelings for each other. Or what passes for them in your part of the food chain.'

'I'm taking her out of here.'

'I don't think so. Thirzarr? Here. To me.' Jennesta pointed to the ground next to her.

Thirzarr lurched forward. Stryke tried to hold her back, but she shook loose violently. With a quicker pace than she had previously shown, she made for Jennesta.

'Thirzarr!' Stryke yelled. 'Don't! Stay here!'

Oblivious, she carried on to the enemy ranks and arrived at Jennesta's side, then spun to face Stryke's squad, her eyes still opaque.

'So nice to have you back, my love,' the sorceress purred.

Thirzarr had been obscuring Jennesta's view of Dynahla. Now she saw him properly, and something like a flicker of doubt passed over her face.

Staring intently, she said, 'The Wolverines become more motley by the day. Do I know you?'

'Do you?' the shape-changer replied levelly.

'I expect an answer, not a riddle.'

'It was an answer. Here's a question for you. Do you know yourself?'

What might have been a troubled expression briefly visited Jennesta's features. 'Correction, Stryke: you've brought five fighters and one deranged human. She looked to Dynahla. 'You *are* human?'

The shape-changer said nothing.

'No matter.' She turned to Stryke. 'Your best option is to surrender, here and now. Any other course won't go well for you.'

Stryke tore his eyes from Thirzarr. 'You think so?'

'Oh, I don't doubt the rest of your band's not far behind. But you'll not prevail.'

He scanned her followers. Though they certainly outnumbered his band, he replied, 'You sure about that?'

'That's one thing I like about you orcs; you're not shy of a fight. So let's make it a little more interesting for you, shall we?' She raised an arm above her head, then let it drop, indolently.

More figures came out of the dark. Gleaton-Rouk led his goblin crew, numbering about a dozen. Behind them were the vague outlines of what the orcs still thought of as elder races; an assembly of diverse creatures of the sort they knew, and often fought, back on Maras-Dantia. Their number looked equal to that of the band.

Gleaton-Rouk carried his bow, Shadow-wing, with an arrow ready nocked. 'I'm gratified to meet you again, Captain Stryke,' he hissed.

'You can go and fuck yourself.'

Jennesta laughed. 'That's *it*, you see? Always ready for a brawl. Very . . . *orcish*.' Her tone hardened. 'But this isn't a time to fight. Your only option is to surrender.'

'What I told him,' Stryke said, nodding at the goblin.

'You can be tiresomely stubborn.'

'We going to talk or fight?' From the corner of his eye he noticed Jup slyly edging a hand towards his satchel.

'You seem absurdly confident, given the odds.'

'We judge our enemies by their quality, not their number.'

'In that case,' she replied, smiling, 'let me provide you with opponents worthy of your arrogance.' Again, she raised her arm.

The murk disgorged another group of creatures. Copiously armed, and warband-sized in number, they wore the same dead look in their eyes that Thirzarr had. They were muscular, flinty-faced and savage in appearance.

They were orcs.

18

The Wolverines' main force, lead by Haskeer, were cooling their heels at the designated stop point. Too far away from Jennesta's camp to see it, they were near enough to hear the signal.

The band passed time quietly checking or sharpening their weapons. Some took the chance to gnaw at the hard rations they'd missed out on earlier, and water pouches were passed round. A few stretched out on the sward, helmets pulled down to cover their eyes, and might even have been snoozing.

Unconsciously, Pepperdyne and Spurral conceded their status as outsiders and drifted together. They had marched side by side, and now they perched on a boulder a little apart from the others. Nearby, Haskeer was balling out Wheam for some minor infraction, but the necessity of keeping his voice down meant he got no pleasure out of it.

'You look grim, Jode,' Spurral observed.

'You don't seem too joyful yourself.'

'Well, we've both got somebody to worry about, haven't we?'

'True. Though maybe we shouldn't.'

'What'd you mean? Oh, yeah. Jup and Coilla aren't exactly novices when it comes to a fight, are they?'

'Exactly. Least, that's what I'm telling myself.'

'Me too. But it's Jennesta they're up against, not some common foe.'

'We'll *all* be going against her soon enough.'

'At least we've got Dynahla. He could help in that respect.'

'Hmm.'

'You're doubtful?'

'We know he's got magical powers, but are they a match for hers?

In fact, we don't really know anything about him beyond what he's told us. Doesn't that worry you?'

'The way I look at it, if Stryke trusts him—'

'Yeah, that's what Coilla says. I hope you're both right.'

Done with harassing Wheam, Haskeer wandered in their direction. He looked grim, too. Though in his case it was more or less normal.

'We were just talking about Dynahla,' Spurral told him. 'What do you think about him?'

'He's not one of the band. I don't like outsiders.'

'That's us told.'

Haskeer cast a contemptuous eye Wheam's way. 'At least you two can fight.'

'Rare praise indeed,' Pepperdyne said, 'coming from you.'

'Yeah, well, I ain't wooing you, so don't let it go to your head.'

'I think you're being unfair on Wheam,' Spurral declared. 'He's not doing too badly.'

'How long do we have to live before he does *well*? If I had my way—'

A horn blast cut through the night air.

'Here we go,' Pepperdyne said.

The band came to life. Scrambling to their feet, they snatched up their weapons and shields.

'Move it, you bastards!' Haskeer bellowed.

The horn sounded again, its note longer and shriller than before.

They began running towards the camp.

Jup was lucky to get off a couple of blasts of the horn. He was too occupied to manage more.

Paradoxically, a small group confronted by a much larger one isn't necessarily at an immediate disadvantage because, by necessity, the number of combatants who can engage at one time is limited. Not that that meant Stryke's party was in any less peril.

Jennesta must have known Jup's signal would summon the rest of the Wolverines, but seemed confident in her greater force. With a snap of her fingers she had sent a faction of her human troops forward, so that Stryke and his companions were faced by at least two opponents each. She herself held back, content to let her servants undertake the initial assault. Gleaton-Rouk was also still, a bow being a less than ideal weapon for close combat. In any event Shadowwing's enchanted arrows hadn't been anointed with the blood of a foe.

Jup discarded the horn and brought up his staff, whirling it with enough speed and skill to befuddle an advancing trooper. Quick as thought he brought it down hard on the man's head, cracking his skull. A second opponent instantly took over. Wary of the same fate, he kept his distance, swiping and jabbing at the dwarf whenever he could get near enough. They began to circle each other, looking for an advantage.

Silently thanking the gods that she always retrieved her throwing knives whenever possible, Coilla tried keeping her adversaries at bay with them. She struck true with her first throw, piercing a man's neck, but her second went wide as her target dodged. Quickly grabbing another blade she set about making a better job of it. In the end, his evasion wasn't up to her skill and the knife found his eye.

Eldo and Reafdaw fought in typical orc fashion by engaging in a slogging match. They battered at their opponents' shields, steel ringing on steel, and drank up the returning blows. Initially, brute force quickly won out over finesse. One of the humans, his guard breached, went down with a gaping wound to his chest.

Stryke faced the most opposition, with three or four of the sorceress' minions homing in on him. They were variously armed, but the most dangerous wielded a barbed pike, giving him more reach than Stryke's sword. Feigning a move towards one of the other attackers, Stryke spun at the last moment and with a vicious swipe parted the pike-man's hand from his wrist. Then he laid into the others.

His real fear was that Thirzarr would be sent against him again. But Jennesta hadn't committed her to the fight. At least, not yet.

As her underlings went down, dead or wounded, Jennesta ordered replacements in, keeping up the pressure. Not the zombie orcs, however, who stood and watched with vacant, implacable expressions. Next to fending off Thirzarr, Stryke's biggest concern was facing them. He didn't know how the Wolverines would deal with having to square up to fellow orcs. He didn't know how he would handle it himself. All he could do was battle on and hope his reinforcements weren't much longer coming.

Stryke, Coilla, Jup, Reafdaw and Eldo were at full stretch, slugging it out with a succession of troopers and a few of Jennesta's human zombie slaves for good measure.

There was a single exception. Dynahla. He remained still as the mayhem churned all around. A couple of troopers were confronting him, but from at least a sword's length away, and seemed uncertain of their next move, thinking perhaps that someone apparently unarmed had to be dangerous. He took no notice of them, and had his eyes locked on Jennesta. She caught his gaze and returned it, an unknowable look on her face.

As he fought off a succession of challengers, Stryke weighed the option of getting to Thirzarr and dragging her clear, however hard that might prove. He glimpsed Jup from the corner of his eye and thought the dwarf could be considering the same move, and might aid him. Cutting down one of Jennesta's shambling, once human zombies, its flesh rending like ancient parchment, Stryke edged towards his mate.

Then the balance tilted.

The Wolverines' main force arrived, streaming out of the dark, bellowing war cries.

Jennesta reacted immediately. She unleashed her entire complement, including the magically enslaved orcs. All but Thirzarr, whom she kept at her side.

What had been a conflict became a battle.

With the only illumination coming from camp fires, and the brands carried by Jennesta's followers, the light was poor. So it took the incoming Wolverines a moment to realise that those they were confronting included members of their own race. Some hesitated, albeit for a split second. Haskeer wasn't among them. When his blood was up he was hell-bent on fighting anything.

The momentum of the reinforcements' charge had them crashing into the enemies' ranks. Haskeer was to the fore, laying about him with an axe in one hand, a long-blade knife in the other. The less nimble human zombies were the first to catch his wrath. He sliced into their limbs with his blade and used the axe to pound their heads, which in some cases exploded under the impact.

Spurral and Pepperdyne's alliance continued as they entered the fray. He relied on his accustomed sword, and as usual abstained from carrying a shield, preferring to rely on speed and agility. She also kept to a familiar weapon, her staff, and used it to good effect. In a strategy she had developed with Jup, and which Pepperdyne had seen and admired, they worked together. So that when a chance arose, Spurral tumbled foes and Pepperdyne delivered the killing blow.

But for all their concentration on fighting, both still tried to keep an eye on Wheam. Although he wasn't altogether in need of nannies any more. His fighting skills had developed and his confidence had increased. In any event he was part of a wedge driving into the enemy line, surrounded by comrades who were veterans. As he disappeared into the scrum, his beloved lute incongruously strapped to his back, Pepperdyne and Spurral saw the tyro ramming his sword the way of a trooper's guts.

The battle fragmented as ripples of chaos ran through the warring mob. Jup and Coilla took advantage of it to fight to their mates' sides. And Stryke got himself a little closer to Thirzarr, who remained immobile beside Jennesta. But the toughest opposition, the zombie orcs, were beginning to act. They moved forward a little unsteadily, but without compromise. Any who got in their way, even if they were allies, were ploughed through, or even felled. Some of Jennesta's human zombies, slower to shift, were simply cut down. Gripped by the sorceress' enchantment, the orcs recognised no barrier in obeying their mistress' will.

Gleaton-Rouk and his goblin crew were also beginning to join the fight. But he was unable to use his bow, the second source of magic Dynahla had detected, both because of the crush and the fact that it hadn't been daubed with blood. Stryke worried that it soon would be.

Outnumbered as they were, the Wolverines had one thing going for them. Unlike Jennesta's widely diverse followers and collaborators, they were a unified force, accustomed to fighting as an entity. It gave them a slight edge in the mayhem. Not that it meant they would prevail against such odds. So far, the band had been lucky. But Stryke knew it was just a matter of time before they started taking casualties.

He wrenched his blade from a goblin's chest and let the creature topple. Then he looked to Thirzarr. She was unmoved, physically and apparently emotionally. But it was Jennesta, at her side, who drew his attention. She was staring fixedly at something beyond Stryke. He turned, and saw Dynahla returning her gaze.

In that instant there was a blinding flash of light. It was so intense that everybody stilled, and the fighting halted. Even the enchanted orcs slowed to a shuffling crawl. When Stryke's vision cleared he made out what was happening.

Jennesta and Dynahla were engaged in a duel of sorcery. They were battering each other with shafts of energy. Both had hands raised, palms outward, their faces rigid masks of concentration. The beams of magical vigour they generated pulsed with coloured light; primarily scarlet in Jennesta's case, green in Dynahla's, though other, subtler hues swirled within them. A sulphurous aroma began to fill the air, and the beams gave off blasts of heat.

One of the sorceress' human zombie slaves, a Wolverine axe buried in his back, staggered into range of the alluring stream. Lurching forward, he came into contact with it. He immediately ignited, a sheet of orange flame quickly spreading to cover his entire body. Blazing head to foot, moaning pathetically, the creature was consumed, collapsing into a heap of ash and yellowed bones.

Dynahla was sweating freely. Jennesta wore an expression of extreme attentiveness. The rich tints of the energy they threw at each other grew more vivid and the heat given off increased. All those looking on remained mesmerised.

Still maintaining her magical defence, Jennesta raised a hand and made a gesture. Some of her followers started to move, sluggishly. She repeated the signal with an angry insistence. This time they all responded. Stryke thought they were about to resume the fight, and readied himself. Instead they disengaged and swiftly pulled back. Wary of what might happen next, he motioned his band to do likewise. They obeyed and came to him.

The two sides were soon apart, the space between littered with Jennesta's dead and wounded. Stryke's glance flicked left and right, checking the Wolverines. They were all panting from the exertion of combat. Several had injuries, a couple of them harsh, but none seemed dire.

As if by unspoken agreement, Jennesta and Dynahla simultaneously ceased their clash. The beams snapped out of existence, leaving trace-lines on the eyes of all those watching. Jennesta let out a sigh and looked drained. Dynahla was exhausted. For a second or two his features blurred and flickered, before settling back to their familiar form. He swayed, and might have fallen if Jup and Noskaa hadn't taken hold of his arms and steadied him.

There was movement in Jennesta's ranks. Gleaton-Rouk and his clan were withdrawing to the rear. The human zombies lumbered after them, along with the enchanted orcs and the smattering of other races from her diverse horde who were still standing. They kept going, and were lost to the night.

Stryke suspected a ploy, reasoning that they might be circling to attack from another direction. But moments passed and it seemed they had retreated altogether.

Jennesta and her human troopers remained, with Thirzarr fixed at the sorceress' side. Stryke resolved to order a charge, seize his mate and put an end to the charade.

He noticed that Jennesta was holding something. At first, it was hard to tell what it was in the poor light. Then he realised she was slotting together the duplicate set of instrumentalities.

Their eyes met. Jennesta smiled.

Stryke cried out Thirzarr's name and lunged forward.

The last star clicked into place.

Jennesta and her force disappeared.

19

Pelli Madayar's intuitive sense, a natural receptiveness sharpened by years of training, detected a certain disturbance in the ether. She had no doubt what it meant.

The Gateway Corps unit was at sea, pursuing its objective. Pelli left her cabin and sought out her second-in-command, the goblin Weevan-Jirst. She found him amidships, alone at the rail, standing stiffly. He wore a severe expression.

'There's been a transition,' she told him.

'Really,' he replied without turning to look at her.

'Yes, and by all indications it's Jennesta, using her counterfeit set of instrumentalities.'

'And what would you have us do about it?'

'Do? Follow her, of course.'

'What about the orcs, and retrieving the artefacts *they* have? Wasn't that supposed to be our mission?'

'There's a difference. The Wolverines' possession of instrumentalities is dangerous, I don't deny that. But there's no sign that they're using them maliciously. Jennesta, on the other hand, has evil intent. I judge her the greater threat. We can deal with the orcs after we settle with her.'

Now he did tear his eyes from the star-speckled night sky and looked at her. 'What does Karrell Revers have to say about all this?'

That was something she had hoped he wouldn't ask. 'I haven't communicated with him about it.'

'Why?'

'There were practical problems.'

'Ah, yes. The loss of the crystal.' He was referring to the most direct and reliable method of contacting headquarters.

Pelli had told him, after flinging the crystal overboard in a moment of anger, that it had been lost. Which was true in a way. 'Yes,' she answered, holding his gaze.

'But there are other means of communicating with our commander.'

'Yes,' she repeated.

'Means which you alone can exercise, as possessor of the highest magical skills among those of us present.'

There was something about Weevan-Jirst's tone that made Pelli wonder, for the first time, if he could be envious of her. In reply, she simply nodded.

'Since you . . . mislaid the crystal,' the goblin went on, 'it would seem we must fall back on your talents to contact Revers.'

'If we *were* to commune with him, yes we would.'

'What do you mean?' the goblin hissed.

'I see no need to seek his guidance in this matter.'

'*I* do. Moreover I demand my right as second-in-command to speak with him myself, as laid out in the Corps' constitution.'

'Those same rules state that the commander of a unit such as this has complete discretion when it comes to operational decisions.'

'So you are denying my rights.'

'Only your right to constantly question my leadership,' Pelli came back irritably. 'And we won't achieve our goal if we keep pulling in different directions.' She took a breath, softened and went for conciliatory. 'Look, we have our disagreements, but we both want this mission to succeed. Can't we put aside our differences and go forward in that spirit?'

'It seems I have little choice.' Reading a goblin's mood was hard at the best of times, but it didn't take an expert to tell Weevan-Jirst was disgruntled. 'Though I want to record my misgivings about the course you are set upon,' he added.

'Officially noted. For my part, I pledge that we'll turn our full attention to the orcs just as soon as we've sorted out the Jennesta situation.'

'I will have to abide by that decision,' he replied sniffily. 'My only wish is to end this fiasco.'

'Believe me, the sorceress poses a far greater threat than anything the Wolverines might do.'

'I hope you are right, for all our sakes.'

*

The Wolverines stared at the place where Jennesta and her followers had been.

Jup broke the silence. 'What do we do now?'

'We go after her,' Dynahla replied.

'Can we?' Stryke said, snapping out of his daze. 'You know where they've gone?'

'Not specifically. But I can follow the trail.'

'So let's do it!' Coilla chimed in.

There was a murmur of agreement from the band.

'All right,' Stryke said. 'What does it take, Dynahla?'

'Hold on. If we pursue Jennesta there's no saying where we might end up. What about Dallog and the others on the ship?'

'We could always leave 'em there,' Haskeer muttered.

Wheam appeared shocked.

Stryke gave his sergeant a hard look. 'We'll get back to the ship. That means a delay. Will this trail you spoke about go cold, Dynahla?'

'We should be all right for a little while. Though of course the longer we leave it the further away Jennesta could be from the spot where she fetched up.'

'Or she could have moved on to another world altogether,' Spurral offered.

The shape-changer shrugged. 'Quite possible.'

'Could you still track her if she did that?' Stryke said.

'Maybe. Providing we don't delay too long.'

'Let's move it then. We'll make for the ship at the double.'

The journey back to the shore was punishing. But they made it in good time, and as they dragged their boats from the undergrowth, dawn was breaking.

Back on board the ship, Stryke briefed Dallog, the other tyros and Standeven about what had happened. He got Dallog to bind the wounded. Then he ordered the grunts to gather all the weapons and provisions they could carry, and to be quick about it.

As they were finishing the chore, one of the privates cried out and pointed. Three ships were moving away from the far end of the island and heading out to sea. They were unmistakably goblin vessels.

'That has to be Gleaton-Rouk and his crew,' Coilla said.

'And no doubt Jennesta's collection of zombies,' Pepperdyne added.

'Do we go after them?'

'No, Coilla,' Stryke replied. 'It's Jennesta I want, and Thirzarr.'

'Jennesta's force was bigger, wasn't it?'

'Yeah,' Pepperdyne agreed. 'Apart from making common cause with the goblin, she seems to be recruiting. There were all sorts in that camp.'

'Why would anybody want to serve her?' Jup wondered.

'The promise of power, a chance for riches, or just for the hell of it,' Stryke said. 'Maybe they're even under an enchantment, like her zombies. Who knows?'

'Those zombie orcs were less than . . . right, weren't they? I mean, they wouldn't be, given they were under a hex, but even so they lacked some vital spark.'

'You can bet she's working on that.'

'We're wasting time here, Stryke,' Dynahla said.

'You're right.' He beckoned the band and they drew together. 'Let's do it.'

'I'll need your set of instrumentalities.'

Stryke cast the shape-shifter a wary look. 'I'm happier holding onto them.'

'Haven't I proved myself yet?

'Well . . .'

'I can see that I haven't.

'It's not that I don't trust you, it's just—'

'I understand. But it's going to be really hard manipulating them through you, especially if it has to be done fast. You've *got* to trust me or this won't work.'

Stryke struggled with that for a moment. Then he reached into his belt pouch, took out the stars, and after a second's hesitation, handed them over.

'Thank you,' Dynahla said. He began slotting them together with impressive dexterity.

At the edge of the group, Standeven watched with covetous eyes.

'What's to stop Jennesta messing with where we land?' Coilla asked. 'The way she did before.'

Dynahla paused. '*I* am. I can counter that. At least to some extent.'

He carried on readying the instrumentalities, until just one remained to be fitted. 'Brace yourselves.'

The band moved closer. Wheam put on a brave face. Spurral reached for Jup's calloused hand. Standeven looked terrified.

'We don't know what we're letting ourselves in for,' Stryke told them. 'So no matter how bad the crossing is we've got to be ready to fight the instant we arrive . . . wherever.' He nodded at Dynahla.

The fetch clipped the last star into place.

No matter how often they made a crossing, and for all their indifference to fear, they found the experience profoundly disturbing.

Having endured what felt like an endless, dizzying drop down a well made of multicoloured lights, they met hard solidity.

Most of the band were shaken but ready to fight. Some, principally Standeven, Wheam and a couple of the tyros, were less composed. But even they, ashen-faced and nauseous, were quickly if unsteadily on their feet.

They stood on a flat, bleak plain. A sharp wind blew, stirring up a grey substance, more like ash than soil or sand, that covered the ground. Here and there, great slabs of black rock jutted out of it. The rocks seemed to be vitrified, as though some unimaginable heat had melted them, making them flow like liquid before cooling.

Above, the sky had a dour, greenish tint. The sun, a sickly red, looked no bigger than a coin held at arm's length. It was cold, and the air was bad, not unlike the way it stank when a thousand funeral pyres had been lit after a battle.

There was no sign of Jennesta's force, or any other living thing, including trees, vegetation or animals.

On the horizon there was something that looked like a city. Even in the weak sunlight it appeared to be crystalline. But it was wrong. Many of its numerous towers were truncated, resembling broken teeth, or leaned at crazy angles.

The band gaped at it.

It took Haskeer to mouth what they were all thinking. 'Where the *fuck* are we?'

'Somewhere pretty damn grim,' Coilla said, buttoning her jerkin against the chill.

'It doesn't matter where we are,' Stryke told them. 'The point is, where's Jennesta? Dynahla, you sure you haven't brought us to the wrong place?'

'No. She's here.'

'Any idea where, exactly?'

'From my own abilities, no. The psychic charge here is too . . . *murky* to be specific. But that seems the obvious place.' He nodded towards the city.

Stryke gave the order and they headed its way.

It was a much longer march than it first appeared, making them realise how large the city really was, and the ashen terrain was hard going underfoot. But the powdery blanket turned out to have one advantage. When they were about halfway to their destination, as far as they could judge, they spotted tracks in it. They led in the direction of the city.

'Human,' Jup announced, kneeling by them, 'and more than one set. Has to be her.'

Stryke nodded. 'Let's keep moving. And eyes peeled.'

They trudged on, warily.

Before they reached the city the tracks petered out, erased by the wind. But they had no doubt of their destination.

Shortly after, they arrived at the outskirts. Even before it fell into ruin it would have been like no place of habitation they had ever seen. Much of its architecture was inexplicable to them. There were sleek structures lacking doors or windows, buildings in the shape of spirals or cubes, or crowned with pyramids. The remains of one edifice was smothered in strange decorative symbols. Another took the form of a cone, its angles so acute that nobody could possibly have lived in it. They saw the remnants of signs in a completely incomprehensible language, if it was a language, and toppled objects that might have been statues, except they were insanely abstract. And when they looked closer, and ran their fingers over walls and pillars and fallen cornices, they discovered they were fashioned from no materials they knew.

For as far as they could see, the city was deserted, and in ruins. The evidence of decay was everywhere, with crumbling walls, cracks spider-webbing buildings and fissures disfiguring the avenues. But there were signs of more violent destruction, too, in the form of ragged apertures, sheered spires and pockmarks that looked as though they had been made by incredibly powerful projectiles. Charred debris and unmistakable traces of smoke damage in some areas showed that flames had played their part.

'This place makes no sense,' Spurral said. 'What kind of creatures could have lived here?'

'And what put an end to them?' Jup wondered.

'A war?' Dallog speculated. 'Or nature rising up and turning on them with an earthquake, or—'

'Could have been the gods,' Gleadeg reckoned darkly, 'upset in some way.'

'No point trying to figure it,' Stryke said. 'Let's keep to why we're here.'

Coilla cupped her eyes and scanned the scene. 'It's vast. Where do we go?'

Stryke turned to Jup. 'How do you feel about trying farsight?'

'Sure.' He got down on his knees and wormed his hand into the ash. Eyes closed, he stayed that way for a moment. 'Bugger that!' He leapt up, waving his hand about as though it had been burnt.

'What is it?' Spurral asked anxiously.

'The energy's fouled. It's even worse than Maras-Dantia.'

'You all right?'

'Yeah.' He took a breath, calming himself. 'Yeah, I think so.'

'Whatever happened here, the magic or weapons used, has tainted this place,' Dynahla said.

'Don't suppose you got a hint of anything, did you, Jup?' Stryke wondered.

'Not a thing. Sorry, chief.'

Haskeer elbowed his way to the front. 'So what now, Stryke?'

'We'll form squads and start searching.'

'That'll take for ever.'

'You got a better idea?'

'*Stryke*,' Coilla said.

'What?'

She pointed at a jumble of half-collapsed buildings. 'I saw something move.'

'Sure?'

'Yeah.'

'I think I did too,' Pepperdyne added.

'Weapons,' Stryke ordered. They all drew their blades and he led them towards the sighting.

Moving guardedly, they reached the spot. There was nothing to be seen except devastation. They rooted around a bit in the rubble, but fruitlessly.

'You two are imagining things,' Haskeer grumbled, glaring at Coilla and Pepperdyne.

'I don't think so,' Coilla replied evenly.

'Ssshhh!' Jup waved them into silence and nodded at an area a little farther along, where heaps of clutter were shrouded in darkness.

Faint noises were coming from it. Scratching and rustling, and the sound of rubble being dislodged.

Stryke at their head, the band quietly moved forward. Again, they found nothing, and the sounds had stopped. But they noticed a narrow passageway, formed by the sides of two adjacent buildings, and at its end there was a faint light. They entered it. As they walked the passage the light grew stronger. When they emerged at its far end, they saw its source.

They came out to an open space that might originally have been some kind of public square. It was strewn with junk, and the scene was illuminated by a number of fires scattered about the place. The flames threw shadows on the walls of the surrounding buildings left standing.

'Where the hell's Jennesta?' Coilla complained.

'She's here somewhere,' Dynahla assured her. 'You can count on it.'

'What I don't get,' Pepperdyne said, 'is why these fires haven't burnt out long since. What's to feed them?'

'I'm more concerned with whatever *that* is,' Stryke told him. He was staring straight ahead.

A shape crept out of the dark at the far end of the wrecked plaza. As it moved into the flickering light they got a better look. It wasn't Jennesta or one of her followers, as they half expected. It was a beast. But of a kind they had never encountered before.

At first sight, some thought it was feline, others canine. In fact, the creature seemed to be a blend of both, and in several respects it was almost insectoid. Standing about waist-high to an orc, it had six legs, ending in lengthy, horn-like talons. Its pelt was a yellowish-brown.

The brute's head resembled a lion's, except it lacked a mane and had a much more extended snout. There was a wide, fang-filled mouth, and instead of two eyes there were six, ruby red.

The band remained stock still, watching the thing, braced for an attack. But although it seemed aware of them, its interest was elsewhere. Letting out a throaty snort, it made its way to the biggest of the fires. Then, to the orcs' astonishment, it thrust its head into the flames and began lapping at them.

'My gods,' Coilla exclaimed, 'it's drinking the fire.'

'How can that be?' Jup said.

'Anything's possible in an infinite number of worlds,' Dynahla told them.

Two more of the animals came out of the shadows. Joining the first, they too gulped the flames, the trio snapping and snarling at each other as though squabbling over a kill.

Haskeer looked on in stupefaction. 'They must have hides tough as steel.'

'Let's hope not,' Pepperdyne said.

His wish was pertinent. Having supped their fill, the creatures turned their attention to the band. Their multiple crimson eyes held a malignant intensity.

Coilla went 'Uh-uh'.

The fire-eaters charged.

One of them, in the lead, opened its massive jaws and belched a plume of flame. The orcs in its path scattered, narrowly avoiding a roasting.

'Now we know what keeps the fires going,' Coilla said. 'They do!'

She and Pepperdyne leapt aside to avoid another creature that singled them out. It swerved and, spitting fire, galloped after the fleeing pair. They made for one of the ruined buildings bordering the square.

Stryke and Haskeer barely dodged incineration from the beast targeting them. The flame it spewed flew over their ducked heads and seared a nearby wall. They set to weaving about the creature and harassing it as best they could. Jup and Spurral joined them, along with Hystykk and Gleadeg.

The rest of the band was tackling the third fire-breather, their greater number allowing them to surround it. They were attacking from a distance, employing arrows and spears, though many of their projectiles bounced off its hardened skin, and they had to retreat periodically as it spat gouts of flame.

To no one's great surprise, Standeven didn't get involved. He scurried off to cower behind a pile of masonry slabs.

Adding to the confusion, a fourth creature turned up and darted towards the fray. Dallog spotted it and shouted an order. He and the tyros, Wheam, Chuss, Keick and Pirrak, peeled off and ran to meet it.

Stryke and his crew were making progress in frustrating their opponent if not actually overcoming it. When it turned away from them and loped off they thought it had been beaten. But it stopped at the nearest fire, supped there, and came back at them.

'The fire doesn't last!' Stryke yelled. 'They have to renew it!'

They knew what to do. Jup, Spurral and the two grunts moved to block the creature's access to the replenishing fires. After that it was a case of staying out of its way and landing blows when they could. Before long, the beast exhausted its flame. Its fangs and claws meant it was still a formidable challenge, but a less dangerous one. They moved in on it, hacking with their blades. A swing from Stryke sliced across the brawny chest, causing the head to dip, and Haskeer brought his axe down on its skull, cracking it open. The creature collapsed and lay twitching, tiny puffs of flame huffing from its nostrils.

'The bastards can stick their faces in fire but they ain't unkillable,' Haskeer announced triumphantly.

The band members fighting the second beast had also noticed that it needed to refresh its flame and followed the example of Stryke's group. They were busy parting its head from its writhing body with a series of brutal strokes.

As they all rushed to aid Dallog and the tyros with their kill, Stryke looked around. 'Anybody see where Coilla and Pepperdyne went?'

Jup shook his head.

Running full pelt, the heat from the fire-breather practically scorching their backs, Coilla and Pepperdyne found an open doorway. Open but two-thirds blocked. Urgency sharpening their agility, they managed to wriggle through. The bulky creature got its head and part of its upper body in but struggled furiously to get any further. It vented its fury with blasts of flame. They quickly retreated into the building and only just avoided them.

The interior was a complete shambles. But there was some light other than that coming from the fire-breather. It came from a small opening, possibly a window, set about halfway up the far wall. A sloping mound of rubble that had probably come in through the aperture made a natural ramp leading to it.

'Think we could get through that?' Pepperdyne asked.

Coilla nodded. 'It'd be tight, but yeah, I think so.'

The creature gave another blast that lit up the room. It afforded a brief glimpse of the chaos and some of the strange objects strewn about, which could have been the remains of curiously designed furniture.

'So let's get out of here,' she urged.

'Hang on.'

Above the door, and over the probing creature's head, was a large quantity of wreckage, including blocks of something like stone. All that supported it was a couple of uprights. To Pepperdyne, the whole thing looked tenuous.

Coilla followed his gaze and guessed what was on his mind. 'If you're thinking what I *think* you're thinking that could bring the whole place down on us.'

'I reckon we could get away with it.'

'Why bother when we can just get out through that?' She jabbed a thumb at the window.

'It wouldn't solve the problem. What's to stop this monster circling round and waiting for us outside?'

Coilla weighed the odds. 'All right. Let's do it.'

'Good. You climb up to the window and I'll take care of it.'

'No way. We're doing this together.'

'It won't take two of us. Look at the state of those uprights. One good kick and—'

'I'm not some helpless female, Jode, and don't you *dare* treat me like one!'

Regardless of their plight he almost laughed. 'I'd never make the mistake of seeing you *that* way, Coilla. It's just practical. If something goes wrong we'd both be in trouble. Better one of us is clear to help if needed.'

The creature at the door grew more frantic. It sent in another sheet of flame.

She nodded. 'You take care, mind.' Then she edged her way to the pile of rubble and started scrabbling up it.

Pepperdyne waited until she reached the window and called, 'Can we get through?'

'Yeah,' she replied, 'I'm pretty sure we can.'

He turned back to the door. To reach the uprights he had to get nearer to the furious creature than he liked. He considered pelting them with chunks of debris, but knew that wouldn't do the job. So he started sliding towards them on his back, legs first. When he got as close as he dared, he gave one of the supports a hefty kick. It let out a loud snap and fell away. Crab-like, Pepperdyne hastily retreated. But nothing happened. It was obvious that the other upright was the only thing holding up the tremendous weight above the door.

The frenzied creature was still trying to force itself into the too small opening, and let out a further gush of flame. It didn't reach Pepperdyne, but he felt the heat through the soles of his boots. He shuffled forward again, aiming for the remaining prop. A powerful kick had no effect on it, so he pounded at it with his foot. The repeated impacts started to tell. A creaking sound came every time he hit it, and the post started to shake.

The upright suddenly gave with a resounding crack. Pepperdyne rolled aside, his hands instinctively covering his face. The debris collapsed with a thunderous roar. Tons of wreckage came down on the creature's head and upper body, instantly crushing it to pulp and disgorging its sticky, green life fluid.

The whole structure didn't cave in, as they feared it might, but a cloud of dust filled the room.

'You all right, Jode?' Coilla shouted anxiously.

He didn't answer right away, and when he did it was only after a coughing fit and having to spit the muck out of his mouth. 'I'm . . . fine.'

Getting to his feet, he climbed up the rubble slope, taking Coilla's outstretched hand. She pulled him the last few steps and they squeezed out of the window. There was just a short drop to the ground.

They found their way back to the square without much trouble.

The rest of the band was there, along with the bloody corpses of the fire-breathers. Standeven had come out of hiding and looked on pasty-faced.

'Been off for a spot of canoodling?' Haskeer taunted, raising a ragged laugh from some of the grunts.

Coilla and Pepperdyne ignored him.

'I was about to send a search party for you two,' Stryke said.

'We're all right,' Coilla told him. 'Any sign of Jennesta?'

'No.' He shot a critical glance Dynahla's way. 'I'm starting to think—'

Right on cue, one of the privates yelled, *'Over there!'*

They all turned. At the far end of the square, near the point where the creatures had emerged, stood a group of figures. Jennesta was at the forefront, and Thirzarr could be made out beside her.

Stryke began running towards them, the band close behind. He called out to Thirzarr.

Jennesta's hands moved. She and her force vanished.

'I think we saw that coming,' Coilla remarked, arriving at Stryke's side.

'Dynahla!' he bellowed.

The shape-changer had the instrumentalities out and was manipulating them. Swiftly, the band gathered together.

'Here we go again,' Jup said.

Dynahla slapped the final star into place and their surroundings disappeared.

20

They came to a place quite unlike the one they had just left.

It was pleasantly mild. The air was clear, the sky blue, the terrain green and abundant.

They were on high ground. A pastoral scene was spread out before them. Rolling hills, lush grassland, copses, forests, a placid lake, and the distant sparkle of a meandering river. Meadows and hedged fields were evidence of cultivation, but there was no sign of buildings. However, there was a well-made road, surfaced with compacted earth. In one direction it ran straight and open for as far as they could see. In the other it soon came to a bend at woodland and disappeared.

'Where's the bitch got to now?' Haskeer grumbled as he surveyed the landscape. Pointedly, he didn't ask the question of Dynahla.

'Out there somewhere, I guess.' Stryke swept a hand at the panorama.

'Not that I can see,' Jup said, 'and her group should be big enough to spot.'

'The logical thing for her to have done was take the road,' Pepperdyne suggested. 'That way, towards the bend.'

Coilla nodded. 'And a good place for an ambush.'

'Then we'll round it with care,' Stryke said. 'Come on.'

The march wasn't welcomed by everybody. Many of them were still drained and aching from the fight with the fire-breathers, in a world that seemed impossibly far away. Which, of course, it was.

Standeven wasn't pleased either, though his discomfort came from a lifetime of indolence rather than anything as strenuous as fighting, or as dangerous. Abandoning his usual place near the rear of the group, he wormed his way to Pepperdyne who walked alone, Coilla being occupied with Stryke at the front.

'Oh,' Pepperdyne said on seeing him, 'it's you.'

'Yes, me. Your master and title-holder, though you seem to have forgotten it.'

'You just can't get it through your head, can you? None of that means anything anymore. It's a whole different game now.'

'It might be to you. I happen to think a pledge still means something.'

'Do you have any idea how ridiculous your blend of conceit and acting pitiable makes you look?'

'There was a time when you wouldn't have dared to say a thing like that.'

Pepperdyne's patience was running out. 'Why are we talking? What do you want, Standeven?'

'I want to know how much longer this . . . *charade*'s going to last.'

'Charade?'

'This leaping from one stinking place to another, of course.'

'This world doesn't look too bad to me. If you're so tired of what's going on why don't you settle here?'

'Oh, you'd like that, wouldn't you? Anyway, unless we're careful we might all end up being left somewhere we don't want to be.'

'Meaning?'

Standeven nodded at Dynahla, walking at the head of the column with Stryke and Coilla. 'You really think that freak can be trusted?'

That echoed Pepperdyne's own doubts, but there was no way he was going to admit it to this man. 'Seems to me Dynahla's done more for this band than you ever did.'

'Enough to be handed the instrumentalities?'

'It always comes back to that with you, doesn't it? Stryke knows what he's doing.'

'Does he? Whatever you think about me, Jode, I'm not insane. I want to get out of this mess alive as much as you do. If you think Stryke's going the right way about that, it's on your own head.' He said no more, and let Pepperdyne walk on.

They were approaching the bend in the road. Stryke halted the column and sent four scouts ahead. He told four more to cut through the lip of the wood, in case there were any unpleasant surprises lurking in there. They soon returned with word that the way was clear. The band resumed its march.

The road took several other turns, although none were blind, until it curved round the base of a hill, obscuring whatever lay beyond. Taking no chances, they left the road and climbed to the hill's summit. Looking down to the far side, they saw a lone building in the middle distance.

It wasn't a farmhouse, as they might have expected. Seemingly made of stone, it more closely resembled a chateau or small castle. There was a low, round tower at each corner, and a large entrance with its doors wide open. Given its rustic setting it looked strangely incongruous.

Some figures could just about be seen moving around in front of the building. Beyond the fact that they walked upright and appeared to be dressed in white, they were too far away for any more details to be made out.

'Signs of life at last,' Coilla said.

'Yeah,' Stryke replied. 'I wonder what kind.'

They moved down the hill, crossed the road bordering its foot and headed over the grassland.

'Sheathe your weapons but keep them handy,' Stryke ordered. 'We don't want to scare them off if they're not hostile.'

'They look peaceable enough,' Spurral reckoned.

'If they are, maybe they'll be able to tell us where Jennesta is.'

'You think she could be there, and Thirzarr?'

He shrugged.

'Keep your resolve, Stryke. We'll find your mate.'

'Maybe.'

As the band approached, they were spotted by the white-clad beings, who simply stopped whatever they were doing and stared. They didn't seem perturbed by the sight of an orc warband, a couple of dwarfs and several humans arriving out of nowhere.

When the Wolverines were close enough they finally got a good look at the creatures.

'They're human.' The way Coilla said it expressed the surprise most of the band was feeling.

'Why shouldn't they be?' Dynahla asked. 'In an infinite number of worlds—'

'Yeah, I know. Anything's possible. I just wasn't expecting it.'

There were five of them, and the striking thing was how alike they were. All were male, if slightly androgynous in appearance, tall, slim and blond. They were ivory skinned and beardless. Their attire was identical, consisting of a white, smock-like garment covering them from neck to ankles. But their arms, and oddly their feet, were bare. By human standards they were handsome. Some would have said beautiful. From the expressions on their smiling faces their dispositions might have been called sunny.

'Humans grinning like fucking idiots,' Haskeer grated dourly, 'that's all we need.'

'Something's not right here,' Pepperdyne said.

'Your race smiles,' Coilla told him. 'I'm sure I saw you doing it once.'

'What I mean is not all humans look exactly the same.'

'You do to most orcs.'

'I'm serious, Coilla. This bunch are peas in a pod. It's not natural.'

Standeven had gravitated to Pepperdyne's side again. He was looking troubled as well.

Coilla noticed it. 'What's the matter with you two? Jode?'

'There's something about them. I don't know. Something . . . familiar.'

Standeven nodded in agreement, his gaze fixed on the supposed humans.

Stryke went ahead of the others, hand raised in a conciliatory gesture, and addressed the nearest being in Mutual. 'We've come to you in peace.'

'Peace,' the creature repeated, his smile unfaltering.

'Yes. We don't want anything of you.'

'You want nothing,' one of the others said.

Stryke looked to him. 'Right. Except to ask a question.'

'A question?' That came from the third of the creatures.

Before Stryke could reply, the fourth said, 'What question?'

'Er . . . we want to know if another group's passed this way.'

'Another group, you say,' the fifth remarked.

Stryke was getting perplexed, but he was determined to persist. 'A party led by a female who looks kind of . . . odd.'

'Odd?' the second, or possibly the third, echoed.

'You would have noticed her,' Stryke persisted.

'Would we?' the first asked.

'This is *weird*,' Jup muttered.

The irritating exchange continued, with Stryke trying to get some sense out of the creatures and not knowing which one would answer next.

Finally his patience snapped and he bellowed, *'Look! It's simple! Have you or have you not seen any other strangers today?'*

The reply came from all of them sequentially, their smiles never wavering.

'Strangers . . .'

'. . . are . . .'

'. . . never . . .'

'. . . welcome . . .'

'. . . here.'

Then something startling happened. As one, they all unfolded a massive set of wings, hidden until now. The wings were pure white and seemed to be constituted of downy feathers.

'An angelic host,' Standeven whispered, awestruck.

Coilla looked at him, then noticed that Pepperdyne appeared nearly as beguiled. 'What?' she said.

He tore his eyes from the sight. 'They mean something to my race. Particularly to Unis and the like.'

'Good or bad?'

'Oh, good,' Standeven said. 'The *epitome* of goodness, we're told.'

'Well, I think you've been told wrong. Or these things are something different. Look again.'

The comely, benevolent faces of the winged beings were twisting into snarling, hate-filled grimaces. Their jaws dropped, revealing mouths full of razor-sharp incisors. Their eyes, soft and as blue as the sky an instant before, turned into inky black orbs set in scarlet. And as their faces turned nasty, so did they.

They shot into the air in unison, their powerful wings flapping mightily. For a moment they circled overhead, and the band saw that they had produced concealed weapons; gold-coloured maces studded with barbs. Then they dived.

The orcs with shields held them above their heads. They swiped at the tormenting creatures with their blades and axes, but couldn't connect. Arrows were loosed and proved no match for the flyers' agility. Again and again they swooped down, menacing the Wolverines with their maces.

Stryke knew that if the band didn't find cover they were certain to lose the fight. He waited until the flying things were at their highest point preparatory to diving again. *'To the house!'* he yelled. *'To the house!'*

They made for the doors at full pelt, desperately trying to outrun creatures that were potentially much faster. Coilla and Pepperdyne, through some act of instinctive charity, grabbed Standeven's arms from either side and dragged the wheezing human along. For all the band knew there were more of the things inside, but it was a chance they had to take. There was no other shelter.

Getting to the house a heartbeat ahead of the flyers they hurled themselves through. They flung their weight behind the doors and slammed them shut. There was the satisfying sound of at least one flying creature crashing into the woodwork on the other side.

Panting from the effort, and with Standeven fit to have a seizure, the band took a moment to catch their breath.

Recovering, they looked around. They were in a long, high, stone-clad corridor, with several doors on either side and a set of much larger ones at its end. The side doors led to windowless rooms or dead-end passages, so they made for the double doors. Kicking them open they found a spacious chamber, perhaps a banqueting room, wood panelled and hung with weighty candelabra. At its far end, and to the right, there was a further, wide corridor running off at an angle.

'Now what do we do?' Dallog wanted to know.

'I guess we start by seeing if there's another way out,' Stryke replied.

'And if there ain't?' Haskeer said.

'There will be. Or we'll make one.'

'*Stryke*,' Dynahla said, urgency in his voice.

'What is it?'

'I feel a presence.'

'Her?'

'Has to be.' The shape-changer pointed to the corridor. 'That way.'

They rushed to it.

It was ill-lit, and long, but some way down it there was a crowd of figures. Jennesta was among them. She saw the band. Fiddling with the objects in her hands, she and her pack blinked out of existence.

Dynahla dug out the instrumentalities, and at a nod from Stryke, slapped them together.

The Wolverines materialised in a swamp, knee deep in warm, stinking water. Waist deep in the case of the dwarfs. The air was humid and uncomfortable. There were countless flies, causing the orcs to slap at their exposed flesh. Small, unidentified creatures zigzagged through the water. All about them was a green gloom, thanks to a canopy of vegetation high above their heads.

Haskeer smacked the side of his neck, crushing an insect. 'This is not an improvement.'

'So where in damnations is Jennesta now?' Coilla complained.

'Yeah, there's no trace of her,' Wheam said. 'How come she isn't right where we land every time?'

'We don't always arrive in exactly the same place as someone else who's made a transition,' Dynahla explained. 'That's partly down to me, because it's hard to be accurate. But it's mostly a function of the instrumentalities.'

'So she could be anywhere,' Coilla said.

Dynahla shook his head. 'No. We always arrive within a certain radius. She's here, and not far.' He looked around. 'The question is where.'

'You seem to know an awful lot about the stars.'

'Serapheim was a good teacher. He taught me that—'

'Can we talk about this some other time?' Stryke interrupted.

'So where to, chief?' Jup said.

'There's a patch of drier ground over there. That's where we'll start.'

They waded to it, and found it was the tail end of a much longer strip of land, muddy and tangled with roots, but preferable to the foul water. The band was glad to haul themselves onto it.

'*Now* what?' Coilla wanted to know.

'We could follow this spit of land and see where it takes us,' Stryke said.

'Bit hit or miss, isn't it?'

'Yeah.' He turned to Dynahla. 'Can you feel anything?'

'What I'm getting is confused,' the fetch confessed. 'It's not clear enough to pinpoint her.'

Stryke sighed. 'Great.'

'But there's another way I might be able to help.'

'Do it, whatever it is.'

'All right. Here.' He took out the instrumentalities and handed them to him. 'Best you take care of these until I get back.'

'Get back?'

'I'm going to use my shape-changing ability to scout the area. Any objections?'

'Er . . . no.'

'Then give me some room.'

The band stepped back.

Dynahla got down on the ground and stretched out. He began to change. His writhing body compressed and elongated simultaneously. The arms and legs drew in and disappeared. The flesh turned black as it redistributed itself and stretched into a long, cylindrical shape, a tapering tail at one end, a smooth, hairless head at the other. Shiny scales appeared along its whole length.

Seconds later an enormous water snake regarded them with unblinking, golden eyes, a forked tongue flicking from its lipless mouth. It turned, slid into the water and disappeared.

The silence that followed was finally broken when Jup said, 'That was . . . bizarre.'

They waited, exchanging whispered thoughts about what Dynahla had just done, looking out for an ambush and swatting flies.

Before long there was a disturbance in the water. The snake surfaced and slithered ashore. Immediately, the reversion to Dynahla's original form took place. At its completion he was on his hands and knees, head down, wet hair hanging lankly. He shook off droplets of water, not unlike a dog, and stood.

'That way,' he stated simply, pointing out across the water. 'Not far. On another plot of dry land. Well, drier.'

'You all right? Coilla asked.

He nodded. 'Transformation can drain me, particularly the more extreme ones. I'm fine.'

'Up to moving again?' Stryke said.

'Yes.'

'Then you'd better have these.' He held out the instrumentalities.

Dynahla seemed taken aback. He accepted them and half whispered, 'Thank you.'

Everyone collected their gear and they set off, with the shapeshifter and Stryke in the lead.

When they neared their destination, as signalled by the fetch, they tried to move as quietly as they could given they were practically swimming. Even so, when rounding a vast outcrop of foliage they came upon Jennesta's party almost unexpectedly.

The two sides spotted each other at the same time. A couple of arrows winged the band's way. Taking cover in the thick vegetation, they returned fire. The exchange grew heavier, the enemy's arrows zinging through the greenery all around the Wolverines, and theirs flying back.

One of Jennesta's archers was bold enough, or foolish enough, to let himself be seen as he made to loose a shot. An orc arrow smacked square to his chest and he toppled into the water. It stirred, rippled and churned as the scavengers living in it were drawn to blood and set to devouring his corpse.

Jennesta herself took a hand, lobbing a searing fireball the warband's way. Dynahla deflected it and sent her one of his own. Jennesta swept it aside.

The duel was short-lived. Jennesta employed the stars and her force was gone.

Dynahla quickly checked that everybody was together and did what was necessary to follow.

'She is taking the piss!' Haskeer raged.

They were on a tundra, an immense, glassy plain covered in ice. The only feature to be made out was a black mountain range straddling the horizon.

Snow was falling, a bitter wind blew, and the band, still wet through from the swamp, felt the cold to their bones.

'There!' a grunt yelled, his breath jetting like steam.

Jennesta and her henchmen could just be seen, actually not too far away but almost obscured by the driving snow. Stryke thought he caught a glimpse of Thirzarr.

'After 'em!' he shouted over the storm. *'Before they—'*

The sorceress and her followers became one with nothingness.
'*Shit!*' Jup cursed.
'*Dynahla!*' Stryke bellowed.
'I'm on it!'
The band took a leap to somewhere other.

They were in semi-darkness.
It took a moment for them to realise they were underground, what little light there was coming from a myriad of tiny crystals embedded in the walls of a large cavern.
Pepperdyne knew Coilla was less than keen on confined spaces, and he gave her hand a supportive squeeze.
A number of tunnels ran off from the chamber they were in.
'What the fuck way do we go?' Haskeer demanded.
'*Ssshhh!*' Spurral held a finger to her lips.
He was about to badmouth her when he realised what the others had already heard. Echoing sounds, like footfalls.
'*That* way!' Keick bawled.
They ran for a tunnel with a larger entrance than the others.
It was long, and twisting, and the clatter of their boots bounced off the walls like a hailstorm.
They came out in another, even bigger cave, resembling a scaled-down canyon. A subterranean river ran through, with a wall-hugging ledge running round it. Where it reached the far side it widened to a natural platform, a great slab of yellowish rock. Jennesta and her horde stood there. But not for long.
'Not *again*!' Spurral exclaimed.
Dynahla applied the remedy.

At first they thought they were back in the world of the malicious angels.
It was temperate and their surroundings were not unpleasant, but it was a scrubbier, less verdant scene. There was grass, though it was patchy, and trees that could have been fuller. They could see modest, whitish-grey cliffs in the distance.
The band stood on a road, more accurately a trail, wide and well trod. Their prey was nowhere to be seen.
'Listen,' Coilla said. 'What's that sound?'

21

'Drums,' Jup said, tilting his head to one side and listening intently. 'And getting nearer.'

'Not just drums,' Pepperdyne added. 'Can anybody else hear horn blasts?'

They could. And Jup was right; the noise was growing louder. Soon, they could make out rhythmic chanting and the tramp of marching feet mixed into the din.

'An army?' Dallog wondered.

'It's an undisciplined one if it is, making that much of a racket,' Stryke said. 'But whatever it is there's a lot of them. Best to get out of sight.'

At the side of the road there was a row of substantial boulders. The band concealed themselves behind them as the sounds increased.

'Can anybody understand what they're chanting?' Coilla asked.

'There's more than one language in it,' Spurral said. 'A hell of a lot more.'

'Damned if I can make sense of it,' Jup admitted.

'Watch out!' Dallog warned. 'Here they come!'

There was a bend a little way along the road. A number of figures were rounding it. The band recognised them immediately.

'Elves?' Coilla said. 'It's not like them to raise such a clamour, is it?'

'It's not just elves,' Pepperdyne told her, nodding at the road.

The elves, twenty or thirty strong, may have been leading the mob but they were by no means representative of it. Right behind them came a herd of centaurs, trotting in pairs, many of them holding long silver trumpets to their lips. An ogre followed, wearing a harness. It was acting as a guide to a line of trolls, their eyes bound against the hated light, who clasped two thick ropes extending from the harness.

Next came a company of swaggering goblins. After that, the races were more or less mixed together. Gnomes walked with satyrs, dwarfs with kobolds. Humans strode alongside bands of dancing, tambourine-twirling pixies. Brownies accompanied gremlins and leprechauns. There were howlers, hobgoblins, harpies, fauns, chimeras and giggling nymphs. Swarms of fairies, mouth-watering to the orcs, fluttered above the horde. There were many other species the Wolverines didn't recognise, mammalian, insectoid, reptilian and unclassifiable.

While most walked, slithered, hopped or flew, some rode, on carts, horses, lizards and giant fowl. Wagons bobbed along in the mass carrying tanks that housed water-going creatures such as merz and river sprites. Flags and banners were waved. Musical instruments were blown, pounded and plucked over the babble of a hundred tongues. The throng was many thousands strong and the noise was deafening.

'There are races down there who never get along,' Coilla said, 'at least on Maras-Dantia.'

'This isn't Maras-Dantia,' Dynahla reminded her.

'Could have sworn I saw orcs,' Haskeer blurted, shocked at the notion.

'Why not? Anything's possible—'

'In an infinite number of worlds,' Coilla finished for him. 'Yeah, we get it.'

The shape-changer didn't take offence. In fact he smiled.

More and more creatures flowed past, over-spilling the road.

'What the hell's going on here?' Jup wondered. He had a thought. 'Could this be something to do with that bunch who were following us? That Gateway Corps?'

'No, this is something else,' Dynahla assured him. 'And if the Corps were following you, they still will be.'

'Oh good, something else to worry about.' He turned to Stryke. 'We haven't a hope of finding Jennesta in this lot. Where do you think they're going?'

'There's one way to find out. Join 'em.'

'Why not? We'd hardly stand out in a mob like this.'

Stryke had to shout so they could all hear over the tumult. 'If we have to get out of here fast, with the stars I mean, we need to keep together! So stay close or risk being left behind in this madhouse!' He noticed his sergeant eyeing a cloud of fairies. 'And Haskeer! Don't eat anything.'

They left their hiding place and, staying close, elbowed their way into the procession. The crowd was good natured about it. They looked passionate but apparently they weren't hostile. For the band that made a change.

The flow of bodies swept them along. The movement, the noise, the swirl of colours and the smell, of incense and excrement, was near overwhelming. What they could see of the terrain beyond the press of flesh was unremarkable and more or less unvarying. It didn't look cultivated, or even inhabited, consisting mostly of scrubland, a scattering of trees and the road. Always the road.

Some of the band, principally Coilla and Jup, tried to engage fellow marchers in conversation. But they got little out of them beyond grunts, and what sounded like exaltations, as far as they could tell above the uproar.

Dynahla, walking beside Stryke, shouted into his ear. 'I think this is a crossroads world!'

'A what?'

'*A crossroads world.* Not all travel between worlds is purposeful, using the instrumentalities,' he explained, articulating as clearly as he could. 'Sometimes there are worlds that have wormholes that beings fall through from all over. By chance, I mean.'

'I remember Serapheim saying something about Maras-Dantia once being like that. Which is why there were so many races there.'

The shape-changer nodded. 'And I think these —' he indicated the throng they were part of '—may be pilgrims, and this is some kind of religious festival.'

'Could be,' Stryke conceded.

'The question is, what could have united such a mixture of beings?'

The road was on the rise, and they were starting to climb, but it was still impossible to see what their destination might be. Stryke looked back, and with the advantage of the extra height caught a glimpse of the multitude of beings following behind. They seemed endless.

He wondered how the hell he came to be here.

Dynahla touched his arm and pointed. The road had taken a turn, and now they could see a tall hill, or possibly a mountain. On its summit stood a building. It looked like a fortress. On second thought, it might have been a temple. Then again, it wasn't like that at all.

Pelli Madayar stood amongst the ruins of the crystal city. Weevan-Jirst was at her side, the rest of the Corps unit spread about them. The never-ending wind blew in from the plain, bringing a constant swirl of grey ash like fine snow. It all but obscured the feeble light of the ailing red sun.

'She was here,' Pelli asserted. 'The traces leave no doubt.'

'And not just her,' the goblin replied. 'It seems the warband was here too.'

'Yes, it does.'

'We abandon our search for the orcs to follow Jennesta and find ourselves back on the orcs' trail after all. Is that not ironic?' There was an element of smugness in his manner.

At least he didn't say *I told you so*, she thought. But she was damned if she was going to apologise. 'You could say it was an example of unintended consequences having a positive outcome. As the two set of instrumentalities chase each other, we are on the trail of both. I call that an economic use of our resources. Anyway, I've said all along that if we found one group we'd find the other.'

'How very fortunate for you that blind luck should be so obliging.'

She ignored the jibe. 'We've learnt something else. The Wolverines aren't just world-hopping at random. They're moving with a purpose. So either they've suddenly taught themselves mastery of the instrumentalities, which is unlikely to say the least, or somebody or something is aiding them. Not just that. We know Jennesta tampered with the orcs' set and had a measure of control over them. That appears to no longer be the case. Whatever help they have is countering her influence, at least to some extent.'

'Yet another player. This is getting complicated. I would have said that if you were willing to contact Karrell Revers, now would be the time to request that another unit be put into the field. We could obviously use some help.'

'We're quite capable of dealing with this ourselves. *I'm* competent to deal with it.' She hoped that came across with more confidence than she was feeling.

'If you say so.'

There was a stirring in the ruins. A bulky shape came out of the darkness. When it moved into the watery light it was revealed as one of the six-legged, multi-eyed fire-breathers. It came towards them, snorting orange flame.

Casually, Pelli raised a hand, palm outwards, and sent an energy pulse its way. The purple beam struck the beast and converted it into a cloud of minute fragments. They were instantly scattered by the persistent wind.

She felt a little ashamed of herself for slaying the creature. It was an act of pique, and in any event it couldn't have harmed them as they were wrapped in a protective shield of enchantment.

'What do you think happened here, Weevan-Jirst?' she asked, as much to cool the mood between them as anything else.

'Who can say? I assume a conflict of some kind, given that all life forms seem intent on destruction.'

'That's a pessimistic view.'

'It is one I have formed through experience and observation. Wherever there is life, it courts death.'

'What about the Corps? We use force only when we have to, and for the good.'

'As you just did?' He nodded towards the spot the disintegrated fire-breather had occupied a moment before.

She had no answer to that, but granted, 'Perhaps we do all have a primitive brute lurking below the surface, no matter how civilised our veneer. But surely that's an argument for the Corps and anybody else that tries to bring some order and justice to bear?'

'How does that square with your sympathy for the orcs? They can hardly be called a constructive force.'

'It's in their nature to be combative.'

'The same could be said of the creature you just killed.'

'I've no more affection for the orcs than any other sentient race, and no more hostility either. As I said, my interest is in justice, and my gut feeling is that they're somebody's pawns in all this.'

'How can you cast a species that lives for war on the same level as those that strive for tolerance?'

'I thought you said all life forms were capable of death-dealing? Aren't you contradicting yourself?'

'Some try to control their impulses more than others.'

'I've never met a race yet, no matter how savage, that wasn't ultimately capable of some degree of compassion. Why should orcs be an exception?'

'Their actions speak for them.'

'With respect, the goblin folk don't exactly have an untarnished reputation themselves. No doubt you'd argue that it's unjustified, and your membership of the Corps is testament to that. But that's my point. Everything isn't black and white, as you seem to believe. Life's messy. We do our best.'

Weevan-Jirst didn't answer. He just maintained the inscrutable expression common to his kind.

She looked around, saw the broken towers, the mountains of wreckage and the desolation of a wasted world. 'You know what I think? Suppose what happened here came about through an inter-world conflict, because somebody who shouldn't have got hold of a set of instrumentalities. I'm not saying it did, but it's possible, isn't it? In any case it can stand as an example of the kind of thing that can happen if we fail. I think that makes it a fitting reminder of our purpose. So let's do our job, shall we?'

'I've never wanted anything else.'

'Then it's time to continue the hunt.'

22

The nearer the Wolverines were carried up to the structure on the hilltop the larger they realised it was.

It had the look of having been refashioned and expanded over generations, each leaving their own mark by adding whatever architectural mode happened to be favoured at the time. The result was a curious hybrid of styles. Much of it was white stone. But there were sections coloured red or black, and extensions made of timber. It had a central needle-shaped spire, and onion domes embellished with gold decorations. There were a number of towers of various heights and different contours. An assortment of windows studded the many walls, some with tinted glass, jostling for space with balconies. Flying buttresses helped hold the whole affair together.

As the crowd climbed, so did their excitement. The chanting reached a new pitch, the drums beat louder, the horns grew more shrill.

When the band finally reached the massive plateau that stretched out in front of the building they found a scrum of beings.

'What do we do now that we're up here, Stryke?' Coilla asked.

'Go in, I guess.' He looked over his shoulder at the mass pressing in from behind. 'We've no choice.'

'Yeah, but take a look at the entrance. They're only letting in small numbers at a time.'

She was right. At the great curved doorway stood a group of brown-robed figures. Their cowls were up and their features obscured, so it was impossible to see what kind of beings they were, beyond basically humanoid. They were strictly marshalling the flow. One of them, in distinctive blue robes, seemed to be a superior of some kind, issuing orders. From time to time he disappeared inside, presumably to gauge the situation.

'Not much chance of us all staying together while they're doing that,' Jup said.

'Why don't we rush 'em and blag our way in?' Haskeer suggested with typical forthrightness.

'I think we need something a bit more subtle,' Stryke decided.

'I can help,' Dynahla said.

'How?'

He explained.

Stryke nodded. 'It's worth a try.'

'We need to get closer then.'

The Wolverines barged their way to near the front of the queue. That strained the otherwise good-natured spirit of the crowd somewhat, but nobody made too much of a fuss. Once in place, close to the entrance, they waited until the supervisor entered the building.

'Now, quickly!' Dynahla said.

The band gathered round and hid him from view. Seconds later they parted, revealing a duplicate of the blue-robed official. Then they elbowed their way to the door with him.

Their worry was that, not knowing the language the custodians of the entrance were using, the ruse would be exposed. In that event Stryke was considering doing what Haskeer suggested and forcing their way in, and damn the consequences. He'd gamble on the crowd being pacifistic enough not to put up too much opposition.

When the band got to the entrance, several of the brown-robed beings looked askance at their elder appearing from the crowd when he had apparently just entered the building behind them. Dynahla countered that, and the communication problem, by employing some robust sign language whose meaning was universal. After a bout of arm-waving, pointing and fist-making the cowed doorkeepers stepped aside to let the Wolverines in.

Once inside, the band surrounded the shape-shifter again and he emerged in his normal guise.

'That's a really handy skill,' Jup said admiringly.

'Thanks,' Dynahla replied, stretching after the transformation. 'It seemed almost too easy.'

'And it could have been,' Stryke warned. 'So stay alert.'

They took in their surroundings. There were plenty of beings present, but given that entry was strictly controlled it wasn't jam-packed.

The interior was opulent. Everything was white, pink and black marble, highly polished. The walls were lavishly decorated with frescos, tapestries and velvet hangings. Way above, the ceiling was likewise ornate, and tall columns soared on every side. Light streamed in through elaborate stained-glass windows.

They saw that there was a similarly large door at the far end of the great hall they were standing in, with lines of pilgrims filing out.

'That explains something,' Coilla said. 'I was wondering why we didn't see anybody coming *down* the mountain. That must exit to a road on the other side.'

'Looks like we're supposed to go this way,' Jup told them.

Silken ropes threaded between stanchions channelled the faithful into a corridor that proved as splendid as the hall they had just left. It was lined with friezes depicting what they assumed were fables of some kind. In truth they didn't take much notice. Their attention was on the chamber the corridor led to, at the heart of the building.

Again, it was marble, although compared to the entrance hall it was austere. Yet somehow that made it more impressive. There were no windows; the light came from a profusion of candles, and from several massive chandeliers. Nor was there any furniture or ornamentation of any kind. The air was heavy with incense, issuing from a pair of heavy brass burners suspended by silver chains.

In the centre of the room was a large sarcophagus, also of marble, set on a podium. A dozen or so beings of diverse race were clustered about it, some on their knees. The tomb itself was topped by a life-sized statue. They approached it.

'A human?' Haskeer exclaimed, causing heads to turn. 'All this in aid of a bloody *human*?'

So it seemed. The statue was the likeness of a human in his prime, a male of perhaps thirty summers. He was tall, and lean rather than muscular. Dressed simply in trews, high buckled boots and a shirt slashed open to the waist, he cut a dashing figure. He wore a form of headgear, something between a helm and a cap, and he held a sword in his raised right hand.

'There's an inscription,' Coilla said, bending to it.

They crowded round.

'"The Liberator",' she read out. 'And there's a name . . . "Tomhunter."'

'Tomhunter-tomhunter-tomhunter,' Spurral recited. '*That's* what the crowd was chanting.'

'They've got some really stupid names, those humans,' Prooq sniggered.

Hystykk grinned. 'You said it.'

Gleadeg, Nep and Chuss agreed. They elbowed each other's ribs and snorted in derision.

Pepperdyne and Standeven had a slightly different view. The former was mildly amused, the latter looked indignant.

'What the fuck did this Tomhunter do to deserve all this?' Haskeer thundered.

'Let's find out,' Stryke said. He spotted a young elf standing alone nearby, gazing respectfully at the statue, and collared him. 'So what's the story behind this Tomhunter then?'

The elf looked bewildered, and not a little shocked. 'What?'

'This place.' Stryke indicated their surroundings with a sweep of his arm. 'What's it about?'

'You don't know?'

'No.'

'*Really?*'

'No. We're . . . er . . . new converts.'

'You don't know about the Selarompian wars or the revolution in Gimff?'

'No.'

'The Rectarus Settlement or the battle of the Last Pass?'

'Not really.'

'Or the—'

'Just imagine we don't know anything, all right?'

'So why are you here?'

'To learn.' He jabbed a thumb at the statue. 'Tell us about this Tomhunter.'

'The Liberator? The all-conquering redeemer? The most revered being in the history of civilisation?'

'Yeah, him.'

'If you truly don't know the fabled story of Tomhunter, blessed be his name, then I envy you. To hear the tale of his exploits for the first time is an experience that will transform your lives and stay with you for ever.'

'So tell us,' Stryke said through gritted teeth.

'There was a solitary incident that, once you know it, will illuminate the character of this martyr, this saint, this paragon of all that is noble and benevolent.'

'*Which was . . . ?*'

'The single most magnificent, heroic, selfless act he performed, the one feat that enshrined his memory in the hearts of everybody for all time was—'

An arrow zipped between them, narrowly missing both their heads. It struck the tomb, bounced off and clattered on the marble floor.

'*Attack!*' Haskeer bellowed.

A bunch of Jennesta's thugs had entered the chamber, five or six of them, and two were aiming their bows.

'*Take cover!*' Stryke yelled, shoving the terrified elf to the ground.

The band scampered to the other side of the tomb, using it as a shield. Several more arrows clanged against it. The band began returning fire.

There was panic among the pilgrims. Those who weren't hugging the floor were running for the exit. Shouts and screams rang out, appeals to the Liberator filled the air. The mayhem could be heard spreading with the fleeing believers, to the corridor outside and into the grand entrance hall.

When Jennesta's group had spent their arrows, Stryke led a charge against them. The enemy turned and fled, the Wolverines on their heels. They dashed along the passageway and into the entrance hall, then headed across it, bowling over any adherents too slow to get out of the way.

Coilla pointed. 'They're making for the exit!'

'*Move it!*' Stryke urged the band.

They put on a spurt, Standeven plodding along at the rear, panting heavily. Their quarry, knocking aside all in their path, got to the back door and scooted out. At the forefront of the band, Stryke, Coilla and Pepperdyne were the next through. A brace of arrows came near to parting their hair and they ducked back in.

'Did you see her out there?' Pepperdyne asked. 'Jennesta?'

Stryke nodded. 'I thought I saw Thirzarr, too. Ready to try again?'

They were.

Moving fast and low, they tumbled out, weapons drawn. There was a paved area there, similar to the one at the front of the mausoleum, and scores of pilgrims were stretched out on it, hands and paws covering their heads, prostrate with dread. To the right, near the downward path and no more than a dagger's lob away, stood Jennesta and her clique, Stryke's mate amongst them.

But even as the band dashed to them, they were gone.

'*Shit!*' Stryke raged.

As Dynahla made ready to transport the Wolverines yet again, Coilla muttered, 'It was never like this in Ceragan.'

Things had never been quite like this in Ceragan.

As mere hatchlings, Janch and Corb hadn't been told what was going on. But they knew something wasn't right.

They couldn't help but be aware that certain of the adults were no longer to be seen in the settlement, but nobody would tell them where they had gone. Corb, the eldest, suspected that no one knew; and his sibling had picked up the general mood of unease even if he couldn't articulate it. As their own parents had departed to they-knew-not-where, their father willingly, their mother taken, they found this new development particularly unsettling.

Quoll, the clan's chieftain, seemed to find it hard to deal with too. Not that he would have let on, especially to a pair as young as Corb and Janch. What he couldn't hide was that he, along with the elders and soothsayers who advised him, seemed at a loss, despite their many congresses and evocations of the gods.

Now Quoll was trying another tack. In an admission that the mystery had become a threat, he dispensed with counsel and summoned the tribe's remaining able warriors. In effect that meant all barring the very old and the lame, and youngsters yet to wield a sword in anger. Corb and Janch, consigned to the care of this group, had slipped away and were loitering near the longhouse where the parley was due to take place.

They seated themselves on a stack of firewood and watched as everyone went in. Barrels of ale and flagons of wine were brought to oil the proceedings, and several whole game, steaming from the spit, to keep bellies from rumbling. Never lacking a sense of the theatrical, Quoll arrived last, accompanied by his closest attendants. He appeared drawn and uncharacteristically deflated.

He noticed the hatchlings and slowed, and for a moment they thought they were going to get a dressing-down. But he just looked, an expression on his face they weren't worldly-wise enough to read. Then he carried on and entered the hut.

The brothers stayed where they were, despite evening drawing in and the air cooling. Perhaps they hoped the adults would come out and miraculously have some kind of answer about what had happened to their sire and their mother.

They could hear the murmur of voices from the longhouse, and occasionally they were raised. With the distorted time sense peculiar to the very young, it seemed to them that they sat there for a very long time. Janch began to grow fractious. Corb was getting bored and thinking of their beds.

There was a commotion inside. It was different to the usual sounds of dispute they were used to when orcs got together to discuss anything. This was an uproar directed at a common object, rather than a disagreement among themselves. The furore was attended by thumps and crashes, as though furniture was being flung about. It reached a pitch and stopped dead. The silence that followed was more disturbing.

It didn't occur to them to run and hide. Even in ones so young that wasn't the orcs' way. Nevertheless, Corb hesitated for long moments. Finally he stood, and Janch did too. Puffing out his chest, he walked towards the hut, his perplexed brother beside him.

There was another brief wavering at the longhouse's only door. Corb took out the scaled-down axe Haskeer had given him, and Janch produced his own, which stiffened their resolve. Corb went on tip-toe to reach the handle, turned it and gave the door a shove. It swung open and they peered inside.

The interior was empty. A long, solid table was askew. Chairs were overturned. Scraps of food and tankards littered the floor. The windows were still shuttered.

An odour hung in the air, which if they could have named it they would have called sulphurous.

*

These were strange days in Acurial.

Nobody really knew what was responsible, despite a glut of theories, and the not knowing was breeding mistrust and something close to fear. It was a toxic combination for the new, still fragile order.

Brelan and Chillder, twin rulers, were coming away from the latest occurrence. They'd tried to keep it a secret, like all the others, but rumour and hearsay were more fleet than any clampdown they could hope to impose. The incidents had increased to the point where concealment was not only near impossible but probably counter-productive, given the twins' espousal of openness. But whether the truth was preferable to speculation was a moot point.

This time it had happened near the outskirts of Taress, the capital city. Twenty-three orcs of all ranks had gone, from a mess hall in an army camp originally built by the Peczan occupiers. It had followed the now familiar pattern. No warning. No hint as to how the victims could be spirited away from a confined space in a supposedly secure area. No obvious similarities as to who had been taken, except that they were militia. No real signs of violence, beyond a small amount of disorder. No one left to tell the tale.

To give themselves space to think, away from eavesdroppers and questioning gazes, the twins had taken a walk along the semi-rural roads.

'We'll have to announce a state of emergency,' Brelan said. 'Impose martial law.'

'You know I've got doubts about that,' his sister argued. 'It'd only cause alarm, and maybe start a panic.'

'The citizens have a right to protect themselves.'

'How? We can't do that now. The *military* can't protect themselves. What chance would the ordinary orc on the street have? I say we inform them rather than do anything draconian.'

'And you think *that* wouldn't cause a panic? Let them know what's going on, yes, but back it with troops on the streets, a curfew, checkpoints and—'

'That smacks of the occupation days.'

'It's for their own good.'

'Which sounds like the kind of language Peczan used to justify their oppression.'

'We're not Peczan.'

'Of course we're not. But it's a matter of how we're *seen*. Don't forget that our race has finally regained its combative spirit. Give the wrong impression and we could risk another uprising, against us this time. You're overlooking the political dimension to this.'

'Gods, Chillder, is that what we've come to? Thinking like damn politicians?'

'Like it or not, it's what we are. All we can hope to do is be a different kind. The sort that puts the citizens before self-interest.'

'I wonder if that's how all politicians start out. You know, with good intentions that get corrupted by power and expediency.'

'Our mother didn't go that way. And we're not going to.'

'I can't wait for us to set up the citizens' committees. Give the ordinary folk a say, spread the load and the decision-making.'

'Yes, well, that's going to have problems of its own no doubt, though I'm with you on it. But there's no benefit in going over that now. We've a more pressing concern.'

'Which we're no nearer solving.'

'Look, it's the militia that's taking the brunt of . . . whatever it is that's happening. I'm right in saying that, aren't I? There have been no civilian disappearances?'

'As far as we know. It's difficult to be sure, mind.'

'Let's assume that's the case and beef up security for the military even more.'

'How?'

'Some kind of buddy system maybe, with one unit keeping an eye on another unit.'

'And who keeps an eye on *them*?'

'Or we get all military personnel to check in at really short, regular intervals. Or have them all eat and sleep in the open, in plain sight. Or . . . whatever. My point is that it shouldn't be beyond our wit to come up with safeguards.'

'Measures like that would cripple the army. How effective a fighting force would they be, if we needed them, under those sort of restraints? Not to mention we'd be a laughing stock, and that's hardly going to reassure the populace.'

'What, then?'

'A state of emergency is all I can think of. Even though you're right: it's not the ideal solution.'

'It's not a solution at all, Brelan.' She let her frustration show and added irately, 'If only we knew *what* was doing this!'

'You mean who. It still seems to me that Peczan's behind it, somehow.'

'We've been through that. How could they be? And I don't buy the idea that they have agents among our own kind.'

He sighed. 'Neither do I. Look, I need to think. Would you mind making your own way back? I'd like to linger here for just a while.'

'If you say so. You'll be all right?'

'Course I will. I'll see you later.'

They had walked quite a way as they talked, and were now on what was essentially a country road. There were hardly any houses to be seen, and the nearest was almost out of sight. Open fields stretched from both sides of the road. There wasn't much else except a sluggish stream and the occasional stand of trees. Brelan took himself to the edge of one of the fields and stood looking out across it. Chillder gave him a last glance and set off towards where they'd come from, lost in her own thoughts.

She didn't know what it was that made her stop, just a short way along the road. It wasn't a sound, it was a feeling. She turned.

Brelan was nowhere to be seen. Chillder stayed where she was for a moment, expecting to see him reappear. He didn't, and she began walking back. Then she broke into a run.

When she arrived at the spot where she had left her brother, there was no sign. She scanned the fields on either side of the road, but saw nothing. There was no shelter of any kind, certainly nothing near enough for him to have reached in so short a time. It occurred to her that he might have set off across the field for some reason and fallen into the long grass. But she knew how unlikely that was. She called his name, and got no reply. Again she yelled, louder, with her hands on either side of her mouth, and kept on calling.

A chill was creeping up her spine. And she noticed something in the air, an odour both familiar and forbidding.

The feeling she had experienced as she was walking away returned. She couldn't put in words what it was, but it was no less tangible for that. An awful oppression fell upon her, and her head was starting to swim. She felt faint and slightly nauseous. Her surroundings seemed to blur and she was unsteady on her feet. She tried to fight it.

It was no use.

Darkness took her.

23

The Wolverines landed with a splash.

They were in water, a great deal of it, and it was salty in their mouths.

'We're in a damn ocean!' Jup yelled.

'There's the shore!' Pepperdyne pointed to a sandy beach a short distance away.

Stryke looked around at the bobbing heads of the band and did a quick count. 'Where's Standeven?'

'Shit!' Pepperdyne exclaimed. 'He can't swim.'

'The gods are being kind to us at last,' Haskeer said.

'I can't let him drown.'

'Why not?'

Pepperdyne took a gulp of air and disappeared beneath the waves. The rest of them trod water.

He seemed an awfully long time reappearing and Coilla was getting worried. She was about to dive herself when two heads broke the surface a little way off. Pepperdyne had hold of Standeven, who was blue in the face and gasping for breath. Jode hauled him to the band, where others lent a hand, most reluctantly. They all made for the shore.

'There's something in the water!' somebody shouted.

Behind them, but moving in their direction fast, was the blur of a large and scaly creature, its spiked head and a sail-like fin dimly visible through the mist. The band increased their speed, and soon their feet touched bottom.

They staggered onto the beach and moved as far up it as they could, dragging Standeven with them until they dumped him. But the creature didn't come ashore, perhaps couldn't, and stayed out in deeper water, cruising back and forth.

'I thought you said the stars couldn't land us somewhere that might kill us, Dynahla,' Stryke complained angrily.

'No, I didn't. I said they couldn't take us somewhere that *would* kill us. If they eliminated all possibility of danger they wouldn't take us anywhere.'

Stryke snorted. 'Yeah, well . . .' He looked about the place. They had jogged almost to a white cliff-face that backed the beach. Apart from a few patches of dull vegetation, there wasn't much else to see. 'Where do you think we are?'

'Could we be back on the world of islands?' Spurral wondered.

'No,' Coilla told her. 'That had two moons. This has two suns.'

She was right, but they had to look hard to see the pair of dim globes through the milky white cloud that dominated the sky.

'So where's Jennesta this time?' Wheam asked, tipping water from the innards of his precious lute. They were all surprised it had survived intact this long.

'She's close,' Dynahla replied, 'as always.'

'Any clue where?' Stryke said.

'Not exactly, no. But does it matter?'

'Does it matter? *Of course* it matters!'

'No, you don't get my meaning. We don't need to know precisely where she is because she'll soon pop up where we can see her. She's playing with us.'

'I think we worked that out,' Haskeer remarked sourly.

'Yeah, it's all a game to her,' Spurral added.

'Maybe,' the shape-shifter conceded. 'Though her motives could be more than just mischievous.'

Stryke eyed him quizzically. 'Such as?'

'Who knows? Perhaps this *is* all for the hell of it. Even I find her hard to fathom.'

'Even you? What makes you such an expert on Jennesta?'

Dynahla hesitated for just a second before answering. 'I've spent a lot of time with her father, remember, and Serapheim's . . . very informative.'

'Heads up!' Jup yelled. 'There she is, right on cue.' He indicated the headland at the end of the beach, a decent arrow shot away.

A group of figures were there. They stayed long enough to be seen, then vanished.

'Do we have to follow her, Stryke?' Dallog said. 'I mean, if this is some kind of crazy game, do we have to play along with it?'

'What choice do we have? And what about Thirzarr? You want me to abandon her?' He glared at him.

'No . . .' The elderly corporal looked abashed. 'No, of course not, chief.'

'Do what you have to, shape-changer,' Stryke ordered.

Dynahla worked on the instrumentalities.

'If I could just get my hands on that bitch . . .' Haskeer muttered, staring at the spot where Jennesta had been a moment before.

'You'd have to stand in line,' Coilla said.

They materialised in night-time, which would have been a lot blacker if it wasn't for a big, full moon and a sky crammed with stars.

There was nothing special about the landscape as far as they could make out. Underfoot was rough grass, there were some ghostly trees in the middle distance and what could have been a mountain range at the limit of their vision. The temperature was balmy and the air dry, with no wind to speak of. Which was fortunate as they were all wringing wet.

Standeven, still huffing and wheezing after his dip, had plonked down on the ground. They let him be.

'So where is she?' Haskeer said, anticipating Jennesta's appearance with his sword drawn.

'Hard to see anything,' Coilla replied.

Breggin pointed into the gloom. 'What's that?'

They all strained to see. A cluster of shapes, darker than the night, appeared to be coming their way.

'Right,' Haskeer declared. 'This time we don't wait for her to call the shots.' He began to run in that direction.

'Wait!' Stryke called after him. 'There's no point! She'll only . . . Oh, what the hell.'

The others seemed to share Stryke's opinion, or else they were tired enough by now not to give a damn. None of them followed Haskeer.

As they watched him dashing nearer to his goal they expected the group of shapes to flick out of existence. Given the distance and bad light, it was near impossible to make out what did happen, but it wasn't that. The figures remained, and he seemed to engage with them.

'Do you think she's actually staying for a fight this time?' Coilla said.

Jup raised his staff. 'If she is, let's get over there!'

The band was all for it, and they were about to rush into the fray.

'Hold it!' Stryke barked. 'Looks like Haskeer's coming back.'

He was, at speed, and the figures were right behind him. As they got nearer, the band noticed something odd.

Spurral blinked at the scene. 'Are they running on all fours?'

'And they look bigger than humans,' Pepperdyne added.

'Ah,' Jup said.

Haskeer arrived, arms pumping, breathing hard. Half a dozen fully grown brown bears were chasing him.

It was one of those times when the band instinctively fell back on their training and experience, and they'd dealt with plenty of wild animals in their time. They immediately formed a defensive ring. Blades and spears thrust out, they began shouting and beating their shields. The bears' charge slowed right down, and they took to circling the band from a distance, looking for a weakness in their defence.

'Toche! Vobe! Your bows!' Stryke instructed.

They nocked arrows and he pointed to the biggest of the brutes, which was rearing up on its hind legs. Both arrows struck true. The shafts jutting from its chest, the bear fell, rolled on its side and was still. Its companions let out howls and quickly withdrew. But not completely. They resumed their circling from afar, dimly visible in the dark, still hoping for a chance to attack.

'Must be hungry,' Noskaa observed.

'Lucky they didn't bite a chunk out of Haskeer's fat arse,' Jup said. That raised a laugh. 'They would have spat it out, mind.' The grunts roared.

Most of them stopped when they saw Haskeer's face.

Stryke wasn't overjoyed himself. 'Eyes front! They're still out there.'

'*Something*'s out there, Captain,' Gant said, nodding at the gloom.

He was right, and it wasn't the bears, which by some means, quite probably magical, had been scared off. What was in the dark now came as no surprise to any of them. They knew the sound of her mocking laughter well enough.

Dynahla got to work on the instrumentalities.

Rain pounded down on them. A bitter wind was blowing. Thunder rumbled and lightning flashed.

'Oh, great,' Coilla grumbled. 'Another soaking.'

It was difficult to see what kind of place they were in through the downpour. Wherever it was, it was awash, with flowing water ankle deep. The ground seemed to be bedrock, in all probability any topsoil and vegetation having been washed away.

A chunk of tree and a couple of dead fish floated past.

Stryke wondered if it always rained here. As if in reply, the furious black sky opened up and dumped even more rain on them.

He got the band to search the immediate area for shelter, but there was nothing, so they huddled together miserably for a while, uncertain what to do next and getting wetter.

Then they became aware of a purplish glow in the deluge. It grew stronger, until they saw that it was Jennesta, dry inside a bubble of ethereal energy. A protection she hadn't extended to her soaked retinue, including the comatose Thirzarr. It was an act of casual meanness that enraged Stryke almost more than anything else the sorceress had done. Even though he knew it was futile, he snatched a bow from one of the grunts and sent an arrow Jennesta's way. The force field vaporised it.

As he thrust the bow back into the grunt's hand, she and her followers vanished.

The Wolverines followed.

They were somewhere high. Dizzyingly high.

It was the top of a building that seemed to be impossibly tall, and the view it afforded was startling. As far as they could see in all directions the landscape was completely urbanised. There were other towers just as tall, and a number even taller than the one they stood on. Looking down, they saw nothing but buildings, jam-packed together, of every conceivable shape and design, and many with an appearance they couldn't have imagined.

Highways sliced through the gigantic metropolis, and wove over and under each other, like strands of ribbon dropped at random by a wayward giant. The roads were host to numerous vehicles of a kind they couldn't identify, and they seemed to move without the aid of horses or oxen. The whole place was in motion and resembled nothing less than a gigantic ants' nest. Even from their great height the band could hear the distant, discordant sounds of it all.

More astonishing were the things that inhabited the sky. They weren't dragons, griffins, hippogryphs or any of the other airborne creatures a sensible being might expect. Some didn't even have wings, and they reflected glints of sunlight as they flew, as though, unfeasibly, they were made of metal or glass.

'This must be the billet of mighty wizards,' Wheam reckoned, awestruck.

'If it is they've built themselves a hellish place,' Stryke said, expressing the sentiment of them all. 'Who'd want to live so cut off from natural things? Where are the trees, the rivers, the blades of grass?'

'And where's Jennesta?' Coilla pitched in.

'I think she'd feel right at home in a hive like this. It's vileness would appeal to her.'

'But not enough, apparently,' Dynahla announced. 'She's left.'

'I won't be sorry to follow her this time.'

The place they turned up in would normally have struck them as either lacklustre or potentially hostile. Compared to where they had just been it felt welcoming.

It was a desert. Sand from horizon to horizon, broken only by occasional dunes. It was hot, but not unbearable, and there was even a gentle breath of wind. There didn't appear to be anything immediate that might threaten them.

'Everybody all right?' Stryke asked.

'I feel sick,' Wheam said.

'You would,' Haskeer came back.

Standeven didn't look too bright either, but he knew better than to complain.

Although they didn't know how fleeting their stay would be, the band took the chance to rest, and most sat or lay down on the fine sand. Stryke was content to let them.

Coilla found herself beside Dynahla, both of them a little apart from the others. It was an opportunity to ask him something she had been pondering.

'Tell me, does carrying the stars have any kind of effect on you?'

'What do you mean?'

'Well, they certainly did something to Stryke's mind once, and to Haskeer when he was close to them for a while.'

'Objects as powerful as these can have an influence on those exposed to them, particularly for long periods. They're not playthings, you know.'

'What kind of . . . influence?'

'Good or bad, depending on the nature and preparedness of the individual. I'm guessing that with Stryke and Haskeer it wasn't good.'

'Maybe strange would be a better word.'

'Each set of instrumentalities has its own signature. And because every set is unique, its effect will differ. But whoever possesses them will feel it strongly nevertheless.'

'But not you?'

'I'm trained to resist their negative power *and* to utilise the positive. And remember that Serapheim created this set.' He patted the pocket containing them. 'What better teacher can there be than their maker?'

'So they'd affect Jennesta too?'

'Oh yes. That's one of the reasons why her having a set is so dangerous. She would certainly prosper from their negative emanations. Although she has an ersatz set, of course, copied from these. I don't know if that would make a difference. It's almost unprecedented.'

'Thanks for telling me that. Though I can't say I understood it all.'

Dynahla smiled. 'The greatest adepts have never got to the bottom of all the instrumentalities' secrets, even Serapheim, and I certainly haven't.' He paused, and briefly closed his eyes. 'She's on the move again.'

'It amazes me that you can tell.'

'As I said, I've been trained.' He turned and called out, 'Stryke! Time to go!'

Stryke came over. 'Already?'

'Yes. I think things are going to take a slightly different turn now.'

'How would you know that?' he replied suspiciously.

'I'll explain later. Meanwhile—'

'Trust you. Yeah.'

He shouted an order and the band gathered round.

The crossing was the longest and most disquieting they had yet experienced.

They opened their eyes to a place like no other.

They were on an enormous, totally flat plain, devoid of any features. Above them, the sky was unvaryingly scarlet, with no clue as to where the light that bathed the scene came from. The ground they stood on was a uniform grey and of some unnatural substance. It was spongy underfoot. The only landmark was a distant, pure-white, box-shaped structure. It was hard to judge the scale of things, but the building looked vast. A tangy, sulphurous odour perfumed the air.

There was no one else in sight, least of all Jennesta and her minions.

'Where the *hell* are we?' Coilla whispered.

'What do you know about this, Dynahla?' Stryke demanded.

'Only that there was a good chance we'd end up here.'

'You *knew*? And you didn't think to tell us?'

'Only a chance, I said. It was by no means certain and—'

Stryke grabbed the shape-changer by the throat and thrust his face close. 'You'd better start telling us what you know about this place.'

'I can tell you that not everything here is real, but all of it can harm. And that nothing you've faced up to now compares with what you're about to be confronted with.'

24

'What the hell are you talking about?' Stryke demanded. 'Where are we?'

'It'd be easier to explain,' Dynahla rasped, 'if you let me draw a breath.'

Stryke had the shape-changer's collar bunched so tight it was crushing his windpipe. He grunted and let go.

'Thank you,' Dynahla said evenly, massaging his throat.

'So what *is* this place?'

'It has lots of names. The Barred Sector, the Proscribed Zone, the Perpetual Discontinuity . . .'

'Bugger what it's called,' Haskeer interjected. 'What's it *for*?'

'A long time ago, a *very* long time ago, it was . . . fashioned. A quartet of great adepts worked together to create it.'

'Why?' Stryke pressed.

'Its purpose isn't completely understood. But the story goes that the four fell out, and they built this environment as a place in which to settle their differences.'

'Like some kind of arena?' Pepperdyne said.

'Sort of, though it's more complex than that. We don't know the outcome of the battle the sorcerers fought here. They've long gone, but this zone remains, and it's potentially very dangerous. That's why it's off limits to those few capable of entering it.'

'Why are *we* here?' Stryke wanted to know.

'Serapheim brought us.'

'What for?'

'Because this is where he is.'

Stryke cast an eye over the strange terrain. 'I don't see him.'

'Well, it's . . . almost where he is.'

'You taking us for fools?' Haskeer growled menacingly. 'He's either here or he ain't.'

'Explain yourself, Dynahla,' Stryke said, 'in a way we'll understand.'

'Serapheim's done something similar to what the four wizards of old achieved here. He's built himself a pocket universe.'

'I said in a way we'd understand,' Stryke warned him.

'He used magic to create a private world, a secret retreat outside of time and space.'

'Why?'

'It keeps him alive. He's old, older than you'd believe, probably, and even he can't hold back the effects of ageing for ever. The world he's made cocoons him from the worst of growing old. It slows down the process.'

'How can that be?' Dallog interrupted, showing especial interest.

'As I said, his world exists apart from space and *time*. He can reduce the rate at which time passes. So although the conditions there can't make him immortal, they can help preserve his life.'

'I still don't get where he is,' Jup confessed. 'How can he be *almost* here?'

'It's more accurate to say we're almost where he is. Though, to be honest, it's a big almost.' Dynahla saw the looks on their faces and tried again. 'Serapheim piggybacked on this place when he built his pocket universe. He fused his magic with the magic here to attach his sphere to this one. Think of it as like putting a new wing on a house, or adding a tower to a fortress. The entrance to his domain is here, in this world. We just have to get to it.'

'How do we do that?'

'By always travelling north.'

Stryke took in their bizarre surroundings again. 'How do we know where north is?'

The shape-changer pointed to a spot just above the horizon. A speck of light hung there, brilliant as a diamond. 'The northern star. Not that north here is the same as north on Maras-Dantia, Ceragan or any other world.'

'My head's starting to hurt,' Coilla said. 'Is anything about this place normal?'

'You can die here.'

'That sounds like the kind of normal we know. What does the killing?'

'Almost anything; it's unpredictable. Things happen at random here. That's one of its properties, and why travel is so dangerous.'

'Why do we have to?' Pepperdyne wondered. 'Travel, I mean. Couldn't Serapheim have just taken us straight there, to this pocket universe of his?'

'No. Even with all his great powers he couldn't transport us directly to his world.'

'What's stopping him?'

'If it was easy to enter his world it wouldn't offer him much in the way of protection. We have to make our own way to its entrance.'

'Why should we?' Stryke said.

'Because Serapheim's your only salvation. If you want a chance to have a reckoning with Jennesta, and to help prevent the catastrophe she could bring down on all our heads, you need his aid. In any event we have no choice. The instrumentalities have been nullified. They won't work in this world.'

'We can't leave?'

'No. Even if we could, that wouldn't help you find Thirzarr, who's here somewhere, along with Jennesta.'

'I'll have them back then.' Stryke held out his hand.

Dynahla produced the stars and gave them to him.

Stryke put them into his belt pouch and made sure it was secure. 'Any other pearls of wisdom before we get going?'

'Only that whatever this world throws at us I'll do my best to help counter it. I know Serapheim will too, as much as he can.'

'We fend for ourselves. We don't lean on outsiders.'

'Of course. But try to have some faith in Serapheim.'

'Trust in a human. Yeah, right.'

'There's no question about it,' Pelli Madayar said, gazing at the endless expanse of desert, 'they were here, not long since. And now they've entered a prohibited sector: the Sphere of the Four.'

'*All* of them have gone there?' Weevan-Jirst replied.

'The Wolverines and Jennesta certainly have. There are indications others are migrating there too.'

'Others?'

'I think the sorceress is importing the rest of her army, and the recruits she gathered on the world of islands.'

'I had no idea she possessed the power to do that.'

'Her magic is extraordinarily potent, the more so when coupled with the strength of even a duplicate set of instrumentalities. But I don't think she's the only one bringing lifeforms in. There are signs of another force at work.'

'The situation is descending into chaos,' the goblin hissed. 'Unauthorised beings in a forbidden zone, armed with two sets of artefacts. Think of the havoc they could cause. This has become a crisis of the highest order.'

'It always was,' Pelli said. 'It just got messier.'

'It's more than we bargained for. Have you ever entered a prohibited sector?'

'No more than you have.'

'But like me you must be aware of the peril such a place holds.'

'Of course.'

'And the Sphere has a particularly unpleasant reputation.'

'I know.'

'Surely now is the time to consult Karrell Revers.'

'Later.'

'When? You *must* report this to him.'

'I will. But we're going to the Sphere first.'

25

The grey substance that passed for ground had a slight spring to it, and the crimson sky was unwavering.

The Wolverines found it difficult to judge their progress. There was too much uniformity in their surroundings, and no landmarks except for the white structure they were heading towards and the star hanging above it. The place was bright and uniformly lit, but they couldn't see where the light was coming from. They marched in silence.

Stryke turned to Coilla, walking beside him, and spoke in an undertone. 'Think we're doing right?'

'Do we have a choice?'

He shook his head. 'What about Dynahla?' The shape-changer was forging ahead, and out of earshot.

'Don't know. There always seems to be another twist to him.'

'Looks to me like we're being led a merry dance. You know I'd go to the end of this or any other world for Thirzarr, but . . .'

'But is following Dynahla the right way to go about it?'

'Yeah.'

'Again, what choice is there?'

Stryke sighed. He looked back at the column marching behind. 'I've been neglecting the tyros. I'll check on them.'

Coilla nodded, and he headed down the line.

Dallog and Pirrak were at the end of the column, several paces to the rear of Wheam, Chuss and Keick, and Stryke came to the trio first.

'All well?' he asked.

'We're fine, Captain,' Keick replied.

'Though we never dreamed we'd see anything like this when we signed up,' Chuss added.

'Always bet on the unexpected,' Stryke advised.

'It's incredible,' Wheam said, sweeping an arm at the bizarre expanse they were moving through. 'I can't wait to include it in my epic ballad.'

'Still working on that, eh?'

'When I can. In my head, mostly.' He pointed at the item in question. 'I composed some more today.' He reached for his lute. 'Perhaps you'd like to—'

'No. We're in enough trouble.'

He left Wheam looking bereft.

Stryke found Dallog and Pirrak in whispered conversation, which they broke off when they saw him.

'Corporal.'

'Captain,' Dallog returned.

Pirrak gave an edgy nod and said nothing.

'You're still bunching,' Stryke announced.

'Captain?'

'I wanted the Ceragans mixed in with the band, Dallog, but that hasn't happened.'

'Aren't we all Ceragans? Whether native or adopted?'

Stryke wondered if that was a dig. 'New recruits, then. They won't learn the band's ways from each other.'

'With respect, Captain, you've seen how well we work as a unit. It made sense to keep us tight.'

'What doesn't make sense is disobeying one of my orders.' He cut off the corporal's response with a flick of his hand. 'But I'm not minded to make an issue of it now. We'll sort this later.' He looked to Pirrak. 'You're not saying much, Private.'

Pirrak fumbled for a reply.

'He's . . . shy,' Dallog offered.

'Shy?' Stryke said. 'I've heard orcs called a lot of things, but never shy.'

'These new recruits are young. They're far from home. All this is unsettling for them, and it takes them in different ways. That's another reason I've kept us as a unit.'

'The best way to toughen 'em is in the field, with combat.'

'You can't say we haven't had plenty of that. And maybe there's more to come.' He indicated what lay ahead with a nod.

Stryke looked up. The white structure was suddenly and inexplicably nearer, no more than a modest arrow shot away. He couldn't work out whether the peculiar geography of this place had made it seem further off than it really was, or whether magic played a part in drawing it, or them, closer.

Stryke made his way along the column, passed its head and joined Dynahla.

'What is that thing?' he asked, gazing at the white slab.

'An entrance, to this world proper,' the fetch replied.

'You mean this isn't it?'

'This is no more than a vestibule. Our real journey begins in there.'

The building, if building was the right word, was an enormous, pure white block, not unlike a giant brick. It was as wide, deep and tall as any fortress they had ever seen, but bore no other resemblance.

Stryke approached it and laid a palm against its surface. It was as sleek as glass and slightly warm. He had no idea what it was made of.

The rest of the band arrived and began their own investigations.

'It's completely smooth,' Coilla said, running a hand over it. 'No sign of joins or seams or—'

'You won't find any,' Dynahla assured her, 'or a door. It's designed to be impenetrable.'

'If that means it's supposed to keep us out,' Haskeer declared, 'it's bullshit. This'll do the job.' He lifted his axe.

'I wouldn't do that,' the shape-changer cautioned.

Haskeer ignored him, took a swing and struck the wall a hefty blow. The axe rebounded and flew out of his grasp, causing several Wolverines to duck as it soared over their heads. At the same time Haskeer was thrown back, as though hit with a mighty punch. He landed heavily on his rump.

'Meet it with force and it returns that force,' Dynahla explained. 'Increase the force and it repays with interest.'

'Now he tells me,' Haskeer grumbled as he got to his feet. His glare wiped the grins off the watching grunts' faces.

'So how *do* we get in?' Stryke said.

'I'll need the instrumentalities for that.'

'You said they don't work here.'

'They don't in the sense of taking us somewhere else. But they have other uses.'

Stryke shrugged, got out the stars and handed them to him.

Dynahla slotted them together with such speed and dexterity that the others couldn't follow. Then he held the assembly of instrumentalities against the wall for an instant before stepping back.

A pair of parallel grooves appeared, working their way up from ground level, about as wide apart as an orc with his arms stretched out. When they got to above the height of the tallest band member they turned left and right, and kept moving until they met, forming an oblong. It had the shape of a door, but no visible means of being opened. Stryke was about to comment on that when it began to change colour. The white turned to grey, and the grey to black. In seconds it came to look like an entrance, albeit to an interior in total darkness.

Dynahla returned the instrumentalities to Stryke and said, 'Do you want to go first?'

'How we gonna see in there?'

'That won't be a problem.'

'You go first then.'

Dynahla nodded. Without hesitation he strode through the door and disappeared from sight.

Stryke hesitated for a moment, decided to draw his sword, just in case, and followed.

He stepped, not into darkness, but full light. That was something he would normally find remarkable, but he was coming to expect the extraordinary.

Dynahla was waiting for him, in a huge square chamber whose floor, walls and ceiling were dazzling white, like the exterior.

'This is big, but not as big as it looked from the outside,' Stryke said.

'No. This is merely a segment of the interior, but it's the only part that concerns us.'

The rest of the band started coming through, led by Coilla and Pepperdyne. When they were all in, the door returned to white and its outline vanished. Even under the closest scrutiny there was no sign of it ever having been there.

They looked around, not that there was a lot to see. The room was completely empty and unadorned. At its opposite end was another, more conventional looking door. Dynahla made for it, and they all trailed after him.

The door, when they came to it, seemed incongruous. It was made of wood, or something approximating it, and it had a chunky brass handle. Dynahla opened it. Beyond was a tunnel, again white, again brightly lit by an unseen source.

'Now what?' Jup said.

'Not much further,' the shape-changer told him.

He entered the tunnel, Stryke and the rest close behind. As they started to walk, Spurral glanced back. She wasn't surprised to see that the door they had just used was no longer there.

The tunnel ran straight and level for a distance none of them could estimate. In terms of time, they could have sung perhaps ten verses of one of their marching songs before they came to its end.

'Oh look,' Haskeer mouthed sarcastically, '*another* door.'

This one could have been made of iron. It was stout and set with studs, and had a latch with a thick metal ring. Dynahla reached out and turned it. Hands hovered over sword hilts as the door swung open.

A different kind of light greeted them. It was natural, compared to what they had come from, and was accompanied by a mild, fragrant breeze. They filed out.

It was what they thought of as a normal landscape. There was greenery and trees. The sky was a proper colour, and a big yellow, summer sun beat down from it. Yet the northern star was somehow still visible, twinkling above emerald hills. They heard what might have been soft birdsong.

'Don't be complacent,' Dynahla warned them. 'What appears ordinary may not be what it seems.'

'We keep going north?' Stryke asked.

'Yes.'

'How far?'

'Who can say? It could be a short journey or a lengthy march.'

'Can't we speed things up?'

'We could find mounts.'

'In this place?'

'Like I said, there's life here.'

'You've been here before, haven't you?'

'Yes,' the shape-changer confessed. 'Just once, when I first came to Serapheim's private universe. That was a long time ago, and I stayed there until I was sent to you.'

'So you came out this way?'

'No. Serapheim used the power of the instrumentalities to transport me directly to your location.'

'But you've been here once before, so you know what to expect.'

'Only in the broadest sense. Like I said, this place has a random element. I very much doubt it would be the same as it was on my only previous visit.'

Stryke chewed that over as they continued walking.

Eventually they came to a river.

'This is a likely place to find our ride,' Dynahla told them in a low tone, while signalling them to quieten down.

It was softly agreed that Dynahla, Stryke, Coilla and Jup would scout for mounts. They moved stealthily towards the riverbank, leaving the rest of the band sheltering on the edge of a copse.

Luck was with them. They found what they were looking for near the water's edge. Four or five creatures, each as large as three warhorses, with elongated, ribbed bodies of whitish-brown, and a forest of legs. The millipedes' rudimentary faces were dominated by a ravening mouth and a pair of unblinking, black button eyes.

'Dangerous?' Stryke said, peering round the rock they were hiding behind.

'Troublesome, more like,' Dynahla replied. 'But they can be made to carry us.'

'How?'

The shape-changer explained.

Stryke went to fill in the rest of the band and got them down to the riverbank for a look. They took the sight of gigantic multi-legged insects in their stride, even if Wheam went a little pale. Standeven, who didn't know whether to be appalled or disgusted, swore he wouldn't go near the things. A threatening fist shut him up.

When they were set, Stryke said, 'Ready, Dynahla?'

'Yes.'

'Sure you can fake something that big?'

'Just about. It's takes a lot of stamina to maintain it. But once we get them working I can give it up. Now if you could give me some room . . .'

They moved away and watched as he went to the ground and twisted, contorted and expanded. They saw the sprouting of a myriad legs, the emergence of coal-black eyes and rapacious mouth.

Finally he was done. He rose up as a creature identical to the ones scooping water on the riverbank. The question was whether they would accept him as their own. Moving sinuously, numerous limbs working in unison, the bogus millipede scuttled towards them. He brushed Standeven's leg as he passed. The human shuddered, eyes closed.

They need not have worried. After some snuffling, twittering and a winding insectoid dance, Dynahla's counterfeit was accepted. Shortly after, he led them to the band.

The millipedes turned out to be surprisingly docile. They did prove hard to mount, however, and harder to stay on. For Standeven, getting aboard was an ordeal, and he got a lot of unwanted help. The creatures were big enough to take the whole band between them, with six or seven sitting astride each extensive back. The orcs wove vines for reins and to lash themselves in place.

Dynahla's millipede carried no riders. His job was to lead the genuine creatures, a task made possible by assuming a female form. The real ones were all male.

They set off at a fast crawl, the band trying to adapt themselves to the left-to-right, right-to-left meandering gait of their mounts.

The terrain they passed through was basically unvarying. It was all rural, as far as they could see, and they came across no cottages, farms or any other signs of habitation. There was an abundance of animal life, mostly evidenced by rustlings in the undergrowth as they scampered past, or the briefest glimpse of fur or hide as something darted for cover. At one point they saw a herd of beasts, gathered in a field on sloping ground. But they were too far away to make out what they were.

Their journey stretched on, and as time passed they became aware that the day had not matured since they arrived. The sun was in exactly the same place in the sky.

'Dynahla told me that it's always the peak of the day here,' Stryke explained.

'Is it ever night?' Coilla said over his shoulder.

'I asked him about that. He said we wouldn't want to be here when it happened.'

Shortly after, the landscape began to change. It grew sparser, and rocky. A clump of pallid cliffs loomed ahead, with a narrow canyon punched through it.

The Dynahla millipede, in the lead, came to a halt, causing the procession to slow and then stop. He transformed, contracting, writhing and thrashing until he assumed his usual form. The true millipedes seemed unfazed by the loss of their amour.

He was dusting himself off when Stryke slid down and went to him.

'What's up?'

'That.' He pointed towards the cliff.

Stryke had to strain to see what it was. Even so, he could only make out a dark shape against the lighter background of rock. 'What is it?'

'Something you have to take. Assuming you can get away with it alive.'

26

'*What* do we have to take?' Stryke said. 'What's so important?'

'I believe that what lies over there is going to be vital to us. But we need more information. Will you let me take a look?'

'Go ahead.'

The shape-changer transformed himself into a bird. It was difficult to say what kind. A large seagull, perhaps, although it was black. He took off at speed.

'Why does he always seem to know more than he's telling?' Jup wondered.

'That'd crossed my mind,' Haskeer said.

'A short journey, then.'

Dynahla was soon back. Once he changed form he stated, simply, 'It's a weapon.'

'What kind?' Stryke asked.

'A kind you're unlikely to have seen before. You should go and look at it.'

'Why?'

'As I said, it'll be useful for what follows.'

'And what's that?'

'I don't know.'

'Fat lot of use you are,' Haskeer muttered.

'I don't know *specifically*,' Dynahla said, 'but I know there'll be challenges. What I *do* know is you need that device to be able to advance further.'

'*How* do you know that?'

'Serapheim told me.'

'Why didn't you tell us until now?'

'I didn't know I had to until we got here. And all Serapheim told me was that in this place gift horses shouldn't be ignored. That weapon's here for a reason. Everything is here for a reason. You have to take it.'

'Well . . .'

'At least have a look. Would that hurt?'

'All right. But it better be worth it.'

'I think you'll find it is.'

The band headed for the cliffs.

When they got to the object it proved extraordinary. It was essentially a long dark metal tube or pipe, with the circumference of a hogshead, mounted on wheels. From its arrangement of gears and handles it looked as though the tube's angle could be adjusted. On one side at its blunt end was a large wheel, on the other a lever. The top of the tube had a sight, in the form of a raised ring with an inset cross. There were wide grooves on both sides of the chassis that bore the weapon. They each held around a dozen sizeable black globes, possibly of iron.

'How does it work?' Coilla said.

'I think I know,' Dynahla replied.

Haskeer looked to him. 'Weapons expert now, are you?'

'No. But when I was here before I changed myself into something that could get inside this thing. Well, not that small, but an appendage with an eye attached did the job.'

'And you figured it out?' Stryke asked.

'I think so. Inside that tube there's a very powerful coil, made of some sort of tough, flexible metal. You drop one of these balls down the tube, then turn that wheel at the end. That draws back the coil, taking the ball with it. When it's in place, the lever releases the coil. It comes free with enough energy to launch the ball. And with a lot of force, I imagine.'

'Clever,' Jup declared admiringly.

'They're a size,' Haskeer said, pointing at the weighty metal balls.

'Nearly as big as your head. Though less dense.'

Haskeer contented himself with giving the dwarf a murderous look.

'This thing must weigh a ton,' Stryke said.

'We can couple the millipedes to it,' Dynahla suggested. 'They're strong. And maybe there'll be a bit of hauling where necessary. But believe me, Stryke, we should take it.'

'All right, I believe you. I hope this isn't wasted effort, for your sake.'

Wheam was staring at the weapon. 'How come it's just sitting here? Doesn't it belong to somebody?'

'Quite possibly,' the shape-changer replied. 'In which case you might have to fight for it.'

Wheam looked around. 'Fight who?'

'If we're lucky, nobody. But we should stay alert.'

'That we can do,' Stryke told him.

Using rope the band carried, along with some pleated vines, they fashioned crude harnesses. They found that two millipedes were capable of pulling the load, as well as carrying riders.

When they were finally ready, Stryke said, 'We have to skirt these cliffs. Which means going away from north and then turning back to it once we're round 'em.'

'What about that canyon?' Coilla suggested. 'Isn't that heading north?'

The peculiar daytime star hung directly above it.

'I guess it does. If it's not a dead end.'

Dynahla offered to find out. He changed to his black bird guise and took off. Before long he was back to confirm that the canyon did indeed go clean through the cliffs.

'What's it like on the other side?' Stryke wanted to know.

'More or less like this, though rockier. There are some caves.'

'All right, let's move.'

They set off, unsteadily at first, hauling the weapon.

The canyon was narrow and high-sided. Its floor was stony, with occasional clumps of miserable vegetation. It didn't run straight; there were bends.

As one of these came into sight they saw a shadow cast by something moving their way. Something very large. Stryke halted the convoy. No sooner had they stopped than a creature rounded the bend.

It could have passed for vaguely human, apart from its size. High as a fully grown oak, and looking as hardy, it was male. The creature was naked save for a loincloth of pelts. He was an extremely hirsute specimen, with a bushy head of hair, a full beard and a mane on his chest, all rust-coloured. There was a belt at his waist, and tucked through it a club as big as a young tree. His piggy eyes held a malevolent glint.

When he saw them he gave a furious roar.

'Shit, an ogre,' Jup said. 'That's all we need.'

'I think we can guess who the weapon belonged to,' Spurral added.

'Why didn't you see this when you scouted, Dynahla?' Stryke demanded.

Before the fetch could answer somebody yelled *'Watch out!'*

The ogre had lifted a sizeable rock and was getting ready to throw it at them.

'Back!' Stryke ordered. *'Pull back!'*

'You tried getting these things to back up?' Haskeer shouted, pulling hard on a millipede's reins.

Those hauling the weapon had an even harder time trying to turn in the confined space. But they managed to retreat a short distance, albeit ending up in something of a shambles.

The rock came down with a thunderous crash, short of the band but too close for ease. His simple face twisted with fury, the ogre scrabbled for another one.

'Archers!' Stryke bellowed.

The bows came out and defensive fire was unleashed. Arrows soared towards their bemused target, and many hit. More than anything, the ogre seemed surprised. The shafts may have stung him but they were doing no real harm. Adjusting their aim, the archers tried for more sensitive areas, around the face and neck.

The ogre lobbed his second rock. It was short again but a lot nearer, throwing up a cloud of shale and dust that pelted the band. Immediately, the creature started to advance, hampered a little by the irritation of arrows. Then one penetrated his cheek, drawing an angry bellow. He plucked it out, stared stupidly at it and flung it away. A trickle of blood flowed down the side of his face. He drew the vicious-looking club, and tried batting at the incoming arrows with it.

'This could be the time to put our weapon to the test, Stryke,' Coilla suggested.

'Just what I was thinking.'

'If we can get it working in time,' Jup added, sliding from the millipede's back.

The archers had only a limited supply of arrows but they kept firing. Stryke ordered everybody else to uncouple the weapon, a task complicated by the fact that the ogre's approach was causing the millipedes to become skittish.

To buy them time, Dynahla changed himself into an eagle and flew off to harass the ogre with wickedly sharp talons. Down below, the band struggled to disengage the weapon and turn it.

The ogre took to swiping at Dynahla with his club. Successfully turned, the weapon was being primed. A couple of grunts heaved one of the metal balls into the tube's mouth. Several more privates, along with a bellowing Haskeer, were straining to turn the wheel that drew back the coil.

Dynahla narrowly avoided being struck by the club. He circled, swooped again and was almost caught by it a second time. The shape-changer called it quits and flew down to the band. He landed, and transformed in one fluid motion, as the weapon was being tilted upwards. Nep and Seafe were bouncing up and down on its non-business end to encourage progress.

Finally they were set. The ogre, frantic with rage, was bearing down on them. Stryke had his hand on the firing lever and was peering through the sight.

'What you waiting for?' Haskeer said.

'We only get one chance. I want him nearer.'

The ogre was obliging. He began jogging towards them, the club raised, his footfalls like thunder.

'For the gods' sake, Stryke!' Coilla exclaimed.

Still he hesitated.

The ogre was close enough for them to be in his shadow.

Stryke pulled the lever. The weapon bucked. The ball shot from the cylinder.

It reached its target in a blink, striking the ogre full in the chest with a sickening thump. He expelled a huge breath, face contorted in pain. Then he fell, crashing to the ground and making it shake. He was still.

The band gave it a moment before cautiously approaching.

'Dead as a doorknob,' Jup declared.

'Well, at least we know this thing works,' Coilla said.

'Let's hope he was the only one.'

The killing ball was retrieved. Then Stryke got the band to roll the monstrous corpse to one side of the track so they could get by. Next they had to re-couple the weapon and sort out their mounts. After that they took a short breather and passed round the water bottles. Stryke judged that a small alcohol ration was deserved, too, and let them break out the rough brandy. Wheam had a coughing fit when he took his tot. Standeven drained his in one go and asked for more, but was ignored. A drunk crazy human was an additional burden Stryke could do without.

They set off again, steering past the gargantuan cadaver.

A while later, riding across the scrubby land on the other side of the canyon, Coilla observed, 'This never-ending high noon is putting everybody out, Stryke.'

'It feels strange, yeah.'

'But mostly they need sleep. We all do. We didn't have that much before we came here. And the band needs feeding.'

'I want to push on.'

'They'll be good for nothing if we do.'

He sighed. 'Right. But it won't be for long. Organise the shifts.'

They found a defensible spot by a heap of boulders. The weapon was secured, the mounts fussed over a bit, and sentries posted. Stryke didn't want to waste time hunting for game, if there was any, and got the band to dip into their iron rations. Sleep proved difficult in the unrelenting sunlight, but they were tired enough that most managed at least some.

Far too soon for everybody, Stryke ordered them to break camp, and they resumed their journey rested if not refreshed.

They rode for a long time, heading straight for the northern star. The land became more verdant, and they found themselves moving across a grassy expanse. Fortunately the vegetation wasn't full enough to hamper them. Whether that was because something grazed here, or because the magic of the old sorcerers had willed it so, they didn't know.

Pepperdyne was the first to spot something out of the ordinary. In the distance, running to right and left as far as they could see, was an unbroken, yellowish-brown line. Dynahla once more volunteered to check on it. He chose the form of a dove. The band took the chance to stretch their legs.

'You have to admit he's handy to have around,' Coilla said as she watched Dynahla flap away.

'Still gives me the creeps though,' Haskeer said.

She glanced at the millipedes. 'Do these need feeding or watering? They haven't taken anything since we got them.'

'Suppose so. Don't know what though.'

'They seem content nibbling the grass,' Spurral told them.

'Yeah,' Jup said. 'Dynahla reckons they're not meat-eaters, despite looking the way they do.'

'I think they're kind of cute.'

Jup made a face.

'Ugly bastards,' Haskeer muttered.

'That's the kind of thing that gets said about us,' Coilla reminded him.

'Not to my face it ain't.'

'They can't bear looking at it,' Jup suggested with a smirk.

'How'd you like your own rearranged, pipsqueak?'

'Any time you've got the strength to try, horse breath.'

Stryke was about to slap them down when someone shouted, 'He's coming back!'

The dove fluttered in and became Dynahla.

'Well?' Stryke said.

'It's a wall, and well defended.'

'By what?'

'Werebeasts, as far as I could see.'

'We've tangled with them before. What kind are they?'

'The kind that can switch from basically human to something like a bear.'

'That kind we haven't seen before. Any chance we could parley with them?'

'You could try, but I doubt it. Though I suppose if you had something of value to offer as tribute—'

'We've nothing.'

'I thought not. And it's in the nature of this place that obstacles have to be fought through not talked through. I think you can see now why we've had to haul the weapon with us.'

'There's no way round this wall?'

'No. Well, maybe if we travelled a much longer way we might find that it ends. But I wouldn't count on it. '

'Let's get closer to it.'

'There's at least one gate. I'll show you where.'

When they were near enough to make it out, they saw that the wall looked ancient, but no less solid for that. They could make out figures on its high ramparts and, as Dynahla said, a massive pair of gates, made of timber, with iron straps.

Stryke decided to try talking after all. Thirzarr was on his mind, as always, and some kind of pact would be quicker than having a battle.

'I wouldn't get your hopes too high,' Dynahla cautioned, 'and approach with care. They didn't look particularly welcoming to me.'

Stryke took one of the millipedes, along with Haskeer, Jup, and Calthmon, who was in charge of the beast. They made a white flag, the universal sign of truce, or so they hoped. Haskeer hated white flags. In his detestation of the idea of a token of surrender, or even reasonableness, he was fairly representative of the band as a whole. He refused to hold it, and that fell to Jup.

They made for the wall.

Figures on the battlements watched as they approached. They looked like humans, which gave Haskeer little confidence in the outcome of any talks.

Stopping a short distance away, Stryke cupped his hands and called out in Mutual. '*We come in peace! Can we talk?*'

Several of the werecreatures conferred, but there was no answer.

Stryke called again. '*We're here peaceably! We want to parley!*'

The figures seemed to grow darker and bulkier.

'Looks like they're changing,' Jup said.

'Is that good?' Haskeer asked.

A swarm of arrows came down on them.

'No,' Jup said.

They were lucky not to be hit. But one arrow had struck the millipede, causing it to squirm. Stryke leaned forward and pulled the shaft out.

More arrows came, and several spears. They fell short.

'Get us out of here, Calthmon!' Stryke yelled.

They retreated to the sound of something like cheers from the battlements.

'The weapon?' Jup asked as they headed back.

'Yeah,' Stryke confirmed.

They dragged it to a point where they thought they could hit the wall but far enough away for the werebeasts' arrows to be ineffective. The ritual of loading and priming the weapon was undertaken.

Gleadeg and Prooq were steady, dependable hands. Stryke let them take care of the firing.

'First shot, Captain?' Prooq said. 'The doors?'

'Let's try for the battlements.'

They adjusted the angle.

'Ready?' Gleadeg asked.

Stryke nodded.

The lever went back and the weapon bucked. With a hearty *thomp* the ball shot out and flew almost too fast to be seen.

It struck the battlements. There was a crash of masonry and a cloud of dust. When it cleared there was a hole in the battlements and the werebeasts weren't to be seen.

'Now the doors,' Stryke said.

They were already realigning the tube, and a ball was being lifted. That done, Stryke made sure the rest of the band was mounted and ready.

The weapon went off. The doors exploded in a shower of timber chips and iron fragments.

'Move! Move! Move!' Stryke bellowed.

Most of the band tore towards the doors, with Stryke on the lead mount. The remainder worked frantically to hitch up the weapon and follow them.

For a moment they thought the doors hadn't been completely downed. But as they got nearer they could see daylight through the aperture, and a glimpse of the land beyond. The plan was simple. Clear the battlement. Take down the doors. Get through them, fast. The first two had been achieved, the third was going to be tricky.

They raced to their goal. The pair of millipedes pulling the weapon were at the back. As the wall loomed, Stryke wasn't alone in wondering if the entrance was wide enough to take them.

More werebeasts appeared on the battlements, running in from outposts. They loosed arrows. The Wolverines brought shields up. That, and their speed, got them through the first spate of arrows untouched. The second came just as they reached the gate. Shafts and spears clattered against their upraised shields. Then they were scampering over the ruined doors and through the opening. Another shower of arrows met them on the other side, and proved as ineffective, although two of the mounts took minor wounds.

The rest of the band shot through, braving the deluge from above, which now included rocks and the contents of buckets. Last in was the tubular weapon, its mounts scuttling like fury, a dozen orcs clinging to their backs. The weapon bounced over the debris from the destroyed doors, and at one point looked close to flipping, but it kept steady and escaped.

The Wolverines didn't slacken their speed until they were well away.

27

It took all the skills of Pelli Madayar and her Gateway Corps unit to gain entry to the Sphere of the Four.

Now they stood under a scarlet sky, with a malleable, grey material serving as the ground beneath their feet. The plain spread out all around them, featureless except for the vast white building in the distance. It was a unique experience for the multi-species members of the unit and they were busily examining the terrain.

Weevan-Jirst sniffed the air. 'The energy level seems extraordinarily high.'

'It *stinks* of magic,' Pelli agreed, more pithily. 'I'm not sure that even our weapons could be entirely relied on here.'

'To find out we need to know which direction will take us to our quarry.'

'We have clues. There must be a reason why the only landmark is that structure over there. And I would say the star, or whatever it is that hangs above it, confirms our path. I can see no other signs. Do you agree?'

'Would it matter if I didn't?'

'Of course it would. Unless you think me a tyrant.'

The goblin sidestepped her tacit challenge and merely said, 'I concur with your deduction. We should be guided by the star.'

'Good. Now let's move, and fast. If we've been led to a place like this, events must be coming to a head.'

'Then let us hope we're in time,' Weevan-Jirst replied grimly. 'Because if we're not, the consequences will be dire.' He fixed her with his beady gaze. 'For all of us.'

*

When they were far enough from the wall that they could no longer see it, and Stryke was satisfied nobody was chasing them, the Wolverines stopped to regroup.

Once the weapon had been checked and secured, the millipedes tended and minor injuries seen to, the band was allowed a brief period to stretch their legs.

Most just squatted or sprawled on the grass. But several drifted a short distance, including Coilla and Pepperdyne, who were deep in conversation. Stryke noticed that Dallog had also wandered off. He was standing farther away than any of the others, with his back to the band, and for once he didn't have Pirrak with him. That individual, Stryke saw, was sitting by himself at the edge of the group. He decided to talk to him.

The new recruit looked uncomfortable when he saw Stryke coming, and stood, awkwardly.

'At ease,' Stryke told him.

'Sir.' He didn't noticeably relax.

'Everything all right with you, Pirrak?'

'Yes, sir. Shouldn't it be, sir?'

'Well, it *should* be, but I get the feeling it isn't.'

'I'm fine.' The response was a little too quick and a little too edgy.

Stryke tried another tack. 'The band's treating you well? They're comradely?'

'Yes, sir.'

'And Dallog?'

There was a pause before he got an answer. 'What do you mean, Captain?'

'He's taking care of you?'

'Yes.'

'Look, Pirrak, maybe I've not been as easy to talk to as I should have been. But you know things have been frantic since we left Acurial.'

The private's expression visibly stiffened. He said, 'Yes, sir,' his voice taut.

Stryke put that down to the youngster's callow nature. 'My mind's been on the mission, and on other things, and maybe I've been forgetting my duties to the band. But I want you to know that if you ever need to talk to me about anything, you can. Or any of the other officers. Though you might not want to make Sergeant Haskeer your first choice.' If Pirrak saw the intended humour in that, he didn't react. 'If Dallog's not around, that is,' Stryke quickly tagged on.

'I understand.' As an apparent afterthought he added, 'Thank you, sir.' There was a more genuine quality in that, and perhaps even a little warmth, than anything else he had said.

'All right. Just bear it in mind. And get a shake on, we'll be moving soon.'

'Sir.'

Stryke turned and left him standing there, looking graceless.

Almost immediately he crossed paths with Coilla and Pepperdyne, on the way back from their tryst.

'See you were having a natter with Pirrak,' Coilla said. 'Pep talk?'

'Kind of. Don't know how much sunk in.'

'Does seem kind of woolly most of the time, doesn't he?'

'He's not the easiest of the new recruits to talk to,' Pepperdyne said, 'but they're all a bit green, aren't they, Stryke?'

'I'd hoped they'd be a little more ripe by now. But I guess that's what comes from letting Dallog keep them apart from the rest.'

'We carrying on now?' Coilla asked.

'Yes,' Stryke replied, 'start rousing 'em.'

Coilla headed off for a bout of shouting, Pepperdyne in tow.

On impulse, Stryke decided to go over to Dallog.

When he came to him he saw that he had his eyes shut, and seemed to be muttering to himself.

'Dallog?'

The corporal came to himself with a start, and for just an instant appeared sheepish. But his crisp 'Captain!' had its usual ebullience.

'What were you doing?'

'Praying.'

'Praying?'

'Asking the Tetrad to look favourably on our mission.'

Stryke knew it was something many in the band did. He did it himself occasionally when things looked rough, and he had turned to the gods more than once since Thirzarr was taken. But it wasn't the sort of thing anyone talked about much. He tended to think of it as a personal matter and none of his business. So he simply said, 'Sorry to disturb you, then.'

'No problem, Captain. What can I do for you?'

'I've been talking to Pirrak.'

Dallog's gaze flicked to the grunt in question, who was gathering up his gear. 'Have you?'

'Yeah. And I'm still wondering if he's fitting in.'

'Oh, *that.* Like I told you, he's a little on the quiet side. Bit of a thinker, if you know what I mean. Not that it makes him any less dependable in combat.'

'Maybe not. But he'll fight better if he mixes with the band more. All the tyros will.'

'You've already made that point, Captain.'

'Just so you know I mean it. There are going to be some changes in future.'

'If there is a future for us.'

'What?'

'I mean, I sort of figured this mission was a one-off. I don't know if you have any plans for the band after that, or whether we'd be part of it.'

'I don't know myself. And you could be right: maybe there's no future for any of us. Who knows how this thing will pan out?'

'That's a glum way of looking at it, Captain. I'm sure that under your command—'

'Yeah. We'll see. Meantime, keep an eye on Pirrak.'

'You can count on it.'

'And get 'em ready; we're moving out.'

They rode on for what could have been a quarter of a day, if they had any means of judging it accurately. The constant sun sat high in the sky, as it always did, and their sense of time was shot.

The landscape stayed the same, not quite lush and not quite scrub, until a change loomed. Ahead of them was the edge of a forest. It spread a long, long way to the west and east. Stryke halted the convoy.

'Through or round?' he asked Dynahla.

'Round is going to delay us a lot, and would probably be as perilous.'

'Forests are too good for ambushes. I don't like 'em. Unless I'm doing the ambushing.'

'I could scout it for us. But if there's no obvious trap in there—'

'You might not see it. I know. That's why I don't like forests.'

'Well, shall I?'

Stryke nodded.

The shape-changer took on a bird guise again, a small one this time, presumably to make it easier to negotiate the forest. They watched as it flew towards the tree-line, but lost sight of it before it got there.

There was such a long wait that they were starting to think they'd seen the last of the fetch. Then the bird reappeared, travelling at speed.

Back in his familiar form, Dynahla reported. 'It's big. Took me a while to get all the way over. I didn't see anything that looked threatening, but that might not mean much. It's pretty dense in parts, and dark.'

'We going to be able to get that through?' Stryke stabbed a thumb at the curious weapon.

'I think so. Though I expect there'll be a certain amount of weaving about.'

'I suppose we'll have to do it then.'

'Like I said, everything in this place has a purpose. The forest's there because we're supposed to enter it.'

'That's another way of saying we *will* run into something.'

'Not necessarily. It could be just a forest. But it pays to expect trouble.'

'What the fuck,' Haskeer said. 'We *love* trouble.'

'You're unlikely to be disappointed,' Dynahla told him.

Stryke made sure everybody had at least one weapon close to hand, and got the archers to nock their bows.

They resumed their journey.

The nearer they got to the forest the more it came to dominate, and it became obvious that many of the trees were enormously tall. Entering it was like being swallowed by some gigantic beast composed of timber rather than flesh.

Mulch from untold numbers of rotting leaves carpeted the ground. That made for soft going, but slowed rather than totally hindered them. Generally, the trees were spaced sufficiently far apart to allow them to get through, although there were exceptions. Most obstructions could be steered round, but several times they had to backtrack and look for another way. Even so, they made reasonably good progress.

That came to an end when, by Dynahla's estimate, they were about halfway. The area they were passing through was boggy, but deceptive because a covering of recently fallen leaves disguised the threat. The millipedes bearing only riders partially sank but scrabbled on. Seeing the danger, Stryke bellowed for the mounts pulling the weapon to be stopped. But it was too late. Under the weight of both the weapon and riders, the mounts floundered in the mire. The load they were pulling began to sink, and the band had to cut the millipedes free. By the time that was done, the weapon was stubbornly bogged down.

They tried hauling. But even the combined strength of the band couldn't free the weapon's carriage.

'We need something to lever it out with,' Haskeer said.

'We're in a forest,' Coilla reminded him. 'Take your pick.'

'That one should do it.' Stryke pointed at a nearby tree. 'Get it down.'

Haskeer was first there. He swung his axe and whacked it into the trunk.

There was a distant wailing sound that stopped them all in their tracks. It was doleful. In its terrible despair it was almost beautiful. Others joined it, but they were angered, and soon the eerie chorus was one of fury.

'That sounds familiar,' Jup said.

'Yeah,' Coilla agreed. 'Nyadds.'

'What are they?' Wheam asked. He looked spooked.

'Spirits of the forest. Or that's what some called them back in Maras-Dantia. They're forest fauns, and they're all female. At least, nobody I know ever saw a male. They're usually so bashful you wouldn't know it if you walked right by them.'

'Except when you mess with their trees,' Stryke added.

'Is that so bad a crime?' Pepperdyne said.

'Each nyadd is bound in spirit to a certain tree. If it dies, the nyadd dies. When a tree's hurt, like this one, they all feel the pain.'

'And they get very pissed off,' Coilla explained. 'Jennesta's said to be part nyadd, which should give you some idea.'

'What do we do, Stryke?' Spurral wanted to know.

'They sounded a way off, and we've still got to dig the wagon out. Let's gamble on them taking a while to get here. Haskeer, the tree.'

'Seems almost cruel after what you said about the nyaads,' Spurral mildly protested.

'Got a better idea?'

'Hell, no.'

Haskeer's axe bit into the tree. Several of the grunts joined in, and made short work felling it. Then they set to cutting the wood they needed. Soon they had a couple of stout levers, and a lengthy pair of planks to give the wheels traction.

Even with these aids it was a struggle freeing the weapon. Only once it was out and re-hitched, and the racket they had made had died down, did they realise that the wailing had stopped. The forest was silent.

Not for long. A crowd of figures emerged from the trees all around. They were tall, lean and olive-skinned, and their nakedness was partially hidden by ankle-length auburn hair. Their handsome faces were contorted with fury, revealing unusually white, and unusually sharp, teeth. They were armed; mostly with curved daggers, though some had snub swords.

A keening version of the wail went up and they raced at the band.

The nyadds had their fury. The wolverines had weapons with a longer reach. On Stryke's order these were deployed. Nine or ten nyadds fell with arrows in their chests. It didn't deter the others, and while the archers were reloading, the first of the attackers reached the band.

Stryke put down two with a single wide stroke. Coilla caught another with a throwing knife, and Jup leapt up to crack a skull with his staff. The dagger-wielding nyadds couldn't get close enough to inflict much damage, but they threatened to overrun the band. More and more of them were streaming from the trees.

By a cowering Standeven, Pepperdyne lunged and ran-through an advancing nyadd. Nearby, Haskeer laid about them with his axe. Dallog's unofficial unit were hacking in unison. But for all that it was like spearing fish in a barrel, the tide was relentless, with fresh attackers stumbling over the bodies of their fellows to get to the band.

'We're not going to hold this for ever,' Coilla said as she slashed at a nyadd's probing dagger.

Stryke parried a nyadd's thrust, wrong-footed her and took off her head. Golden blood spattered his tunic. 'Then we'll go for their heart. *Archers! Burnables! The trees!*'

They understood, and drew their flammable arrows. Flint sparks ignited the tar-soaked cloth and flame blossomed. The burning arrows streaked out and hit a dozen trees. Most took fire immediately.

An even greater wail went up from the nyadds. They backed off and stared in horror at the burning trees. As they watched, the orc archers loosed a second round, spreading the flame.

The nyadds weren't simply routed; they forgot about the fight. Now many of them were showing signs of distress, and even pain. Some shook violently, some sank to their knees, some just collapsed. A cruel malady swept through them, and as the fires grew stronger their torment grew as well.

Here and there, nyadds were bursting into flames. In some cases they fell and burned, with a kind of sad resignation. In others, the fire-swathed nyadds lurched and stumbled, and shrieked as they blazed. Some ran into the forest, illuminating its depths. The smell of charred flesh filled the air.

The Wolverines waded in and helped the process along with their blades. But what was happening to the trees was a more effective weapon. Shortly, only a handful of nyadds were left standing, and those not for long.

Stryke scanned the carnage. 'Let's get out of here!'

'What about this fire?' Spurral said, nodding at the burning trees. 'We can't just leave it to spread.'

'We've no time for fire-fighting.'

'You'd destroy an entire forest?'

'Look at it. I doubt we could put it out now if we tried.'

'And you're not going to?'

'I wouldn't worry too much,' Dynahla interrupted. 'You're forgetting the magical nature of the world we're in. This place takes care of itself. Only I think we should get out while we still can. The fire's going to surround us soon.'

They left before it did. The fire burned on at their rear, throwing its light after them so that they cast long shadows. But before long it faded, then died as the forest overwhelmed all but its memory.

The band met no more hostility, and eventually came to the forest's end.

They emerged on the top of a gentle slope running down to a green expanse. Crossing this was a dead straight artificial waterway. They couldn't see far enough to say where it came from or went to.

There were several barges on the water, and one very large one tied-up next to a small cottage. This was weathered red brick with an unkempt thatched roof. Figures moved around it.

Coilla cupped her eyes. 'Looks like . . . gnomes.'

'Miserable bastards,' Haskeer said.

'That canal runs north,' Stryke realised. 'And they've got a barge.'

Coilla nodded. 'Think it'd take all of us and the weapon?'

'I reckon. But we'd have to let the millipedes go.'

'Shame.'

'Let's see if we can parley.'

They headed down to the waterway. The panic started before they reached it. Seeing an orcs warband charging towards them, mounted on giant multi-legged insects and towing a black tube, was enough to unnerve the gnomes. It sparked an exodus. They scrambled into wagons and headed off along the towpath at speed.

'Rude buggers!' Haskeer exclaimed. 'They could have given us a hearing.'

Jup shrugged. 'Saves us having to negotiate.'

Stryke didn't waste time. They got the weapon onto the barge, which proved a tough task. Then the band embarked and they cast off, using the barge's oars. There was a small sail too, and Stryke had it unfurled, despite little wind.

As they moved away they saw the liberated millipedes undulating towards the forest. Everybody was sorry to see them go. Except Standeven.

28

The waterway took them through terrain that was mostly flat and lacking in any particular landmarks. All they saw was an expanse of green, dotted with the odd tree or rock. An occasional low hill, glimpsed in the distance, became an event to be remarked on. Taking advantage of their stately progression, the band rested, fed themselves and maintained their weapons. Curiously, they met no other boats.

As best as they could estimate it, more than a day went by as they slowly glided towards their unknown destination. Some in the band wondered if there *was* a destination, and whether the canal might not go on for ever. Those who thought there must be a destination speculated on how they would know it. The only certainty was the north star, and they were still heading straight for that.

Into the second day they saw the peaks of a mountain range ahead, and also noticed something strange about the star above it.

'It's definitely getting bigger,' Coilla decided.

'I think you're right,' Stryke agreed. He turned to the shape-changer. 'Dynahla?'

'It's to be expected the nearer we get to our goal.'

'You mean we are, at last?'

'It's in the air. Can't you feel it?'

Haskeer gave a prolonged, noisy sniff. 'I can't.'

'Take my word for it, Sergeant; our destination's imminent. Though we shouldn't get too excited. It may be closer only in distance.'

After that, the star and the mountains it crowned rapidly grew larger.

Eventually the problem of where their destination would lie was solved: the canal came to an end. It terminated in a modest dock, which had the benefit of a winch that proved sturdy enough to unload the barge. But that was the end of their luck as far as the weapon was concerned. Without beasts to help with the burden, it had to be moved bodily. The band was hardly keen on the idea, but they had experience of hauling siege engines over long distances. Once roped up, they found it took about half the band to pull it, which meant they could labour in shifts.

Now as big as a harvest moon, and rivalling the sun, the star was suspended above whatever lay behind the mountains. Fortunately there was a wide pass cutting through them. They made for it.

Halfway along, the pebbly stone floor of the vale began to be covered in patches of fine sand. By the time they got to the end of the pass there was nothing but sand underfoot, and it was quite thick. They had to work even harder to negotiate it. The temperature was also noticeably hotter.

Ahead of them was a low ridge of granite. Leaving the weapon at its base, they climbed the gentle incline to see what was beyond. Lying on their bellies, they looked out at the beginning of a vast desert. More arresting was what stood on it in the near distance. It was a pyramid, the largest any of them had seen, and it seemed to be made of milky glass. At its apex was what looked like a massive, multifaceted gem. Sunlight glinted on it.

'What in hell is that?' Coilla said.

'Something legendary,' Dynahla explained. 'If I'm right, it's the Prism of Sina-Cholm.'

'Which is?'

'An artefact created by the wizards who built this world.'

'What does it do?' Stryke asked.

'It kills.'

'How?'

'Can you get one of the archers to send an arrow its way?'

'Sure. It's in range. But I don't think an arrow's going to hurt it.'

'That's not the point.'

Stryke shrugged and ordered one of the grunts to string-up.

'It might be an idea if we all kept our heads down,' Dynahla suggested.

The archer loosed his bolt and it soared towards the pyramid. It had almost reached it when an intense white beam shot from the gem at the apex, striking the arrow and obliterating it.

'It targets anything that approaches,' Dynahla said.

'Is there somebody in there operating that thing?' Pepperdyne wanted to know.

'No, it functions entirely by itself. It works by drawing energy from what passes for the sun here, concentrating it and using it to defend itself.'

'Do we have to tackle it?' Stryke said.

'You know the nature of this place by now. It's there because it's the next thing we have to overcome. Maybe the last thing. Fortunately, we have a chance because of that.' He nodded at the weapon parked below them.

'Won't the pyramid just destroy what we fire at it?'

'What if we were to fire more than one thing at the same time?' Coilla suggested.

'That's not a bad idea. Think it might work, Dynahla?'

'Your faith in my knowledge about this place is touching, Stryke. Frankly, I don't know. But it's worth a try, isn't it?'

They needed a spot where they could get the weapon to see its target, and where there was some kind of shelter for the band. Scouts found such a place not far from the incline they climbed. It was a ground-level slab of stone big enough to accommodate the weapon, and with a perfect view of the pyramid. There were enough sizeable boulders strewn around it to give the Wolverines cover. They set about hauling the weapon to it.

'All right,' Stryke said when they were installed, 'let's get the thing loaded and lined-up.'

While that was going on he picked six archers.

There was a lot of fussing with the weapon's alignment, and when he was finally satisfied, Stryke stood ready at the lever. The archers nocked their arrows and drew back the strings.

'*Now!*' he yelled, pulling hard on the lever.

The weapon coughed its missile as six arrows were loosed.

The arrows travelled faster than the ball, which described an arcing path. A flash came from the gem and one of the arrows vaporised. There was another dazzling streak and a second arrow disappeared. Then it was the ball's turn. A beam sought it out, shattering it to fragments. The remaining arrows got through and clattered feebly against the pyramid's face.

'Fuck it!' Haskeer cursed.

'We proved it can't handle several things at once,' Stryke said.

'But it got the important one, didn't it?'

'We'll do it again, with more archers this time.'

Ten archers lined-up as the weapon was reloaded and its angle slightly adjusted.

Again the launch was simultaneous. The beam from the gem got two, three and then four arrows, and they were picked off before they had travelled as far as the first volley. But the ball got through. It struck the pyramid low down, near its base, and did some damage, although nothing terminal. A cheer went up from the band.

The weapon was primed once more and its angle altered on the basis of the previous shot. Arrows were readied.

'*Now!*' Stryke bellowed. He pulled the lever and rushed forward to see the result.

The beam singled out no less than five arrows this time, and intercepted them much nearer their firing point than before. Tumbling through the air on a high trajectory, the ball travelled unscathed.

There was a blinding flash and a roar. Stryke found himself on the ground, along with the others, not knowing what had just happened. As they looked up, they saw the ball hit the pyramid at the point where the gem was fixed to its peak. The sound of the impact was tremendous. Swaying for a second, the gem tumbled, and as it fell the pyramid itself rippled with numerous cracks and began to fall apart. Great shards of the glassy material plunged to the ground to shatter into thousands of pieces. In a brace of heartbeats the entire structure gave way, the remains shrouded in a cloud of dust from the debris.

The band cheered. It took them a moment to hear Coilla shouting at them and to realise something was wrong. Stryke turned and saw what it was. The weapon was on its side, the tube broken into several pieces, the woodwork blackened with charring. Its ammunition, the iron spheres, were scattered all around. Some were split in two.

Coilla was on her knees next to something half under the toppled weapon. Stryke and the others dashed to it.

'The pyramid fired at us just before the ball hit,' she explained. 'Vobe was standing next to the weapon.'

Stryke looked. Their comrade was crushed, bloodied and unmistakably dead.

They would have liked to give Vobe the send-off he deserved, but they knew that wasn't always possible in the field. So Stryke and Coilla said a few words about one of their longest-serving brothers-in-arms, and Dallog commended his spirit to the Tetrad with Haskeer looking on disdainfully. Then they buried the body as deep as they could in the desert sand.

'Strange to think we've buried him in a place that doesn't actually exist,' Coilla said as they moved away.

'Nothing that happens these days surprises me,' Stryke replied. 'But I wish we could have seen him off on a pyre on Ceragan, where he belongs, with feasting and drinking in his honour. He deserved at least that much.'

'We'll raise a tankard to him when we get out of this.'

'Think we will get out?'

'Of course we will. And you don't want to let the others hear you talking like that.'

'No, you're right. But what with Thirzarr, and now Vobe—'

'I know. But the best way we serve them is to complete this mission, the way we set out to do.'

'That feels like a long time ago, and it seemed so much simpler then.'

'Tell me about it.'

Dynahla approached them. 'I don't want to intrude on your grief,' he said, 'but we should be thinking about moving on.'

'Yes,' Stryke agreed soberly. 'But which way?'

'To what Sina-Cholm was guarding. Now the prism's gone we should be able to get through.'

Heavy-hearted, the band set off over the sand towards the ruins of the pyramid. They realised how big the thing had been when they had to negotiate a vast quantity of debris, much of it viciously keen shards of the glass-like material it had been constructed from. But they struggled onto its base, and after rooting through the chaos uncovered an aperture in the floor with a flight of stone steps that descended into darkness. They filed down, weapons in hand.

At the bottom of the stairwell they found that their way was lit, just as other areas had been on their travels in this world, from an unknown source. They were in a wide, tall tunnel, seemingly constructed without blocks, bricks or any evidence of joins. There was only one way to go and they took it.

'This I do know something about,' Dynahla told them. 'I was in this labyrinth when I first came to Serapheim's pocket universe. Take heart. We're very near our destination now.'

They trudged along the tunnel for what seemed like an eternity, their surroundings never changing and the light staying at the same uniform level. More than one of them noticed the sulphurous whiff in the air that indicated a magical charge. And it was getting stronger.

There was a brighter radiance somewhere far ahead, and it shone more and more strongly as they approached it. When they arrived at its source they found that the tunnel ended at a waterfall of multicoloured light.

'We're here,' Dynahla announced. 'All we have to do is step through this curtain of energy and into Serapheim's world.'

'Is it safe?' Spurral asked.

'Perfectly. Stryke, I think you should have the honour of going through first.'

'I reckon this . . . entrance or whatever it is should be big enough for us all to go through together.'

'Good idea,' the shape-changer said. 'Shall we?'

The band lined up in front of the dazzling cascade, not quite believing it could be an entrance of any kind. Standeven, as usual, hovered a few steps to the rear of the others, looking fearful.

On Stryke's word they moved forward and stepped into the luminous whirlpool.

The sensation was not unlike world-hopping with the instrumentalities. It felt as though they were falling from a great height through a madness of churning colours and exploding stars.

They opened their eyes on something like paradise.

The sun beat down on a verdant scene of grassy pastures, soft rolling hills, trees in full leaf and silvered lakes. So blue it almost made their eyes hurt, the sky was host to a few fluffy white clouds. The air was fresh and a gentle breeze blew, fragrant from a thousand wholesome, growing things. There was no sign of the vibrant curtain they had walked through.

'This is quite something,' Pepperdyne said admiringly.

Spurral nodded. 'It's . . . beautiful.'

'It's based on Maras-Dantia before it fell into corruption,' a voice boomed from behind.

They spun round. Serapheim stood before them, a broad smile on his face. 'Congratulations on getting here,' he said, 'and welcome to my world.'

29

Tentarr Arngrim, or Serapheim as the world of sorcery knew him, looked very much as the band remembered from their first meeting on Maras-Dantia, albeit he showed the signs of ageing. But he had at least the appearance of vigour, despite what Dynahla had said about his failing health. His back was still straight, his build lean. He had shoulder-length auburn hair and a tidily trimmed beard. There were lively blue eyes above a slightly hawkish nose, and his mouth was well shaped. He was dressed in a blue silken robe and shiny black leather boots. The shape-changer was at his side.

'Greetings, Wolverines,' he said. 'It's good to see you again, and a pleasure to welcome some new faces.' He looked to the Ceragan recruits, Spurral, and Pepperdyne and Standeven. Then he took on a more solemn tone. 'Allow me to commiserate with you on those who fell on the way here. I know the loss of your comrades must be a grievous burden.'

'I think you've got some explaining to do,' Stryke told him.

'Yes, I have. You deserve no less. But come, let's do it in more comfort than standing here.'

He led them to a white marble villa. It was elegantly fashioned and tastefully furnished, and it was hard to credit it all as a product of magic. In a room the size of a banqueting hall he invited the Wolverines to rest themselves and take refreshments. Several young male and female humans, similarly dressed in blue robes, appeared with trays of water, juice and ale, and platters of bread, cheese, fruits and freshly roasted meat and fowl. It was hard to believe that the food and drink, like the villa and the world in which it stood, literally didn't exist.

Serapheim let them pick at the food and take some of the drink before moving on to weightier matters, despite the obvious impatience of Stryke and several others.

At last he said, 'I can understand your frustration and your puzzlement at the turn events have taken.'

'Can you?' Stryke replied frostily. 'We signed on for this mission to get our revenge on Jennesta. But it all got a lot more complicated than that, didn't it?'

'Not really.' He raised a hand to gently forestall Stryke's objection. 'You signed on with two objectives in mind. One was helping to liberate the orcs of Acurial, and you achieved it. You should be proud of that. It again gives the lie to the slander that orcs are selfish, purely destructive creatures. As to the second prong of your mission, settling with my daughter, that was and remains the prime purpose of the assignment.'

'There's still hope that we can do that?'

'Every hope. It's why you're here. And let me add, Stryke, that I'm fully aware of the situation your mate, Thirzarr, is in. Her wellbeing is as important as defeating Jennesta, and I give you my word that every effort will be made to reunite you.'

'Maybe she wouldn't be in this mess in the first place if I hadn't agreed to this crazy scheme.'

'If anything I've done has been responsible for putting Thirzarr in danger then I apologise. That was never my intention. But you have to understand that she would have been in danger anyway, sooner or later. From Jennesta. We are all in peril because of my daughter. You know of her scheme to create an army of obedient zombie orcs?'

'Course I do,' Stryke replied angrily, 'Thirzarr's one of them.'

'No, she's not. She's being held in a state between normality and mindless servitude. It suited Jennesta to have it that way, so she could more easily manipulate you. Or so she thought. Her demise would see an end to the hold she has over Thirzarr, and all the others who have fallen under her influence.'

'We kill her—'

'And they live, yes.' He looked around at the others in the room, all of whom were intent on what was being said. 'Some of you, particularly those new to this warband, might find it difficult to understand how I can talk so calmly about the death of my own flesh and blood. But Jennesta is no longer my daughter. It's as if I had never fathered her. I renounced her long ago, and my heart is heavier about that than you can imagine. The fact is that I helped bring evil into being when she was born. My only wish is to put that right.'

'You tried once before,' Stryke reminded him.

'Yes, and somehow, by some fluke, she survived the vortex. This time my thought is to serve her a fate from which there is no escape.' He fell into a kind of reverie for a moment, undisguised sorrow in his eyes. Then he roused himself. 'But about her plan for a slave army. Do you know who inspired that idea in her?'

'No. Should I?'

'In a way, you already do. I'm afraid we've been a little deceptive with you, Dynahla and I, and for that, too, I offer my apologies.'

'What do you mean?' Coilla asked, finding her voice.

Serapheim turned to Dynahla and said, 'Shall we show them?'

The shape-changer smiled and nodded. He stood, and immediately began to transform.

The band watched in awe as the process twisted and contorted Dynahla's body. At the end of it they were looking at a handsome, some would say beautiful, woman. Only her crimson hair was retained, tumbling to her milky white shoulders. It was hard to estimate her age, but she appeared to be in the prime of life for a human.

'Allow me to introduce Vermegram,' Serapheim said. 'My mate, my partner, my bride. And Jennesta's mother. She is as old as me, which is to say very old . . . I hope you'll forgive my indiscretion, my dear . . . and as high an adept in the ways of sorcery as I am.'

'Why?' Stryke said. 'Why the deception?'

'To protect her, and your band. If Jennesta knew that you were consorting with her mother, whom she despises, she wouldn't just have toyed with you, or with Thirzarr. The likelihood is that you'd all be dead by now.'

'I'm sorry,' Vermegram said. 'We weren't trying to trick you. It just seemed the safest way to offer you some protection and guide you through this world.' The band found it hard to get used to the soft, almost melodic voice of someone they had thought of up to now as a male. 'As to my inspiring our daughter's obsession with raising her slave army, I think at least some of you know a little about that from Serapheim. Basically it was because I tried to do something similar myself, a long time ago, when Maras-Dantia was still as fair as this artificial world. Unlike Jennesta my intentions were benign. I wanted to do good. But as the old saying goes, the road to Hades is paved with the tarnished gold of noble intentions. I was damned for that and I've been trying to rectify the error ever since.' She glanced affectionately at Serapheim. 'We both have.'

The silence that followed was broken by Haskeer asking bluntly, 'Are you a real fetch or what?'

Vermegram smiled. 'I'm human. Basically. I wasn't born with shape-changing abilities; I acquired them as a result of my magical studies.'

'Your kids—'

'Why do they vary so much in appearance? Why does Jennesta look the way she does? Why did her late sister, Adpar, turn out a hybrid? And she was another bad lot, I'm ashamed to say. It was because of tampering with myself, altering the very core of my being, when I took on the power to shape-shift. There were unanticipated consequences. One of which was that I passed on certain unusual traits to my offspring. Only my youngest daughter, Sanara, has a normal human appearance. Fortunately, her path has always been one of good, unlike her siblings.'

'Which reminds me,' Serapheim said. He reached out a hand. A velvet bell cord appeared from thin air. He gave it two tugs and it disappeared.

'Nice trick,' Coilla muttered.

A door opened and Sanara entered. She was wearing a similar set of blue robes to her father's. When she saw Jup she made straight for him, throwing her arms around him and giving him a kiss on the cheek. Spurral looked on flint-faced. Jup was blushing. Then Sanara waved a greeting to the other band members who remembered her and took a seat by her parents.

'Vermegram and I cannot confront Jennesta's forces alone, for all our powers, because hers have grown at least as strong,' Serapheim explained. 'My own, I confess, are wavering. As this pocket universe is kept in existence by the force of my will, I find I need the additional mental strength of my apprentices, the young people who served you the food, and the support of what's left of my family.' He exchanged smiles with Vermegram and his daughter. 'Sanara is one of our allies in this fight. Would you like to meet some others?'

He led them through a door and along an airy passage. Another door took them out into the open air and a large area resembling a parade ground, except it was grassed over. It was crowded.

Quoll, Ceragan orc chieftain and Wheam's father, was there, along with what looked like all the able-bodied males of the clan. So were Brelan and Chillder, formerly of the Acurial resistance, and several hundred of their troops.

There were greetings, warriors' hand clasps and hugs.

'This is amazing,' Coilla said.

'We were only too pleased to help,' Chillder said, 'after what you did for us.'

'Though we could have done with a gentler way of getting here,' Brelan added. 'Serapheim's method of transport was kind of disconcerting.'

Wheam approached his father, looking anxious.

'There's no need for timidity,' Quoll assured him. He clapped a meaty hand on the youth's shoulder. 'From what I've heard you've much to be proud of, and I know you'll make me proud in the scrap to come.'

Wheam smiled.

Stryke made his way to the chieftain. 'Quoll,' he said, almost afraid to ask the question. 'Janch and Corb. Are they—'

'They're fine, Stryke. Safe and well, and under the clan's protection. How could it be otherwise? Though they're missing their sire and mother, of course.'

He felt a wave of relief. 'Thank you.'

'But I regret we weren't able to stop Thirzarr being taken. I'm sorry about that.'

'No need. Few are a match for Jennesta.'

'The bitch. She took the lives of some of our best, and devastated our lodges. I can't wait to make her pay for that.' He slapped the broadsword he wore.

'Do you know what you've let yourselves in for here? Do any of you?'

'Yes,' Brelan offered. 'Serapheim explained everything.'

'That's more than he's done with us.'

'And that's remiss of me,' the magician said, appearing at Stryke's side. 'You need to hear the plan. Come with me and I'll tell you.'

He took Stryke back indoors and to what looked very much like a sorcerer's study, complete with shelves of massive, leather-bound grimoires, vials of potions and powders, and assorted skeletons of unidentifiable small creatures of bizarre appearance.

'It will come as no surprise to you that Jennesta is here,' Serapheim announced when they were settled. 'She's gained entry to the Sphere of the Four, to which this world is adjunct. And she's used her fake instrumentalities to import the followers she left behind. From a world of islands, I'm given to believe. It's only a matter of time before she gets in here.'

'Can't you stop her?'

'Stop her? I *want* her here. That's part of the plan.'

'Why?'

'Several reasons. First, if there's to be a battle between her forces and ours, better it should be here where only combatants and not the innocent are affected. Second, the set of instrumentalities she has doesn't function here, although I don't think she knows it and I want to keep it that way. That takes away her option to flee if she has to. Third, the plan we have in mind must be executed by Vermegram, Sanara and myself, and as I can't conveniently leave this world I contrived to lure Jennesta here.'

'What is your plan for dealing with her?'

'No disrespect, Stryke, but I'm keeping that to myself. Only because what you don't know can't be got out of you. Oh, I know you're tough and not given to betraying confidences, but this is Jennesta we're talking about.'

'Fair enough. So what do you want us to do?'

'I want the Wolverines to be part of our little army and engage her forces. But I want you to pick two or three members of your band to help you carry out a special task.'

'Not fight, you mean?'

'I expect they'll be fighting all right, it's just that I don't want you in the battle proper. I've something else in mind, though it's more dangerous. If you're willing.'

'If it gets at Jennesta, I'm willing.'

'There will be a point in our run-in with her when it's vitally important that she be distracted. Have more coming at her than she can cope with and still think straight, in other words. That's where you come in.'

Stryke nodded.

'I'll let you know when the time is right,' Serapheim added, 'and make sure you can get to her. You might like to go and select your helpers now.'

'Hold your horses. I want to ask you something. We've been dogged by an outfit called the Gateway Corps. What do you know about them?'

'It's said they've been around almost as long as instrumentalities themselves have existed. The Corps' self-appointed mission is to track down the artefacts and limit the damage they can do. An ambition I don't altogether disapprove of.'

'They're a problem I didn't need.'

'Understandably. They're tenacious, and have allegiance only to their cause. But we can deal with it.'

'From what I've seen, they're powerful.'

'So are we. But I believe the Corps to be basically virtuous, and potentially useful allies. They are not our first concern, however. Put them from your mind.'

Stryke shrugged and made to leave.

Serapheim waved him back into his seat. 'There's one more thing. It has no real bearing on the task in hand, but you might find it . . . interesting. You know that the world you've just travelled through was created by a group of high adepts called the Four. But do you know what their names were?'

'No, why should I?'

'They were Aik, Zeenoth, Neaphetar and Wystendel.'

'The Tetrad?' Stryke was shocked, despite believing he was beyond being affected by any revelation at this point.

'I tell you this not to undermine your beliefs. I think they *were* gods, in a way. They are certainly seen as that not only by you orcs but a number of other races too. You only have to look at what they created to see their god-like qualities. I tell you this as a lesson. The lesson being that you shouldn't always rely on what you think you know or think you see. That could be valuable in what's to come.'

'I think I understand.'

'Keep it in mind. Now you'd better—'

The door flew open and Sanara came in. 'Father! Jennesta's here. She and her followers have just breached the western membrane.'

'That was to be expected. Indeed, hoped for. Take your position, Sanara. Stryke, brief your band and wait on my word.'

The Gateway Corps unit had also penetrated Serapheim's hideaway, though with immense difficulty.

'This place is glorious,' Pelli remarked as she surveyed the scene.

'Looks can be deceiving,' Weevan-Jirst reminded her.

'Still, it's hard to believe anything nefarious could be going on in this kind of setting.'

'Yet we know it is.'

She gave up on his obduracy and held her peace.

They had wandered away from the body of their unit to explore the options and decide which way to go. There were no roads that they could see or any signs of habitation. Pelli thought the place was like an enormous garden.

'What's that?' Weevan-Jirst said. He pointed to a nearby hill.

There were figures on it.

Pelli strained to see. 'They look like . . . goblins.'

'So they do.'

'I wonder how they fit into this.'

'We could ask them.'

'Is that wise?'

He gave her the goblin equivalent of a condescending look. 'They're my own kind. I'm sure I can converse with them in a civilised manner.'

'All right. We'll go up and—'

'I think it would be best if I did this alone. My folk don't always react well to other races.'

'As you wish. But take care. I'll either be here or back with the others.'

He set off and she watched him go. But she didn't leave. She was curious to see how he would handle it.

As he walked by a cluster of bushes a figure leapt out and began to struggle with him. Shocked, Pelli called out and rushed to help. As she approached the figure ran off.

She arrived at her second-in-command panting. '*What . . . happened?*'

He showed her his arm. It had a gash across it and the blood was flowing freely. 'He attacked me.'

'Who did?'

'A goblin.'

'Was he trying to kill you?'

Weevan-Jirst was binding his arm with a field bandage he'd produced from his belt pouch. 'I don't know. I don't think so. It was senseless. He leapt out, slashed my arm and made to run off. I tried to stop him but he got away.'

She noticed movement on the hill. One figure was running up it, towards the others. 'Is that him?'

He looked. 'I suppose it could be. I've a mind to go up there and—'

'I think it would be wise not to.'

'They're *goblins*. My kind. Why would he do that?'

'There are good and bad in all races. And I'm beginning to suspect who they are and their relationship with Jennesta.'

Before she could go on he said, 'Does one of them have a bow?'

She looked. 'I think he might. We should either get out of here or be prepared to defend ourselves magically. He seems to be aiming this way.'

'Then he's a fool. No archer on any world could achieve a shot like that. The distance is too far and the angle's wrong.' There was the sound of something cutting through the air. 'Why does he think—' A spasm shook him and he let out a strangled gasp. A black arrow jutted from his chest.

'Weevan-Jirst,' Pelli said, stunned. '*Weevan-Jirst!*'

He fell. She went down on her knees to him, felt for a heartbeat, not the easiest task through a goblin's carapace, then tried the vein in his neck. He was dead.

She looked up to the hill again. The archer and the others had gone. Her thought was that anybody who could use a bow like that, over such a distance, commanded a strong form of magic and was best avoided. Keeping low, and still numb from what had just happened, she hurried back to the others.

*

The area Serapheim occupied buzzed with activity as the diverse force readied itself for battle. Serapheim's apprentices, perhaps a dozen in number, had joined its ranks with the intention of using their magic in aid of the cause.

Stryke stood apart from all that with three others. The band had been dismayed when he told them he wouldn't be fighting alongside them. But once they knew why, they were approving.

He had decided to take Gleadeg, Coilla and Pepperdyne with him on the mission Serapheim had allotted. The human he might not have chosen, good a fighter as he was, but Coilla insisted that they stay together, and Stryke wanted her along. None of them had any idea where Standeven was, or particularly cared.

There was a commotion. A chorus of *'They're here! They're here!'* went up. Stryke and the others rushed to see what was happening.

On the plain that stretched out not far from Serapheim's villa, a force was advancing. They recognised Jennesta at its head. Her human troopers from Acurial were with her, along with shuffling human zombies and the more sprightly orc kind. There was a mass of flotsam and jetsam of various races she had recruited from the world of islands, including what looked like the remnants of the Gatherers. Racing to join them at the rear was the goblin Gleaton-Rouk and his piratical gang.

Stryke knew Thirzarr was somewhere in the horde but couldn't spot her. At least he hoped she was there. He didn't like to think about what had happened if she wasn't.

Jennesta's army was even more ragtag than the one Stryke was a part of. But hers outnumbered his by at least two to one.

'Stryke!'

He turned and saw Serapheim approaching, and he wasn't alone. Pelli Madayar was with him, along with her multi-species Gateway Corps comrades.

'I have granted admission to a group I think you know,' Serapheim explained.

'Hello again, Captain,' Pelli said.

'What are you doing here?' Stryke asked suspiciously.

'I've long felt that your band has been a mere pawn in this game. The Corps' principles, and my training, have prevented me from acting on that impulse. But recent events have made me question my impartiality. There comes a time when a side has to be chosen and to hell with the consequences. I've decided . . . we've *all* decided that yours is the one to offer our services to.'

Stryke thought about that for a moment, then said, 'Glad to have you aboard.'

30

The two armies faced each other.

For Jennesta it was the culmination of the revenge she sought to inflict on her father and the hated Wolverines. For the defenders it was a matter of survival.

Hostilities started from a distance, using a combination of magic and arrows, the former blocking most of the latter. Streaks of energy, yellow, white and red were exchanged, resembling a hatchling's coloured streamer caught by the wind. Shimmering defensive bubbles were up, cast by Jennesta on one side, the Gateway Corps on the other. The difference being that Jennesta's was to protect her and a small coterie, while the Corps was trying to shield everyone.

When the sides finally began to advance it wasn't at a charge. The pace was more deliberate, almost stately, save for the taunts and foul curses each side rained on the other. But ultimately they had to meet, and when they did it was bloodily.

The roof of Serapheim's villa was an excellent vantage point. From it, Stryke, Coilla, Pepperdyne and Gleadeg had the best view of the battle. All of them would have liked to be there.

Serapheim came to them. 'There,' he said, pointing. 'You can just see Jennesta over on the far side. Having set the fighting in motion she's retired to a safer distance.'

Stryke looked, but had to strain his eyes. He could make out Jennesta. There were others with her, and he thought one of them might be Thirzarr, but he couldn't be sure.

'You must get to her,' Serapheim continued. 'You can either go round the field of battle—'

'Too long,' Stryke told him.

'Or through it, I'm afraid. Shall I assign you some extra bodies to help?'

They looked at each other and Stryke answered for all of them. 'No. We can manage.'

'I hoped you'd say that. We can't really spare anybody.'

Coilla gave a gentle dig. 'Some army.'

'Valiant as they are, it isn't them we're relying on. It's you. Take care.'

Stryke and the others set off.

When they got to the plain, the battle was hotting up and there was a great roar coming from it. Stryke had hoped to cross by moving through their own ranks, but things had got mixed. It was still the case that most of Jennesta's force was on the right and Stryke's was on the left, but both armies had been contaminated with each other's fighters.

They drew their weapons. Stryke tried to pick a spot with more friends than enemies, and they plunged in.

The Wolverines were where they always liked to be, in the heart of the battle.

For Haskeer it was all the excuse he needed to crack skulls and sever limbs with his axe. He preferred the living opponents. The zombies were basically dusty demolition jobs with little fight in them. The orc zombies were livelier but still lacked a spark. Haskeer had no qualms about fighting them.

Jup and Spurral were side by side, as usual, working in unison with staffs and knives. They made a point of seeking out goblins, and were duelling with a pair of them, staffs against tridents. Nearby, the Ceragans fought together, with Dallog leading them. Wheam stood with his father, and he had made the supreme gesture of leaving his lute back at the villa.

Gateway Corps members were all over the battle, discharging magical punches that downed men and caused the human zombies to explode in clouds of dust. Pelli Madayar was fighting conventionally, something the Corps was required to be proficient at. She finished off a Gatherer with a sword thrust and, spinning, bumped into Wheam. They exchanged nods and turned to their fresh respective opponents.

Shortly after, in a rare lull, they both happened to catch sight of Weevan-Jirst, skulking at the battle's ragged edge, looking for prey.

'Do you know him?' Pelli said.

Wheam nodded. 'His name's Weevan-Jirst. He killed one of our band.'

'With an arrow?'

'Yes. His bow's enchanted. Didn't you know?'

'I guessed as much.'

'An arrow smeared with his victim's blood always finds its target. *Always.*'

'That explains something.'

'What?'

A uniformed human came too close. Pelli fended him off and he was caught up in the swirl. 'Doesn't matter.'

'I've got an idea about Weevan-Jirst,' Wheam confided. 'Something that could hurt him.'

'Can I help you with it?'

As they battled their way through the melee, so did Dallog and Pirrak, but moving in a different direction.

Initially, Stryke and his tiny crew made good progress. They were well into the crush before they hit a foe, then trouble came thick and furious.

But now, sweating and breathing hard, they were in sight of Jennesta. She had Thirzarr with her, rod straight and blank-eyed. There was also one of her once human zombies and a handful of troopers.

'So how are we going to do this, Stryke?' Pepperdyne said as they worked their way closer.

'I'm thinking just straight in, fell the guards.'

'What about the biggest threat?'

'I'm counting on Jennesta still wanting me and the band serving her. Why else would she keep Thirzarr alive?'

'You better be sure about that,' Coilla said. 'She might be keeping her as a pet.'

'If you can think of another way in the time we've got—'

'No, let's do it. I've come to trust your hunches.'

They fought their way to the battle's rim, lingered in the crowd for an opportune moment then charged across the open ground. The guards were their first target. There were five of them, all human, so the odds were no problem. Gleadeg got the first with a single blow and surprise. Pepperdyne had as easy a time with his mark, felling him with a brace of strokes. Stryke and Coilla had a bit more of a slog. Their opponents had some fire and it took a moment to put them down.

There was a human zombie present, but for some reason Jennesta hadn't set him on them. He stood immobile, and they recognised him as what was left of Kapple Hacher.

The sorceress had a jewelled dagger at Thirzarr's throat.

'Give it up,' Stryke advised.

'You dare to speak to *me* like that, you snivelling animal? And while I'm holding a blade to your bitch?'

'I was never much of a one for niceties.' He wished Serapheim and the others would turn up. Equally, he hoped none of Jennesta's supporters in the battle would notice what was going on and come to her aid.

'If anyone should give up,' Jennesta announced haughtily, 'it's you.' She pressed the dagger closer to Thirzarr's throat. The crease in her flesh was plainly visible.

'I think if you were going to kill Thirzarr you would have done it by now.' He prayed she wouldn't call his bluff. And thought of the Tetrad and what Serapheim had told him.

'You think I wouldn't?'

It was sliding into a stalemate. Stryke was wondering how far to push it when they were all distracted by movement and noise.

A couple of Jennesta's troopers had detached themselves from the battlefield, as Stryke had feared, and were rushing to save her. But as they neared and Stryke fought to bring up his sword, another figure ran into their path and viciously engaged them. It was Pirrak. He felled one man in quick order. The other put his sword through Pirrak's guts. In his turn, the attacker was felled by a Wolverine's blade.

Dallog came out of the scrum and joined the others around Pirrak.

The youth was mortally wounded and they all knew it. He was losing blood fast and could hardly talk, but he tried. '*Sorry . . . sorry about . . . Acurial.*'

'What was that?' Stryke said.

'*Acurial . . . didn't want . . . he . . .*'

'I can't make it out,' Coilla said. 'What do you mean?'

'*No . . . choice . . . in Acurial . . . sp—* Uhh.'

Pirrak had a dagger in his heart, with Dallog's hand on it. The deed was quick and smooth.

'*What the hell?*' Stryke exploded.

'What are you *doing*?' Coilla exclaimed.

'He was suffering and I put an end to his misery. It was a kindness.'

'Are you insane? He would have been dead in a heartbeat anyway.'

'Or was it something he was about to say that you wanted to put a stop to?' Stryke ventured.

'Ah,' Dallog said, and rose from the corpse.

In the turmoil they had almost forgotten about Jennesta. Now Dallog crossed to her. When he reached her side he turned and faced them. 'Yes, it would have been embarrassing if Pirrak had talked. Not that it matters now that my allegiance is no longer a secret.'

'Your *what*?' Coilla said.

'I serve the Lady Jennesta. At least this once.'

'You serve me whenever I want you to,' she informed him coolly.

'This started in Acurial, didn't it?' Stryke hazarded. 'It was you.'

'Who?' Coilla said. 'What happened in Acurial, Stryke?'

'We know what happened. We just didn't know who did it. When that orc was found dead in the resistance safe house.'

'You think *he* did that?' She pointed at Dallog.

'I'm not denying it,' Dallog told her.

'And we've been blaming Standeven,' Pepperdyne said, 'the poor bastard.'

'How did you do it, Dallog?' Stryke wanted to know.

'I got the youngster to help me. We were passing information about the resistance to the Peczan forces, and to my lady here. Something I've done more recently about the band.' He flicked a finger at his head, then indicated Jennesta's with it. 'We have a way of talking. I called it praying, you'll remember, Captain.' He smiled. 'The dead orc back in Acurial was a cohort, strictly for coin. He got greedy and said he'd expose me. It suited me to let Standeven take the blame.'

'You said you *got* Pirrak to help you. How did you do that?'

'He was no saint. He fell in with my scheme easily enough.'

'You mean he was young and green, and easily swayed. Or bullied. You slur Pirrak's name. He died an honourable death.'

'Saving *you*,' Dallog sneered.

'Why did you do it?' Coilla wanted to know. 'What did she promise you?'

'Something you could never offer. Something that's wasted on Pirrak and Wheam and all the other whey-faced hatchlings I've had to wipe the arses of. She's promised me my youth back. I'll be young again, now and for ever.'

'You're a fool,' Stryke told him.

'This is all very interesting,' Jennesta said, 'but I was about to cut your mate's throat.'

'Reward me now, my lady,' Dallog said.

She gave him a look usually reserved for dog shit. 'What?'

'I've done all you asked, and more. We had a pact. I've fulfilled my part.'

'You don't have a great sense of timing, do you? It may have escaped your notice but I'm a little busy at the moment, what with a war and everything.'

'My true loyalty's in the open now; there's no point in delaying. And with my youth restored I can serve you so much better. You can do it easily, I know you can.'

'*Enough.*' She extended her free hand. 'Come then, claim your reward.'

Stryke and the others looked on impotently as Dallog, beaming, took a step closer and bowed slightly so that Jennesta could lightly touch his forehead.

'As age is your problem,' she said, 'let this put an end to it.'

A change came over him, but not necessarily the one he was expecting. More wrinkles appeared on his face, not less, and his skin began to grey. Blue veins started to stand out on his neck, arms and the backs of his hands. His fingernails were turning yellow. The smile had vanished now and there was terror in his fading eyes. He tried to struggle, but whatever enchantment she was using prevented him from breaking free.

The others watched in horror as flakes of skin fell away and his face sagged. His body shrank, the bones showing through rice paper flesh.

His rotting teeth dislodged as his mouth gaped in a silent scream. He shrivelled, his flesh turning to dust until his skeleton could plainly be seen. Then that crumbled too, falling like poured sand. In seconds he had been rendered to a scattering of ashes.

Jennesta was still holding a portion of his skull with discoloured skin attached. She casually tossed it aside and it shattered when it met the ground. 'The old are such a trial, don't you think?' she said.

'We're taking a hell of a risk,' Pelli said as they got themselves nearer to their target.

'We can do it if we're quick,' Wheam assured her.

'Are you sure you're right about this?'

'Yes.' He pointed. 'That goblin over there is some kind of healer, I reckon, and he seems to be looking after only Weevan-Jirst. I've been watching him. And that bucket by him has got bloody bandages in it.'

'Doesn't mean it's Weevan-Jirst's blood.'

'No. But I think there's a good chance. When we saw Weevan-Jirst before I noticed that he had two bound wounds, on his upper and lower arm. But even if it isn't his blood on those bandages it'll be from some other goblin and that's got to be a result, hasn't it?'

'I guess so.'

'Are you ready?'

'Yes. But remember to close your eyes when I tell you to. You'll be all right when you open them again. But if you don't close them when I say—'

'Yes, I know. Let's get going.'

The healer was off the battlefield and to the side, some way from his master though in sight of him. He was alone, and rummaging through a bag of kit. They got as close to him as they dared.

'Now!' Pelli ordered. 'Close them!'

She closed her own eyes too, and cast what was basically a simple spell but a very effective one. It generated a burst of incredibly intense light that briefly blinded everybody in range. That meant more than just the healer, but they thought that was justifiable as it gave nobody a real advantage, except in the unlikely event of someone who happened to be fighting with their eyes closed.

The potency of the flash did its job. When Pelli and Wheam

looked, the healer was rubbing at his eyes and blundering about. He wasn't the only one.

'Quickly!' Pelli urged. 'It doesn't last long!'

Wheam darted towards the medic, dodging several of the temporarily sightless. He reached the bucket, grabbed a bandage and raced back. Then they lost themselves in the confusion.

Finding a corner of the field away from the still churning battle, Wheam got out the distinctive black arrow he'd found on the battlefield earlier. They smeared it with blood from the bandage.

'The next bit's even trickier,' Pelli said.

'You can do it.'

'Let's see.'

They made their way to where they had last seen Weevan-Jirst. He was still there, and aiming his bow, seemingly at random over the heads of the combatants. The arrow flew, circled a couple of times and came down to strike someone in the crowd.

'That's one more on our side he's claimed,' Wheam remarked angrily.

'Come on, let's get nearer.'

They approached the goblin as closely as they dared, and saw that the arrow sheath he wore was almost empty. But another, full one, stood on the ground beside him, presumably containing a store of arrows tainted with blood collected by his gang.

Pelli took their arrow from Wheam. 'Guard my back, will you? This takes some concentration.' She added under her breath, 'I hope nobody sees it.'

She laid the shaft across her outstretched palms and stared at it. Nothing happened for a second, then it twitched. The twitch became a more animated judder. Suddenly the arrow soared from her hands, and under her direction headed straight for the quiver. It did a neat flip and fell inside. It was all so swift that no one appeared to notice, least of all Weevan-Jirst.

'Well done,' Wheam congratulated.

'We don't know when he'll fire it, or even if he will.'

'We've done our best. Now let's get away from here.'

They rejoined the battle. But whenever there was a rare moment of stillness they glanced the goblin's way. Twice they saw him loose arrows that seemed to hunt their targets like a living thing, and both times found them. Wheam and Pelli began to think their plan wasn't going to work.

A bit later, in another brief pause that starved them of anyone to fight, Wheam nudged Pelli and nodded towards the goblin. He was drawing his bow again. They watched with no great expectation.

The arrow Weevan-Jirst fired went way over the battlefield, made a couple of circuits and headed back in his general direction. He looked on, presumably to see who the latest casualty would be. But the shaft was coming towards him. When it was close enough for there to be no doubt of its goal the goblin's expression turned to dread and he tried to run. The arrow took him square in the back. He went down heavily. Other goblins ran to him, but what they found looked pretty conclusive even from a distance.

Wheam and Pelli slapped their right hands together and let out a whoop. It was joined by a cheer from pleased onlookers.

Stryke was thinking of rushing Jennesta and overpowering her. It was a sign of his desperation that he would consider such an unwise move. The chances were that Thirzarr would suffer for it, and likely they'd all die. But Serapheim and his kin still hadn't turned up and the situation was even more edgy after what Jennesta had done to Dallog.

He got the impression that Gleadeg, Coilla and Pepperdyne might also be thinking about attacking Jennesta. Catching their eye, he tried to convey through facial expressions how reckless a move that would be. He hoped they got the message.

'I'm getting bored with this,' Jennesta said, her knife still at Thirzarr's throat.

'That must be tough for you,' Coilla told her.

'How shall I relieve it? By killing this one?' She twisted the dagger a touch. 'By killing you four? Maybe both.'

'You're big on talk,' Stryke said. 'Why don't you let Thirzarr go, and face me, one to one?'

She laughed. 'And you think you'd stand a chance?'

'Try me, then,' Pepperdyne offered. 'I'd take you on.'

Jennesta looked him over. 'Hmmm. Not bad. For a human. Perhaps I should let you *take me on*, pretty boy.'

Coilla stared daggers at her.

At that moment there was what could only be called a shift in the air. It was rapidly followed by a burst of light. When everybody blinked back to normality there were three more beings present. Serapheim, Vermegram and Sanara had finally arrived.

'Ah,' Jennesta cooed. 'What a pleasant surprise. A family gathering.'

'Let the female go, Jennesta,' Serapheim said. 'She's nothing to do with this.'

'I don't think so.'

'Don't make me make you.'

'You're so melodramatic, Father.'

'That's rich coming from you,' Vermegram said.

'And you have no sense of melodrama, Mother? There's no attention-seeking when you take the form of some mangy animal?'

'I don't hold knives to innocent beings' necks.'

'You should try it, it might brighten up your dull, sanctimonious little life.'

'That's enough,' Sanara said.

'Oh, *please*, little sister. You're nothing but an even more prissy version of our mother. I couldn't care less for your condemnation.'

'Put the knife down,' Serapheim demanded, his tone like ice.

'Go to *hell*.'

He made a swift movement with his hands. The dagger Jennesta was holding became malleable, then melted like an icicle in a heatwave. It ended as a metallic coloured puddle at her feet.

At the same time, Vermegram wove her own spell. Thirzarr started, staggered and seemed to come to herself.

'Stryke!' Serapheim cried urgently.

Stryke dashed to his bewildered mate, took hold of her and dragged her away.

Alarmed at the speed of events, Jennesta's perplexity turned to anger. Lifting her own hands, lips moving through some incantation, she prepared to retaliate.

'*Get clear!*' Serapheim shouted.

Stryke and the others didn't need telling twice. They withdrew from the line of fire.

Jennesta hurled energy at her kin. They repelled it by instantly throwing up a glossy protective bubble, and answered with fiery bolts.

These Jennesta batted aside as though they were no more harmful than a swipe from a kitten.

'What in hell is going on, Stryke?' Thirzarr asked. She looked exhausted as well as baffled.

'I'll tell you later,' he promised, pulling her closer.

The duel built in intensity, so that even those fighting a short distance away took a step back from their opponents to watch.

Then there was a development from an unexpected quarter. The zombie Hacher, who had stood to one side, forgotten through all this, now stirred himself. Perhaps there was just enough humanity left in what remained of his senses, or enough unforgiving malice. Lurching towards her from behind, he grabbed hold of Jennesta, encircling her in a death-like grip.

'Get off me, you scum!' she shrieked, struggling to free herself.

When she failed to break his hold she resorted to a more extreme measure. A small hand gesture was all it took. What had once been Hacher let out a moan of agony and began to writhe. He let go of her and his hands went to his head. They weren't enough to hold it together. It erupted as surely as a melon hit with a mallet. A sticky black liquid seeped through his fingers and down his chest. He collapsed, truly dead.

Serapheim and the others were still mounting their magical attack. It was all becoming too much for Jennesta. She reached into her gown and took out her ersatz set of instrumentalities. Four were already in place. Grinning triumphantly at her enemies, she quickly slotted the fifth into place and disappeared.

'I thought you said they didn't work here,' Stryke complained. 'You've let her get away!'

Jennesta's parents and her sibling looked truly mournful. Vermegram and Sanara might even have had moist eyes, as was the way with humans.

It was Serapheim who spoke, his tone weighed down. 'No, they don't work here, and she hasn't got away. That was our plan.'

'I don't understand.'

'Working together, because that's what it took, even with a counterfeit set of instrumentalities, we managed to alter them from afar. Jennesta thought she could use them to get away, and no doubt had the coordinates for a safe location. We changed those coordinates.'

'Where's she gone?' Coilla asked.

Serapheim looked up at the sky. 'I'll explain.'

The world Serapheim created was in every respect artifice, fuelled and maintained by magic and the force of his will. But for all practical purposes it was real. The food it produced could be eaten, the rain that fell was wet, the perfume of flowers was just as sweet. Pleasure could be experienced there, and pain and death. The reality extended to its sun. It was no less the giver of warmth and light than any that existed in the so-called natural universe.

And so it was that as Serapheim explained what had happened to his depraved daughter, on the surface of the sun he had brought into existence there was the tiniest blip. A minute, incredibly short-lasting flare of energy as a foreign body, newly arrived, was instantly consumed by that terrible inferno.

Jennesta's going had a number of effects on the battlefield. Her human zombies simply stopped functioning, and fell to dust. The entranced orcs had the chains binding their minds severed, and came to their senses. Others, of many races, also felt her influence seep away, and they threw down their arms. Yet others, those far gone in depravity who followed the sorceress willingly, fought on. As the battle descended into part dazed chaos, part fight to the death, it was one of the latter who was responsible for what happened next.

Stryke and Thirzarr stood with Coilla and Pepperdyne, a little apart from the others, watching the turn of events when a fighter on the battlefield took aim and unleashed an arrow.

Given the unpredictability of a conventional longbow, it could have struck any of them. It chose Pepperdyne. The arrow plunged deep into his chest, passing through the side of his heart as it travelled. He fell without a sound.

The cold hand of horror clutched at Coilla's own heart. She went down on her knees to him, and if confirmation of what had just happened was needed, she saw his white singlet rapidly turning scarlet.

On the battlefield, the archer who sent the bolt, a Gatherer perhaps or some other form of lowlife, was cut to pieces by an avenging pack of Wolverines.

Stryke got hold of the arrow jutting from Pepperdyne's chest, thinking to remove it. Pepperdyne winced and groaned. Stryke let go. Spurral caught his eye, and almost imperceptibly, shook her head.

Coilla took her lover's hand. Pepperdyne's eyes flickered and half opened. He stared up at her face.

'Take it easy,' she whispered. 'We'll patch you up and—'

'No . . . my love,' he replied almost too softly to be heard. *'I'm . . . beyond . . . patching up.'*

'Don't leave me, Jode.'

'I'll . . . never . . . leave you.'

Coilla squeezed his hand tighter. 'How can I go on? How can I live without you?' She turned to Serapheim and his kin. 'Can't you do something?' she pleaded. 'With your great powers, surely—'

Serapheim shook his head sadly. 'There are limits to even our abilities. Some things must take their course. I'm sorry.'

Desolate, she returned her gaze to Pepperdyne. He tried to speak again, and Coilla had to put her ear to his mouth to catch what he said. Whatever it was, it brought the flicker of a smile to her face before grief replaced it.

Epilogue I

Stryke, Jup, Spurral, Pelli Madayar and Standeven stood in the semi-arid wastes of a drought-ridden slice of Maras-Dantia. The sun beat down without mercy, the air was verging on foul.

'This isn't fair,' Standeven whined. 'You could at least have brought me somewhere other than Kantor Hammrik's fiefdom.'

Stryke pointed across the desert. 'I reckon if you walk for about three days in that direction you'll be out of it.'

'I've no supplies, no proper clothing, no—'

'Here's a bottle of water. You better make it last.'

Standeven snatched it. 'I was as upset about what happened to Jode as any of you, you know.'

'Yeah, right.'

He was still whining and muttering curses when the others vanished and left him to it.

Stryke, Jup, Spurral and Pelli looked out at a considerably more pleasant world. It was blessed with fecundity and almost entirely unspoilt. In the valley below was a small village of round huts and longhouses. Smoke lazily climbed from cooking stoves, and in an adjacent field cattle were grazing.

'A world comprised solely of dwarfs,' Pelli said, sweeping an arm at the scene. 'The Corps has had contact with the inhabitants before, and we're on good terms. They're expecting you down there. Just mention my name.'

Jup and Spurral thanked her, then turned to Stryke. Pelli moved off to a discreet distance.

'Well, we've already had our goodbyes,' Jup said, 'and you know I'm not one for emotional gestures, so I'm offering you my hand, Stryke.'

Stryke took it in a warriors' grasp and squeezed hard.

'You and your *I'm not one for emotional gestures*,' Spurral teased as she shoved past Jup. 'Well, I am.' She gave Stryke a powerful hug, her head not quite up to the level of his chest. 'Thank you, Captain. For everything.'

'And you,' he returned.

Spurral had tears in her eyes. Jup pretended there was a speck of dirt in his.

They didn't linger, but set off down the hill to their new life.

Stryke and Pelli watched them go.

'Is Coilla going to be all right?' she asked.

He sighed. 'I hope so. There's a great sadness weighing on her now. But just before we came here she told me about something that I think is going to keep her mind off it for a while.'

'I trust time will heal her. Oh, there's just one more thing, Stryke.' She held out her hand.

He dug into his belt bag and produced the instrumentalities. For a moment he studied them, then handed them over.

'Sorry to part with them?' she asked as she slipped them into her tunic.

'No.' He thought about it. 'Well, yes *and* no.'

She smiled. 'They do have an enticing quality. But the Corps is right. They shouldn't be abroad.'

'I'll drink to that.'

'Come on, let's get you all home.'

Epilogue II

In the months that followed, the destruction Jennesta had brought to the orcs' settlement on Ceragan was cleared up. New longhouses were built and corrals repaired.

The more personal hurts took longer to fade.

Stryke wandered through a fine summer's day. The sky was blue, the birds were singing, there was abundant game in the vales, forests and rivers.

He passed Thirzarr, sitting at a wooden bench outside their lodge, chopping a carcass with a razor-keen hatchet. They exchanged a smile. Nearby, Haskeer was fooling on the grass with Corb and Janch, the hatchlings fit to burst with laughter. Stryke increased his pace a little at that point, lest Haskeer collar him to say, once more, how right he'd been about Dallog.

Wheam and his father, Quoll, were sitting on the steps of the chieftain's longhouse. Wheam was plinking on his battered goblin lute. Quoll was acting as if he enjoyed it.

Farther along, in a quieter corner, he spotted Coilla sitting on the ground by Pepperdyne's grave, a spot she still came to frequently. He went to her.

When she saw him she said, 'What do you think Jode would have thought of it here?'

'I reckon he would have liked it. Might have been a bit of a change from what he was used to though.'

'I don't think he minded change. None of us should. Didn't somebody say the only thing that stays constant is change?'

'Probably. And it's just as well you feel that way.' He reached out and gave her greatly swollen stomach an affectionate pat. 'Because nothing's going to be the same again.'